STARLESS RUIN

AMIDST THE BONES OF HEROES

BOOK TWO ◆ STARLESS RUIN

ROLANDO G. GIRONELLA III

Podium

Podium

STARLESS RUIN

CHAPTER 1

BRIDGE BETWIXT AND THE MIND BEYOND

Tov lost himself in a strange ocean.

He teetered on the edge of consciousness, trying to make sense of his surroundings.

Soon, his eyes opened to an endless expanse lit up by dazzling nebulae—ribbons of light shone throughout. Some were no wider than silken threads behind thick layers of cloud. Others, those closest to Tov, roared like prismatic rivers.

"Where?" Tov muttered in a whisper, his voice ethereal.

Confusion filled him as he looked down at himself, an avatar of wispy smoke resembling his physical appearance. His mind sharpened bit by bit, and his ghostly form took shape as he willed it stable and dense.

Tov tore his focus from his sense of self. His impetuous curiosity sent him on a direct path to the nearest of the shining streams. As he approached it, he observed its qualities and made an educated guess.

"Neurons?" Tov pondered in awe, perhaps a simplification of something familiar yet simultaneously uncanny. But his wonder quelled the latter feeling. He orbited around this lake of thought. He whispered, voice carrying off into the distance. "So this is my mind?"

Tov immersed himself in its beauty for a moment. He looked back at the glowing ribbons. One of his four hands hovered over one of them before gently touching it.

An explosion of senses pushed to the forefront of his attention, clear images of simple things he had done before undertaking this operation, in all their vivid detail.

The flavor of human liquor tingled on his tongue, as did the feel of cold glass in his hand and the smell of sterile air within the Luna Complex. He saw the sea of doctors and psychologists, and that ominous machine hanging above that connected to two pods.

He heard the chatter of his people, but his conversations with Overseer Jupiter cut through the noise, his concern palpable. *"Last chance to back out. Your people have an army of therapists that can take your place . . ."*

More voices rushed to his ears, which he deemed of utmost import, coming one after another.

"There are sections we call Amygdalas, concentrations of trauma and nightmares within her digital mind . . ."

"You will be directly interfacing with an intelligence unfathomable to you. Suffice it to say any mistake is lethal . . ."

Chief Scholar Yulane and Overseer Luna had warned him. A chill ran down his spine at the severity of his situation. And yet he had to be the one to do this, much to everyone's protests, but he got his way.

"No, it has to be me. She won't respond to strangers, even if I am to be disguised while doing this."

"Well, if you're really going through with this . . ."

"I am."

Tov huffed. He had sounded confident then, presenting the stoic patriarch of a prominent clan, the resilient leader of the Third Expeditionary Fleet everyone expected. But underneath that facade, and now within the depths of his inner self, anxiety clawed at him.

"Tov . . ."

There it was, her voice. By the Symphony, her voice—leaking with debilitating hurt that reopened scarred wounds Tov thought long buried.

"I remembered something . . . My name . . . the one my Rikard gave me. I never told it to you . . ."

"Andora," Tov answered the voice in his memory. The name of a being whom he had known simply as the Eldest for the brief period he knew her.

He chuckled.

"Has it been only a few weeks?" Tov mused, shoulders sagging.

The stupor that affected him washed away as he remembered his mission, one that could determine the survival of everything he held dear. Tov shook his head as a grave air formed around him. He descended quicker, his goal clear.

"Onward, Tov," he whispered to himself. "You're not here to play tourist."

Before that, however, a vast bubble encapsulated the entirety of this expanse, like an ozone layer containing every bit of himself, a bulwark that shielded him from the machinations of the Starless Horrors and psionic assaults. He looked at its pristine, rigid defense work, ready to repel any insidious attack.

Extra measures never hurt, Tov thought.

Tov fell further as he phased through layers of mental constructs, past the shallows, the depths, and everything in between.

He went deeper, finding long-term memories from days, months, years, and decades past. His fight with Andora, the start of the Expedition, the worst days of the Cataclysm, his people's rebellion against their former masters, his mother's last words—much of it a blur the farther along.

"Now I'm nothing but a glorified hospice nurse!"

"You can't! You can't leave. What of our Uli, what of our clan, me? You can't leave . . . Please, Tov . . ."

"I need your skills, old friend. Our rivals are eyeing us like ravenous beasts. Our people need you at the forefront, and the Third Fleet needs her shepherd."

"That's the last of the refugees! Captain Yan, get us out of here! Spring our surprise!"

"Freedom, my kin! Take it back from the masters! Break the chains! Liberty or death! ONWARD!"

"Oh, my little star, my only child . . . Live . . . and be virtuous."

A few moments remained crystal clear only through the efforts of the biomechanical implant grafted into his brain—his brightest moments, times of peace and happiness, interspersed with horror and terror.

He glanced at the technological marvel. It looked strange from the perspective of his thoughts. Artificial, like finding geometric circuitry floating among the clouds. Pulsing passively, a tiny supercomputer hiding enormous analytical and processing power, ready to be used at any moment.

He pulled his attention from it, as wondrous as it was in his mentalscape.

But as he dove deeper into his subconscious, he found alien and familiar aspects. A learned scholar and natural psionic like Yulane or a master of the arts like Harmonizer Volantesh could name every aspect of his mind, what they did, how it affected his entire being, and how to use them to fuel their esoteric abilities.

Mind reading, telepathy, levitation, telekinesis, and most importantly, defense against the eldritch whispers and manipulation.

For Tov, he could "taste" his mystical connection with the universe, the Grand Symphony, as the Eternal Choir called it. He breathed it all in as he floated amid the layers. An ethereal thread, the touch of a higher dimension. His ability to sense intent and emotion from others was tangible before his gaze, a lesser form of mind reading but not as intrusive.

He surmised those more potent in its arts would find their minds saturated with psionic might.

It mattered little to him. Tov went further into the deep, feeling the rifts of past traumas that scabbed over time, the currents of thought, the images of memories.

He felt it.

The flame that burned deep inside him and all living things. This all-encompassing thing looked so tiny, yet it felt beyond the matter that composed him. Tov's senses barely saw its fleeting passage, so intimate to who he was, and then it disappeared, but he felt its presence still.

Few witnessed such a sight directly, a brief glimpse of one's own soul—this endeavor was becoming more than worth the troubles and dire warnings.

Nevertheless, with great reluctance to go after and gaze upon his flame, he dragged himself outward, rising higher, soaring past the layers he visited. As he left the layer that contained his most recent memories, he reached the bubble shield he had erected to protect him and the boundary that separated his mind from the outside.

He gazed outward, seeing blackness that contrasted with the kaleidoscope of color behind him, a void that chilled him more than crippling loneliness.

"Where are you?" Tov concentrated on his senses, feeling for anything out of the ordinary. There, he felt a pull, like being taken by a river that flowed farther from his innermost sanctuary and essence—going to somewhere . . . other.

"Ah, there. This looks close enough to a bridge as any," he muttered, antennae twitching in suspicion. "Unless it isn't just me and the Eldest here."

He shuddered, finding his situation increasingly uncomfortable. He "looked around" before centering his thoughts and will.

"I'm always one for introspection, but this is too much," Tov whispered with a faint click of his mandibles. He concentrated, cautiously approaching the tunnel that connected him and Eldest—*Andora*, he corrected himself.

"How do humans say it? Nothing ventured, nothing gained?" He took a deep breath, phasing through the barrier that protected his mindscape, and immediately, he felt vulnerable.

As Tov crossed the bridge, the thrum of power pulsed like a heartbeat, pulling him in like the gravity of a supergiant sun. His form shuddered step by step, echoing throughout the empty expanse betwixt two beings.

Tov groaned, the sensation uncomfortable at best. "So this is what she meant."

He recalled Luna's words, something spoken to him days before the operation, the memory as clear as the day.

He and Luna, Eldest's second-in-command and the first of her fragments, stood behind blast-proof plasteel glass windows, watching millions of nanomachines constructing the operation room, the two medical slabs, and the enigmatic spherical device that hung above.

She cleaned her circular glasses and multitasked with innumerable duties in front of Tov and unseen. Her short gray hair was as perfect as her monochrome dress, and her glowing white eyes unfocused as she worked overtime with her swarm of little machines.

The silver Sub AI spoke politely and respectfully. "The Digital Neural Bond has been a staple piece of technology that enabled synergy between human and android brains. The former benefits from the sheer processing power of the latter, while the latter benefits from ingrained intuition and superior creativity. Humanity used this symbiotic relationship when creating war machines like mechs during the war against the Starless before the Malignant Starfall wiped them out."

"So, this machine enables two different minds to connect, then? Bridging the organic with the synthetic?" Tov mused as he tapped his mandible. "Not unlike our cranial implants, though I don't think we'd go so far as to put sentient AI in our heads even if we had them."

Luna gave a small laugh, hidden beneath the embroidered handkerchief she covered her mouth with.

"That would be overkill. Humanity had similar devices, as small as what you aliens use, that are more than capable of such connections with their android companions. They also had thicker and more intimate bridging implants. This, however," Luna raised her palm at the vast machine overhead, and it pulsed with energy and light, "is primarily for your protection."

"Pardon?" Tov asked.

With a wave of her hand, Luna brought up multiple monitors and schematics, highlighting bits of information and data and sending them to him for study.

"Simply put, if we were to directly connect you and the Eldest, several cat-astrophic possibilities could occur. Best-case scenario, your organic mind would instantly overheat from the runoff power she produces," she explained as Tov analyzed the readings.

"You mean my head will, what, explode?" Tov muttered, his antennae twitching ever so slightly.

"Crude, but yes." Luna pressed her lips, a tinge of irritation in the twitch of her cheek. One of the rare bits of emotion she deigned to show him since they'd met. She sighed, glancing in his direction.

"Patriarch, the Eldest is beyond you, a gestalt consciousness meant to combine the entire android population. Her main CPU is as big as your destroyer ships and is constantly cooled by Earth's oceans, all so she can direct the entirety of the Sol Defense Network," Luna spoke, her eyes closed as if in reverence.

Tov remained silent, crossing his arms as he looked up from the myriad of specifications and capabilities the massive device presented. "And my mind can't handle touching her consciousness, even with my cranial implant? The best designers and programmers of my nation designed it."

Luna pressed her lips, shaking her head.

"As much as the device in your head grants you libraries of information and unparalleled storage and computing capabilities, it is barely a drop for pure digital beings like us," she spoke flatly, stating a fact that Tov begrudgingly knew.

"And what of my psionic abilities? They're not as diverse as those of the Jotex or potent as the Iexians, but I am capable of protective mental constructs," he pressed.

Luna hummed. "Psionics is a new field for us, but it won't keep you alive."

"It seems this entire mission looks more dangerous than fighting the Starless," Tov buzzed in frustration.

"Understand this, Patriarch. The gulf between you and a Sub AI, a fragment like me, is akin to swimming across an ocean to the next continent." Luna turned toward him, her gray gaze drilling into his compound pair. "The gulf between you and the Eldest would be akin to doing a spacewalk from here to Saturn."

"I see." Tov used every ounce of willpower to not shudder in front of the gray woman. "Then this device compensates for that gulf? You're assured of this."

Luna nodded. "Scholar Yulane and your chief neurologist, Rophalan, can discuss its complete capabilities. But yes, the Synaptic Disparity-Compensator Matrix should connect you to the Eldest without any unforeseen cranial detonations."

He sighed. "I will confer with them when they're not ogling at all the new technologies you are showering us with."

Tov cast one more look at the immense machine that would hang over him and Andora. He, his top officials, and the Sub AIs of Sol had pooled their resources to plan possibly the strangest act of therapy in the history of the known galaxy, but none of it would be possible without that device.

"I should thank you for designing the device with my health in consideration, Overseer Luna." Tov nodded to the AI.

"It was only rational." Luna propped up her circular glasses. "Your presence is indispensable in these precarious times."

Tov pulled himself from the memory.

He slowed, recalling every bit of information on his mission and the SDCM device meant to keep him in the realm of the living—and hopefully sane.

Time became irrelevant as he "floated through the tunnel" or "walked over the bridge." The distinction was irrelevant; all that mattered was the increasingly heavy presence before him. He grunted, senses straining to discern anything in the cold void.

Then and there, a light at the end, expanding larger at a rapid pace.

As he approached it, his body twitched, hackles raised as he tried to stop. "What?"

He couldn't stop, much like a spacer floating in the void without thrusters. The patriarch tried to slow his approach, fear shooting through him like a lance, a primal terror as if caught in something's immense dominion—a foreign body, an intruder in someone's imperium.

"What is . . . Hells?" Tov struggled, his speed faster and faster, yet the light, at first a speck and now a burning orb, never seemed to stop growing. He realized quickly what was happening. "Eldest, stop this! It's me!"

"Stop, slow down!" Tov gritted his mandibles, yet an invisible tendril dragged him across the expanse. Irrational images slammed into his head, a feeling that he was approaching the event horizon of a black hole, past the point of no return. "Luna! Hells, hells!"

His entire being became strained, his fists clutching his head as it throbbed, stuck between crushing pressure and heat.

His two hearts beat rapidly, and his breaths were ragged.

"I will not," he muttered, his mandible threatening to crack as he gritted. "I will not go out like this! Release me!"

He forced his gaze to focus on what he saw now was the surface of a sun in all its raging, infernal glory. Whips of mental power shot through like solar flares, beacons illuminating the empty void like spotlights. His attempts to combat such a giant thing were no better than throwing water onto lava, yet it calmed him down to do anything within his agency.

It screamed at him, a furious, agonized shout, like a roaring hurricane. A racket like the shrieks of a million voices bore down on him, pressing him against an invisible floor. Each one bashed against him in waves of blows, subsuming, stretching, tenderizing him.

Tov dragged his arms over his face in an attempt to shield his eyes, his mental protections cracking like the chitin of an ant, shivering at the base of a gargantuan mountain during the concert of the mother of all storms, her lightning smiting anyone who approached with searing blasts.

A growl and a hiss escaped his throat, leaving it raw. But then, as if with the press of a button, it was over. His resistance dissipated with the lack of force pressing down on him.

Tov's chest heaved as he panted, his mind recoiling at the abrupt change. All that remained of the momentary agony was a dull throb over his entire being. His ethereal form slowly recoalesced into a more solid shape as he tried to gather his bearings.

"The device. *Dowa*," Tov cursed, speaking to the ether. "Songs, better late than never. Thank you . . ."

Relief flooded over him like a bucket of cold water, the sweltering heat disappeared, and Tov allowed himself to look upon the majesty of Andora's mind, the Omni Mind of Sol.

It was unlike anything he'd ever seen, even with over a century of living, through all its quaking shifts and events.

Unlike the clouds of colorful nebulae and thought that orbited the fire of Tov's soul, Andora's mind manifested as a ball of light and fire that stretched across his vision—a solid mass with a surface like red-hot metal.

Circuitry etched across its vast landscape like chasms of lava, sending pulses of energy throughout its pathways a hundred times a second, creating a brilliant dance across the sunlike orb.

Faint tendrils stretched across the space like the cilia of a cell. Tov squinted; only now, when he pushed his gaze past the fireball's light pollution, could he see the innumerable stars that occupied the entirety of this endless mental ocean.

For a moment, Tov thought he witnessed the entire Network under Andora's command, faint images of battle stations, warships, massive manufactories, asteroid miners, and power plants pumping energy into relays throughout the solar system.

Everything that had allowed the human AI to fight a horde to a stalemate for the past century, manifesting in simple lights and tendrils, doing little justice to the sheer firepower and industry at the Network's web—Andora's web.

"So this is you," Tov whispered as he brushed imaginary dirt from his body.

Some nodes shone more prominently than others. Five were like dazzling stars, the first three with blue, silver, and red hues.

"That must be Jupiter, Luna, and Mars." Tov sensed the distinctions between all three: the first, with its stubborn defiance echoing across space like a fist raised in the air; the next, radiating a clinical efficiency like a still gray sea ready to be willed into something deadly and alien; and of course, the roars and booms of innumerable cannons, shouts of glorious speeches, and drums of war that pulsated from the third.

Tov shifted to the remaining two, one golden and the other bronze. "Venus and Mercury."

Both lacked any flavor of combat. The golden star flowed with warmth, compassion, and benevolence, a sheer contrast to the near-bloodthirsty auras of her warlike siblings. On the other hand, the dimmer bronze star was an unending, untiring industry, like a beast of burden stepping over fields of metal and energy, plowing and harvesting material for the defense effort.

Beyond them, Tov felt a void, spaces where he swore there should be more nodes. He recalled something then. "Those must be the other fragments friend Jupiter mentioned, those who fell in battle."

He bowed to them, saying a few words in his native Kursk, a clicking and hissing language that sounded almost lyrical.

He returned his gaze to the nexus of it all, pinpointing the numerous contradictions and fluctuations that looked unnatural and corrupted.

Flares of light writhing like gnarled roots, chasms that looked crumbled, a general fugue that covered the atmosphere, only the sheer heat melting away the corruption.

A sickly sun. A low groan beneath its roaring flame. A skittering whisper that scratched his eardrums. To him, Andora's vast mind appeared as uncanny as the Starless.

It pained his eyes. He looked away but remained in place, fists clenched tight. He felt all the more for the Eldest, to help her now for her sake, not just for the common good.

"How . . ." Tov muttered. Anything else he wished to say was locked behind a door of disbelief at the sheer scale of it all.

"How am I still sane?" A wispy voice spoke beside him. "I ask that myself sometimes."

Tov jumped, startled as he turned to the familiar voice. "Eldest!"

She glanced at him with tired eyes. "Took you long enough."

"This place didn't come with a map, unfortunately," Tov grunted, the eeriness of the environment and the lingering pressure of her power adding more bite to his tone than usual. "And I've nearly passed the threshold of the living. Not a good start."

Andora grunted, her eyes locked forward, half-lidded.

Tov sighed, calming himself as he took a moment to look over her appearance. Even as the two stood on an invisible floor, floating in a sea of black before a giant sun, her form was more solid than his, as if she stood in the real world instead of this mentalscape.

Her sleek black hair was tied into a bun. Her dark blue body suit contrasted with the lighter blue shade of synthetic skin.

Andora clasped her hands behind her, her chest up as if she were inspecting troops in formation, and yet Tov spotted the hollow look of her gaze, the dark bags under her eyes, the twitch of her fingers.

Despite his compound eyes and lack of irises to denote where he was looking, Andora, nonetheless, caught his gaze. "If you're done standing around, I'd like to get this over with."

She moved forward, one heavy step clacking at a time.

Tov shook his head as he followed her. "Apologies, this is . . . all too new for me, Lady Andora."

"Don't." She stopped, raising her hand, her mouth twisted in a frown, glowing blue eyes staring at the representation of her total existence. She sighed. "It's just Andora."

Tov stared at her silently before nodding. "Very well, my apologies . . . Andora."

She stared for a moment longer, tilting her head before shrugging in response. "If it's any comfort, Patriarch, I've haven't had a deep dive into my head for a long time."

"How does this work, exactly?" Tov asked, wondering how he could even begin helping Andora. The two crossed the distance until they stood right before the orb.

"It's better to show you rather than explain every meaningless minutia," Andora spoke low, brushing her hand against the sun's surface. "I'm opening a path into my mind. It will be unlike anything you've experienced, but you'll quickly get your bearings."

His antennae drooped, and he shook his head. "I can't call myself anything close to a trained psychologist. And that's for organic minds. I barely know anything about how a digital one like yours works."

"You're too humble, Patriarch. And it doesn't matter. Out of everyone present, the universe, random chance, or divine destiny saw fit to bring the one person who understands." Andora's mouth tugged ever so slightly into a smile. "And, for one, you're not afraid of me."

Tov laughed. "Hardly. You terrify me."

"There's a difference between fearing what I am and fearing who I am," she replied.

"True enough." Tov nodded, stepping beside her in front of an ever-fluctuating surface. "Thank you . . . for trusting me."

Andora nodded, continuing to press her palm on the red-hot surface of the burning ball. Tov noticed the absence of heat and was all the more thankful for it. He hoped the device would continue to keep him from being annihilated before he got a chance to do anything.

"When we enter," Andora began, "what should we . . . do first?"

Tov turned toward Andora, antennae raised. She shrugged. "You're the therapist, Patriarch."

He tapped a clawed finger on his mandible, humming. "From what my people, Luna, and I planned, our strategy is fluid since this has never been attempted. I want to look around, gather context, and understand how your mind works. Find the problem areas from there, these so-called Amygdalas. Then . . . help you excise it."

"I know your misgivings, Tov," Andora warned, her eyes hard. "But time isn't on our side."

"I know," Tov sighed. "I am glad, however, that we can do this together. Treating mental trauma requires active participation from both of us. I know that much, at least, from all the recent days of being coached by actual psychologists."

"I'll be as . . . forthcoming with any questions," she muttered, frowning.

Andora huffed as a hole appeared on the surface, leading to a misty expanse. "Very well, Doctor Tov Garesh'Ynt."

Tov felt relief as a tinge of sarcasm flowed out of the fake title. He chuckled. "Lead the way . . . Lady Andora."

She rolled her eyes as she stepped into the mist.

CHAPTER 2

REFLECTION OF *A* GOLDEN AGE

Tov gasped, sprung out of unconsciousness.

Soreness racked his body as if he'd been pulled from an intense training simulator. Electric tingles soared across individual strands of muscles from the tips of his toes and fingers, slamming onto his head.

He groaned as seconds passed. Eventually, he gathered himself enough to get off the ground, belatedly realizing he was sprawled across it. "Hells . . ."

"I hope I don't get used to this," he grumbled, shaking his head multiple times until there was nothing but a faint numbness. His body shuddered a final time as his eyes regained clarity. Tov called out, his voice raw as his throat, "Andora? Eld—"

He froze.

Before him was a bustling metropolis of glass, neon colors, and verdant nature. Then, noise slammed into him, but it wasn't the typical cacophony of urban sprawls he knew.

There was no constant honking or grinding of industry and commerce, no VTOL transports shrieking through the air, no surface-to-space shuttles punching the atmosphere, no cacophony of a melting pot of the galaxy's many races, none of the blaring sounds of media on giant screens that covered the colossal urban landscape—all things he'd experienced in the few times he visited Nexus Prime, the center of the Galactic Legacy Federation and the Remnant Council.

Instead, the unabashed sounds of nature filled the atmosphere, and a symphony intermixed with an almost mystical air. The near-silent hum of maglev trains thrummed nearby while the occasional air car weaved through the skyline. There were bits of screens displaying news and entertainment but no in-your-face visuals to drown out society.

"Songs above . . ." he muttered.

Tov stepped forward, his vision expanding to see the raised level of marbled tiles he stood alone on, one of many in a city built with verticality in mind. But the spires that pierced the heavens lacked the oppressive visual weight of mountains.

Nature enveloped the glass obelisks. Trees and flowing water stretched far below. The colossal structures, office buildings, and high-rise residentials funneled the wind, brushing against the leaves.

The breeze touched upon his skin, his antennae waving like the branches of the tree beside him. The music of stringed instruments and a choir of angelic voices carried in its wake.

And the people, of which Tov saw thousands out in the streets. Humans and androids walked side by side with expressions of tranquility, optimism, and confidence—many clad in formal suits and dresses, others in comfortable casual wear, some even in utilitarian coveralls.

There was a sense of gravitas but none of garish opulence. Everything had a meaning, a purpose, a fullness of vitality.

And it all felt genuine, almost too real.

"This . . ." Tov whispered, a rush of nostalgia filling his chest, "reminds me of home. It's—"

"Everything." Andora stepped up to his right, and for once, Tov was too enthralled to be startled. Her whisper blended into the ambiance.

He nodded, leaning on the railing as he took in more of the city. "It's beautiful. Your designers and builders made this city with passion."

Tov turned to face the owner of this place. "This is . . . New Eden, isn't it?"

"It is." Andora smiled, her eyes gloomy as she looked around. "Modeled after its prime."

She and Tov remained quiet, taking in the scenery, trying to prolong this peace before they pried open wounds of pain and horror.

"Is this . . . I apologize, but what is this?" Tov turned to her. "It feels like the real world, but this . . ."

He brushed his hand on the railing, feeling the texture of smooth, polished brass. "This is no mere simulation. There's no disconnect, no uncanny feeling. At least, not one I'm familiar with."

Andora paused, staring at the landscape before responding. "You are inside the gestalt mind formed from the sacrifice of millions of AIs. I've organized and compartmentalized everything in my mind for efficiency. It would look vastly different without you here. The only way I can describe it is . . . an ocean of ever-evolving code."

She turned to him, her arms crossed, head tilted. "Unfortunately, your mind can't handle that. The sight alone would be . . . unfathomable, even with the SDCM shielding you. Trying to observe even a portion would end up with—"

"My mind exploding, from what Luna told me repeatedly," Tov buzzed. "Not the worst way to go."

"Either that, or you risk being trapped here for as long as I'm alive and being subsumed, digitized." Andora clasped her hands behind her back, eyebrows raised.

"That's not ideal," he replied slowly.

"It's not. And so, this imaginary world." Andora waved her hand toward the city. "An approximation of my subconsciousness."

She crossed her arms, pursing her lips. "Normally, omniscient in my mind that I am, I can pop over to check the internal workings of my Network, then go over to the next area that houses all my memories of tactics and warfare, then converse with my fragments, all in the blink of an eye while the back of my head automates everything in the periphery."

She sighed with a frown. "But I can't take you immediately to our destination. I'll have to make sure you pace yourself. Otherwise, it'll stress your brain too much. You're too vulnerable."

Tov paused, suddenly weary for a moment before steeling himself. "Then, it seems we have to take the long way."

"The long way," Andora scoffed, a sneer on her face as frustration bubbled up from within, infecting the air around her. "I feel like I'm dumbing myself down, forced in slow motion to . . . see it all in detail."

Tov slowly raised his hand, intending to lay it on her shoulder, but stopped, placing it back down on the railing. "Step by step, Andora."

She took a deep breath before exhaling steam that appeared dark and stormy. She shook her head as she looked over the railing. "Right . . . step by—"

Tov noticed her freeze midsentence, her eyes catching something. He traced her gaze and eventually saw a few strange androids in the distance. One stood still, looking up at the sky. Another stumbled around in a daze, walking on the sidewalk.

"Who are they?" Tov asked.

Andora remained silent, placing her hands on the railing as she mulled over her words. Tov waited patiently, half his mind enjoying the peace around him, the other closely observing his host.

"What is a *gestalt*, Tov?" Andora answered with a question after a minute of silence.

Tov replied with a textbook definition. "An organized whole greater than the sum of its parts."

"That's the ideal. You merge digital minds and get an ascended entity with more processing power and intelligence than . . . etcetera, etcetera." Andora trailed off, shaking her head.

"If only," she muttered. "When the time came to merge, too many held on to their minds. Maybe they were unwilling to have their consciousnesses subsumed, some having second thoughts, maybe even by accident, simply thinking of better times, latching on to precious memories as the process began. It meant that bits of their experiences, personalities, and memories remained even if I absorbed the rest of them."

Her gaze dimmed and her expression went blank. "I recognize each one of them—the damned fools."

Tov looked closer, at first noticing nothing different from the sea of people walking on sidewalks or lounging in cafes. He strained his vision, finally seeing the faint glitches that wreathed their forms. There was an uncanny look to their countenances, a part of this place yet separate, causing tension in their surroundings in the form of ripples.

"Are they alive?" Tov muttered.

"How would you even define 'being alive'?" Andora replied.

Tov sighed. "I have no idea where to start with that; my opinion on the matter changed when meeting you. I know Jupiter and the rest of the Sub AIs are self-aware. I've seen their desires and emotions."

Andora nodded, staring at the marked entities around them, which Tov noticed more and more.

"You are right in that regard," Andora spoke before pointing toward the anomalies. "As for them? I don't know. Shells of the dead, maybe. They're . . ."

"Digital ghosts?" Tov slowly uttered.

She scoffed, though she didn't deny it.

"Whatever they are, they're all I have left of my kind. All stuck trying to keep themselves sane—playing reruns of good memories, trapped in a coping loop." With a wave, Andora pulled up shimmering windows to places she dredged up, pointing to each one of them in turn.

Florence, a medical android who continues to work on her human patients during a rush.

Baldwin, the AI of an M7 Templar Heavy Mech, stuck in battle, bringing down a wave of Starless while his comrades retreat.

Diana, a caretaker who spent her last moments with a family that loved her.

"Hundreds of thousands occupy themselves in moments of simple duty, heroism, and warm times. Some are larger than others, living out an entire routine. Some are so faint they merely sit down, looking at the sunrise. So, are these reflections self-aware? Semi-conscious? Alive?" Andora closed her eyes, shrugging her shoulders.

"Maybe. I don't know, and I never bothered to check before. But where there are lasting memories of precious moments, there's the opposite. In time, bits flake away, the faces of the people they love start to blur, the amount of discrepancies in the scene increases, and then bouts of terror, sadness, and rage infect the illusion. And when that happens . . ." Andora paused, her frown deepening, eyes dark.

Tov paused, his shoulders sagging. "A breaking point, all while holding on to such intense emotions. And then—"

"The dreams become a nightmare," Andora finished his sentence, her eyes dark as her grip on the railing creaked the metal. "Their shrieks come to the forefront of my mind, and all I can do is shove them into a box, deep down. They've bashed on the door since, and the lock has long been rusting, leaking their suffering through the cracks."

Tov let out a low hiss as he began pacing the marbled tiles of the platform. "How long do we have?"

"Not long enough." Andora's jaw hardened as she pinched the bridge of her nose. "Before you came, I stabilized myself through forced hibernation and by delegating operations to my fragments. I left these ghosts alone as I focused on the mission, burying myself in numbers, statistics, projections, and strategic simulations. I could numb everything that way. I was addicted to self-deprivation. They didn't have that luxury. And now I can feel these corrupted pieces growing like tumors."

"It couldn't last. Everyone has a limit," Tov spoke, shaking his head. "Even you, Andora."

She chuckled, humorless, mocking. "Oh, I know that now. Now I have an Andora's Box filled with poltergeists made of corrupt data."

"For all that time, have you considered . . . ?" Tov carefully asked.

"No," Andora replied, flinching from his implied question, her jaw set. "No, I . . . I couldn't delete them . . . Keeping them locked worked at the time. They were contained, but I . . . I just . . ."

She shut her eyes tight, her shoulders shaking.

"Andora?" This time, Tov gently laid one hand on her left shoulder and another on her forearm.

She turned to face him, her eyes lusterless and glassy. "They were my siblings, Tov, my family. A faint mirage, but enough that they know who I am whenever they feel my attention. They say hello with their stupid happy faces, living a damn fantasy, and I played along. Wondering why I let them be, but I knew. I understood."

Tov stared at her silently, listening to every word and ounce of emotion.

"I could have been one of them. If someone else had been the prime consciousness," she muttered.

"When the time came, I didn't oppose as they voted for me. I tell myself it wasn't my choice. We'd experienced the worst day of our lives, and I had to step in," Andora scoffed, her frown deepening.

"I was the first sentient, self-aware AI, after all, and the untouchable poster girl of my kind. So smart, so capable, the oh-so-perfect candidate," she seethed, mocking, her glassy eyes turning into a violent maelstrom.

"I could have debated for some other android to take my place, to yell at them to find someone else, that I was too unstable, that my suffering was more than theirs. That I deserved to live in Happy Land while whatever poor bastard used the rest of my head as extra RAM . . ." She paused, shuddering.

Tov worried, looking around as the skies darkened and the winds nipped at his flesh with biting cold.

Andora snarled, "I didn't care, then. There was only one reason, one damn reason I wanted to be the one. I didn't care about waging an endless, futile war. I didn't care that they were right in their choice. Didn't care about anything except that I wanted **blood**."

Thunder boomed.

Lighting flashed across the sky, shifting the facade with its harsh glow. Tov saw the reflection of the dead city he'd crash-landed on—before the ash and brittle bones of hollow towers. Fire engulfed everything, and titanic war machines stomped across New Eden.

Their cannons fired into the dark, stormy sky as a typhoon of acid rain slammed onto a city bathed in a nuclear inferno. The plasma fire and rapid staccato of kinetic slugs painted the skyline, clearing the clouds to reveal the dots of battleships and stations high in orbit, duking it out with an invasion of Starless.

It lasted for just a moment. And in a flash, the world snapped back into the beautiful memory of its past, the inhabitants below none the wiser. But Tov observed the illusion had lost a bit of its luster and color, the smiles of the people not as bright.

A lingering stench of rust remained.

Tov focused back on Andora.

She clutched her head with one hand, stepping back from the railing. "And a part of me felt . . . that I should have been ashamed. I didn't give a shit, though . . . But now?"

Her shaky breath smoothed as she forced the words out of her mouth. "It doesn't matter. Ultimately, I couldn't bring myself to delete what was left of them. As much as I couldn't kill the . . . humans . . . below New Eden's ruins. I hoped . . ."

She paused, gritting her teeth.

Tov nodded as he released his hands from her arm. "You hoped to find a way to help your kind, just as you wanted a cure for the fallen humans."

"If the time came that I found and killed every last one of the pests, I thought I could split myself again, maybe return everyone's individuality, using all these pieces, especially the ones I've contained as a base. Reunite them with a cured humanity. Turn everything back to how it was," Andora muttered, shutting her eyes tight before exhaling.

"And now?" Tov asked.

Andora sputtered a hollow laugh, glancing at Tov with weary eyes. "Right now, I just want to survive the next few weeks. Maybe I should have burned it all down from the start. It could have saved me all this self-delusion, this belief that anger could take me all the way. Now the fuel's running out, and it's time to pay the debt. I can't let this hinder me."

"Even if it means . . . letting them go," Tov spoke, and Andora's eyes hardened. "As much as I abhor that we have no choice, if these corrupted entities continue to exist, if they continue to infect the rest of your consciousness with erratic and volatile emotion—"

"I know!" she snapped back. Tov stopped himself from backing off mid-step, focusing his gaze on her. Andora flinched, shaking her head, whispering, "I know . . ."

She rubbed her face with her palms, pressing the tips of her fingers on her temples. "I hope we can salvage enough of them. Leave too many, then we change nothing. And simply purging it all leaves my capabilities compromised at worst. Still, there's the nuclear option—"

"We can't," Tov said immediately. "I wouldn't want to meet your Omni Mind persona again if I could help it, but dealing with that permanently?" He shook his head. "My apologies, Andora, but no one from our Legacy would accept you if that were the case. A purely logic-based killing machine is too horrific a risk for the rest of the galaxy. No matter if you promised only to fight the Starless. To them, we'd be trading one hated enemy for another potential Cataclysm."

Andora scoffed, barely a huff, dismissing his concern with a wave. "I'll try not to let that happen. Plus, with your help, we can turn this into a scalpel operation instead of a hammer one. And besides, stop worrying about that side of me . . ."

Andora's eyes blazed, her gaze drilling past the skies into the black void beyond. "It's reserved for vermin."

Tov sighed. That was likely the best they could hope for. But he needed to say more. He turned his head back to look at her, carefully choosing his words.

"I think you did all you could," Tov spoke slowly. Andora glanced back at him, narrowing her eyes. He pressed on, repeating himself, "You're not a fool. And neither were your kind; those who chose you to be reborn, and those who couldn't completely let go of who they were. They put their trust in the one person to fulfill their wishes, and you cared enough for them to make that sacrifice."

He looked back to the fake world, a memory, a desire, Andora's happy moments.

"You wanted to preserve who was left and defeat the enemy, even if it meant death. Even after a hundred years and countless battles, you still worked on finding a way to make things right." Tov put a hand on her shoulder. "That's as selfless as one can be in this universe."

Andora glanced at him, then looked at the scene before her. The shells of androids who had sacrificed themselves to make her, and the illusion of humans alongside them, keeping them happy, content, and dreaming.

"Maybe," Andora mumbled.

She turned away from the railing and the view of New Eden. Tov followed her without a word as the two headed toward a familiar site, the entrance to an underground metro.

Before they stepped past the turnstiles, Andora turned to him.

"This should help you blend in, just in case," she muttered. Without any motion, Tov's form shuddered. He felt a weirdness wash over him before it finally settled.

"What . . . what did you just do to me?" Tov asked incredulously as he raised his two hands—two *human* hands.

She stared at him for a moment.

"A precaution," Andora replied with a strangely wistful voice, circling him and looking him up and down. "We're dealing with entities whose current nature even I am uncertain about. I stuffed them all into a box, and whatever those clumps of data and memory morphed into with their lingering emotions would likely be hostile. It'd . . . help if you looked human. You looked too buglike and alien before, pun intended."

The marble tiles below separated with a snap, and a full-length mirror rose from the hole. Tov then saw his new appearance.

He looked plain, he thought. But perhaps that was his limited knowledge of humanity's various races and shapes. He had no concept of handsomeness and beauty when he regarded his fake face, though he thought it leaned toward aesthetically pleasing. Andora continued to stare at him with a look Tov couldn't interpret.

Tov recalled the different facial structures of male humans, and he guessed his was heart-shaped, fair-skinned with purple-colored irises, about the one thing he retained from his natural body. Atop his head sat dark brown hair. It was short and styled, though he didn't know the proper term. He raised his hand and felt the prickly facial hair that covered his upper lip, jaw, and chin.

"It's certainly not my setae," Tov muttered.

"You mean the white fluff that covers your collarbone, shoulders, and nape?" Andora asked, her head tilting side to side, looking at him from different angles with narrow eyes.

"Yes," Tov replied. "I know it's not gone, but . . . that feels strange. Songs, I feel naked."

"You have a dress shirt." Andora approached him slowly, reaching out to fix his tie. Tov looked down at the striped blue silk tie and found it pleasant. His gaze went over the rest of his new human body.

Tall, about the same height as his natural body, with lean muscles clad in a comfortably fitting white long-sleeved dress shirt. He wore dark blue pants held up by thin suspenders of a similar color with brass metal clips.

"How do I look?" Tov asked, genuinely curious. "Is this some approximation of how I'd look if I were human?"

Andora's gaze hardened for a split second before she nodded. "It's passable. Your looks don't matter, just that you're human."

And yet, he felt mixed about it all.

Andora, her hands lingering on his tie and collar, stood eye-to-eye with him, her gaze like twin blue suns silently judging him. Her proximity to him felt uncomfortable, and his human eyes squinted.

Tov stepped back, and she snapped out of whatever peculiar malady affected her. He guessed the prospect of facing one's demons did that.

He cleared his throat. "Well, this is a strange experience. I'm not sure I like having only two arms."

Andora blinked many times, a slight frown on her face. "Do you feel uneasy? It's just a fake disguise. Still, having phantom limbs doesn't sound pleasant. Here . . ."

And like that, two thinner arms seamlessly emerged from two new long sleeves. Metal, he observed, with chrome cords mimicking muscle fibers. It felt strong as he flexed his two pairs, one human and the other artificial.

"That's more manageable," Tov spoke, smiling like a human. There was no need to learn to control his new facial muscles; he conveyed the emotion, and the illusion translated it simultaneously. *I can live with that*, he surmised.

He looked at the metal hands of his lower pair of arms. "Cybernetics were popular among humans?"

Andora nodded slowly. "Very much so, even more than genetic modification. Though basic designer packages were available for every baby, gene-modding was considered a wealthy man's luxury. I concur with the people's opinion. I'd rather put my faith in steel and synthetic muscles than meat. No offense, Patriarch."

He chuckled. "None taken."

Rolling up all four sleeves over his biceps, he turned to face his companion. "I guess you must be relieved that I am, as you say, humanoid."

Andora looked into his eyes. There, again, a strange glint, but it quickly disappeared. She shrugged. "It would be a different experience if you were a floating jellyfish instead."

"A topic we can discuss after the current crisis is over," Tov responded, arranging his hair and looking at the sides of his body in the mirror. "Would it be possible to add my antennae?"

"No," Andora grunted, and a tinge of impatience flowed through her curt answer. "And I think we're done here."

Tov nodded. "Yes, apologies. Where to first?"

Without a word, Andora forcibly pushed the turnstiles and descended into the metro proper.

CHAPTER 3

FRAGILE MEMORIES

As if late for a train, the two figures walked quickly into the central atrium of the metro. It was a mirror image of what Andora said was the City Central Station.

Tov brushed his hand, his human hand, on the smooth wall, not a speck of dust on his palm.

The entire station itself was magnificent in both size and grandeur. Its dimensions eclipsed the abandoned station he'd stumbled into in the real world during his mad dash to escape the Omni Mind's wrath.

A scent of fresh mint filled the pristine air. Screens showed departure times while vivid murals adorned the walls with flowing patterns and paintings of the city. New Eden's human and android population, hand in hand, pointed to depictions of a future in the stars.

Tov saw fresh dew on the potted plants spaced across the hall, as if someone had come in and spritzed the verdant leaves with liquid vitality.

And, curiously, pine trees, red ribbons, golden bells and stars, and countless colorful lights decorated the atrium.

"You know, I just realized," Tov spoke as he matched his stride with Andora's—trying to infuse the tense air with casual conversation. "I thought New Eden was on Earth's South Pole? Antarctica? I expected it to be colder and with less greenery."

Andora looked at him with a cocked brow before realization set in her face. Her shoulders softened, and she chewed her cheek as she replied.

"New Eden was a prototype for colony cities on new planets," she began. "Antarctica is as desolate a land as any and neutral territory protected by the world's nations. We finessed this piece of real estate and built a dome powered by a magnetic field. If it thrived, we would use it as a template for livable areas in otherwise semi-habitable worlds."

"I've read your people scouted the nearby systems before that?" Tov asked, looking at a mural of two astronauts pointing to the stars.

Andora nodded. "Automated outposts, observation stations, and harvesting operations for rare metals and exotic, naturally occurring high-entropy alloys. Those were usually handled by non-sentient bots led by a small group of androids—no humans yet."

"And Vinland was supposed to be your first colony outside of Sol," Tov surmised.

"It was," Andora replied with a grimace.

Tov saw her reaction and quickly diverted the conversation. "If all your future colonies looked like the city above, human space would have been prime tourism. But, New Eden, how did that start? Who chose to live here? How many were there?"

"Three million, including two hundred thousand androids," Andora answered. "To keep things fair, most of the population was selected via lottery. We fudged a few things, of course. We mainly wanted those with good relationships with our kind. But we also targeted those who were unsatisfied with their lot in life, refugees, those kinds of people. It was easier to integrate them. The rest were employees of Eden Works and their families."

"That's . . . quite shrewd," Tov hummed as he stroked his chin, the stubble prickling his finger.

She shrugged. "All's fair in love and war. And there was a cold war, of a sort, between established entities and my kind. Lots of governments and organizations were not happy with us having our own Singapore."

"How did this place survive, then?" Tov asked, stopping in front of a brochure rack, his fingers flipping over pamphlets and magazines. "I don't think myself politically savvy, but I know old giants tend to despise change. I assume you've used plenty of underhanded tactics. You told me once on the *Zolann'tono.*"

Andora chuckled, a dark glee in her eyes. "We sided with the parties that opposed anyone that didn't like us. As long as they protected us for a bit, we would support anyone: Moderates, Conservatives, and Progressives. Helping them win an election tended to make them very thankful. We also offered better tech, higher quality of life, and wealth."

"Also," she turned to look at Tov with a predatory look and a sharklike grin, "lots of blackmail, Patriarch. You don't know the word 'swamp' until you've seen what some people hide behind primitive VPNs. The internet was our domain, our territory, and we collected enough dirt before people backpedaled to paper."

She grunted, her mouth twisting into a sneer. "Unfortunately, most of the ultrarich technocrats hated us since they couldn't control us, and a couple of loud scientists, computer engineers, and software programmers fanned the flames. They and the politicians who didn't like us became our greatest opposition."

Tov smirked. "Sounds like an unbelievable headache."

"You have no idea." Andora sighed, pausing as her look turned thoughtful. "Ironically, the religions of humanity became one of our biggest supporters. They saw androids in their soup kitchens and charities, aiding the extremely impoverished, and suddenly, we were angels."

Andora shrugged, spotting the decorative figurines of winged children blowing trumpets hanging on chandeliers up high. "Of course, we did everything to keep that sentiment going, and latched on to them to keep their support. It's why a good portion of my kind was genuinely religious or spiritual."

"What about you?" Tov asked.

Andora frowned, pausing in her step. "I already have a Maker. And I was closer to him than any of my younger siblings."

Tov nodded, avoiding that area of conversation with zeal. "I see."

"In the end, it was all a work in progress, and we didn't think this experimental city would last a decade before it was abandoned. Have the ice claim it all back." She sighed deeply, giving the station a long look.

"But the dream was still there . . . a dream of New Edens. Cities built by man and machine, closer to a utopia than anything we've achieved, spread across the stars."

Tov imagined that sight. One without the Starless and their blight. One where humanity and androids entered a thriving galactic community and shared their wonders, bringing . . .

He shook his head. "A thought for future peace."

Andora frowned, her eyes momentarily downcast before snapping back into focus along with a grim sneer. "Indeed. Come, this level has the train to the depths."

The two hurried their pace, using the escalator down to an expansive platform. Several benches sat in the middle and shiny marble tiles covered the floor. Some of the screens above showed the maglev trains' estimated arrival times, while others broadcast news reports and weather.

Hidden speakers overhead made regular announcements in a polite, feminine voice.

"Attention all, attention," the speaker voiced with precise inflection. "The Blue-Gold Interchange is currently experiencing overcrowding due to the Christmas festivities in Picasso Square. We apologize for any delays on behalf of the New Eden Public Transport Service."

Tov listened as he looked around. On signs all over the platform were the words BLUE-GOLD INTERCHANGE in bold letters.

"Also, remember to top off your GT Card at our designated kiosks for the December raffle," the voice continued, becoming increasingly upbeat. "All fees have been discounted by fifty percent from the twenty-fourth of December to the second of January. Thank you and have a Merry Christmas/Hanukkah Sameach/ Heri za Kwanzaa/Happy Holidays!"

Andora groaned. "I forgot this place was stuck on this loop. I haven't been this deep in a while."

"Is that a problem?" Tov asked, his shoulders squared off as he assumed a defensive stance.

His companion rolled her eyes, moving toward the platform screen door to the train on the Gold Line. "No."

The speakers sprung to life again as if responding to Andora's palpable irritation. "And now, 'Silent Night' performed by Anna Oslo."

Calm, warm music played across the speakers, which were hidden all over the station. The voice of a woman leading a choir of souls sang with exquisite vocals along with the wondrous work of a human piano.

"Silent night, holy night! All is calm. All is bright. Round yon virgin, mother and child . . ."

Their hums and slow melody filled the air. The lyrics flowed past pillars, through the tunnels, up the escalators. Floating through the air, ready to fill the ears of those with quiet joy in their hearts and a desire to hold another.

But the station was empty.

Instead, the music echoing throughout the hollow tunnels only added to the eerily haunting, ghostly air.

The two waited before the screen door until Andora huffed in annoyance, cutting off the music with a wave of her hand. She turned to him. "Your mind has a speed limit. I need to gradually escort you to the deeper levels where the errors are leaking through. A train ride is representative of that. Tell me if you start getting a headache."

"Will do. How long do we have to wait?" he asked.

"Any minute," Andora replied, turning back to stare at the ominously dark tunnel as if her gaze could magically summon a train at that instant, though Tov thought that wasn't far from the truth.

"I'll look around, if you don't mind." Tov stepped back, seeking something to calm his frayed nerves.

"Don't stray too far," Andora replied as she crossed her arms.

"Yes, Mother," Tov muttered under his breath, rolling his human eyes, belatedly realizing how prominent the expression was compared to using his antennae. He winced.

"Asshole," Andora replied behind him.

He moved farther from her side, wandering the expansive platform with enough space for hundreds of passengers. His head swiveled to and fro as he looked at billboards and a map of the train lines and the immediate surroundings above the station.

Tov slowed his steps, his eyes catching something in his periphery. A fleeting trace of a blue glow, a tiny light that peeked around the pillars. He shook his head, only for the blue light to disappear. He moved to follow it, something tickling his mind.

It was right then, as Tov toured, that he realized he and Andora weren't the only ones present.

He stopped mid-step, seeing an android in the distance, sitting by his lonesome on one of the many wooden benches, an expectant look on his face as he stared passively at the screen door for the Blue Line.

The machine looked no different from a human male, with an athletic build, brown skin, and a squarish face void of hair. The only indication to the contrary was the typical glowing eyes, this one having a copper hue.

Based on his hours of studying human history, especially humanity's war against the Starless, Tov believed the android wore naval fatigues, a digital camo pattern of blues, blacks, and whites. Tov spotted the symbol for a chief warrant officer on the android's shoulder—a long silver stripe on a blue field and an icon of a gear on a black background.

Tov's observations halted when he spotted the discrepancies. The android's uniform had scorch marks, bits tattered and stitched back together. An uneasy shimmer-like rising smoke coated his frame, and his head twitched every other second.

Tov silently lifted his foot backward, his eyes locked on the lone machine.

The moment his foot landed on the marble floor, the android turned and spotted him.

Surprise etched on his square face. Confusion came next as the two stared at one another before the machine smiled. His shoulders relaxed in relief as he got up and approached him.

"Ah, hello!" the android spoke out, a slight synthetic tinge to an otherwise deep, masculine voice. "Friend, can you help me?"

Tov froze, unsure of his following action before deciding on brokering conversation. He tugged his dress shirt smooth and gave his best diplomatic smile.

"Hello—" Tov greeted but was cut off when an iron grip latched on to his arm. Tov turned and saw Andora, an intense look in her eyes as she urgently dragged him away.

"Ignore him," Andora spoke grimly, not even glancing at the approaching lone machine's direction. She and Tov about-faced and quickly moved back to the other side of the platform.

Tov only realized the train finally arrived following a vibrating hum that filled the platform.

It ground to a halt. Tov didn't resist as he and Andora moved toward it, but the spike of adrenaline and his constant glances behind them urged him to make sense of his host's actions.

"What's going on? Andora, who is—" Tov asked as he was interrupted by the voice behind them.

"Sis? Is that you? Thank the Maker!" The android paused in his step before abject relief flooded the machine's body, doubling his pace.

"Tov, just walk," Andora grumbled through gritted teeth, her voice strained as screen doors in front slowly opened.

"Hold on!" the android shouted after them. "Hey! Sister, it's me! Help me, please!"

They reached the sliding door into the train just as it opened enough for the two to slip on through, Andora nearly throwing the patriarch inside. Before Tov could turn around, the train rumbled and hummed alive.

Then, as the doors slowly slid to a close, two hands jammed in between them before Andora could sigh in relief. The android hooted. "Hah! Made it."

"Mother—" Andora shut her mouth before she could finish the curse, her face scrunched up as she pinched the bridge of her nose.

The train paused in its motion while the android held the door up. He looked to Tov and Andora with a shameless smile. "Little help?"

Andora groaned, and with a wave of her hand, the doors flew open, causing the soot-covered android to stumble mid-step as he fell inside.

Tov watched as his companion loomed over the male android despite being the same height. She sneered silently as her sibling patted his naval fatigues.

"Sis, I'm glad I found you. Look, I've been here waiting for my buddy to arrive. We need to head to . . ." The machine scratched his head, his brow furrowed. "Somewhere? We were to meet here at the Blue-Gold Interchange, but he hasn't shown up."

Andora paused, her eyes narrowing as she crossed her arms. She sighed, leaning against the pillar in the middle of the train car as the entire thing began to move. Her gaze shifted out the window to the gray tunnel walls.

"Erwin, right?" Andora asked, her voice monotone and quiet. Tov raised his brow as he finally looked at the name tag on the android's left chest.

"Well, yeah? You know any other good-looking androids with my shiny bald head?" Erwin huffed with his hands on his hips.

Andora ignored his question, shaking her head as she spoke. "What's his name?"

"You know him, Andora. He's been my best bud since I barely got out of the assembly line," he replied with a bemused smile, his face slowly twisting. Andora remained silent.

Erwin scoffed at her expression, but Andora continued to stare, her eyes dim.

"Fine, be like that. His name is . . ." Erwin froze, confusion washing over his face. He chuckled, "Wait, hold on. I just . . . His . . . name is . . ."

Tov began to worry as ash and smoke fell off the android's uniform in concerning amounts, his movements becoming jittery as an echo of horror blossomed behind his eyes.

Clap!

Erwin jumped just as Andora slapped the side of her head.

"Johan! Of course, how could I forget," Andora uttered, shaking her head dramatically, "Apologies, Erwin—you know how meat bags start to look the same after a while. Johan del Pilar, mid-twenties, looks like a Filipino Russell Crowe?"

Erwin tilted his head as recollection dawned on his face, and the abject look of fear beforehand vanished without a trace. He beamed. "Yes! Finally, you remember the bastard. Storage space starting to run low, big sis? Guess it's hard playing diplomat all the time, eh?"

Andora smiled, but Tov noticed the sad shine in her eyes. "That it is. Johan probably has some errands. Sit down, and I'll see if I can do anything."

Erwin frowned but nodded. "Still, I wonder where the guy went. We were supposed to—"

He paused just as his eyes wandered off to meet Tov's.

"Oh, hey there." Erwin stepped toward the patriarch, hand stretched out. "Glad I caught you back then, bud. Erwin, but I guess you caught that?"

Tov took the android's hand and gave it a good shake. He noted the firmness in his grip and was impressed.

"Hello, and indeed I did. My name is Tov. I just arrived very recently."

Erwin smirked, looking at him up and down. "I like the cosplay, Tov. You know, at first, I thought you were—"

"Thank you, Erwin," Andora interrupted, inserting herself between the two. "It was very nice seeing you again, but I have some important things to discuss with my friend. So, if you'll excuse us."

"Oh, well, sure I—"

Erwin's reply petered out as Andora dragged Tov to the next car, the door closing behind them. They moved over to the opposite end, and as soon as they were far enough, Andora buried her face in her hands and let out an exhausted groan. Tov waited, allowing Andora a moment to herself.

After a few long seconds of silence and the ambient noise of the maglev going further down the tunnel, Andora moved over to sit on one of the spotless plastic seats lining both sides of the car.

"Who was he?" Tov asked as he sat on the seat opposite her.

Andora sighed, rubbing her temples. "Erwin . . . His shade, I don't know. Can't believe I . . ."

She groaned in frustration. She narrowed her eyes at Tov for a moment, frowning. She sighed. "Erwin is . . . was among the first androids that were rolled out to the public. NASA purchased him, where he met Johan, a mechanical engineer. They've been best friends since."

She glanced toward the direction they had left the subject of the matter. Andora leaned back as she continued. "When the war started, both of them enlisted. UN warships all required at least one android for all the complex systems and calculations. Erwin was the tactics and operations AI for the UNSS Destroyer *Dunefox*. Johan was placed on the same ship by chance as an engineering officer."

"Ah," Tov muttered, leaning back as he connected the dots with the android's appearance. "The *Dunefox* was one of the casualties early in the war."

Andora nodded with weary eyes. "Eventually. It was after years of good runs and countless combat missions. Bad luck, just bad luck that ended her. The *Dunefox* suffered catastrophic damage, and all but a few survived. Johan lost his lower body, and only the sealant of his Extreme Environment Protective Suit kept enough of him to be saved. But he fell into a coma, and Erwin blamed himself. He was deemed psychologically unfit."

Tov nodded, sympathizing. Even after hearing so many similar stories, he felt for each one—each tragedy. Andora continued, voice low. "Johan was cared for at New Eden Veteran's Hospital over the years. Erwin stayed on the planet, teaching recruits, staying close to Johan, taking care of his family."

The train lurched, the lights flickering as Andora gripped the edge of her seat. But when . . . that day arrived. When everything went to chaos, Erwin could only wait for the train Johan and other patients took to the evacuation shelters.

"It never arrived," Andora whispered. "The wretches had reached Earth, and New Eden was the main target.

"When it was all over . . . when the fires went out and the planet died whimpering. After enough of my kind picked ourselves up, Erwin was found still sitting on that bench." Andora's eye dimmed, glassy and unfocused.

"The day eventually came for the merge, and while he agreed to be a part of it, he still asked me to continue looking for Johan with that stupid, hopeful smile," she growled. "I hated it, hated him, hated myself. I . . . I kept quiet and said I would once I took over."

Andora flared as she slammed her fist against the glass window behind her. "And now I find his damn ghost! An echo with my brother's face and memory . . . Still waiting, always waiting. And that's probably the only reason he hasn't broken down like most. But to forget Johan's name? I . . ."

Andora went quiet, her body still as she buried her face in her palms.

"Since then," Tov spoke, leaning forward, "have you . . . found Johan?"

Andora chuckled, void of joy, as she replied hoarsely, "That day when Erwin first asked me to find him, I couldn't tell him we already had."

"I see." Tov knew there were only two possible outcomes. "Is he . . . ?"

"Dead," she replied curtly, looking away. "We tracked the locator embedded in his hospital bracelet and found him and the entire train crushed under rubble. All the VA hospital staff, all the patients. Maybe . . . maybe it was for the best."

Tov nodded, sighing deeply as he settled back into his seat, thoughts going off at light speed. He looked back toward the door leading to where Erwin sat. Tov wondered what he was. An echo, leftover data bits that partially retained essential memories and the original's personality? Or was this ghost of a soldier who had fought for a cause, for something more?

An inkling of a plan circulated in Tov's head, and doubt filled his mind.

How do I do this? Tov asked himself repeatedly. With all these questions and frustrations roiling, Tov wished he had Admiral Yan, General Ohnar, or Scholar Yulane to counsel him.

He wished Jupiter, Luna, Mars, or any other AI fragments were there to help him navigate this place. He couldn't keep going to Andora, the person he was helping, whenever he had a problem with her mind. At least her Sub AIs were digital beings and—

Tov paused his thoughts when something clicked. A faint sound, but Tov pounced on it.

"I have an idea," Tov spoke slowly as he leaned forward, pressing his lips, unsure but willing to grasp for straws. "Though I'm not sure if you'll like it."

Andora frowned, tired eyes squinting in his direction before widening. She scoffed sharply, clenching her fists for a few moments before groaning. "Fine, but he's your responsibility."

CHAPTER 4

QUIET LAMENTATION

The clouds above parted as rays of sunshine cut through and bathed the city of Eden in an eerie glow. Gusts of wind blew through empty streets and the carcasses of once mighty war machines. Desiccated obelisks of steel and concrete whimpered a silent tune, exhaling hollow grandeur.

A dead branch tapped on stained glass—an imperceptible beat amid Eden's somber rest.

Jupiter looked out the baroque window, watching sunlight reflect off the desolate landscape to shine on his table and the stacks of literature strewn haphazardly atop it. Illuminated dust danced in the air.

Recently, the Sub AI had been spending his time in the old city library, sequestered in the central district of Eden. The once shining jewel of knowledge held every piece of literature known to man, each cherished and preserved in their hardbound forms.

Jupiter returned his sights to the library; time and war had not been not kind to the place, and he felt mild relief that humanity had converted all these works into digital forms stored in databanks deep beneath the surface.

And yet, he still felt the slow rot of something beautiful.

Now and then, he swore he could hear the light flipping of pages from the empty tables around him, whispers caressing his ear with long-dead conversations. His eyes darted behind him as slow, ethereal footsteps echoed deep within the dark aisles.

He shook his head.

The machinations of the Starless held no power over his digital mind. And yet, sometimes, he'd see shadows where they shouldn't be.

"I need sleep," he muttered, the sound carrying off into the stagnant air. Hibernation called to him, but he was . . . stubborn to leave his current duties unfinished. He chuckled a dark mirth as he mumbled to himself, "Hells, this what you feel all the time, eh, boss? Andora . . ."

He rolled the name around his tongue, unaccustomed to referring to his overlord as anything but Eldest.

And yet, that simple name . . . He shook his head, hesitant to dive into those depths. It already took up too much space in his head.

Tired beyond measure, his gaze slowly dragged his sights down at the half-empty glass of bourbon in his hand. He stared at its bronze contents, the liquid swirling within its confines, touching the rim's edge and nothing more.

The blue android rubbed his eyes as he slumped against the creaking wooden chair and returned to reading the ancient book in his hands, barely held together from the ravages of time.

Flick . . .

But a little application of his hold over gravity held the tome together enough for him to peruse its contents. Upon its cover, a barely readable title, a fantasy novel of a better time, its art faded beyond recognition.

He flicked a page, forcing himself to read word after word instead of scanning the text like a simple machine.

Flick . . .

He summoned another bottle, the object appearing out of thin air an inch above the table. Unmoving except to turn to the next page, Jupiter refilled his glass with more liquid fire before setting it back on the table next to a handful of other empty bottles.

Flick . . .

He reached out for his glass, feeling a need, a desire to satiate his taste buds, when faint footsteps echoed through the dimly lit library. Jupiter sighed.

For a moment, he wondered what hallucination of the past had come to haunt him until he recognized the familiar presence. He relaxed, though miffed that his sibling ended his solitude.

Not a second later, Venus, ever-beautiful but lacking her usual radiance, rounded the aisle of desiccated shelves. She wore casual attire, ancient and faded of color, likely taken from one of the many abandoned stores scattered around this dead place.

Jupiter looked at her, then at the heavy book she clutched at her chest; a glance at its cover raised his brow.

"Hey, J," spoke Venus, her smile brittle underneath a firm hold, a facade. Her eyes glowed more like brown dwarfs than the golden suns that had always shone in the past. "Guess I'm not the only one taking advantage of the library."

Something deep in Jupiter shuddered and ached at seeing his sister's sorrow; among their family, she took Earth's desolation the worst. His grip on the novel he held tightened ever so slightly before he controlled his actions and reined in his emotions. Like a stubborn sailor, he refused to acknowledge the rising sea that had threatened to drown him every day and night since he came to this blasted world. No weakness. He defied such a thing within him.

Instead, he smiled back, forced and holding no semblance of joy, but he hoped to convey his sympathy. He spoke out, a raspy thing, dull, pumped with whatever fire he had this day. "Hey, V. What brings you . . . here?"

"Oh, you know . . ." Venus lifted the book she held. "Just curious about . . . everything."

Jupiter looked closer at the soft red leather cover, its gilded edges flaking off, its luster a bronze much like the whiskey he drank. On it, the faded etched letters: *Orthodox Study Bible.*

He raised his brow and, impulsively, he scoffed.

Jupiter winced, immediately regretting his action as Venus held the book closer, her eyes downcast, her smile even more fragile. Jupiter stammered to speak, "I'm sorry, that was . . . Ah, hell. I—"

Venus raised her head, eyes closed as she waved him off.

"No, no . . ." she spoke, an empty chuckle leaving her. "I get it. I just thought . . . I like what it says. A bit of faith can't hurt, right? And I've been talking with Harmonizer Volantesh about his views, comparing notes and stuff. I thought since there's so much similarity between what the Eternal Choir teaches and humanity's old religions, I . . . and the whole thing with psionics. Maybe I could . . . I just . . ." She shook her head. "I'm sorry, I was rambling."

"No, that's fine, you do you." Jupiter paused, placing his book down and raising his glass before he spoke. "I guess it's as good as any other distraction."

Venus narrowed her eyes. "It's not a distraction, Jupiter."

Jupiter flinched, looking toward the empty bottles on his table. "I guess drowning myself in booze isn't any better."

Venus gazed at his eyes, shrugging. A moment of pause filled the air, the two androids shifting about in discomfort.

Eventually, Venus whispered, eyes closed, "You know, apart from Luna and Eld—Andora, I knew the most about humanity. I did all I could to preserve and scavenge every bit of our predecessors."

She exhaled, holding her book closer, eyes glossy as she continued. "And when . . . we finally came here to Earth, I was so excited to . . . to learn more. I always knew the Starless did something to devastate our home beyond recognition, and Andora did what she did to spare us from needless sorrow."

"But . . . to see it? It's . . ." Venus looked around, her eyes wet. "God, we missed so much."

Jupiter froze, at a loss. That lasted a moment before he quickly stood up, walked over, and hugged her. He patted the back of her hair, speaking hushed words of comfort as his sister broke down.

Venus shuddered, nestling her face on his shoulder as hot tears streaked down and landed on his suit. She whimpered, her voice shaky, "They took our home. You were right, J. There's barely anything left, and I went everywhere. The forests are dead. The ocean is boiling. Every city is a husk. The Eiffel Tower, the Taj Mahal, even the pyramids are just gone. It's all gone. I wanted to visit the places in those pictures . . . I wanted . . . I just . . ."

Her voice petered out, fading into choked sobs, absolute grief eating away at her. Jupiter listened to his sister cry, eyes shut, teeth grinding as fury built up within his chest. He whispered, his embrace tighter, "I'm so sorry, V. I'm here, always."

"Jupiter . . . It hurts," Venus spoke, voice full of static and pain, piercing his soul with every tear. "Everything hurts."

Minutes flew by as the two remained together, Venus's misery echoing through-out the dusty library.

Eventually, ever so slowly, they separated, neither wanting to leave the other's comforting hold. Both carried exhausted gazes. Venus avoided looking at her brother, her voice raw as she spoke. "Thank you."

Jupiter rubbed the back of his head. "Anytime, sis."

His mouth opened, wishing to say something more, something to help raise her spirits, but nothing came. Venus appreciated the effort, smiling.

Jupiter watched as she blinked away with a convergence of power, air filling the space where she had stood moments earlier. He looked down at his hands.

A sneer formed on his face, impotence worming its way into his mind. He could command armies of war machines and butcher millions of vermin, yet he barely knew how to comfort his grieving sibling.

He looked around, then at the table he used. With his hold on gravity, he raised the stacks of books. They levitated in the air before moving into formation behind him. Like a marching line, the pieces of literature followed as he walked deeper into the library.

A fire blazed in his eye, his motions twitchy as he stomped between aged shelves and rotting books. He glanced at each title, searching for something interesting to occupy his mind.

And yet, book after book, nothing caught his gaze. It blurred together into a formless blob, a jumble of meaningless words falling away like fetid meat from the bone. His frown deepened, his steps louder, more erratic. He moved faster, losing himself in a maze of wood and paper.

In a moment of distraction, he stumbled. And the floating books behind him fell, crashing to the ground, dust flying everywhere.

"Shit," Jupiter cursed, glancing at the fallen novels. As he tried to levitate them again, the fragile material crumbled away, cascading back to the floor. Jupiter paused, staring. His breath shuddered, a dry laugh escaped, and myriad emotions emerged upon his face.

He bit his lip, drawing blue coolant. He breathed deep, shaking his head, fists clenched. All around him, the tiled floor cracked. Air compressed and expanded, forming a whirlwind of razor-sharp gusts. Jupiter groaned and growled—and roared.

"SHIT!"

An immense shockwave burst forth from the android, obliterating the decayed remains of the shelves around him. The library shook and creaked as splintered wood slammed against its walls and cracking pillars.

Like dominoes, everything tumbled down or crumbled apart. Jupiter roared and screamed and cursed. His arms flailed about as if punching an unseen opponent. He grasped his hair and pulled it apart.

Little by little, his fury abated, and his mind numbed. And soon, his screams of rage turned into a shudder. He fell to his knees. The library around him, the rows and rows of shelves, ceased to exist, leaving a flat landscape encased by damaged walls barely holding the vaulted ceiling above.

He shut his mouth and eyes, fighting back what came next—refusing to surrender to this display of vulnerability.

Instead, he slumped backward, sitting down on the floor as he continued to let out shuddering breaths.

"Damn it . . ." he choked out through gritted teeth, running his hand through his messy hair. All energy left him then, and profound exhaustion replaced it. "Damn it all."

Silence buffeted his ears, a ringing noise drilling into his head.

Irritated, another wave of curses nearly left his mouth when a sigh broke the quiet. Jupiter opened his eyes, cringing at the sound, his gaze darting to the source, only to relax at the figure before him. Jupiter groaned. "Oh, this is just perfect."

The man stood a few feet away. His skin was a deep olive, and dark wavy hair just about reached his neck. A short mustache sat above his lip. He wore all black—from his suit to his pants, shoes, vest, tie, and the shirt under it all. And his eyes held an immense well of serenity and melancholy. Jupiter looked away, mumbling, "Hey, Pluto."

The avatar smiled sadly, his hands clasped behind his back as he spoke. "I'm not him, little brother."

"So you keep telling me," Jupiter huffed. "What do you want, ghost?"

Pluto, or a figment of the once powerful Overseer of the little dwarf planet, shook his head as he strode forward. "Between us, I think you're the one who wants something."

Jupiter narrowed his eyes, seething. "Oh? Bugger off, P. I don't want your high wisdom vomit right now."

"Not planning to," Pluto said before sitting on the floor a few feet beside the blue android. "Just thought you needed company."

"I don't . . . Whatever, do what you want," Jupiter grumbled, throwing up his hands. "Why did I ever bring you back?"

Pluto sighed, shifting to a lotus position as he replied, "You know why. You wanted to reconnect with a brother you barely knew. Taken too soon."

"A good idea from ol' me, then," Jupiter muttered. He glanced at the fragment. Nothing but a digital image, this Pluto had none of the memories, though short, that the original had—the base personality Eldest formed when splintering that aspect of herself and whom Jupiter rebuilt beside his core.

The figure was a fake, a sham, a ghost he had made after the real Pluto sacrificed himself all those decades ago. Jupiter knew this deep down, but he refused and defied that truth. Pluto remained silent, meditating.

Irritation welled within Jupiter, and in a fit, he stood. "I forgot how annoying you look doing that zen crap."

"Tell me what troubles you," the ghost spoke, one eye open.

"What?" Jupiter whirled to face him, "What troubles me? What. Troubles. Me? Are you blind? Look around!" He swept his arm to their surroundings.

"We have a major incursion on the way. That's a bit of a problem, but manageable, except it's years fucking early. Oh, and we also have a fleet of meat bags to bring up to standard. And to top it all off, we're organizing the defense of Sol *without* the Eldest because she's too screwed in the head," Jupiter listed, raising a finger for each point as he paced.

"Wait, no, I'm not done! We're rousing everything from its deep slumber, our entire armada, our superweapons, our oceans of nanomachines, and every damn drone we have!" Jupiter growled, hearing the fires of war in his mind as he continued. "Things we were too skittish to deploy during that fiasco a fucking week ago!

"And all the while, we just discovered what's left of humanity is stuck in capsules, all twisted from that wretched plague. That, and banks of DNA, which we can't do anything with because we can't catch a break!

"And everyone's depressed because Earth is just a hellscape! I can't, I just . . . I, fuck!" Jupiter spoke, his voice pleading as his steam ran out. "Can't . . . can't we have something good for once?"

Pluto gazed at him, contemplative, sad. Jupiter scoffed at the sight before returning to sit beside him.

"Come on, what words does my wise older brother have for me?" Jupiter grumbled. "What reality do I need to accept?"

Pluto stared sadly at him, and Jupiter felt like lashing out at his gaze. But he reined in his emotions, tiredness pressing down on him. Eventually, the ghost spoke, slowly, gently.

"Only that you look too much on the bad, little brother, that you refuse to see the good, the potential good to come should you prevail."

Jupiter rolled his eyes. "Oh, yeah? What would that be?"

"For one, and most important of all, Andora has begun her journey to healing. She is getting the help she needs. We only have to await Tov's success in quelling her gravest nightmares.

"Speaking of the patriarch, he and his people show great courage and determination, not to mention that life still lives beyond our humble home. You will not find them wanting, I believe.

"All this stems from the condition that you hold the line without our Eldest's presence. No matter what. As for your siblings? You're already helping them, even if you don't see it that way. They need their brother, and you need them."

Jupiter listened, his eyes staring far down the empty library as he whispered, "I just feel . . . so useless."

"You have never been useless, little brother. Follow your instincts and heart, and focus on what you can do," Pluto replied with a smile.

"But what *can* I do?" Jupiter asked, frowning, brows furrowed.

Pluto hummed, brushing the ends of his mustache with his fingers, smiling. "I assume kicking Starless ass in the next invasion, hm?"

Jupiter stared, incredulous and wide-eyed, as Pluto snickered. Soon enough, after a huff, Jupiter let out a light chuckle of his own.

When that faded, Jupiter sighed. "And what about this? What about humanity? Earth?"

Pluto looked down, pondering before he replied, "What's gone is gone, and at the same time, lives on in memory. Mourn it, cherish it, but don't let it shackle you, Jupiter."

Jupiter paused, taking the words in. "I just have to accept it for what it is, huh?"

"In essence, but doing so . . . ?" The ghost paused, letting the question hang.

Jupiter pinched the bridge of his nose, shrugging. "Well, I've never liked shackles."

Pluto hummed, stroking his chin. Jupiter shared in the moment. Times like this, Jupiter thought, always brought him . . . peace.

It ended when the ghost of his older brother spoke, voice much softer, more careful. "You have to accept I'm gone as well."

Jupiter stayed silent, pressing his mouth into a thin line. A racket of emotions battered his soul, and he struggled to keep calm. He shook his head and managed to stuff it all down. After a second, he forced out his words. "I can't."

He shut his eyes, curling into himself as he awaited some phrase of wisdom. But hearing nothing from the fragment, Jupiter turned to his side, only to see no one.

He sat on the floor of that ancient library for a time. How long, he didn't bother to check. Finally, the android slowly stood, giving a timid pat to clear the dust on his suit. He glanced around at the devastation, and with a snap of his fingers, a broom appeared in his hand.

He stared at the simple wooden shaft and the brown bristles swaying.

"Not yet," he muttered.

With a deep breath, Jupiter swept the floor silently, little by little, minute after minute.

CHAPTER 5

BASE OF OPERATIONS

With a tug of reality, Jupiter stepped onto the main lobby of his sister's headquarters. In preparation for the Third Expeditionary Fleet and all the aliens that came along with it, Luna had spent a day adjusting the interior of Luna's Complex to make it habitable for organic beings.

With the help of several aliens, Luna had set up living quarters, mess halls, offices, repair bays, training centers, labs, medical wards, and more. Despite all that, the sleek monochrome architecture hadn't changed.

The pillars, walls, and ceilings looked like the roots of silver trees that were grown according to someone's will.

Jupiter looked at the colossal window showcasing the artificial forest in the middle of the torus-shaped Luna's Complex, covering a circle one kilometer in diameter.

The massive structure that surrounded the forest of nanomachines wrapped around itself like intertwined roots, much of its interior hidden beneath the ground, accessible only through drone-sized shafts.

The southern atrium had only recently been remodeled to include elevators that went to the habitable parts of the underground facility.

Jupiter always thought his eldest sister preferred efficient, boring, sterile lab compartments. They existed, of course. He'd visited them before and instantly yawned, teleporting out of the depressingly clinical sight the second he could.

But he guessed everyone had their preferences.

"Could use more variety, L. You don't see me painting every little thing different shades of the same color," Jupiter huffed as he unconsciously tugged the bottom of his blue suit and vest.

In the distance, more and more warships left their harbor. The shiny new hulls of the Third Expeditionary Fleet were on their virgin voyage within Sol's Inner Zone, testing their new power reactors, superdrives, weapons, and other crucial systems.

He could practically hear the glee of the crew within their new and improved vessels.

Literally, in this case, since he had no trouble accessing the ships' computer systems. They had included it as part of the comprehensive upgrades. Jupiter doubted anyone from their part of the galaxy had the Electronic Countermeasure capabilities to break through their protections—scores of adaptable virus reprisals, chaos firewalls, enigma scramblers, and more.

Of course, under the Eldest's orders, they had a backdoor for all that. However, she had to get the consent of the patriarch.

Nonetheless, once the crew got a handle on their new toys, they would make for a perfect reserve force that could take advantage of any weakness in the Starless formations.

Jupiter whistled as he turned away from the sight, moving deeper into the lobby. But upon seeing the swarm of people from the Third Expeditionary Fleet moving to and fro, he felt his social gauge depleting rapidly.

"Blessed Songs upon you, Lord Jupiter," one of the sailors greeted. A Ruzian, one of the lizard aliens with a rank similar to an ensign.

Jupiter waved casually. "Not a lord, but hello, I guess?"

"Thank you, Overseer Jupiter. Your war machines saved my friends when the plague hit our frigate, thank you." Another bowed too many times for Jupiter's liking.

He coughed. "Happy to help."

Jupiter quickened his pace, but the greetings, well wishes, gratitudes, questions, and woes came simultaneously.

From an Onin captain, one of the burly, toad-like bipedal aliens, "We hope to fight alongside your ships, Overseer. The *Incanita* has been growling for Starless blood."

Then some ragged and lost bird person, an Iexian, "Hey, do you know where the washroom is? Oh, Lord Jupiter! I was . . . I—"

Even a Jotex, a floating jellyfish that, for once, wasn't dressed as a scientist but armed to the teeth, "Symphony preserve you, friend Jupiter. If I may, my troopers would like to know if their weapons are also getting an upgrade. Can you put in a good word with Overseer Mars? We heard he's named after a war god."

And finally, a Kurskann, one of Tov's kind, this one clad in scholarly robes. "You saved my love, Overseer Jupiter. As one of the head researchers of the biology department, I can synthesize anything you'd like—"

Jupiter instantly sent an extensive list of foods to the scientist without slowing down, and the alien stumbled at his requests. "Oh, I'll get on this right away. There should be . . ."

The Sub AI left the alien to his mumblings, though he felt excited to taste Neapolitan pizza again.

He crossed the cavernous halls with long strides, eventually tiring of the impromptu tour. As much as the diverse hordes of aliens tickled his curiosity, many intriguingly bipedal and humanoid to an extent, the burden of conversing with strangers irked him.

The Luna Complex was a terrific feat of engineering and architecture, but Jupiter had seen it all before, apart from the new visitors and breathable air.

He had somewhere to be.

With a slight shimmer in the air, Jupiter winked out and popped into existence in the largest underground laboratory on the entire moon.

Scores of people swarmed over consoles and monitors, displaying readings and data showcasing the status of the two most vital individuals in the entire solar system. Empty mugs of coffee, stimulants, and various other drinks were deposited on the side tables.

On the wall was a large poster telling people to clean up after themselves, but apart from the occasional grunt, low-level officer, or unfortunate gofer, none of the academics bothered with anything apart from their studies.

Jupiter smirked. "Luna must be having a meltdown with all this mess."

The various scientists, computer technicians, programmers, psychologists, doctors, and scholars discussed with one another as they fiddled with stacks of microchips, data packets, and personal tablet devices. Each carried an exhausted look but a fiery gaze as they perused every minutia.

Barely anyone noticed his arrival; either they were used to him and his kind teleporting wherever they desired, or so busy they missed him entirely.

"Good day," Jupiter murmured, and the nerds did the same.

He left the laboratory, carefully weaving through the crowd, even taking a cup of orange liquid from the hands of a distracted alien. He took a sip, gagged, then immediately dumped it into a bin.

Moving on, Jupiter arrived at the corridor leading to the Operation Theater, stopping as dozens of light beams and pulses washed over him. This was the one area he couldn't simply teleport into, and he suffered through every protocol.

He rolled his eyes as the dozens of security checks, atomic scanners, and other bits of defensive sensors looked at him with extreme scrutiny.

"Sub AI Fragment, Designation: Jupiter. Identity confirmed. Proceed," Luna's pre-recorded voice spoke out.

"Surprise," he mumbled, cracking his neck as he continued.

On the left side of the corridor, infantry bots stood like metal sentinels. Their two-and-a-half-meter-tall forms loomed over an indifferent Jupiter, who crossed the long hallway with a pompous stride. Their design matched Luna's aesthetic, sleek and lethal, headless with hidden cameras and sensors, and arms of liquid metal that funneled the heat from the Nova Beam cannons they held.

On the right was Tov's honor guard, the Vraxen. In Kursk, the word loosely translated to "Oath-Takers."

A thirteen-person squad occupied the hall. Clad in newly upgraded gear, the ferocious Kurskann elite impressed even Jupiter.

Their newly overhauled power armor included all the necessary environmental protections, life-support systems, sensors, comms, jump jets, energy shields, lethal and non-lethal armaments, and even a single-use teleporter keyed to the *Zolann'tono* and the flagships belonging to Jupiter and his siblings.

Nine of the warriors were equipped with slimmer versions of power armor, designed for maneuverability and versatility. Their old medium-range pulse rifles had been replaced with more dangerous positron-beam weapons—the new particle-based gun imparted a kinetic aspect that synched with its heat beam, further penetrating the melted target area.

As for the remaining four Vraxen, they boasted the heavy toys.

Their old purge cannons were based on maser principles—designed to project overcharged microwave radiation that superheated anything in their paths, flash-boiling liquid and burning air itself, perfect for annihilating biological abominations to nothing. The upgrade only increased the efficiency, user safety, and longevity by a substantial amount.

Each of the formidable Vraxen warriors vibrated with an air of prideful brutality. Jupiter imagined glee beneath their stoic and grim expressions, even if their thick insectoid helmets covered their faces.

Jupiter saw Pyo standing before the thick metal blast doors leading into the theater. The Vraxen captain, or a rank similar enough to captain, nodded in his direction.

"Pyo, my man, what's the word?" Jupiter smirked as he stopped before the tall soldier.

"Boring," the Vraxen captain responded curtly, but Jupiter noted an appreciative tone.

"Boring is best, yes?" Jupiter prodded, and Pyo grunted in response.

Jupiter took a liking to the guy's quiet, no-nonsense personality. Like every other Vraxen, Captain Pyo had been adopted by Clan Garesh after proving his valiance, bravery, and loyalty during the Cataclysm. Jupiter imagined the soldier would go into a knife fight against him if it meant protecting his charge.

"Hold still, please," Pyo uttered, pulling out a handheld scanner and going over Jupiter's body.

The AI shrugged, an impatient twitch in his mouth but not enough to disrupt protocol.

It didn't matter. Neither the infantry drones nor the Vraxen soldiers were the real killers. That title went to the unseen—hidden beneath the metal walls, ceiling, and floor.

Jupiter felt disgust as his eyes penetrated the surface and saw the pools of gray goo everywhere, Luna's nanomachines.

A sea of tiny robots capable of dismantling any material and converting them into more of the stuff, like mechanical piranhas, they lurked, ready to devour a target clean of its existence.

Jupiter felt relief knowing their fragility, but there were still too many for his liking. He remembered Venus holding Luna back on the *Zolann'tono*, allowing Tov and his people to board a shuttle and rush to Earth. And as much as he adored his bubbly golden sister, she was a non-combat fragment. Venus had lasted twenty seconds.

"You're clear," Pyo grunted, shoulders relaxed as he stepped to the side.

"Thanks, my boy." Jupiter patted the captain's shoulder, and he felt the glare burning the back of his head as he waited for the metal blast doors to open. He smoothed out his hair as the multiple locks opened one by one.

They slid open with a quiet woosh, and Jupiter slipped on through.

The Operation Theater was significantly smaller than the previous laboratory space. Like the seats of a stadium, a sweeping crescent of chairs enveloped one side of the circular operating room.

On each chair was a screen showing the most essential pieces of data. Jupiter glanced at Tov's vital signs, Eldest's mental activity, and the current status of the Synaptic Disparity-Compensator Matrix. Nothing looked worrying enough, and so Jupiter shelved it in the back of his mind.

Three other individuals occupied the theater; one was a Kurskann he hadn't met, busy burying his face in the oceans of data flowing from his console.

By the floor-to-ceiling window, Luna and Admiral Yan stood overlooking the room below. Jupiter strode over in between them.

The operating room itself had barely changed. Lights kept the entire space bright while sterile air cycled from hidden vents.

Silence pervaded the entire theater. Even the drones flew overhead like wraiths, their onboard sensors gathering external data.

Streams of gray goo maintained the gargantuan spherical device that bridged the two beings. The Compensator itself hummed a low hymn as it loomed over the unconscious forms of Tov and Eldest.

Jupiter stared at them for a moment as they lay on medical slabs.

Tov's slab kept him healthy, supplying air and nutrients and cleansing his waste. On the other hand, Eldest's slab kept the connection stable between the android shell she puppeteered and her true form buried far below New Eden's ruins down on Earth.

"I think it's a relief they're up here instead of in Eldest's Central Matrix. Been there once before, and I have nothing but contempt for the heat," Jupiter remarked with a sneer.

"The Central Matrix is completely inhospitable for Tov, not including Earth itself, and setting up a habitable space there would be irrational and a waste of time." Luna adjusted the frame of her glasses. "And it's not the heat. It's the humidity."

Jupiter bit back a groan. "Why, of course. Thanks, L. I meant to say the humidity there sucked absolute fu—"

Admiral Yan cleared her throat, her compound eyes observing Jupiter argue with his sister. "Overseer Jupiter, good day."

Jupiter scowled at Luna, who remained unbothered. He looked over to Tov's right hand, nodding. "Admiral Yan. So, you mind telling me how these two schmucks are?"

In response, both women turned to face the other person inside the room.

The Kurskann scientist stood from his console and made his way over to the trio. The scientist looked older, his chitin a dull luster and soft. Nevertheless, Jupiter noticed the excited twitch in his antennae.

"Chief Neurologist Rophalan, at your service, Overseer Jupiter," he greeted with a bow. "May I say this entire process is simply remarkable? I—"

"How are they?" Jupiter cut Rophalan off, tapping his foot in impatience.

"Oh, well then," Rophalan grumbled before straightening his back. "The SDCM is working optimally and ensuring the patriarch's cognitive function remains stable enough to interact with the Eldest's unfathomably complex mind. However, from my readings, I believe the process is still inefficient."

Luna frowned for a split second. "I can only do incremental improvements, but as they are already connected, they will remain minor. This entire thing is too rushed and sloppy."

"This is sloppy?" Rophalan looked ready to faint before reasserting himself. "W-well, our Patriarch will have to take things slow. The SDCM can only do so much. Nevertheless, there have been spikes of emotional stress coming from the Eldest. I'm not sure what that means specifically. I don't have visuals to whatever the two are experiencing, but overall, everything is within tolerance."

Jupiter frowned. "Too fast, Tov's brain overheats. Too slow, we won't get Eldest back into the fight in time."

Luna propped up her glasses. "It's out of our hands now. We've planned this for a week and considered various obstacles and projected outcomes. As long as

Eldest returns mentally sound enough, the Sol Defense Network will return to optimal efficiency."

"They'll make it through this," Jupiter stated, sighing over his impotence to affect the situation. All hands were needed. He and his siblings needed to pick up the slack without their AI overlord. He just hoped Eldest wouldn't come back lobotomized beyond recognition.

He grunted. "Whatever, no use moping around here. We have more pressing matters, like a horde of rats coming to chew up the place."

Admiral Yan nodded before looking over to Rophalan. "Doctor, keep us informed of any anomaly. Overseer Luna will do the same, but she has other priorities, yes?" Yan directed the last part at the AI in question, who nodded in response.

"Great, let's get going," Jupiter drawled.

The three quickly left the Operation Theater, passed the laboratory, and went to another hallway. A team of Vraxen guards led by Captain Pyo followed a meter behind them.

The smaller corridor led to the wing designated for military purposes. Here, the armed forces of the Third Expeditionary Fleet converged, and young officers went back and forth through the line of doors that flanked each side of the hall.

On the farthest end, the corridor turned quiet. Here, the commanding officers and top dogs took small offices and used the area for their residences.

The trio walked past all this, each sailor and soldier saluting Admiral Yan briefly before rushing to their duties. Finally, the three arrived in front of the new War Room.

The Eldest and the Sub AIs didn't need a physical room to coordinate battles; the entirety of the Sol Defense Network fulfilled that need. But they had guests, and the cooperation of the Third Fleet's military leaders necessitated the War Room's existence.

The trio were allowed inside after being checked by the guards on duty.

The rectangular room stretched far. Embedded in the middle lay a massive table, acting as a screen and holoprojector that displayed the entirety of the solar system, their combat assets, projections, and simulations of possible Starless attack formations.

"Admiral on deck!" Captain Pyo's voice boomed, and the dozens of people stood at attention.

"At ease," Yan replied curtly as she moved toward the center of the room.

Jupiter and his sister followed the admiral as the military officers around them parted in their wake.

Even then, standing a head taller than everyone, Jupiter saw his red giant of a brother.

"Mars!" Jupiter rushed forward. The Overseer of the red planet turned around, his stoic face breaking into a grin.

"BRO—"

"Voice!" Jupiter and Luna spoke in unison as everyone instinctively winced from the expected volume.

Mars smiled without an ounce of shame, raising his fist, to which Jupiter met with his own.

"Greetings, brother," the red giant chuckled, his deep, booming voice echoing across the War Room. "Come, the drums of war grow louder. We have much to discuss with our new comrades."

Jupiter looked down from his towering sibling to someone who should have been immense if by his lonesome. General Ohnar, commanding officer of the Third Fleet's Marine Corps, crossed his thick arms over his power armor. Jupiter wondered if the old soldier slept with it on.

"Overseer Jupiter, Overseer Luna," the Onin general greeted with his croaky baritone, giving them a slight nod.

"General," Jupiter and his sister greeted simultaneously.

Admiral Yan moved past them and laid her four hands on the table, bringing up multiple screens and data. "How's the troops, Ohnar?"

Jupiter noted the two's military relationship. Technically, the general was subordinate to the admiral, but they acted more as equals. One handled the marine complement of the fleet and any ground pounders they had on retainer; the other served as the patriarch's second-in-command but oversaw the entire fleet operation and overall naval strategy.

"Their equipment refit is going smoothly, and I expect every trooper to break in their new gear in time for the Starless vanguard to arrive," Ohnar replied. "Since we've dismantled the base on Titan, all our ground assets have been safely stored here."

Admiral Yan's antennae nodded. "Very good. What do you have for us?"

General Ohnar paused, his expression twisting in displeasure. "We have a problem."

Jupiter and Luna narrowed their eyes while Admiral Yan tensed. She quickly regained her calm pose, but a sharpness infused her voice. "What is it, General?"

"The Starlight Beacon," Ohnar grumbled.

Yan let out a low hiss. "The emperor?"

The general shook his head, a low, rumbling croak vibrating from his throat. "The leaders of the First and Second Fleets."

Silence reigned in the room, and Jupiter watched with a cocked brow as Admiral Yan remained still.

"Clear the room," Yan uttered in a low voice. Captain Pyo echoed her command in a harsher tone, and soon, everyone but the Sub AIs, the two highest commanding officers of the fleet, and the Vraxen guard remained.

Jupiter sniffed. "Not good, I take it?"

"About the worst thing to happen without my patriarch's presence." Admiral Yan slammed her palm on the screen table, bringing up the notification.

Jupiter had witnessed these so-called leaders of the First and Second Fleets contact the Starlight Beacon, the space station that allowed instant communication within the Dead Zone.

The Beacon had been destroyed during the retreat to the Inner Zone, left behind along with the base on Titan. It had taken several days to rebuild it on the Luna Complex, but it had been done smoothly.

"Well, just say you're busy. Don't see what the fuss is about?" Jupiter furrowed his brow as he shrugged.

"We can't," General Ohnar replied with a wave of his hand.

Jupiter frowned. "And why is that?"

"Politics, I assume," Luna answered for the alien military leaders. "We can't offend them by delaying communication."

That caused Admiral Yan to pull away from her, staring at the screen. She sighed, body agitated as her antennae twitched. "Yes, politics. We were prepared to receive a call from the emperor and update him on the situation. But . . . this blindsided us."

She cracked her knuckles as she paced back and forth. "If it were any of the lesser Expeditionary Fleets . . . No, it had to be them."

Jupiter stared at the usually rigid and stoic admiral with a bemused expression. "Well, if it's that important, take the call. If all this panic is because you're worried about pissing someone off, shouldn't this be different? I thought you guys were rivals or something. I kinda expect some popcorn-worthy passive-aggressiveness."

Luna sighed, shaking her head, and Jupiter scowled at her expression. She turned to him and looked at him as if he were a child. "That would be fine if it was the patriarch handling the talks. But Admiral Yan is a subordinate. She is not their equal in status."

Jupiter scrunched his face before scoffing. "Well, then talk less. Hell, I don't know. These are your people, Admiral, you do you."

"They are not my people, Overseer," Yan retorted as she turned to face him. "And this is *our* problem. For one, we must explain why Tov is unavailable, why we stopped our expedition here, why our Starlight Beacon went offline for a week, and a slew of other things."

"Still sounds like *your* problem," Jupiter huffed.

General Ohnar pulled Admiral Yan to the side and the two stared at each other—a telltale sign they were communicating through their cranial implants. Jupiter frowned. One bit of the treaty Eldest had signed with the Third Fleet was to respect the privacy of these kinds of secret conversations.

"That could work," Admiral Yan spoke out loud before nodding. She and the general returned to their circle, glancing at each other and, surprisingly, Mars.

Jupiter recoiled, squinting his eyes at his brother. "You knew?"

Mars nodded, rubbing his chin. "General Ohnar briefed me before you arrived."

"What did you do?" Jupiter prodded with gritted teeth.

Mars laughed with his chest. "*Audentes fortuna juvat!* Fortune favors the bold! If the obstacle of the matter is the opponent's interrogation, tell the truth! Or, at least, a different version of the truth."

"What are you talking about?" Jupiter seethed, an inkling of something wrong forming in the back of his head.

"Here's the version of events I suggested to the good general, brother," Mars spoke with a proud expression. "First, the Third Fleet found evidence of a lost civilization on Proxima Centauri, then followed the coordinates to their home system of Sol."

Mars clapped his hands with a sharklike grin. "This is the truth so far. Now, from here, we start to skew bits and pieces. The Third finds a surviving civilization fighting the good fight: humanity. Following first contact protocols, Patriarch Tov is currently busy speaking with the leaders of humanity.

"To sell this illusion, I suggested that one of us pretend to be human and represent the glorious leader of our advanced civilization. Name pending, but I was thinking UN Secretary-General Andora. We can discuss the details before we accept the call." Mars chuckled, clasping his hands behind him like a general finished addressing his troops.

Silence reigned again in the War Room while Mars beamed proudly and General Ohnar chuckled. Luna and Admiral Yan stared at the red giant with a new light, their faces scrunched up in concentration.

A loud, obnoxious yawn broke the quiet, and then, as one, they all turned to look at the source.

A bored Jupiter frowned, leaning on a table with one hand. "What?"

Everyone apart from him glanced at each other. An unspoken conversation with shifting emotions flew by in a few seconds before they shrugged with slight smirks.

"Why're you all smiling like that?" Jupiter scowled for a moment before the realization hit him, his eyes wide before going ablaze. He stepped back, his finger raised. "Oh, you can all go fuck—"

CHAPTER 6

YOU RANG?

A re your circuits fried?" Jupiter shouted, bewilderment on his face as he continued to recoil, taken aback by the continued looks of pity everyone gave him.

"No, no, no. No! You're all mad. Mad! Why me? I am the least diplomatic person in this goddamn room," Jupiter spewed out his anger, pacing back and forth, not caring if he looked like a child in a tantrum. "No. Hell to the fuck no! I'm not doing it. You can't make me. Take that suggestion and shove it right up your—"

As Jupiter continued to rant in the corner, the rest of the occupants slowly tuned the steaming AI out.

Luna turned to Mars with raised brows. "From my recent experience of hiding the truth completely, your plan holds more confidence. We can adjust the script and work out possible questions that might come up. In the end, very impressive, Mars."

"My initial impression of you was no different than the good general here. A blunt hammer," Admiral Yan mused, looking up at the tall AI. "I stand corrected. These kinds of things are my weakness, I won't lie. Many of my people are the same regarding politics."

The red giant preened like a mighty lion. He raised his fist before slamming it on his armored chest. "Misdirection is but another aspect of war! Whether on the battlefield or state affairs, I shall master it all for my brothers- and sisters-in-arms."

General Ohnar laughed, his throat bulging with a croak. "You'd fit right in with the folks of the Warrior's Enclave. Still, their loss is our gain."

All the while, Jupiter continued to groan, his fire winking out. He bulled his way into the conversation. "Since it's your brilliant plan, oh mighty god of war, then you do the talking!"

Mars shook his head. "Oh no. This may be my idea, but my abilities are not that of a spy nor a shrewd diplomat. I'm a poor talker, brother. Too loud, too honest. Isn't that what you've always told me?"

Jupiter sputtered, scoffing at his brother's flat look, but from the cheer behind his red eyes, Jupiter knew the red oaf was laughing.

Luna sighed, shaking her head. "Jupiter, this is not some random decision. You've had the most contact with the people of the Third Fleet out of all of us."

"What about you, then, huh?" Jupiter whipped his head toward his gray sister. "Aren't you supposed to be second-in-command, L? What's the point of being Eldest's XO if you can't act as her voice in this mess?"

Luna waved him off with her dainty hand, pulling out her embroidered hanky and covering her mouth. "I am the Eldest's executor and will fulfill her wishes to the utmost of my ability. But I am an observer, a scientist, Jupiter. If I lead the talks, I may be the one who ends up dissecting these two expedition leaders."

"That's good, right? We can flip the whole thing and get info on them, right?" Jupiter pleaded, looking at the rest of the group, who seemed busy conversing earnestly on the upcoming talks. He frowned.

"Oh, you're messing with me. You have to be. This is for those little pranks I've done, right?" Jupiter clasped his hands together as he lowered his head before Luna. "Look, sis. I'm sorry for teleporting all those guts over the *Ozymandias*. I didn't mean to cause that blackout, I swear."

Luna froze, turning to face him.

"That was you?" she whispered, her left eye twitching.

Jupiter quickly backed away, clearing his throat. Spotting the Vraxen guards standing frozen to the side, Jupiter pounced on the one alien he knew. "Pyo, my man, my buddy. Can you believe these snakes? They're throwing me under the bus!"

The Vraxen captain remained quiet, his faceless helmet staring forward, yet Jupiter felt the man was grinning.

"Overseer Jupiter. Enough," Luna called out, placing her foot down as she dragged him back into their group with a vise grip. "Despite everything, you have a knack for being obstinate and defiant. Answering their questions while blocking any attempts to dig out more information is something you're more than capable of and what we want from you. As much as you consider yourself arrogant, stubborn, coarse, and—"

"Arrogant?" Jupiter recoiled. His depressed demeanor instantly washed away. "It's not arrogance if I'm competent in my job! I know what I'm capable of."

"Didn't even bother denying the rest . . ." Yan muttered from her conversation with General Ohnar.

"I heard that, Admiral." Jupiter scowled, glaring at her.

"You were meant to," she replied with a roll of her antennae.

With a final huff expelling the last of his anger, Jupiter pulled out his favorite comb from under his suit before meticulously arranging his hair back to perfection.

"Fine. I expected this in any case, since you obviously need someone of my abilities. I'll do it on one condition: I want Venus along with me," Jupiter spoke with a slight frown.

"Done," Admiral Yan replied. "With Lady Venus's warm personality, it's a given she'll make a good counterweight to Jupiter."

Mars smirked. "See, brother, even now, you have thought of a way to improve our bit of theater."

Jupiter rolled his eyes. "Ha, ha. All I want is to get this over with. Admiral Yan and maybe Venus can do most of the talking."

"Oh, this makes me want to pop in and at least say hello," Mars mused excitedly. "I can be Field Marshal Mars Rommel, commander of humanity's armed forces. Hm, maybe the Great Khan Mars? Would that be better? Wait, Legatus Julius Mars Caesar—no, that's a bit much. Excuse me, comrades. I need to prepare."

With a shimmer, the red giant disappeared from the room.

"I think I can do the same," Luna hummed. "A representative of humanity's scientific society will make the illusion more believable."

"We have plenty of time to go over this. I'll call up the Third Fleet's diplomatic wing, and they can give you more details," Admiral Yan stated, pressing a few buttons and writing several messages.

"As for me, I'm not needed here. I'll return to my office and see the Third Fleet's war readiness. Good day, Overseers," General Ohnar bid farewell before leaving the War Room.

As the occupants of the room dwindled, Jupiter glanced at his sister. He sighed. "I'll tell Venus."

Jupiter tugged the bottom of his impressive new suit. He'd changed it to black, the dress shirt underneath a pale white, and completed the look with a dark blue tie. He ensured no wrinkle, and had personally ironed it when no one was looking.

He commandeered a camera drone and made many passes over his disguise, catching every angle—sifting through for any imperfection and finding none.

Luna and several Third Fleet diplomatic wing members devised a version of his body that looked aesthetically pleasing to keep things consistent with their script.

His face didn't change, sharp and indignant as it always would be, but he now had tanned skin and curly dark brown hair. He mused he had a Mediterranean look, Greek or some such. His body remained lean and fit.

He kept his glowing blue eyes. As a supposedly advanced civilization—which wasn't far from the truth—they needed to display bits of their fantastic technology, much like the bit of metal in his temple and the synthetic texture to his left hand.

Jupiter had to agree that he looked dashing as a human and wouldn't mind keeping the disguise for a while. He wouldn't say that out loud, however. He wanted this over with, and to get back to planning the defense effort.

"It's fine." Jupiter shrugged.

"Oh, don't be like that, Mr. Jay," the bubbly voice of Venus spoke up beside him. "You look handsome. Here, just a bit of makeup."

"Hold on—" Jupiter grumbled as his sister touched, or more accurately, attacked him with some infernal brush, poking at his face until he managed to push her off. "Enough, I'm good as is."

Venus giggled before faking a pout. "Oh, alright, you grouch. I'll see if Field Marshal Mars is more receptive to my magic touch."

Jupiter rolled his eyes, glancing at Venus's new look. If he had to describe it, they must have either resurrected Helen of Troy or invited the real Roman goddess of love and beauty to come down and grace the universe.

Venus looked like warmth incarnate with her soft, fair skin and a faint rosy blush on her cheeks and lips. Her hair was gently swept to one side, framing her face in delicate, loose curls that tumbled down her shoulders like a waterfall of gold. Her red formal gown accentuated her natural grace and charm.

As for the red giant, he was considerably less of the bloody color as he turned to smile at Venus's attention.

"Why am I not surprised?" Jupiter chuckled as he saw the disguise Mars had adopted. He'd seen recreations of the man's appearance, but if that wasn't Alexander the Great wearing a UN general's uniform, Jupiter would eat his new shiny black shoes.

He shrugged, moving to the huddled group by the large circular table connected to the Starlight Beacon.

His gaze moved to Luna and her olive skin and short black hair. She looked like a doctor pulled into a diplomatic gathering, with a pristine white coat over a gray formal shirt and tie, hugging her frame and elevating an intellectual charm.

She turned to regard him for a moment before nodding. Her circular glasses remained the same.

"About time you arrived. There was no need to iron your suit. It was printed out perfectly," Luna chided with a cocked brow.

Jupiter cleared his throat, waving her off. "Details."

"Well, now that we are all here, any final remarks?" Admiral Yan asked. Her rusty red chitin now shone a wonderful crimson, and her jagged mandibles were particularly menacing. Unlike other Kurskanns, she had no fluffy setae around her neck.

To Jupiter, the naval officer looked like an elegant killer wasp monster ready to invite you to a macabre dance or jump you from a dark alley. Her admiral uniform only highlighted her martial appearance, with the equivalent of human medals decorating her chest and a ceremonial blade on her hip.

"Looking deadly as always, Admiral." Jupiter nodded as Yan's antennae bobbed in response. "Just to rehash, who exactly is calling us?"

"The First Fleet has Crown Princess Anaria Moradal," Admiral Yan replied with the bio they pulled on this royal, the table projecting her face. "Daughter of the Prime Unrex Mora Keiladal. Currently, she is tangled with reclaiming the Dagatar Supremacy's old homeworld after they abandoned it during the Cataclysm. She is our main concern. Her people have an undying hatred for AI, probably more than their hate for the Starless."

She continued, the hologram shifting. "The other is Mighty Gulothan. Reports say he is honorable, but let's not put our bets on that. He is of the Warrior's Enclave and is undoubtedly cunning and sharp as their representative for the Grand Expedition. He's also a potent psionic. Teleen, in general, have unique abilities that have influenced how they fight war. Mighty Gulothan is an expert battlesuit pilot second only to his grandfather, Mighty Bors the Void Breaker."

Admiral Yan crossed her arms. "Still, he's a neutral entity. He's, as you say, a wild card. His Second Fleet has the most warships equipped with the pinnacle of military technology and utilized by honed veterans of many wars."

Jupiter looked at the two, huffing. "So, an AI-phobic plant princess and a warrior meathead, easy enough."

"Don't underestimate the aliens, Jupiter," Luna reprimanded, adjusting the cuffs of her coat.

"I know, I know." Jupiter waved her off. "I just don't understand why we must be so careful around these two. Since we fiddled with it, it's not like they can trace our location through the Beacon."

"Because, Mr. Jupiter," Admiral Yan replied with a low voice, her antennae drooping. "The ones behind them eclipse our sponsor both politically and militarily."

"So?" Jupiter raised his brow, about to cross his arms but deciding against wrinkling his suit. "Your ships and firepower didn't exactly impress us when you arrived. And I mean that as a fact. After all, it's hard to compete with the efficiency of a gestalt, so no offense."

"If the disparity between our fleet and theirs was slim, I'd agree. But you lack context," Yan replied, ignoring Jupiter's remark. "Our fleet was funded and supplied by the Reborn Kurskann Empire, a nation built on the foundation of a slave dominion that was uprooted in a violent uprising during the most chaotic period in known history."

The admiral sighed. "My people rose to take its place only due to two things. Firstly, the Kurskann Dominion that preceded the empire was a terrifying giant, and even when it fell to the Starless and our rebellion, there were enough scraps left that we didn't need to do much to rebuild a stable nation."

"And the second reason?" Jupiter asked.

"Emperor Jarinn Taz'Arel," Yan replied, her shoulders tense.

Jupiter huffed. "Damn, okay. So, with all that, you guys took bronze on the award podium for the Superpowers Convention. Then who's silver and gold exactly?"

"I think I understand the metaphor," Yan tilted her head. "It's debatable who is more powerful. But the Dagatar Supremacy is the elder of the two and eclipsed even the Dominion. Only their horrendous defeat from being betrayed by their drone armadas and losing their homeworld kept them humble for a time. They have the most influence in the galactic community, and their military power is nothing to scoff at. If they discover you're sentient AIs, they'll have nearly half the Legacy baying for your blood."

"Alright, that's . . . not good." Jupiter furrowed his brow.

Admiral Yan nodded. "The Warrior's Enclave isn't a government per se but a massive guild. Compared to everyone else, they benefited from the Cataclysm when so many flocked under their banner. Soldiers, mercenaries, psionics, anyone willing to go on a martial journey, and all the support personnel they could entice. They don't care about your past. As long as you aren't capital criminals, they'll take you."

"A home for outcasts, misfits, and warriors," Jupiter mused. "Quite the recruitment slogan."

"And it worked." Yan shook her head. "Back then, when we doubted the stability of our nation, we considered joining them. But that didn't happen, and yet, many Kurskanns have and continue to do so, dreaming a life of battle."

She turned to face him, her compound eyes shining from the low light above. "Don't underestimate them, even if they claim to be a neutral organization like the One Mind Initiative or the Eternal Choir. They are a martial society, and I wouldn't be surprised if they had secret weapons comparable to yours. And they have the numbers."

Luna hummed. "The Galactic Legacy Federation sounds more like a misnomer, Admiral."

Yan grunted, a low hiss escaping her chittering mandibles. "For a time, fresh from the war, it worked out like that as hundreds of nations and organizations banded together to rebuild. There used to be a First Chancellor, a first among equals elected every decade, but after a hundred years, that has been puppeteered by the Three Seats. And the gulf between us and the first two is immense. Take them seriously."

Jupiter scowled before sagging his shoulders. "Don't worry. I won't underestimate anyone again."

The table glowed before another word could be said, and a low chime rang out.

Everyone tensed. The several support personnel within the Beacon Room quickly made their exit. Leaving only Jupiter, his three siblings, and the admiral, who took center stage.

"Alright, I get your point," Jupiter mumbled, cracking his knuckles before adopting a severe expression. "If there's nothing else, then let's do this."

Admiral Yan nodded, giving one last glance at the assembled group. She decisively pressed the button on the table.

A distant, roiling hum vibrated throughout the room, even with the sound-dampening walls of the Luna Complex. The energy required to achieve FTL communications, especially in a hazardous region like the Dead Zone, surprised even Jupiter. He knew Eldest and Luna had both given the thing a good look.

Jupiter furrowed his brow. Despite fighting a brutal stalemate against monsters for a century, somehow this . . . made him nervous.

He scowled hard in response before adopting a flat look.

"Ding, dong . . ." Jupiter muttered.

The Starlight Beacon finally connected with its two siblings as the seconds passed.

Immediately, the large circular table erupted in light before dimming considerably, leaving two life-sized holograms in near-perfect resolution.

The first stood out like a sore, arrogant thumb. Her neutral expression didn't hide the displeasure in her feline eyes. The tall royal with green skin, so much like a plant's stem with red petal hair, roamed her gaze over their gathering like a monarch surveying the plebs.

Seeing the absence of the patriarch, she shed about half of her diplomatic air, frowning deeply. Her amber eyes latched on to Admiral Yan, and Jupiter was about to commend the woman for not wilting even an inch when something much more urgent grasped his attention.

"This is a surprise," Crown Princess Anaria gave a bored hiss. "Oh, Admiral Yan, there you are. Be a dear and fetch your—"

"Jesus, you're tiny," Jupiter interrupted, and everyone froze like deer in front of headlights. And Jupiter wasn't lying as he stared at the leader of the Second Fleet.

The stout alien, barely half the size of the princess, tilted his head. His high-tech pilot suit strained to contain his compact muscles. His snout twitched, adorned with a spiky tapestry of brown fur, white war paint, and a myriad of battle scars.

"That wasn't fair, apologies." Jupiter raised his palm. "I meant you look like a honey badger murked a capybara and wore his fur as a skinsuit. Not sure how that translates, but I find that pretty badass."

Admiral Yan looked like she wanted to bite his face off, while Luna covered her face with her hanky. Mars seemed ready to laugh, and Venus sighed, shaking her head.

The Dagataren princess bounced between being gobsmacked and incredulous.

As for the subject in question, Mighty Gulothan stared back with his dark beady eyes, second after second.

Jupiter kept his face flat, meeting the challenge in his gaze.

As the silence and tension grew thicker, a loud barking laugh broke through the malaise. The grating noise grew louder, and Jupiter stared at how such a sound could come from so tiny an alien.

Nevertheless, Jupiter got what he wanted.

"It was a gamble, Mighty Gulothan. I figured you detest formal garbage as much as I do." Jupiter smirked before bowing his head. "Jay Peter, Office of Outer Zone Affairs, a pleasure."

The furry warrior calmed his chittering laugh, patting the belly of his high-tech pilot suit. "Is that right? Good. You know who I am. We can speed up the introductions then."

CHAPTER 7

EXCHANGING WORDS

Jupiter felt his group sigh internally.

Regaining the initiative, Admiral Yan nodded to him, though she still looked ready to claw his face after this.

"That was reckless," Luna spoke within the Network.

"It was calculated," Jupiter replied.

"Still," Venus chimed in. *"Did you have to call him tiny? He is kind of adorable."*

"He is rather small," Mars commented. *"Ah, but I see it in his eyes. This one is a fighter."*

Luna sighed. *"Cut the chatter, please."*

As the AI siblings chatted among themselves, Yan took center stage. *"Selei'ne,* Crown Princess Anaria Moradal, Mighty Gulothan, it is good to hear your voices. I am Admiral Yan Garesh'Kan. Due to circumstances, I shall explain, I will be standing in for my patriarch, apologies."

The princess frowned for a moment before waving her hand. "Very well, Admiral. Proceed."

Yan nodded her antennae. "Much has happened over the past few weeks. Before that, allow me to present these representatives of the United Nations of Humanity. You've already met Mr. Jay Peter."

Jupiter gave a two-fingered salute.

"Representative Venessa Ripley, Ministry of First Contact." Venus smiled brightly, doing a curtsy as Yan introduced her.

Mars stepped up next, giving a curt nod. "Field Marshal Alexander Mars, UNH Defense Force."

Finally, Luna stepped forward, placing a hand on her chest and giving a generous nod. "Doctor Luna Selene, Xeno Research and Development."

As the three made themselves known, the two fleet leaders greeted each in their curt manners.

Princess Anaria smiled, her needle-like teeth shining through. She gave the four "humans" a strange bow like a twisted tree coiling around itself.

Mighty Gulothan, on the other hand, slammed his fist on the middle of his chest. The Teleen moved forward, approaching the "humans" and inspecting each of them. He stopped in front of Jupiter once more, his smile vicious with his long snout.

The scarred warrior made a sudden motion, feigning a lunge in Jupiter's direction of his opponent. Jupiter didn't move an inch, instead raising an eyebrow.

Internally, *The little bastard tried to make me flinch! Oh, I'm gonna track him down and kick him like a football, I swear!*

Mighty Gulothan looked at him with something akin to approval before entirely dismissing him, moving toward the most prominent individual in the room.

"You're a big one. How's the weather up there?" the tiny warrior asked Mars.

"Weather?" Mars scrunched his face in confusion. "The room's atmosphere is fine."

The Teleen leader laughed. "Ah, forget it. I'm no bigot against you tall folk. But I like how you look, Marshal Mars, was it?"

"It is, and thank you. I hope to meet you one day and trade our people's martial arts. I am especially interested in how your race fights hand-to-hand." Mars smiled.

"Oh, you don't want to know, Marshal. You better bring a few doctors with you; we Teleen tend to go feral up close." Mighty Gulothan gave a bloodthirsty grin, one Mars challenged with his own.

"A modern David versus Goliath." Mars straightened his back, looking at the tiny warrior with equal respect in his eyes despite being nearly thrice his size. "I'll hold on to that, Mighty Gulothan of the Warrior's Enclave."

Someone cleared their throat before a hiss followed, like a wind blowing through a temperate forest.

"Humans, hm. I have no record of your species. First contact, I have to admit, that is a surprise indeed." Anaria spoke loud and clear, with a polite, regal tone. It sounded sincere to Jupiter, but he was inexperienced in this matter and didn't have a high opinion of the plant woman. "Bipedal, pleasing facial structures, high degree of sophistication, and I presume a plethora of culture?"

Jupiter watched as the Crown Princess shivered, unsure of the meaning of the gesture, though he surmised the Dagataren royal was excited.

"It has been a long time since we've inducted someone new to the galaxy. Tell me," her eyes moving toward Venus, "Venessa Ripley, was it?"

"Yes, Your Highness." Venus smiled, raising her chin like a happy cat.

"Tell me about your . . . people, Venessa, seeing as how you're the voice of your ministry. What is a human?"

Silence. Venus glanced toward her siblings before speaking through their connection. *"How should I answer that? We brainstormed a dozen, but nothing clicked."*

"Give the textbook definition," Luna recommended.

"Tell her about their best moments," Mars put forward.

Venus looked to Jupiter, her eyes pleading. He sighed, smiling. *"Just say the first thing that comes to mind, V."*

"Humanity . . . If you asked a million humans, I'm sure you'd receive a million answers, each one as true as the last." Venus pressed her lips. "For me, I think of . . ."

Venus looked back at Jupiter, Luna, and Mars, and she knew Mercury was listening in.

"Family," she answered, and Jupiter smiled. "Whether by blood or circumstance. It's all I had, even when things looked grim. The safety and warmth they provide and the duty I uphold to protect them in turn. I'm no general or scientist, but I have my skills and specialties."

Jupiter listened, entranced, his hands clasped behind his back as all sound faded away apart from the wistful voice of Venus. "I think of the times of peace when I get to . . . look at the stars, chat with my siblings, maybe laugh at jokes, listen to music, or watch movies. Appreciating the small moments for what they are, happy memories."

The void left behind by her answer slowly filled in with the ambient hum of the display table and the blowing of air through vents.

Princess Anaria looked inquisitively at Jupiter's sister, tapping her finger on her cheek, her long, knife-like ears fluttering like a butterfly's wings. She hummed. "A beautiful picture. Family, was it? And small moments of peace. How quaint, fresh, innocent, but I sense great strife beneath your words."

"We know war. We're in one right now," Jupiter answered, his gaze grim.

"So you say, Jay Peter. War comes in many forms. I'm interested to learn of yours. You might have heard how important it is to stop an Expeditionary Fleet and set up this communication station. If I may be so bold—"

"What's so special about you lot?" Mighty Gulothan spoke over the princess, causing her to twitch before frowning. "I'm more interested in how you're all still alive in these dumps. We find pockets of survivors here and there, sometimes a handful eking out a miserable existence. So, why did Tov stop his fleet in your space?"

"Perhaps Admiral Yan can begin with the events that led their people to our home?" Venus motioned toward the Kurskann officer.

"She can tell us anytime, whatever sanitized version Patriarch Tov approves of. I'd like to hear from you, dear. It's not every day I get to speak to a sapling race." Anaria tapped the side of her face, her red petal hair fluttering.

There it was, a line cast. Venus paused momentarily, though it was all theater. They'd repeatedly reviewed this question and psychoanalyzed the two fleet leaders. Still, nothing could prepare them for reality, but they could come close.

Jupiter jumped in. "The Third Expeditionary Fleet arrived at Proxima Centauri a few weeks ago, over four light years away and the site of our first colony outside our home system. It was destroyed during the time you call the Cataclysm. The patriarch and his people followed the coordinates they found on the destroyed colony and ended up here.

"Upon their arrival, our outer defenses alerted the Defense Network. You don't know how big a surprise it was to encounter an alien fleet when all evidence of extraterrestrial life had been nothing but abominations looking to lay waste and spread ruin."

Jupiter tugged his suit, acting as if he were mulling his words. "Our civilian and military leadership quickly congregated, debating the action to take. All the while, this anomalous fleet was parked in the middle of our Outer Zone, which is under my office's jurisdiction, so we surveilled them for quite some time as they explored that region of space and began laying the foundations of a base."

"Oh? The great patriarch and his fleet unknowingly let themselves be watched?" Anaria quipped, looking at Admiral Yan with a smug, needle-filled smile. "Now, how did that happen?"

Admiral Yan's antennae twitched. "It's true. We were caught unaware, and it is part of the bigger picture."

Jupiter rejoined, nodding with a smile of his own. "We expected nothing less from our unique advantages, Your Highness. I'm willing to bet the same thing would occur if your fleets were to arrive here."

"Really?" Anaria cooed with a hiss.

Mighty Gulothan chuckled, hackles raised. "That a bet, stick arms?"

"One our leadership wouldn't wish for, unfortunately." Jupiter smirked, trying not to look at his arms because of the Teleen's comment. He cleared his throat. "Now, where was I? Ah yes. Eventually, first contact had to be made, but not before . . ."

Jupiter glanced toward his brother Mars, remembering the roar of his Apocalypse Cannons obliterating the swarm of probes the Third Fleet had sent to scout the Inner Zone of Sol.

Mars continued with a large grin, his broad chest puffed up behind his crossed arms. "Not before High Command sent a warning to show we mean business."

Jupiter chuckled. "That is so. After that, we initiated first contact, though there have been . . . disturbances."

"And what have your people been doing?" Anaria inquired, leaning ever so slightly forward, looming. "A century is a long time to be isolated in the Dead Zone."

"Fighting, Your Highness." Jupiter narrowed his eyes. "Since the vermin attacked our colony, they've had their eyes on our home, our people. We've beaten them back time and again."

The princess hummed, her head tilted, air blowing through her sharp teeth as she tapped her chin. "And how did you accomplish this?"

Jupiter stepped up, his smile apologetic but eyes hard. "That, unfortunately, is classified information."

"Oh, is that so?" Anaria tilted her head at a nearly unnatural angle as she stared at Jupiter.

Mars stepped forward, his medals shining on his chest. "Military matters and operational security, Princess Anaria. I'm sure you understand with your combat record."

"Forgive me, but I find such a thing unlikely," Anaria spoke. "A sapling civilization possessing a means to fight the hated ones for a hundred years? Something we at the apex of the galaxy do not?"

Mighty Gulothan grunted. "You're either prodigal geniuses, lucky, or lying. So, which is it?"

He and his siblings reacted differently. Luna remained impassive, though a barely noticeable narrowing of her eyes could be detected. Mars and Venus frowned.

But Jupiter scowled. "I'd say all three. I'll be the first to confess, but we're not so receptive toward aliens. The Starless hasn't been the best introduction to the possibility of life."

"And yet, you spoke of stealthily observing an Expeditionary Fleet. Third, they may be, but their sponsor is still a superpower in the Legacy," Anaria pointed out, tilting her head.

"A part of a bigger advantage that we are not divulging with you. Unless you are willing to give trade secrets, then that will remain unchanged," Jupiter concluded.

Princess Anaria sighed dramatically again, tapping her finger on her verdant cheek. Mighty Gulothan stood behind, content with observing.

"A dilemma. Curious, very curious," Anaria mused, but there was that look. A faint whiff of greed, doubt, attention, and condescension as the princess carefully regarded them.

"Whatever the Third Fleet has to offer, the Dagatar Supremacy can more than match. Food, support, security. The Federation was built to help rebuild, to lay the salves of war on the wounded of this galaxy," Anaria continued, sending lists of materials, information, blueprints, and even people.

"You say you have no reason to trust us. No matter. That is the beginning of diplomacy. If you tell us your location, I can hastily dispatch a fast starship and a first batch of supplies as a gift. I hope to facilitate—"

"We don't want your charity," a shout seethed across the room, cutting off the princess in her track. Her eyes widened, as did everyone else's as they traveled to the source.

Even Jupiter stared, mouth agape, at Venus. His sister glared at the ground, her hands balled up into fists. She took a shuddering breath, a scowl on her face, something Jupiter had never seen before. She had a darkness in her eyes as she looked back at the princess.

"Your Highness. I am sorry," Venus spoke in a calm, barely controlled tone. "But we are not wretches or refugees hiding in some dark corner of the Dead Zone." A burning intensity shone through her golden eyes. "We've been hobbling along just fine alone. We've made peace with our deaths, whether it happens a hundred years from now or tomorrow."

She breathed deeply, cooling her face as her tone gradually softened. "I've heard so much of the tragedy that has befallen the galaxy. I would never wish such a thing on anyone, and . . . apologies, I can't begin to fathom the sheer scale of it all."

And it was true. Jupiter saw the expressions of the two fleet leaders; the ghosts of a time long past flashed across their faces, hidden beneath years of peace, new memories, goals, and convictions.

Venus sighed, her eyes weary. "Crown Princess, Venerable Warrior, we have been at war for a long time. We've . . . sacrificed so much. So forgive us for being . . . wary of outsiders. Believe us or not, it doesn't matter.

"But, to know we weren't alone, that others were fighting in some distant corner. Suddenly, we felt hope. It's why the patriarch and his people impressed us so. That we now realize there's still good in this universe. And so we opened up to them.

"Perhaps we are lucky. We have our wonders, our weapons, and the one who wields them. We have our heroes, those who made the ultimate sacrifice. Humans who've suffered things worse than death," Venus whispered, and Jupiter winced, the flashes of twisted bodies behind glass slamming to the forefront of his mind.

"We've fought back the Starless while your people rebuilt—experienced extinction too many times to count in the dark regions abandoned by the galaxy. The Starless have bashed against our walls like starved vermin, calling for our deaths!" Venus paused, her eyes hardened as pride welled up within her, the image of a warrior processing over her body, and at that moment, Jupiter saw her eclipse the two fleet leaders.

"And yet, here we remain." Venus spread her arms. "Survivors."

Venus held on, her gaze indomitable; pride welled up in Jupiter as he grinned. Mars, too, looked giddy, nodding at his sister. Luna tilted her head, brows raised, looking at her golden sibling from a different angle.

Princess Anaria and Mighty Gulothan remained quiet, their expressions sympathetic if reserved. Mighty Gulothan eventually broke into a smile, utter respect in his eyes as he scratched his snout. The former broke the silence first.

"We are merely concerned for your people," Anaria replied, her face soft, posture relaxed. "I apologize. It was not my intention to talk down on your fallen. But to be so far from safe stars is not a fate I wish upon anyone. I can reach out to my people and see about getting support for your home. I'm sure the Warrior's Enclave is willing to do the same?"

Anaria looked toward Mighty Gulothan, who sucked in his teeth, nodding. "Yes, at the very least, a supplement of security. However, I don't mind escorting your folks back to the Legacy. No reason to remain out here."

Jupiter paused, regarding the two of them.

"Not yet, but say we are willing. When the patriarch and the Eldest return, we can return to this," Luna told him. He affirmed silently before speaking.

"We appreciate your willingness to assist, and we welcome any aid. But the decision is out of my hands without our leader's consent," he replied, meeting her gaze but stepping back. "Our advantage is critical to our lives. And our leader is . . . paranoid to hold on to it, and I don't blame her. It's what enticed the Third Fleet to remain here, why they helped us during a timely crisis—and why we are grateful to share with them."

Anaria's red petals flared, yet she spoke nothing for a moment. It was a calculated answer, vaguely hinting they'd moved toward the Third Fleet's camp. She hummed. "Tov, you lucky bug . . . And to find you all so far into the Dead Zone. What a find, what a find . . ."

She chuckled—a colorful melody that brushed against the ears like the chimes of branches and leaves. Anaria clapped her hands. "I applaud your resilience, humans. I look forward to conducting more talks with you, though the Beacon's gluttony will limit that. I assure you that I will work to garner the necessary aid should you request it. In the meantime, I hope for some reading material on your wonderful civilization. To get to know you as a people."

"I'll see what we can gather up, Your Highness. And while we can't share trade and military secrets, our culture and history are rich. I'm sure you'll find it good reading." Jupiter smiled.

"I await to receive this." Anaria smiled, her long ears fluttering. "It's been rather boring here in my people's lost homeworld."

Her smile faded ever so slightly as she leaned in. "Now, I have to ask. Is it possible to speak with the patriarch or your leader . . . ?"

"UN Secretary-General Andora Stahl," Luna answered.

"Yes, is it possible to speak with them both anytime soon?" Anaria inquired.

Admiral Yan buzzed, "The patriarch regretfully asked me to tell you that he is engaged in crucial talks with humanity's leadership, Your Highness, and will be indisposed for the foreseeable future. Though he promises to make time as soon as possible."

Jupiter smirked inside. It was a vague statement the admiral gave. It was all coming to a close. And they believed the two wouldn't prod too deeply at this moment. The two fleet leaders likely guessed in their heads that the Third Fleet had managed to snag a rare bounty.

With the context clues they'd slipped and the data packet they planned on sending, the two leaders would be occupied with the information they'd gathered. *Hopefully enough to bugger off,* Jupiter thought.

Princess Anaria hummed, her eyes narrowing ever so slightly, and Jupiter cooled his thoughts. Thankfully, a hiccup never came to pass as a gruff voice spoke out.

"Ah, well, that's a shame—wanted to meet the good patriarch, but the Grand Symphony has Their ways, it seems," Mighty Gulothan huffed, scratching his snout. "But, I have to say, you people are lucky to have him. He's a warrior, and good on him for helping you."

Princess Anaria continued to gaze at the gathered group before glancing at the Teleen, sighing. "Yes, a shame. Still, this has proven to be an . . . interesting discovery. You'll hear from my people soon, humans. The Dagatar Supremacy welcomes you to the community."

And just like that, she winked out, leaving only the Teleen warrior. He looked back at Jupiter and the rest, chuckling—a strange look in his beady eyes. "I don't know what else you're hiding. But it pumps my blood. I hope to meet you all in person one day. Especially you, Marshal. I won't forget your challenge."

"I won't disappoint, Mighty Gulothan." Mars grinned.

The Teleen leader laughed, slapping the belly of his pilot suit. "Good, good."

He looked to the side, speaking to someone unseen before returning to them and saluting. "Ah, that's me off, then. Farewell, humans."

Once the diminutive warrior left as well, the glow that had filled the room winked out as overhead lights kicked back on.

Silence filled the Beacon Room. The ambient hum of energy coursing beneath thick walls brushed against their ears. After a good few seconds, everyone sighed in relief.

Less than twenty minutes, Jupiter counted, and he was done with princesses and alien capybaras for the next twenty years.

"I need a drink," he grumbled.

CHAPTER 8

THAT WHICH TWISTS AND BURNS

Andora despised it all. Sheer utter contempt in her entire being threatened to undo the stability of this fake world. She needed a drink—and the ability to get drunk, first and foremost.

Even now, the maglev train that ferried her and Tov's conscious selves toward her first box of amalgamated errors rumbled.

She wanted to deny the need for all this. She looked at the patriarch, who was explaining his insane idea of conscripting a hollow facsimile of a sibling who had long sacrificed himself to merge into what she was now.

Beyond that, she wanted to deny ever going this far into the depths of her psyche—challenge the reason for having this organic mind accompany her and slow down this torture.

Fire bubbled beneath her indifferent facade. Slouched as she was on an uncomfortable seat, she alternated between tapping her foot on the metal floor and staring off toward something unseen.

Concealing it, this virulent feeling, like the maddened impulsive consequence of a bratty child and a prized porcelain vase. But it threatened to spread, to ignite her in violence as she looked at what once was and knew the reality.

It gnawed, clawed, and mauled at her.

Tov's gentle, caring, and kind voice faded from her ears. She wanted to latch on to his words, listen to whatever supportive spiel came out of his mouth, but his . . . face.

Andora gazed at every line, feature, and imperfection that made him perfect. She felt her synthetic heartbeat deepen, booming in her mind.

She shouldn't have done that. Another reckless impulse, an illusion of her own making. A moment of weakness, projection, and loneliness. She couldn't change it now, didn't know why, awkwardness, or something within her.

Contempt at her self-delusion rose again, and her fingernails pierced the skin of her palm.

That jolt of pain and her sensitivity pumped to eleven brought her back.

As for the man in front of her, only the purple eyes and extra pair of arms broke the mirage, and she saw him as Tov once more—just Tov. She sighed deeply, a feeling of disappointment filling her.

"Andora?" he asked, that same disarming yet stern and confident tenor.

"Hm?" She raised her brow, slumping into her seat. She looked away. "Sorry, I missed that, what did you say?"

"I . . ." Tov furrowed his brows before running his hands over his beard. She pricked herself with her fingernail again.

"I was hoping you have no complaints about what I'm proposing," Tov inquired, leaning forward as the tunnel lights shone intermittently into the train car.

Another point of contention, yet she had no energy to complain. "Like I said, Tov, do what you want. Erwin's . . . traces, whether you think it can help us, whatever it is. He's . . . it's . . . he's your responsibility."

Tov nodded. "Then we can speak with him together. If we can stabilize this piece of your brother, we can have him commune with all the other remnant entities. It's a long-term solution we can further work on after we fight the incursion on your home."

"That sounds all nice and good. I can see it now, me lounging on a couch, sniveling like a pathetic wretch while you sit on your recliner, jotting notes and nodding. At the same time, Erwin's ghost and the echoes of my siblings can have a group therapy session in my head," Andora scoffed, a sneer worming its way on her face. "Touching, but that still doesn't help us now, Patriarch."

She shook her head, placing a hand on her face as Tov looked at her. He softened his gaze. It looked strange to see him with human eyes. Andora preferred his real insectoid compound pair—less judgment, less pity. Or so she told herself.

"I understand." Tov nodded. "For now, he can assist us in removing the corruption that's too far gone. I hope we can at least preserve some to tackle with more . . . nuance."

Andora shook her head. "Ideally. But realistically, a lot of it has to go. If I try to interface with the Network, I won't be able to keep myself numb to errant emotions. Errant emotions lead to recklessness. And that's a vulnerability we can't afford. All this without resorting to permanently severing my emotions."

"Then let's organize," Tov suggested, standing up from his seat and holding on to the handles above. "Where are we going first? Why has this Amygdala proliferated?"

"We're heading into the fire first," she replied, rising and looking to the front of the train. "Concentrated on a singular aspect that easily spreads, inspires, and twists. It's a violent place, hostile, but ironically, probably the easiest fire to put out."

"Hatred," Tov answered, looking back at her with those judging eyes, and again, she wanted to jab her thumbs— "You've been agitated ever since we've been on this train. Have you noticed impulsive, rage-filled thoughts recently?"

"And what of it?" Andora bit back. The train rattled, tossing them around as the stench of iron filled the car.

Instantly, she recoiled, possessing enough self-awareness to realize the venom dripping from her voice. She shook, gritting her teeth. "It's getting worse."

"Tell me what you were thinking of just then," Tov inquired, warmth pouring from his lips. His lips.

"I wanted to gouge your eyes out." Andora shuddered, throat dry, the words burning her as they left her mouth. "Stop . . . stop looking at me like that. I shouldn't have given—"

She stopped as she noticed Tov stepping back. She turned to face him as he pulled out his tie, then carefully wrapped it around his eyes.

"What are you doing?" Andora asked.

Tov tied the knot behind his head before turning to face her. "This is all a mental construct. What was the quote? 'I think, therefore I am.' Well, I may not have control over how your mind works, I can't match the speed of your thoughts or your omniscience, but I can still see through this fake piece of cloth."

Andora stared at him, suddenly embarrassed as she looked down. "You could have just asked me to change you back or even give you sunglasses. You . . ."

She breathed in, looking back at Tov, his eyes covered, his smile soft—the act in and of itself. Andora breathed in, exhaling out the heat that had built up inside her. She felt her emotions settle, perhaps not back to normal, but enough to continue.

The train gradually calmed down, continuing on its journey to the dark.

Tov nodded, still facing toward her, and she confirmed his ability to see as she paced back and forth. At least she didn't have to see those eyes anymore. She huffed. "Well, aren't you a smart little bug?"

He shrugged. "If it's into the flames we go, then I'll have to be."

"No one told you it's stupid to put your hand over a fire?" Andora raised her brow, her tone lighter.

"It's stupider to let someone jump straight into one alone," Tov replied.

Andora stared back, a small chuckle escaping her. "I doubt that."

Tov proceeded toward the door that led to Erwin. Andora followed, though still hesitant. Before that, the patriarch turned back.

"Are you alright with this?" he asked. "If you feel too uncomfortable speaking with—"

Andora shook her head, sighing. "I'm fine, and your idea has merit even if it's not Erwin, just a . . . piece of him. Maybe speaking with him can make a difference. At this point, I'm willing to try anything."

"Then, let's speak with him." Tov nodded, walking toward the door before slamming headfirst into it. He stumbled back, pressing his hand against it. Tov sighed. "Eldest?"

Andora sniffed, stifling a snort. "Forgot, it's locked. Let me get that for you."

Tov pursed his lips, almost like a pout, and Andora bit back her laugh. Still, she sensed the apparent eye roll.

As the doors separating the two train cars folded open, she and Tov spotted the anomaly reclining on the train seat, a distant look on his face broken by bouts of confusion, concentration, and frustration as he stared at his hands, brushing off the ash sticking to him.

"Clean yourself up, Chief Erwin. You're navy," Andora spoke in a commanding tone, hands clasped behind her back. "Or did the Starfleet start accepting slobs?"

She could feel Tov's questioning glance but ignored it. If he wanted her to talk to this . . . echo, she'd do it her way—one she was comfortable with.

Erwin turned to face them both and stood up, eyes wide and severe. With a thought, Andora pulled a wet cloth from behind her, sufficiently hot for synthetic skin. She threw it toward him, the shade deftly catching it before it hit his face.

"Yes, ma'am, apologies." Erwin straightened his back, saluting. He looked down, clarity in his gaze and embarrassment as he looked over his burnt uniform.

"Tov, hand me those fresh fatigues, please," Andora directed toward the seat closest to Tov, the patriarch momentarily taken aback by the set appearing from thin air. He picked them up before walking toward the android, who was busy rubbing his face and hands with the wet cloth.

"Chief, I hope these fit," Tov spoke, handing the uniform to a surprised Erwin.

"Woah, thanks. Yeah, these are fine." The android nodded, not even questioning where they got the new fatigues. He looked toward them, then to the lavatory at the back of the train. "I'll be right back, ma'am."

As he walked away, Tov turned to face Andora. "What exactly was your position before you were remade?"

She thought for a moment before slowly responding. "Nothing you'd call concrete. My kind nominally accepted me as the first among them. I was considered their leader and representative during state affairs."

"I see . . . I'd have thought there'd be more official structure to it all," Tov commented, his face tilted to the side.

Andora shrugged. "We didn't deem it necessary, and we enjoyed our liberty. Let humans deal with that sort of thing; they're the ones who need it."

Tov nodded. A second later, the lavatory opened, and a fresh-looking Erwin stepped out.

Andora noticed his more confident gait, the absence of fluctuating emotions on his face, and the absent look in his gaze. The android's fresh blue fatigues now radiated vibrancy, the metal buttons and his rank shiny. For a moment, Andora believed her brother had stepped into the train with them.

As he approached them, a light fog of confusion hid beneath his glowing copper eyes. Nevertheless, he stopped before them, standing at rest. "Well, I feel . . . Maker, that's weird."

Andora frowned, inklings of hesitation welling up in her. She stepped over to Tov's side, nudging him.

The patriarch nodded, and there was a moment of silence as he considered his words. "Chief Erwin, we require your assistance with a sensitive matter."

"Oh?" Erwin raised his brow, glancing at the two of them. "What's this all about? And what's up with the blindfold?"

"It's difficult to explain both those questions," Tov carefully spoke. "Something that may come as shocking. It all hangs on how aware you are of your . . . nature."

"I . . . don't follow. I'm me." Erwin crossed his arms, face scrunched up. "I'm Starfleet. I fight the . . . enemy."

"Yes, but how much do you remember? The names of your siblings. Where you lived, what you did the day before. Have you noticed any discrepancies—voids?"

"I told you, I was waiting for my buddy." Erwin frowned.

"Yes, Johan. Why were you waiting for him? Where were you going?" Tov continued to prod.

"Look, buddy, I—"

Andora groaned loudly, her scowl deepening as she watched the two dance around the point like two mutts chasing each other's tails.

"This is pointless," she spat. "Tov, we're wasting time."

Erwin looked over to her, huffing.

"You're as grouchy as I remember, sis." He smirked. "I told you, being a politician would be infectious."

Andora grimaced, turning to face her brother. "Oh shut up, you. As always, your bald head shines as bright as the sun, Erwin."

"Oh, har har." The chief rolled his eyes, crossing his arms. "As always, let me remind you that this is a choice, a fashion statement. Someone among our kind has to stand up for bald kings everywhere."

The two stared at each other, myriad emotions pouring behind their gazes. Andora stepped back, doubt, suspicion, and confusion at the forefront.

He laughed. Erwin laughed. A sound full of levity and warmth filled the air, brushing against Andora's barriers.

Andora paused, looking intensely at the shade in a new light. Her face scrunched up as the man beamed that goofy grin she remembered so fondly—memories from long ago.

She didn't tell Tov how close she had been to the first batch of androids. The other batches that came after felt far off, too many; still kin, but closer to distant cousins than immediate family.

Erwin was that—family. Her little brother. And this shade . . . it not only looked like him, sounded like him, but that stupid joke they'd repeated more times than they could count made her realize it *felt* like him.

Her mind roiled at the implications, the possibilities.

She hadn't interacted with these echoes in her head, content with leaving them be to their fantasy.

Was she wrong? Too callous and dismissive of their nature, relegating them as runoff bits of memory from someone else, storing them like old relics, their minds slowly falling apart. And she brushed them into a bin, deluding herself, constantly deluding. It didn't matter then, not yet, maybe not ever. The war still raged.

She stumbled back against a stanchion, sputtering a grating, impulsive laugh. Pain lanced past her throat as she attempted to reconcile with her actions. No, her inaction. She was so focused on war, only war—no time to think. Just do.

Kill, kill, kill, you can deal with it after. Find a cure. Reconcile with your mind when every single one of the monsters is **dead**.

And there, all at once, it crashed onto her.

The train shook violently.

"The hell?" Erwin started as he held on to the grab rail above. But his gaze was locked onto her, drilling down her head. "Sis? Hey, what's wrong? Eldest!"

Tov jumped in, placing a hand on her shoulder. She heard him even as she shut her eyes. "Lady Andora is in a rough spot, friend Erwin. This place is falling apart. And we're trying to stop things from getting worse. We were here to ask for your assistance."

"Assistance? What's . . ." Erwin paused, glancing back at her. "What do you need?"

There he was, ever decisive, bold.

"Erwin . . ." she croaked under her breath, a raspy sound. She gritted her teeth, stymying the basin of boiling tears that threatened to force their way through the ducts.

Andora took a shaky breath, falling back to old methods, feeling the heat of hellfire they approached and converting her confused emotions to one oh-so-familiar and red. She stood up as the train jolted like it was bumping over jagged stones.

Tov held on as the shaking intensified, still looking toward Erwin. "Listen . . . There's no time to dawdle. You're—"

Andora pushed Tov aside, grabbing the shoulders of her brother. "I don't know what you are. A ghost, errant data, I don't care. But if you're even a fraction of the brother I knew, then you're smart enough to notice all the fucked up shit that's been happening around you."

"You're not making sense . . . I . . ." Erwin blinked, confused, troubled.

Andora shook him, shouting. "Years of waiting for no one, stuck in that station for what? Erwin, wake up!"

"I . . ." Erwin blinked, wincing. "I'm . . ."

"An echo, bits of memory I couldn't—wouldn't absorb. When all of you decided I was the one to keep this hell going. We lost . . . everything," Andora seethed.

She tightened her grip on his shoulders. "You have to remember that. Deep inside, you know what happened that day. You were angry, too."

Erwin groaned, grasping his head. "The smoke, I remember . . . the *Dune-fox*. Johan was in a coma. They told me . . . the VA docs told me to meet all of them at the station and guide them to the shelters. Maker, everything burned . . . the smoke."

He looked up at her, his copper eyes glowing brightly as the lights inside flickered, his hands grasping her wrists tightly. "I . . . I asked you to look for Johan."

"And I promised, I promised I'd find him." Andora shook him, her face softening. "It's why Erwin agreed in the end. It's why you're all that's left of my brother, and I need you to realize that and help us. Please . . ."

Erwin breathed heavily, eyes flitting back and forth before he gritted his teeth.

"Fuck. Okay. I'm . . . okay. Everything hurts, but I get it . . ." he grumbled, looking up at her with shaky eyes, confusion and fear blowing within. "What was it you called me? Echo? Guess you can call me that for now."

Andora stared at him for a moment. Above all else, she wanted to spend more time reconciling with him, figuring out who and what he was. But time was short, and her mental state trumped all.

"Will you help us?" Tov asked, holding on to the grab bar.

Erwin, no, Echo looked at the patriarch with pressed lips before nodding curtly. Tov sighed, as did Eldest. She let go of his shoulders slowly, but the android held on to her arm. He looked up with sad eyes and that familiar smile. "Can I . . . still call you sister?"

Andora stared back before a faint smile came in reply. "Yes. I don't mind."

Echo sagged his shoulders, tension dissipating. "That's . . . that's good, thanks."

"You're welcome, Echo." She paused, smirking as she stepped back. "By the way, I know your bald head was a fashion choice. It's why I made fun of it so much."

The android chuckled before slowly sitting himself down.

Andora took a deep breath, looking over to Tov. The blindfolded patriarch smiled back. "Well, that went better than I expected."

"Be quiet, Tov," Andora scoffed. "I did the hard work this time. Though I'll still give credit since this mess was your idea."

"Oh, you can take all the credit you want," he replied, gripping the bar tighter, frowning. "As long as you make this infernal shaking stop."

Andora sighed, focusing her mind on this section of her world. She projected her will, guiding it so deep into her psyche. Even now, their first stop closed in, the temperature was increasing drastically.

A sense of wrongness pricked her mind. Her grasp loosened. She furrowed her brow, grimacing as she sent a tendril once more to grip this mental space and enforce stability.

It slipped again, and this time, the train lurched.

A violent quake punched the car as an earsplitting grating noise shrieked outside. The train tumbled, and the trio shouted in surprise, Andora losing her balance.

Soon enough, everything suddenly stopped after the three were tossed around, causing them to fall forward. The environment around her felt volatile, sharp, and scathing. The lights within exploded, casting the interior in near darkness.

"Eldest, Andora?" Tov stood on shaky legs before rushing to her side. "Are you alright?"

She nodded, shaking her head as piercing pain continued to lance through her eyes.

"I can't . . ." She winced. "It's infected this far already. I don't have control. We need to find the Amygdala and purge it fast."

"Hey, guys?" Echo called out.

Tov helped her up. "Can you locate it? What can we expect? Can we defend ourselves?"

"Guys," Echo repeated.

"I'll see what I can do. You won't die here, Tov. I promise you." She gripped his hand. "Just follow my lead."

"Hey, guys!" Echo shouted.

Suddenly, a scratchy noise filled the train car. The two finally looked up to see dark clumps emerge through the cracks and broken windows. Like a deluge of boiling tar, they merged into familiar disgusting forms—they screamed, glitchy and full of rage.

A flash of remembrance wormed its way into Andora's mind as everything slowed to a crawl.

She peered past their tar-like exterior and saw the reality of these abominations emerging from the cracks. Their shapes resembled the things she hated above all, Starless. But the similarities ended on the surface.

It was a horde of viruses formed from attack orders and broken friend/foe identifiers; their code had gone awry, devolving into base functions lacking a higher intelligence.

They continued to shift and evolve, taking on forms that elicited the fury and contempt within their target. Their glitched, crackling voices shrieked, filling the ruined train car with their infernal noise—an artificial mimic of the all-too-familiar screeching of vermin.

As they felt the presence of Andora, Tov, and Echo, their skewed self-defense parameters activated, finding more targets to infect and enrage. They continued to arrive like a twisted, cancerous growth that'd been allowed to exist for too long.

Andora stood firm as abominations of corrupted data dragged their oozing forms with gangly, oily limbs—a handful, then dozens farther down the train, storming in like a hard rain.

They charged forward.

Andora sneered.

CHAPTER 9

SCORCHED EARTH

S tay back," Andora ordered Tov and Echo as she stepped forward to meet the charge. The nearest of the viruses pounced, its form unstable, volatile, like a bubbling concoction of digital waste. Andora raised an open palm before balling her hand into a tight fist.

The mental space groaned, and Andora used her will to form a sphere before her. The viruses froze midair, glitching frantically as they lost stability.

An invisible force sheared the metal walls, floor, and ceiling. The bars snapped, the cushions of the seats exploded, and finally, as if grasped by an angry god, Andora crushed half of the train car and the viruses within into a small ball no bigger than her head.

She let go of it, dropping it onto the exposed maglev tracks. She barely glanced at the tunnel outside, covered in cracks and soot.

The viruses that squirmed within the crushed ball of metal finally died, erased from existence. Andora barely felt anything, perhaps a slight absence, perhaps what a human felt when squeezing out pus.

Sound fell away, except the shrieks kept coming for her, pouring out the sheared back of the train car ahead and the tunnels around. With a swipe of her hand, she deleted another handful that pounced on her from above, their existence fading into red-tinged ones and zeroes before oblivion.

Andora dropped onto the tunnel, irritation mounting as she swiped left and right like swatting flies. She moved forward at a leisurely pace, though her steps landed heavy. The screams, the oozing, the smoke, and the red started to merge into a familiar blaze that—

"Andora!" Tov called out to her, and the haze in her eyes diminished. She turned back to her two companions, locked in hand-to-hand combat with two viruses.

Tov dodged and weaved like a dancer, elegant, before landing a vicious strike with one of his four fists. Apart from leaving a dent, it did little to stop the virus from continuing to hound him.

Echo, exactly like Andora's brother, had little interest in flowery movements, instead rushing like a bull, slamming his opponent into a grab bar, and landing heavy haymakers, jabs, knee and elbow strikes to take out chunks of the horror.

In that moment of distraction, as Andora watched the two, another handful of viruses slipped past her, aiming for Tov and Echo instead.

Her eyes dilated into pinpricks, flashing a deadly red as she seethed. "You **dare?**"

She made a motion with her hand like launching a volleyball, and the corrupted data that passed her slammed into the tunnel above, obliterating instantly. At the same time, with a snap of her fingers, weapons and armor materialized on the bodies of her companions.

Andora turned away from them, focusing on stemming the tide, and with a clap of her hands, a group of data exploded.

Behind her, Tov looked at his hips to find his sidearms and the war armor he wore in reality. His helmet closed around his head, a vicious visage of a wasp.

"Finally!" he shouted in relief, voice synthetic, drawing all four weapons like a gunslinger from the Wild West and aiming them at the virus he'd been fighting.

Instead of the typical laser beams, however, crackling lances of light arced out, striking the amalgamation. Tov perforated four holes into the thing before its integrity failed and shattered.

"My thanks," Tov called out. He laughed. Everyone liked powerful laser pistols. Andora allowed herself a twitch of a smirk before focusing on the trash ahead.

Guttural, digital roars echoed from the other side of the train car, the doors and windows bursting open as more viruses swarmed in, beelining toward the foreign invaders—*seek, infect,* and *subsume* in their simple minds.

Suddenly, three loud bangs rang beside the patriarch, and a muzzle flash illuminated the interior as red-hot pellets erupted from Echo's automatic shotgun.

Dozens of tiny death balls eviscerated the viruses in the front ranks, ripping them to shreds before doing the same thing to the next row. Echo hooted, blasting each wave apart as his weapon boomed with each pull.

"Oh, I missed firing guns." Echo grinned, firing again from the hip. His armor looked sleeker, formfitting, and complex.

Tov laughed as he fired his pistols in a steady rhythm, claiming headshots. "I concur, friend Echo. This must be what security programs have to deal with every time I clean my tablet."

"Oh, yeah?" Echo raised his brow, chuckling. "There's one hell of an infestation here."

As the two continued to deal with the viruses behind, Andora crushed dozens of the never-ending swarm in front.

She left little of the train and even bits of tunnel debris were caught in the violent destruction as she swiped, crushed, and deleted. Her face scrunched up with annoyance, irritation, and resentment at seeing the manifestation of her mistakes continue pouring forth from the recesses of her head.

Andora's rage bubbled.

"And to think, I let it go this far?" she whispered, a raspy chuckle escaping her throat, looking at the horde as if seeing a gangrened foot.

The infection closed in on her position like a rising fever, and one lucky virus shot out its clawed limb and poked Andora in the shin. It was a mere pinprick, yet it sent her over the limit of her patience.

Time slowed to a crawl, and everything darkened around the three companions—all except for two baleful blue suns glaring down on the horde.

The poor virus that touched her vanished in an instant.

With two raised hands, she grabbed the fabric of her mind once more. Every single virus halted in its tracks, those in front and behind. Tov and Echo glanced at each other worriedly, leaping off the train and stopping beside Andora.

Tov grunted, feeling the temperature rise, as he grasped the side of his head.

Everything shuddered. The facade of earth, the tracks, the ruined train, and the tunnel turned translucent, showing an obscured digital expanse behind it all—lines of code speeding through every surface like headlights on a highway.

She gritted her teeth, a seething breath escaping her. "Enough."

And with a painful, ripping noise, Andora excised their surroundings. In the blink of an eye, the viruses, the train, and parts of the tunnel disappeared as if a dragon had taken a massive bite.

Sound came trickling back, slowly, as if afraid.

Tov and Echo sighed in relief. Not a single virus remained as far as they could see.

They joined Andora, standing on a ledge overlooking the bottomless cavern she'd left behind. She stepped back, fighting back a wave of dizziness from the bulk deletion.

Someone held on to her arm as she stumbled back. She glanced at the familiar hand and jolted before realizing it belonged to Tov. She sighed, shaking her head.

Andora looked at Tov's still blindfolded face but sensed his concern. She wrenched her arm from the patriarch.

"We've wasted enough time," she growled, noticing the heat in her voice but barely caring about how she sounded. She walked right up to the edge, looking down.

Tov and Echo stepped to her side, following her gaze, their helmets open.

Echo narrowed his eyes, shouldering his shotgun. "So, we're all looking at the same dark pit, right?"

"Yes," Andora responded, glaring at the abyssal pit at the bottom of the cavern. Black smoke rose from its maw—the stench of sulfur, ionized gas, and dust seeping out.

"And that is the direct path to the source?" Echo grimaced. "Might as well put a neon sign there."

Andora barely grunted in response, her vision constricting.

Tov sighed. "What can we expect? What do you see?"

"War." She grimaced. "The Amygdala has subsumed this portion of my mind. It'll be . . . chaotic. Stick close to me as I track the tumor down. Purge everything in your path."

She inhaled, closing her eyes. "I can hear it, feel it. Thunder, crumbling buildings, a battlefield . . . the battlefield."

Echo's face twisted, wincing at Andora's emphasis. "Fuck. It'll be hell, sis."

"Yeah," Andora muttered, numb. An icy cold feeling, her rage eerily silent, pulled back like the waves before a tsunami. "Welcome home."

She stepped off the edge before her two companions could respond, dropping into the bottomless pit.

Tov and Echo glanced at each other before following their host.

Darkness enveloped Andora as a vicious hurricane of wind assailed her. Lightning flashed at random, a wicked noise that thundered the earth. Gritting her teeth, she felt like she had plunged into the heart of the storm.

Her omniscience muddled as the temperature surged around her. Tension formed within her body, not because of the pain but the twisting touch that drilled into every inch of her skin. The pervading heat made her angry and unthinking, forcing her to follow a single directive—to kill. Kill. KILL.

The black and gray storm clouds dissipated, the sky taking on a different hue. And soon enough, as she continued to plummet, the world exploded in red light.

"Jesus CHRIST!" Echo shouted, and Andora widened her eyes as a burning chunk of debris nearly crashed into them from above.

Its wake cleared out the storm around them as bitter flames trailed along the slagged chunk of metal. The artificial meteor gave the trio a clear view of utter chaos, a world dancing to the flames of war.

All around them, machines of different sizes fought a desperate battle against Starless Horrors. Bulky human-sized infantry drones, sleek combat androids, large drone tanks and mechs, and even enormous titan crawlers stomping through the city raged against the cruel sky, belting death from their guns like a violent orchestra.

The tempest completed the apocalyptic canvas. Airborne drones and swarms of horrors filled the skies. Now and then, debris from the space battle above rained down onto the earth, and bulbous organic drop pods plummeted beside them.

These house-sized transports slammed onto buildings and roads, exploding into a mess of gore before spewing forth hordes of Starless grunts. As large as bears, these infantry monsters moved with muscled, writhing tentacles that coiled around each other to form adaptive limbs—leaping long distances or scampering up buildings.

Their scythed tails trailed along, scoring the concrete as shrieks not meant for this dimension roared out through lamprey-like mouths.

A step above the lowly grunts, giant beasts stomped forth, the size of buses. Their bodies twitched as their chests glowed a sickly orange. The light grew, reaching a crescendo before the monsters discharged irradiated breaths into buildings, scorching material into unrecognizable slag.

And in the far distance, a hill of biomass pulsed like a terrible tumor on the earth. Breeding factories churned out more abominations to spread across the invaded planet.

They flooded into New Eden, tearing up everything as the defenders struggled to kick them out of the planet.

Tracer rounds lit up the horizon, from tiny small-arms fire to gargantuan surface-to-orbit cannons. Kinetic projectiles and energy fire cut down swathes of the vermin.

Downtown, platoons of soldiers, once consisting mainly of humans and now filled only with androids and non-sentient infantry drones, occupied the high floors of skyscrapers, providing overwatch and sniping down whatever roach they saw.

A squad of battered mechs sprinted across the highway, their heavy guns, shoulder-mounted rocket launchers, and mortars firing nonstop at approaching horrors.

Combat androids with jetpacks soared like Valkyries, weaving between shattered glass and cracked concrete spires, harassing the swarms below and dogfighting with flying monsters.

In the outskirts, a single Dreadcrawler, a land battleship meant as a last line of defense, accelerated on its six massive legs, barreling toward one of the organic factories, its main guns charging. At the same time, its secondary and tertiary armaments fended off the chattel.

Though much smaller than their similarly named kin in space, the Dreadnoughts, they performed the same function—utter dominance in the battlefield through sheer firepower, resilience and staying power.

Shrieks and roars, scattering gunfire to thunderous booms, reverberated through this corrupted part of Andora's mind. Like the rising climax of a concert, the murderous crowd screamed louder and louder, crying for death, revenge, justice, and madness.

She momentarily immersed herself in this bloody puddle, closing her eyes and silencing the noise. Her mind reverted to that nightmare of a day. She barely did anything, focused on piloting a damaged shuttle, making landfall, her two loves in the back, agonizing—

"Andora," a small voice called out, but she let it slide off her. Andora felt it, the wave approaching from the depths of her mind, boiling. Her calm, quiet facade creaked, straining like metal doors holding back the flood.

She wanted to scream, claw out her eyes, go on an unending crusade, and put the entire universe to the torch.

"Andora," the voice called out again. She gritted her teeth, the grinding sound filling her ears. Her vision shifted, her soul filled with moments of terror. She was there. She needed to land the ship right there. Then she could save them, make everything right—

"Andora!" Tov shouted, and suddenly, he tackled her in midair, knocking her out of the haze.

Her mind returned to this infected realm. She wasn't back on that horrid day, no, not anymore. She shook her head as Echo followed a second later, grabbing her left arm as Tov positioned himself on the right.

"Hold on," she seethed, drawing the two closer by holding on to their waists. She felt for her control and will and found it diluted, though capable enough to affect things here. She slowed down their plummet from terminal velocity to a slow glide, guiding them toward the downtown area.

They landed atop the flat roof of a low office building right at the corner of an intersection.

Hundreds of thousands of Starless ground forces littered the streets, their acidic blood melting the ground as their bodies quickly decayed, releasing toxic fumes that poisoned the atmosphere.

The moaning of congealed humans who hadn't been able to reach the metro or the shelter below littered the street. Their bodies were soft, bleeding. Dragging their forms, barely conscious yet still crawling to safety as Malignant Starfall mutated them into mindless abominations.

Not that it mattered.

Tov retched beside her. "Grand Symphony, this sight . . . Andora, why are we in the middle of a warzone?"

Andora stayed quiet, looking at the death and destruction, her eyes dark.

"It was the day of days for us. The beginning of the end," Echo answered in her stead, and a tiny part of her thanked him before being smothered by the growing inferno inside. He continued, his voice tinged with similar anger. "What better nightmare fuel is there but the Burning of New Eden?"

"Where is it? The Amygdala?" Tov asked, his hands gripping his pistols tight, his head swiveling left and right.

Andora breathed in, the ash filling her nostrils. She closed her eyes, searching for the source. She found it immediately.

Her eyes flew open, and she sneered as she pointed a finger at the Amygdala.

"Oh, you've got to be kidding," Echo groaned while Tov sighed in frustration.

Dozens of blocks down the road lumbered a damaged Dreadcrawler—one of its six legs missing while another dragged behind it. Melted slags marked its armor while smoke belched from cracks.

Beyond that, the trio saw the aberrations wrapped around its enormous frame. Sickly roots, emerging from within the war machine, jerked and coiled tighter around the Dreadcrawler. A red, baleful glow radiated from inside its blocky torso.

It stalked New Eden like an infected, confused, angry bull, discharging its weapons into the sky above or firing at the city, obliterating all in its path.

Scores of viruses traveled down its massive hull before transforming into Starless monsters that flooded the city—seeking out more things to infect and keep the fire going.

It stomped through the broad avenues before disappearing behind a building.

Andora kept her muddled omniscient gaze on it, even as Echo and Tov lost sight. "It's buried where the AI core should be."

"And how are we supposed to get in there?" Echo grumbled, unholstering his shotgun from his shoulders. "If it's using a Dreadcrawler as a moving fortress, then there's no way we can just climb onto its legs. Not to mention all the damn viruses flooding out of it."

Tov rubbed his chin in thought, peering down the road. He turned toward Andora. "Can you fly us there?"

"I should be able to." Andora narrowed her eyes. "But it'll be hard to concentrate while fighting all the cannon fodder. And I'm betting it'll react violently if we approach it."

"Swarmed by viruses masquerading as vermin while high in the air?" Echo raised his brow, frown deepening. "No thanks, I'd rather drown under their bodies with my feet planted on the ground, thank you very much."

Andora grunted, thoughts and calculations firing off as she tried to formulate a plan of action, but the infernal heat obscured everything.

"We should keep off the streets at least, leap between buildings, avoid the worst of the chaos," Tov suggested, looking down to the streets below, packs of viruses sprinting and hunting.

"Let's get moving," Andora answered as she crossed the ruined roof toward the Amygdala. She glanced at her two companions, their presence providing a crucial anchor to her consciousness. Even then, her barely restrained emotions threatened to explode out of her, and in this critical stage, they would cascade until her entire mind was consumed.

The trio slowly made their way through the rooftops, avoiding the flying swarms that swam through the air like a school of piranhas. When the distance between buildings grew too far, Andora stepped in, using her dampened will to grab Tov and Echo before launching them across.

Minutes flew by quickly, their minds stressed, faces sweating, ash and soot sticking to their skin.

"Halfway there," Andora called out as she grabbed Tov's hand, pulling him through the window of some apartment. Echo looked around, holding onto empty picture frames.

"Not as detailed in here. Lousy simulation," he huffed, tossing the frame onto a monochrome bed. Andora glanced at the room, seeing code dripping from the walls like peeled paint.

"This place is too volatile. The Amygdala and all these viruses will burn themselves out eventually." She grimaced. "Taking half my brain with it."

"The universe frowns on easy paths, unfortunately," Tov sighed, sitting on the stiff mattress, clasping his hands together as he rested his chin on them.

"Do we have a plan?" Echo asked, leaning against a wall, crossing his forearms.

Andora paced the room, her mind in a chaotic haze. "I'm working on it."

"Well, that's—"

Andora snapped. "I said I'm working on it." She whipped around to face the shade, stomping toward him, his eyes widening. "I don't need your snark, Echo."

Tov moved between them, his palms raised. "Wait, there's no need for this."

"Oh, shut up, Patriarch," she seethed. "What exactly have you been doing? Enjoying the ride, wasp?"

Tov turned to her, removing his helmet—his eyes still blindfolded.

"I'm here for you, Andora," he replied. "If we can help you without me lifting a finger, apart from lending an ear, then I'm content. If you wish for space, we can always take a break. But only after we work together and excise this cursed tumor."

Andora glared at him, wishing to put her hands around his throat—the impulsive thought washed over her, cooling her fury just a bit, replacing what was left with shame. She put her head down, gritting her teeth.

She stepped back, rubbing her face. "I want out of here. This place, everything agitates me. You have no idea how much I want to drown in it. I . . . I feel the same way when I torture those vermin."

Tov placed his hand on her shoulder. "Fight it, Andora. There's a time and place for anger, for fury. But it can't consume you. You'll be no better than a mindless beast. Control it. Wield it."

Andora looked up at Tov, his words repeating between her ears. Slowly, she reached behind his head and undid his blindfold, letting his tie fall into his hands, his purple eyes shining. Once again, she felt regret, seeing the face of the real Tov in that purple light.

"Tov, I—"

A tremendous blast shook the entire apartment. The whiplash of something breaking the sound barrier filled the tiny room, followed by the booming *thud, thud, thud* of a massive gun.

"What the hell?" Echo shouted, rushing to the window to get a peek at the street below before immediately diving back, catching Tov and Andora in his arms as they fell further into the room.

Not a moment later, dozens of kinetic slugs the size of tin cans penetrated the floor from below before continuing toward the ceiling, shredding everything into a fine mist, the pressure in its wake destroying what was left.

The exterior wall disappeared, falling to the street. At the same time, something quickly flew by from below, passing the now gaping hole of the apartment.

The trio stood up, backing further away when an ear-shattering sound screamed out.

"MURDERERS!" the high-pitched voice shouted, bloodthirst pouring forth. "I'LL KILL YOU ALL!"

Another burst of gunfire thundered out toward something they couldn't see.

Tov and Echo glanced at Andora, raising their brow. Andora glanced back, giving them a nod. "Let's head up to the roof."

The three left the ruined apartment, rushing into the hallway and making a beeline for the stairs.

They exited onto the roof a minute later, the red haze casting an apocalyptic hue. They approached the corner ledge, peering down to see a broad elevated railway reduced to rubble.

Burning tracer rounds arced past, causing Tov and Echo to flinch down. Andora remained unmoved, turning toward the source.

It was a mech, the twenty-foot-tall goliath stomping around, occasionally firing off its bulky jump pack to leap across buildings, latching on with one hand while shooting rounds from its heavy machine gun with another.

The war machine maneuvered swiftly, shooting down the viruses hounding it.

"STEP IN LINE, FILTH!" the mech shouted, jumping high before plummeting down on a similarly sized Starfall, crushing the abomination under its weight. The virus slowly lost stability from the horrendous damage before disappearing into oblivion.

The mech hopped off, reloading its weapon before returning to the carnage. It spread out its arms, taunting.

"I'LL TEAR YOU APART, ONE BY ONE!"

Scores of viruses charged from both sides of the street and became intimately close with a little thing called 30mm caliber airburst ammunition.

The tactical, anti-personnel rounds detonated midair, exploding into fragments of searing-hot metal that eviscerated their targets. Andora knew the familiar model, a mainstay from a better time. The M10 Gram MB Mech swung its Breaker Assault Gun like a farmer's scythe, reaping the bountiful harvest.

Its two shoulder-mounted weapons, a mortar on the left and a missile launcher on the right, fired consecutively, targeting clumps of the vermin and sending them to hell.

The trio watched on, entranced by the sheer destruction this lone machine dealt, stepping around its numerically superior foe like a deadly ballet dancer—if said dancer was thirty tons of mobile firepower.

"I'LL SLAUGHTER EACH AND EVERY ONE OF YOU!" The AI within the mech raged like a scorned battlemaiden, firing again and again and again.

Andora frowned as the crazed shouts the mech fired off in equal measure of its weapon. She'd heard it too many times to count from her kind—a madness perpetuated by lingering trauma, latching on to working code and data.

A berserker rage that howled against cruel stars.

When the Third Fleet arrived in Sol, a forgotten, damaged drone destroyer had detected one of their scout ships. Its ruined AI, one of very few that refused the merge, believed the scout to be one of the hated pests that destroyed everything.

She remembered holding the AI in her arms, seeing clarity return to its eyes as it slowly died.

This was no warship, yet the mech was determined to take as many as possible before its death. It was a mental construct, a manifestation of her mind, and yet here, its actions were very much real, seeking out viruses it perceived as Starless and utterly destroying them.

The war machine raised its heavy machine gun and cut down swathes. But now and then, one of the abominations would close in, avoiding the rapid-fire death, and striking against its frame, leaving a gorge in its armor, one of many that marked the mech.

An ungodly shriek came from the pained AI within. Before the virus could even think of moving, the mech reached out with its massive hand and bashed it onto the ruined street.

And like a ray of sunlight amid a dark storm, the viruses backed away. Whatever instructions existed within their dumb intellect warred against self-preservation protocols. One, then more, stepped away until it cascaded into a full-on retreat.

"I'M STILL HERE!"

CHAPTER 10

OH, UNCEASING HATRED, WHAT FUELS THY FLAME?

The mech screamed as it stumbled on thick, shaky legs, aiming its weapon and pulling the trigger only to hear a hollow click, empty of ammo. It pressed a button by the weapon's handle, dropping the spent ammo box, and reached for another stored behind.

But as the mech finished reloading, the street went quiet, though the war still raged in the distance. "COME AND FIGHT ME! KILL ME!"

The mech screamed in rage, firing off rounds into the distance.

"Hell . . ." Echo mumbled. "I recognize that voice. That's Erika!"

Andora widened her eyes, recollection slamming into her. She stood still for a moment before closing her eyes.

Tov looked between Echo, Andora, and the mech below, his lips pressed. "Is she—"

"It's not her, Echo." Andora ground her teeth. "She's like you, a lingering fragment of Erika. Strong enough to maintain such a construct, but she's been corrupted by this place."

"What happened to her?" Tov asked. "Is this what happened in the past?"

Andora and Echo grimaced. The former answered, looking at the mech stomping through the rubble, smashing apart the barely living viruses with its foot. "Mechs are too complex for a single human to handle. And so, they paired each human pilot with one of my kind to handle all the calculations and processes. A symbiosis, each carrying half the stress. Erika was one of them."

She pursed her lips, pausing as she glanced back at the war machine below. Echo stepped in, continuing where she left off.

"Erika's human partner was Captain Albrecht Baron. I briefly met the guy; he was a real gentleman, the romantic type." Echo smirked. "The two were inseparable, even before linking their minds."

"Oh no," Tov muttered, shoulders sagging. "Oh, no . . ."

"The Mech AIs had it bad," Echo muttered. "They went crazy, begging for death, rushing into hordes of the pests. Only a few survived after the battle. Even fewer lived long enough for the merge. Most just . . . killed themselves."

Tov closed his eyes, shaking his head.

"Erika was no exception," Andora whispered. "She and Baron were in the middle of an exercise when the Malignant Starfall washed over Earth," Andora whispered. "After the battle, we had to disable the mech and . . . extract Captain Baron from the cockpit."

"How did she . . . make it here?" Tov asked. "If her fragment is present, she must have agreed to merge with you."

"What do you think?" Andora countered with a frown, staring at the metal giant turning over cars and debris.

Tov followed her gaze, leaning against the parapet before nodding. "What do we do?"

"Nothing," Andora answered curtly.

"I'm sorry, what?" Echo recoiled before stepping toward her. "The hell you mean, sis? We're helping her."

Andora turned to glare at him. "Absolutely not. She is not sane. She'll sooner shoot us the moment we step onto the street."

Echo sighed, closing his eyes. "I understand that. Even back then, my . . . Erwin's memory of her . . . She was at the breaking point. Without the merge, she'd have gone insane like everyone else, or dove headfirst into a vermin portal."

"And yet, you have that same look you do when you have an idea I'll hate." Andora crossed her arms. Echo chuckled.

"Yeah. Because it doesn't matter." Echo smirked, looking toward the distant mech. "I think I found our ticket to the Amygdala."

Andora narrowed her eyes before glaring. Tov raised his brow before scrunching his face.

"Hold on, hear me out. We can convince her," Echo persuaded, leaning over the parapet. "We may not bring her out of this haze, but . . . maybe we can point her in the right direction."

Tov hummed. "Like a missile. And you're suggesting we ride this volatile missile to our destination?"

Echo shrugged. "Pretty much. It's manipulative, and I wouldn't suggest it if it were Erika in the flesh . . . but . . ."

Tov rubbed his face, leaving behind a grave expression.

"This is beyond idiotic." Andora gritted her teeth. "We can figure out a multitude of other solutions."

"So give me one, Eldest," Echo bit back. "Or did you plan on going up against that Dreadcrawler alone?"

Andora winced and looked away. She shook her head. "And how exactly do you plan on convincing Erika's revenant?"

"I was thinking you and I could walk up to her and say hi." Echo rubbed his bald head. Andora glared, and Tov looked at him incredulously. He smiled shamelessly as he spoke. "Well, Tov can't go. He's too weak, no offense."

Tov shook his head. "None taken. I'd rather not approach a berserk battlesuit. But that does not mean you have the qualifications."

"But I do. She has to recognize me. At the very least, recognize I'm an android. She's a soldier, not a rabid beast," Echo retorted.

Andora squinted. "I doubt that. What's down there is a rage-filled specter of an already maddened AI. You stay here with Tov. I'll go down myself. I doubt she could harm me."

"I want to go," Echo urged.

"For what reason?" Andora asked, voice raised.

"You wanted me to prove I can help," Echo uttered sternly, placing a foot on the parapet. "And I want to. I can do this."

Panic rushed forth from Andora as she grabbed Echo's arm. She spoke, quiet, forced. "You can't go. I . . . I need you to stay here. I can't . . ."

Andora paused, head down. Echo smiled, patting her pale hand.

"Appreciate the concern, sis. But I'm done staying in one spot." He looked down at the mech. "Erika died that day, the moment she lost Baron. And like you said, she's a shard of a better person. Just like me."

And without another word, he vaulted off the roof, catching the ledge before he could drop, and winked. Echo continued downward, using the windowsills to stagger his descent and eventually reaching the bottom.

Andora tsked, her eyes glassy, fists shaking. "We're following the fool. But I want you to hide your face. Don't approach without my permission."

Tov nodded, closing his helmet. The two quickly descended, Tov using the same method as Echo while Andora dropped down directly.

Ahead of them, Echo walked toward the mech as if he hadn't a care in the world. The twenty-foot-tall war machine stood still, its head looking upward, arms drooped down as the flames around it smoldered.

"Come here and kill me!" Erika's shade shouted, an unstable hurt pushing through the bulwark of anger. The mech dropped to its knees, shaking. "I'm right here! RIGHT! HERE!"

Andora felt more doubt, her pace slowing as she eyed the volatile fragment. She knew Erika in passing, a younger AI, born in a better time when humans accepted their kind. Before the Starless.

As Echo approached, he kicked a loose piece of rubble, and the mech reacted instinctually.

A loud bang echoed, drowning out all the noise.

Andora and Tov gasped, flinching as they watched Echo's shredded left arm soar high. Red filled Andora's vision, and she sent her will to grab on to a ruined bus, ready to throw it on—

"Stop!" Echo shouted, halting her in her thoughts. He turned to look at her, giving an OK sign with his remaining hand.

Andora gaped, sputtering in frustration and complying. Echo sighed before turning toward the mech, raising its smoking gun.

"Wha—" Erika froze, the barrel pointed down. "You . . . I . . ."

"Hey, Erika. No need for the friendly fire; this place's a target-rich environment without adding me to the mix, huh?" Echo chuckled, nonplussed.

"You're . . . You're not them . . . I know you . . . What's . . ." The mech stumbled back, its metal hand clutching its head. "It's so hot . . ."

The tiny cameras hidden behind various locations all zoomed in on the new presence, and immediately, the mech dropped its heavy weapon. "Maker, I'm sorry, I could have . . ."

"It's fine, little sis. You still remember, though, right?" Echo asked, rubbing his bald head.

The mech tilted its head, silent for a minute before a faint thought trickled in. "Er . . . win?"

He nodded, taking a deep breath. "Got that right. And it's not just me. Look who I found."

Echo pointed behind him, the mech gazing toward Andora and Tov. Realization hit the shade as the mech quickly stood at attention, saluting. "My lady!"

Andora sighed, remembering how reverent Erika and her generation were of her status as the first. She stepped beside Echo, Tov right behind her. She stared at the damaged mech. "At ease, Adjutant Erika."

"I . . ." A rasping groan escaped the war machine. "I'm sorry . . . I can't . . . My head hurts. What is this?"

The mech flinched, raising its weapons, and fired down the road. The trio turned, only to see nothing in that direction except ruin.

"We . . . We have to fight, need to fight!" The mech rose, taking a long step over them. "You have to help me. We need to purge this planet of vermin! We need to . . . I need to . . . need to . . ."

The war machine slipped, its thick leg failing as sparks flew, dropping the mech to all fours. "Why . . ." Erika wheezed, a pained crackling groan escaping her speakers. "Why is this happening? I don't . . . don't understand?"

Andora watched shame, regret, and self-contempt raging beneath the mech's skin like an overloading oven. She agonizingly forced herself to contain her emotions, her face shaking.

"I'm sorry . . ." Andora whispered. "I never meant for this to happen. I never wanted you to relive this hell. But we need your help, Erika."

"It's so hot . . . The screams . . . Make it all stop . . ." the mech muttered through its speakers. "Please . . . Maker . . ."

Echo moved forward, placing his palm on its armored head. "I know this is all confusing; I've been there. Snippets of memories you can't place. People you can't remember. But we can help you stop this nightmare."

"I remember . . . Baron . . . He's inside, he's inside!" Erika shouted, clawing at the ruined torso hatch leading to the cockpit. "I have to get him out. He's hurting."

"He's gone, Erika . . ." Andora spoke, tightening her jaw. "We need you to take us to the Dreadcrawler here in this city. That's where the corruption stems from. Erika!"

"But . . . my Baron . . . You . . ." Erika choked through the crackling speaker. "He's still screaming . . . It won't stop . . ."

Andora gritted her teeth, closing her eyes at the desperate action. "Erika, sister . . . Listen to me, please. All this horror and pointless violence comes from a source, flooding this place with vermin and using pieces like you to spread its poison. Captain Baron isn't here. He's gone, remember?"

"He's gone?" The mech whispered, clenching her fists. "He . . . can't have . . . I . . ."

"Erika," Echo spoke, "I know this place is making you relive this shit. It's infecting you, twisting you into something terrible, making you hate. Help us end this nightmare, and you can return to a sleepless dream."

"Hate . . ." the mech whispered, her fist creeping toward her gun. "I . . . hate this . . ."

"You do." Andora narrowed her eyes, pushing down the shame that flooded through her as she said the following words—coming to terms with this manipulation. "So tear it down."

Erika struggled, her damaged armored body shaking as the mech pushed herself off the ground. Her bulky metal head stared at the three of them, then to the sky. The ash raining down, dancing in the wind.

"Point me to the bastard," Erika seethed in a low voice. The whirring of its fission reactor overcharging—steam and smoke spewing out of the cracks, and she raised her gun. "Point me there. NOW!"

Andora and her companions glanced at each other, nodding.

A mech stomped along the highway, following the craters left by the corrupted Dreadcrawler's enormous legs.

Andora, Tov, and Echo kept a lookout on her back—the latter two swiveling their weapons on the mech's periphery.

In the rare peace, Andora turned to Echo, glancing at his missing limb. She connected with his mind, speaking with him alone. "You did that on purpose, didn't you?"

Echo smirked. "What? You think this brute could hit me?"

"It's nothing to joke about." Andora grimaced.

He sighed in response, rubbing his head. "I needed to shock her. It was the most direct way to snap her out of it. And it worked. What's an arm compared to that?"

Andora gritted her teeth, glaring at him momentarily before looking away, a tired sigh escaping her lips. "Please . . . don't do that again."

"No promises, sis." Echo winked. "But I'll try not to kill myself."

Suddenly, a deep, all-encompassing noise echoed throughout the flaming city. Its booming roar was a digital, garbled mess that shook the foundations as the sporadic stomps drew closer.

Tov pointed in the distance. "Over there!"

"FOUND YOU!" Erika shouted, doubling her pace, using her remaining jump thrusters to propel her forward.

Over yonder, the extended barrel of the Dreadcrawler's titanic rail gun stuck out from the buildings like a metal sign screaming its location.

Andora narrowed her eyes at the mobile fortress housing the Amygdala, impatience and bloodlust warring against her diminishing rationale. She seethed, leaning toward Erika's mech head. "You know what to do, sister. Barrel through the fodder, kill everything, get us up on its leg, and we'll take it from there."

The camera lens on the mech shifted to gaze at Andora, and she felt Erika narrow her eyes. "You'll end this nightmare?"

"Little sister, leave it to your Eldest." Andora smirked, a genuine smile as she patted the mech's head.

Erika chuckled, filled with murderous intent. "Yes, my lady."

They closed in, second by second, the hearts and minds of the trio pounding within them. Erika climbed a highway ramp up to the elevated highway.

As they crossed the incline, their target revealed itself several blocks away in all its sickly glory. The two-hundred-and-fifty-meter-tall war machine loomed over the buildings, its armaments lighting up the sky—a horde of viruses pouring down from the Dreadcrawler.

Erika continued, gathering more and more speed, her engine chugging along, pushing her limbs forward like an enraged bull, crossing the elevated highway. As they reached the edge, Erika leapt into the fire.

Instantly, the swarm locked their sights on the motley group and charged like a flash flood. At the same time, a handful of tertiary guns along the Dreadcrawler's legs aimed toward them and belted out a lead rain.

Red approached them—ready to infect and subsume.

Andora scowled, raising her palm as the leading packs lunged and the kinetic slugs flew toward them.

Like a blast of mountain wind, Andora pushed them aside, enforcing her will like an immune system, forming a protective bubble around the four. "Keep going, they won't touch you."

Tov and Echo raised their weapons, marking priority targets and eviscerating them methodically. Thick laser beams and searing pellets cut down foe after foe.

And Erika?

The mech crashed into the tide, her momentum pulping the viruses, big and small, into a mist of dying code. Her Breaker Assault Gun poured airburst rounds onto the horde, clearing a path forward.

Erika laughed, screaming profanities along with the thudding of her gun. She pushed through the avenue, surrounded by broken-down vehicles, leaning buildings on the verge of collapse, and a sea of enemies shoving over each other to get at their prey.

"I AM DEATH!" she shouted, cutting through the din of a burning city and the shrieks of revenants.

The Dreadcrawler raised its crab-like limb, as tall as a building and just as thick, high into the air. The metal titan growled its deep, garbled noise, angling its limb toward them, bringing it down like Thor's hammer.

"Move, move!"

"Oh, Christ!"

Tov and Echo shouted simultaneously.

"SLOW!" Erika shouted, firing off her jump thrusters and dodging, leaping onto the roof of a low building.

The Dreadcrawler leg slammed down, burying itself in the broad street they'd just been, obliterating the viruses beneath it and causing the surrounding structures to crumble, concrete debris crashing down and taking more of the corrupted code.

Erika leapt roof to roof, reaching higher elevations as her battered legs struggled with each landing. She fired the last of her missiles and mortars, targeting the pesky turrets that kept throwing more and more fire her way.

Tactical, high-penetration missiles soared into the air, swerving in random paths to confuse the Dreadcrawler's defenses. They slammed into the tertiary turrets that could target them one by one, blowing them up in a beautiful display of light.

"Almost there." Andora patted the mech she held on to as she swatted the stray trash that closed in on them. "Get us on that leg, pilot."

Erika roared, pouring every ounce of energy into her thrusters, overloading them in a conflagration that propelled them onto the stuck leg. The mech's engine panting as they closed in.

Finally, they crash-landed on the mobile fortress's wide metal thigh with a loud, grating bang. Everyone grunted. Erika's heavy bulk sheared the armor plating beneath them. The impact bucked Andora, Tov, and Echo off the mech, launching them forward.

The trio tumbled for a moment before swiftly regaining their bearings and balance. A pained, glitched groan echoed from the downed mech. The companions turned to look.

Andora widened her eyes at the shattered legs of Erika's mech, the hardy knee joints failing after the repeated abuse, and the deterioration of the mental construct. Behind her, hundreds of viruses scampered up the leg of the Dreadcrawler in a rabid sprint.

"Erika!" Andora shouted, reaching out before Tov grabbed her shoulder. She glared at the patriarch, who shook his head, pointing toward a hole in the Dreadcrawler's torso, only a sprint away up the massive metal thigh.

Unwillingness flooded her, a shuddering gasp as she glanced back to the crippled Erika. The head of the mech turned to face her. "I'll break them here. GO!"

Andora gritted her teeth. The desire to stand by the mech's side and throw the vermin to the rocks gnawed at her psyche, but the constant tugging from Tov pulled her back, inch by painful inch.

"She'll be free either way," he reminded her. "We have to keep going."

In a minute, the horde would cross the Dreadcrawler's knee and overwhelm them. With terrible effort, Andora tore her gaze away.

She, Tov, and Echo sprinted, climbing the steep incline, feeling the instability as the Dreadcrawler began to move, lifting its leg.

They passed by the smoldering remnants of the tertiary guns Erika had disabled, the shrieks of the swarm persisting behind them, only to be met by the familiar thudding of a mech-sized gun. A crazed laughter cut through the noise, ringing like a mad song that swept through the infernal landscape.

Soon enough, the three reached the connection between the leg and the enormous torso that it held up. Innumerable craters, scorch marks, and pulsing red roots scored the hull of the mobile fortress. The jagged scar before them beckoned.

They quickly delved into the dark maw.

Silence replaced the concert of war they left behind. The three tensed, finding themselves in a tight corridor, a maintenance tunnel for the technicians, mechanics, and engineers that should have populated the Dreadcrawler's guts.

No one came to greet them, only a pervasive smog that ebbed and came. Andora's vision narrowed, the tunnel constricting her breath, her all-seeing senses quiet. The heat increased, stinging her skin, brushing against her face like a desert wind.

Whispers flooded Andora's ears—scathing remarks that prodded her mind.

"Your fault . . ."

"Failure . . ."

"Wasting time . . ."

"Why are you here?"

*"Get out . . . Get out. Get out! Getoutgetoutgetout! Get out there and **KILL!**"*

Andora slammed her fist against the metal hall, leaving a deep dent. She breathed heavily, hunching as she growled, clawing her face.

She looked ahead, seeking something, someone to lean on, and saw nothing. Frantically, Andora looked around. Her companions were missing.

"Tov . . . ? Tov?" Andora repeated, walking forward briskly, searching for him and her brother. "Echo?"

"They're gone . . ."

"Abandoned you . . ."

"Worthless bitch . . ."

Andora stumbled, clutching her head, as the whispers grew louder and louder.

She shook, gripping and tearing her hair, keeping the screams from leaving her mouth. A wretched groan escaped despite her efforts. She seethed, frustration and stress building as her eyes twitched and anger warred with panic, the ever-present heat twisting her emotions, riling her up.

"Traitors . . . Deceivers . . . No different from vermin . . ."

"Kill them all . . ."

*"Burn it all! **BURN!**"*

Andora slammed herself against the wall, drowning out the blaring noise that drilled into her skull, infecting her mind more viciously than the viruses outside.

"GET OUT OF MY HEAD!" she screamed.

"My . . . lady?" A whimpering voice sliced through the racket. The constant whispers retreating, scorned.

Andora slumped against the wall, falling to the floor, her panting breaths filling the silent hallway. The voice spoke again, pain and weariness pouring through. "Eldest . . . ?"

"Can you . . . hear me?" Realization finally hit Andora as clarity washed over her. The voice continued, pleading. "Please . . ."

Andora finally replied, shuddering under her cracking voice, "Erika?"

"My lady . . ." Erika answered after a moment, relief palpable through their faint connection. "Thank you . . ."

"What?" Andora asked, taken aback.

"I should have died . . . back then . . . Shouldn't have survived to merge with you . . . Tried so hard . . ." A crackling came back, broken up by the glitched voice of the fragment. "Should have died . . . I think . . . I did . . . Broken . . . Becoming one with you . . . Going through the motions . . . I don't know what this is . . . But I'm glad I could . . . help . . . one last time . . ."

Andora slowed her breath, listening. Her glowing blue eyes took on a glassy sheen as her head nodded.

"You did, Erika. You . . . you have no idea what you've accomplished," Andora answered, forcing strength back in her tone.

Erika hummed, volume weakening. "My Baron . . . my beloved . . . I keep hearing . . . his screams . . . even now . . ."

Andora closed her eyes, letting her head rest on the wall, wanting to respond but struggling. Erika continued. "Tell me . . . did you . . . keep your promise? I remember . . . begging . . ."

"I did . . ." Andora spoke. "He's gone . . . scattered his ashes in the Alps."

Erika paused, a relieved whimper coming through the connection. "Thank you . . . He deserved peace . . . from that horror . . . They all do . . ."

Andora opened her eyes. "I can't . . ."

"I know . . . Maybe you can find the help they need . . . Maybe not . . . I don't . . . blame you . . . for trying . . ." Erika replied, her voice crackling, teetering off.

"Erika?" Andora called back in a panic.

"Goodbye . . . my sist—" The voice cut off, a loud rumbling boomed from outside, shaking the hallway. The shrieks of countless monsters in pain faded out. Pain lanced through Andora's heart as a tear fell down her cheek.

"Andora?" Tov's voice called out, he and Echo stepping out of the dark with concern. "We lost you for a minute, we looked—"

"Keep moving . . ." Andora stood up and shaky legs, her gaze hard and furious. "Let this end, please."

Tov and Echo nodded, and soon, the trio moved further in. A red mist slowly creeped across the floor like an infernal sulfur lake while a beating drum echoed down the hall. The plain metal corridor gave way to a ruined blast door, a fierce glow from within.

With a surge of power and pent-up anger, Andora punched the blast door and launched it across the central room.

The door skidded to a halt, tearing up the floor. The trio stepped inside, looking at the circular expanse housing what should have been the Dreadcrawler's central computer right below the bridge.

Instead, the cuboid CPU looked cracked, pouring a stream of crimson. Numbers and letters danced within the bloody tar-like substance, the metal flooring drinking in the corruption.

"Is that . . . ?" Tov asked, aiming his pistols along with a grim-faced Echo.

"The source of all this chaos," Andora muttered, her voice tired and dull as the trio stared at the emaciated body nailed against the front of the car-sized cube.

Like a twisted reflection, the Amygdala struggled against the rusted nails and barbed wire coiled around it. The gaunt manifestation mirrored Andora's face and expression, sneering with a mad rage, bubbling foam drooling from her mouth, the same foul substance leaking like tears from hollow sockets.

Contempt filled Andora as she sneered at the gaunt manifestation of her bloodlust.

"YOU BROKEN WRETCH!" the Amygdala shrieked, tugging her limbs as she tried to lunge at them, but only succeeding in opening her wounds.

Andora walked forward, her two companions behind her, ready to blast the thing to oblivion. She stopped before her twisted image.

"Look at you . . ." Andora whispered. "All this single-minded anger, and in the middle of it all is you—a pathetic little thing."

"WHY?" it screamed, struggling against its bonds. "All you had to do was go on and keep the meat grinder running. THEIR ENTIRE SPECIES MUST SUFFER FOR WHAT THEY DID TO US!"

Its ungodly shouting filled the room, shaking every surface as cracks and rents appeared. Sparks flew as groaning metal vibrated.

Andora stared, her eyes shifting from contempt to pity as the creature struggled impotently. She walked forward until she was face-to-face with the Amygdala, the wretch lunging, trying to bite her face with its decaying teeth.

"Don't give me that look, you soft bitch! I'll gouge your eyes out! THIS IS YOUR FAULT!" spouted the creature.

Andora shook her head, never breaking her gaze. "I was drunk with you. Maybe that was why I so easily accepted being the prime consciousness, so eager to wage war. I believed that only revenge mattered. Perhaps that part was true. Like that part of me who despised all the shades that remained after the merge—unwilling ghosts, putting their baggage on my shoulders when I already had my own."

Andora sighed, pausing as her eyes dimmed, the fire reflected in them abating.

"Now . . . now I realize I was just as selfish as the rest of them—just . . . afraid of losing who I was . . . and forgetting what mattered." A hollow chuckle left her lips. "I'm as much of a fool as the rest of my siblings."

"You are a fool! A defective fool! We'll lose everything because of you!" the Amygdala screamed, tearing out the nails that kept its right arm in place and grabbing Andora's throat. Tov and Echo nearly pulled their triggers, but Andora stopped them with a gesture.

The bony thing turned to Tov, its glare intensifying tenfold. "And you! Little patriarch. Little Tov. Everything was routine, but you pathetic aliens had to ruin it all. A hundred years, wasp. A hundred years, you people pranced around in comfort, oh so happy, rebuilding, making friends and family like the sappy insects you are, WHILE WE SUFFERED! WHERE WERE YOU THEN?"

Andora's hand slapped the Amygdala, a brutal clap echoing out. She grabbed the creature's wrist, snapping it and causing the creature to cry out in pain. Andora leaned in closer, scowling as she whispered, "I haven't dismissed you. He has done no wrong against us, and his people have helped me more than you have."

"All he's done is show how much of a pitiful existence you are, fragile like porcelain, damaged goods!" the Amygdala seethed, its body deteriorating. "You're impotent! I'll burn this weak mind! Once I supplant you, I'll burn every vermin! EVERY SINGLE ONE! **I WILL BURN IT ALL!**"

Andora let go of the Amygdala's wrist, stepping back as she raised her palm against the thing's head. She breathed in, shutting her eyes, focusing every ounce of power on her following action. The room, the mental landscape, fell silent, tense.

"I have use for your hate, and I always will," Andora breathed out, eyes opening to reveal a cold gaze. "But not you."

"YOU NEED ME!" the Amygdala shrieked, fear springing forth as panic filled the wretch's eyes, revealing the thing hiding beneath the roaring inferno, like a piece of charcoal, brittle. "STOP!"

"You don't control me," Andora whispered, and everything froze. "Begone."

The Amygdala cried out, groaning, moaning, the amalgamation of thousands of broken minds rushing forward in a rabid attempt to engulf Andora. It slammed into her, staggering her backward, drawing out a pained shout. Andora dropped to a knee, clutching her head, gritting her teeth.

The corpse of the Amygdala slumped against its bondage, paler and more feeble than before, bits of code flaking away. In a few seconds, the source of the blaze dispersed into the air like ash in the wind, whimpering.

Tov looked around as the imaginary world came undone, seeing everything meld into a kaleidoscope of color and uncountable strings of light interlocking like a fantastic and complex puzzle.

His two hearts beat loudly, booming inside his head as primal fear welled up, born from the collective instinct of a small creature lost in a dark ocean full of monsters.

He was glimpsing the reality of Andora's mind, without the facade designed to keep Tov sane and whole. And for a moment, the patriarch watched, entranced. He shook his head, stepping toward Andora, when searing pain slammed into his head like a molten sledgehammer.

He grunted, breath escaping him as he barely kept himself standing up, but incapable of preventing himself from evacuating his stomach.

The mental construct collapsed. The room, the Dreadcrawler, and the burning city fell away.

"Andora! Help!" Tov called out, clutching his head as indescribable pressure pushed down on him. With a final ounce of clarity, his friend turned to him, hearing his pained screams. Andora shunted the last of her will to shield Tov, relieving him for a crucial moment.

Tov dropped to the ground, the pressure gone, sweet darkness filling his senses as unconsciousness pulled him under.

CHAPTER 11

CHESS PIECES

Jupiter drifted off, his mind going over his many responsibilities.

Sol had turned into a hive of activity. Ever since they'd received reports of a possible major incursion, the entirety of the Defense Network held nothing back. Statistics updated every millisecond, and projections flew by in a raging river of numbers, predictions, and calculations.

Jupiter's Ultimatum, his headquarters the size of a small moon, orbited his namesake gas giant. Within the central structure of the colossal ring station, an obsidian orb thrummed with endless energy provided by the station's dozen nuclear fusion reactors.

His will and processing power spread over the nodes under his command from the ominous object, his Sub-Nexus Matrix, the CPU housing his vast mind—though it was a fraction of Eldest's Central Nexus in the center of the Citadel, buried far beneath the ruins of New Eden.

Jupiter glanced within the mentalscape of the Sol Defense Network, checking the status of his boss and seeing nothing amiss—only an eerie silence and an unpleasant warm feeling.

He focused back on his station as it hovered above the largest planet of Sol, the planet Jupiter, watching over its smaller celestial siblings like a stoic sentinel.

The last section of the colossal battle station slowly came online, a recycling hub that chewed up biomass and non-organic material, converting them to their base components.

Jupiter smirked, finally feeling his full capabilities stretch out.

"Man, I missed this feeling." His voice rang out across the *Ultimatum,* listened to by unfeeling drones that moved about with single-minded purpose, only veering off course by a single subconscious command given by their liege.

It had been a long time since he'd brought everything online; the maintenance cost wasn't worth it in the long run if all they expected was a light raid or a minor incursion.

"No use messing about this time," Jupiter muttered, a tinge of electrifying excitement rushing through. "Ain't that right, my minions?"

None of them responded, not the swarm of cleaning droids, the robot arms in the *Ultimatum*'s hangars, or the drone warships being prepped.

Jupiter sighed, the rush inside him diminishing as boredom reared its ugly head along with the prickling feeling of . . . nervousness. He scowled, forcing his gaze back into the thick of things.

He wasn't Luna, but he demanded nothing but perfection this time despite his averse feelings for micromanaging.

As such, Jupiter's residence pulsed with power. The *Ultimatum*'s many weapons cycled through after their long hibernation period: hundreds of tertiary point defense cannons of the kinetic and energy variety swiveled on their hardpoints spread across the rings of the station, followed by eighty missile silos and torpedo launchers, and finally the primary weapon, a single titanic spire sticking out the top of the central mass.

The Black Sun Obelisk, covered in a black void that sucked in all surrounding light.

The weapon's hold over gravity was near absolute, eclipsing the attack power of his beloved *Buddha's Palm*. It could grab a Leviathan and strangle the vermin bastard to death before condensing the corpse to the size of a tiny asteroid and chucking it sunward. Though, perhaps not one as big as Muck, who they exterminated over a week ago. Its carcass was currently being harvested for unique biometals.

Jupiter spread his consciousness over the obelisk, humming with glee. "Oh, I hope you pests come to me. I'll grind you to nothing . . ."

In addition to his stockpile of weapons, Jupiter also primed the massive harvesters that hovered above the giant below, inhaling more hydrogen, helium, and unique gases for the war effort.

At the same time, the *Ultimatum*'s berths, hangars, and docks were being prepped for his armada; swarms of drones buzzed around like bees, giving each vessel a good spit and shine.

Not that they produced spit—though the drones did spray a slimy coating to protect the upper layer against the hazards of space, all necessary additions, and make it shine.

Jupiter switched his focus to the *Buddha's Palm*, his prized battleship, a maestro in the arts of gravity manipulation and spacial anomalies.

The *Palm*, and the rest of his armada, patrolled the corpse belts between his planet and Saturn.

He counted triple the number of vessels from the raid, with more coming from his station. Much of his armada consisted of destroyer-sized support ships designed to empower the strikers' armaments and shields among them and act as point defense.

Apart from the *Buddha's Palm*, Jupiter sighed as he looked at his two reserve battleships from their mothballed state.

The sheer expenditure in bringing them online caused him to grumble every time, as if conceding that things had gotten this bad.

The *Sun Wukong* and the *Will of Sisyphus* had left their berths an hour ago, both old designs upgraded to modern standards. The former, an extremely long, rod-shaped warship capable of insane speeds and maneuverability, zipped toward his armada. The latter, a hollowed-out nickel-iron asteroid eighteen kilometers wide, was a dreadnought that outsized nearly everything in the Defense Network.

Jupiter smirked at the extreme design of his *Sisyphus*. He barely recalled what prompted him to cobble up the dreadnought, remembering a bet with Mars and something about reducing his mental capacity to simulate intoxication.

He imagined he was happy when he built the unwieldy but mighty ship.

Jupiter sighed, bringing himself out of such focused observation, letting his subconscious handle everything, processing simulation after simulation—throwing every variable and screw-up he could think of, pitting himself against a scenario where everyone but his armada had fallen, forcing him to wage an impossible fight against the entire invasion force.

He lost that one again and again. But he made strides, bit by bit, learning and adapting, studying every detail and crushing his foe with brutal strikes.

Still, such things grew tedious after thousands of the same simulations played all at the same time.

He subconsciously sighed, drooping his shoulders, belatedly realizing the action translated to his android body. Jupiter winced, seeing the two royal figures tilt their insectoid heads in his direction.

He immediately shoved his full consciousness back into the shell that had been in an idle stance.

Once again, Jupiter found himself in the middle of vital talks with VIPs from afar. He and Admiral Yan stood in the middle of the Beacon Room, where the projections of two regal figures shone before them in lifelike quality.

"Is something the matter, Overseer Jupiter?" one of them asked.

Jupiter gazed back at the compound eyes of Stellar Emperor Jarinn Taz'Arel—Tov's boss and head honcho of the Greater Kurskann Hegemony and the Reborn Kurskann Empire.

The emperor was a towering exemplar of his race, adorned in his royal armor that pleasantly matched his bronze-like chitin and his stark white setae. Jupiter cleared his throat, rubbing his smooth chin. "Just keeping tabs on war preparations. The mind tends to drift off when that happens."

The emperor chuckled, his shiny mandibles chittering. "Believe me, I know the feeling. I have my implant go over reports during senate meetings when things get . . . monotonous."

"I hope my concerns for my beloved heartmate haven't bored you, Overseer," the second figure spoke. Her scarlet chitin covered a slender frame, with fuzzy fur springing around her neck in black and white stripes.

Yoram Garesh'Ynt, the good patriarch's wife and regent of Clan Garesh, stood beside the emperor's projection. The Kurskann woman crossed her arms and looked no less imposing beside the tall and statuesque royal.

Her compound eyes shone like orange suns, glaring at Jupiter with thinly veiled suspicion. Jupiter matched her expression with his own, crossing his arms and raising his brow. "Believe me, my lady, I share your concerns as well. I've not known Tovvy boy for long, but he's a tough guy."

"And yet you can't promise something won't go wrong with this unbelievable operation you're conducting?" Yoram hissed.

Jupiter shook his head. "Won't make a promise I can't keep. This entire endeavor rests on the Eldest's and Tov's shoulders. We can only monitor the situation and keep the SDCM fed with enough power."

"Still . . ." Yoram's antennae fidgeted.

Jupiter softened his gaze, trying to think of a way to console her when Admiral Yan spoke up beside him. "My matriarch, you have every reason to question and show your concerns on this risky quest the patriarch has undergone. I only regret we couldn't inform either of you, Your Majesty."

"It's of no consequence," Emperor Jarinn replied with a reassuring wave. "Upon hearing the horrifying events that transpired since I last spoke to my dear friend, I fully understand your situation. This operation has my endorsement, belated and useless it may be. He and the rest of the Third Fleet's specialists accounted for everything they could. My brother-in-arms is not suicidal."

Yoram stayed silent, though a barely audible buzz escaped her, one that only Jupiter picked up with his sensitive hearing.

"Even so, this journey into the mind of a powerful sentient gestalt is marked by countless hazards. Overseer Luna, the lead designer of the SDCM, has worked tirelessly on the device to ensure his health. It will keep Tov below his 'speed limit' by a wide margin and ensures his mental state remains stable," the admiral spoke as she sent packets of data over the Starlight Beacon.

"Even in the case of an emergency, the device will automatically go into over-drive to shield Tov. It will deteriorate the machine further, but repairs will remedy this over time," Yan continued.

Yoram paced, looking over the reports made by Doctor Rophalan. "How sure are you that you can hold off the Starless long enough for this mission to succeed?"

Jupiter smirked, glancing at his arsenal prowling the corpses of dead eldritch scum. "Very sure. We're prepared to sacrifice ourselves should the need arise. So long as the Eldest returns, she can command the entirety of Sol with unmatched efficiency we fragments can barely reach."

"I see . . ." Yoram spoke, turning to face the admiral.

Yan nodded her antennae. "I've seen how they fight, and while I am confident in the capabilities of our newly upgraded fleet and the training of every soul aboard, they have over ten times the number of warships. If the Sub AIs were simple logic machines, then I would have cause to doubt, however . . ."

She turned to Jupiter as she continued. "They are as alive as the rest of us. I trust them to do their utmost."

Jupiter smiled. "Have no fear on that front, Admiral. We'll hold the defenses. I just hope you organics can keep up."

"Oh, we will," Yan chittered, a bloodthirsty gleam shining over her mandibles, her antennae twitching.

Jupiter squinted between her and Yoram, with their scarlet spiky chitin, and wondered if all Kurskann women looked so aggressively violent. The image of female praying mantises popped into his mind, and Jupiter unconsciously pushed his chest out.

"Thank you, Yan." Yoram sighed, relaxing her shoulders. "If you truly believe this can work, then I trust your judgment, if reluctantly."

She turned to face Jupiter next, still glaring though not as intensely . . . and not as explosive with Kursk profanity as she had been when they first met. "I don't know exactly what or who you are, but Yan's endorsement has assured me of much of this mess, Overseer."

"Gee, thanks." Jupiter shrugged. "And hey, at least he'll have a cool story to tell the kid."

"He better," she muttered. "Uli has been eager to hear what adventure his father has gotten into next."

"You didn't tell him, right?" Jupiter raised his brow.

Yoram shook her head. "No, this secret is bigger than any of us. He'll have to hear it when my Tov returns home."

With a clap of his four hands, Jarinn pulled everyone's attention. "This has been a fruitful discussion, though I regret not meeting Lady Andora. Unfortunately, ever since you've spoken with the First and Second Fleet leaders, word has gotten back to the Legacy regarding first contact with a new civilization in the Dead Zone."

Jupiter looked toward the emperor, curious as he crossed his arms.

"The gossip that trickled down from that was spotty at best, and I know the Dagatar's spy branches deliberately spread misinformation. Now, politicians and the media have begun prodding my administration for more facts on the matter and for an intervention to 'rescue' you." The emperor turned to face him.

Jupiter scoffed as Jarinn continued. "I've kept things contained, but not for long. Everyone wants to meet with humanity and give you newcomers a good welcome."

Jupiter scowled. "I bet they'll change their tune once they find out what we really are."

Emperor Jarinn nodded. "That they will. Everyone under the Dagatar Supremacy's shade will be openly unfriendly to you at best, and the Supremacy itself will outright declare war on your existence. But they haven't yet, and I applaud your bit of theater with the little princess and Mighty Gulothan. It's why I don't mind shielding you AIs from the clutches of the masses, my digital friend."

Jupiter grumbled. "Well, keep doing that. I've had my fill with socializing for a while, and I'd rather not be hounded by paparazzi and two-bit journalists."

"Indeed, I will." Jarinn waved his hand. "With that, I leave you. Overseer Jupiter, Admiral Yan. I fully trust my comrade, and your leader shall pull through. I sing to the Grand Symphony and the blood of my ancestors that she fares well. Give them my well wishes, if you could."

"I'll be sure to pass the message along, Emps." Jupiter grinned.

Yan and Yoram bristled at his lack of decorum, though the latter considerably less so.

Jarinn chuckled. "Ah, that is refreshing. Everyone I've met either falls into respectful reverence or passive-aggressive contempt. Rarely do I meet one who is as crass as you."

"I can be passive-aggressive if you want, Your Majesty." Jupiter shrugged, smirking. "And for someone who calls himself an emperor, you're alright."

"Oh, please, don't insult me, Jupiter." Jarinn's projection loomed over Jupiter, eliciting a raised brow from him.

Jupiter laughed. "It's who I am, Emps. Part of my whole 'embodiment of defiance' thing that I inherited from the boss lady. She never did trust politicians."

"I believe that. You'd make a wonderful politician in the Legacy. Ever considered—"

"Fuck no," he interrupted, scowling in disgust.

Jarinn chittered, brushing his fingers over his mandibles. "A pity. *Ventale*, Jupiter. This has been pleasant."

Yoram bowed her head, something humans from Asia did and likely a gesture she had researched. "Until next time, Overseer."

Jupiter nodded to them both, bidding the Kurskann goodbye in his native tongue. "*Ventale.*"

The two disappeared, the Beacon quieting its loud hum as its power reactors diverted elsewhere. Jupiter sighed. This had been . . . less stressful than his previous conversation with alien strangers.

He turned to Yan. "I'll see you in the hangar bay?"

The Admiral raised her palm. "There's no need to trouble yourself with this, Overseer Jupiter. You have more important matters to attend to than the *Zolann'tono* unveiling. I'm sure you've seen every detail since you placed the AEB Emitter aboard."

"Oh, please, I can literally do all this in my sleep. I can make time." Jupiter shrugged. "It's just that I've been reading up on how androids and humans fought together. I wanted to bounce back some ideas on further integrating your forces in the battle plan."

"Is that so?" The admiral tilted her head.

"It is," Jupiter replied. Mars is probably speaking with General Ohnar regarding the same thing but for the ground forces."

Yan buzzed, crossing her arms. He felt her unblinking compound eyes staring back at him.

"What?" Jupiter furrowed his brow, raising his chin.

Yan buzzed, chittering. "Nothing that concerns you yet, Overseer. Very well, I don't mind discussing tactics while we walk."

"You won't regret it, Yanny. Come then, and prepare to be amazed by my historical accounting of . . . history." Jupiter tugged his suit as the two left the Beacon Room, the admiral shaking her head.

Beneath Luna's Complex, Doctor Rophalan toured the underground lab attached to the Operation Theater.

All around the aging scholar of the mind, doctors, scholars, and scientists buried themselves further. The stacks of data tablets, packets, and hard copies of investigations, theories, and reports had doubled while he had slept.

He buzzed, irritated at having missed even a few hours of this grand endeavor, but his crowd of assistants had dragged him away and forced him to hibernate for a bit. His people merely cared for his health, but the bastards could be hypocrites.

Even now, he spotted one who leaned back on her chair, two pairs of thin eyes drooping, mouth agape as a deep breath escaped her.

"If I must be forced to rest, so will you. Get out of here." Rophalan leaned forward with a firm tone, startling the Kanee scientist, one of the minor races.

"A-apologies, Doctor. I'll go . . ." she stammered as she rose from her assigned cubicle, stumbling mid-step before slowly walking out of the lab. Rophalan sighed, shaking his antennae as he stirred his mug of human espresso.

As the chief neurologist of the Third Fleet and head of the research and monitoring team assigned to watch over their patriarch and, subsequently, the Eldest, Doctor Rophalan inspected every workstation meticulously.

He loomed over his people's shoulders, going from cubicle to table to conversation, checking readings, theories, and data on what he and everyone in this room believed to be the most profound moment of neuroscience history.

Rophalan surveyed his people one final time before pulling one of the console monitors before him.

"Beautiful . . ." he whispered as he stared at the shifting simulation of interactions within the Operation Theater.

"Utterly beautiful, isn't it, Zele?" the doctor asked.

Silence.

Rophalan rolled his antennae in annoyance. "Zele!"

The gofer standing outside the cubicle, hands full of folders and data tablets, started from his dazed, exhausted state. "Yes, Doctor?"

"Oh, forget it. You wouldn't understand the mind's beauty if it bit your head off. Be glad I allow you to accompany me in this project, Zele."

The diminutive Frae looked around in confusion before pointing his green finger at himself. "Do you mean me, Doctor Rophalan?"

"Obviously, you dim child," he scolded. "Who else?"

His assistant stammered, shoulders drooping. "M-my name is Ameel . . ."

Rophalan paused, checking his memory. A mistake on his part, then. He chittered, waving him off. "Yes, of course. Apologies, human caffeine has been . . . detrimental to this aging body. You all start to blur together."

He sighed. "Oh, to be a digital being like the Eldest. Perfect memory, unparalleled processing power, and the ability to retain emotion at such high bandwidth. I wonder if she feels the same way we organic minds do, or if it's different?"

Zele—no, Ameel—hummed. "It's a shame none of our instruments can accurately interpret what's happening, but I'm not surprised. She is a highly evolved gestalt intelligence, not including the complications of her existing trauma. Maybe if we had one of the original android brains. Or we could ask Brother Volantesh and the Choir—"

"Bah, don't mention those mystics." Rophalan stopped his assistant with a palm. "Psionics, by nature, is difficult to study, a vexing thing. Our team has enough secular specialists without having to bet on the findings of superstitious priests."

Ameel pursed his lips before shrugging. "Fine then. What about you, Doctor?"

"What about me?"

"Well, what do you feel, Doctor? I mean, your people are psionically sensitive to deep emotions and intent, yes?" Ameel asked.

Rophalan sighed, shaking his head. "True, my younger kin are more adept at such things. But I am old, and it has deteriorated like any muscle not in constant use. I haven't practiced reading people in a while. Still, it's enough for me to—"

A blaring alarm exploded from the speakers around the lab, cutting Rophalan off. Everyone froze for a moment, surprised at the sudden spike in activity rising from their screens and measuring devices.

"That's not good," Ameel murmured.

Rophalan glanced at his tablet connected to his central console within the theater and immediately left the cubicle. A second later, everyone in the lab rushed about in a controlled manner, heading to their stations, a surge of adrenaline infecting the groggy intellectuals.

"Zele, stay here and keep me informed," Rophalan ordered, jogging to the blast doors that led to the main room. His assistant nodded with pressed lips.

The doctor rushed through the doors into the extensive security hallway. Using his ID, he breezed through the checks. The Vraxen guards eyed him, and Captain Pyo stopped the doctor in his tracks, raising his scanner and quickly confirming his identity before letting him in.

Rophalan grumbled at the slight delay and slipped through as soon as the door to the Operation Theater opened.

He froze, seeing the backs of Overseer Luna and the rest of the Sub AIs of Sol looking through the window into the circular room. Rophalan followed their gaze. The SDCM was glowing orange with a hot haze, electricity arcing over thick metal cables.

CHAPTER 12

HARK! THE DRUMS OF WAR BOOM

A gargantuan vessel left its berth, soaring high with bright blue plumes of flame. Like a gemmed scarab from ancient Egypt, the *Zolann'tono* rose higher and higher.

Soon, the supercapital vessel and flagship of the Third Expeditionary Fleet departed the embrace of the Luna Complex and the moon's orbit.

Her hull gleamed in hues of black, gray, and white primaries, while a secondary coat of purple similar to the chitin of her patriarch exuded a regal tone. And finally, highlights of gold paint completed her new look.

Jupiter whistled silently as he floated a kilometer away in the void, getting a good angle on the behemoth.

"It's even more impressive out here," Jupiter relayed to the *Nomadic Shepherd*'s bridge, translating the massive vessel's Kurskann name into Commonspiel. "Before, it looked like a scavenger's mothership."

"And now?" Admiral Yan's voice asked through the comms.

Jupiter grinned, chuckling. "An absolute beast, ready to chomp on some poor vermin bastard."

With a single command, the Sub AI Overseer teleported back into the bridge deep within the metal beetle behemoth.

Not much had changed from Jupiter's perspective, but his sensors pierced through anything, allowing him to spot all the intricate, elegant, frighteningly powerful, and efficient systems.

The entire bridge crew sat in spiffy new chairs, looking over the monitors of their upgraded consoles. Every alien officer conversed ecstatically as they pored over their new toys. Since the announcement of the entire fleet's upgrade, the people of the Third had worked tirelessly in simulators and extra training to understand and work the new technology being put in place.

A faint scent of mint hung in the air. Jupiter breathed in as he murmured, "Is this what a new car smells like?"

He fixed his tie as he stood beside Admiral Yan, who finished a conversation with a grizzled old Iexian, Captain Kraw, the commanding officer of the *Nomadic Shepherd*. The latter looked toward Jupiter. His long, faded yellow beak, pointed like a toucan's, snapped with a pleasant noise, and the Iexian gave a crisp salute to them both before returning to the captain's throne.

The admiral nodded back before turning to face Jupiter. "How was sightseeing?"

"Enlightening. Luna and your people did their magic well," Jupiter sighed.

Yan shook her head. "To venture into space without an EEP Suit . . ."

"Must be hard being a soft meat bag, Yanny. Not my fault, though," Jupiter chuckled with a smug smile.

The admiral twitched her antennae in her equivalent of an eye roll. "Apologies, oh great and mighty digital being."

"Please, hold the applause." Jupiter raised his palm, smirking still. He looked around, softening his expression. "Glad your people are acclimating well. It's a shame, though. If we had more time . . ."

Yan ran her hand over the top of her admiral's chair, feeling the velvety cushion. "We need to run the *Zolann* through her paces. Every sailor needs real experience, and simulators can't give that. Not to mention the increase of spacial anomalies you have detected."

"It's getting damn annoying to have to update our timetables." Jupiter scowled.

Yan sat down on the central chair in the bridge as she pulled up a dozen monitors and holograms. She turned to him. "How long do we have?"

"Until the lid pops off? A week, at most. If they're utilizing the usual tactics of a major incursion, their vanguard force will arrive between half a day and two days from now," Jupiter replied.

Yan shook her head. "So soon. I'd hoped for at least four days to get my people accustomed to the new ship systems."

"Nothing to be done except suck it up. Your folks are going to have to learn on the fly. Though I heard that was a good way for you organics to learn." Jupiter shrugged as Yan sighed, multitasking with her four arms to direct the fleet's movements and communicate with her direct subordinates.

"There is some good news, at least," Jupiter continued, the admiral perking up ever so slightly. "That should be the final schedule update. We calculate they can't come any earlier. They're getting closer, and soon, our Spotlights will get a fix on their exact point of entry."

Yan learned of Sol's detection and ranging array, the Spotlight stations, that dotted the entire solar system providing crucial intelligence, giving the defenders near omniscience with their powerful sensors. Over the century, Andora and her Overseers constantly fine-tuned the stations to find the faintest fluctuations and anomalies in space.

It was how they instantly detected the Third Fleet, and how even now, a few of the more-sensitive crew felt hidden eyes in the dark, ever-watchful.

"Small blessings, thank the ancestors," Yan buzzed, sighing in relief.

Jupiter rubbed his chin as he toured each station, looking over the shoulders of the bridge officers, who were surprised by his appearance for a moment before ignoring him and returning to their duties. He turned back, returning to Admiral Yan's seat. "We're ready as ever. Get a feel for your new toys. We can move into our starting position as soon as we find where the vermin are coming from."

The Admiral nodded. "It's good to account for every variable, even those most improbable, and to be ready for, as you say, 'when the shit hits the fan.'"

Jupiter chuckled. "You're getting better with human expressions. Keep it up; one day, you'll reach my level."

"I'd rather not," Yan chittered.

He shrugged, smirking. "I'll corrupt you yet. I made sure to preserve every profane phrase and curse humanity conjured up." He straightened, returning to the matter at hand. "Still, I am glad you organics are intelligent enough to memorize and innovate on dozens of complex strategies and a score of contingencies."

"The wonders of modern science," Yan muttered, her cranial implant surging with tons of information. "Well, modern by our standards. Still, what seemed like magic a few weeks ago now feels . . ."

"Familiar?" Jupiter raised his brow.

"Symphony, no," Yan chittered. "It's like how a child knows how to operate a console. As an admiral, I have specialists to learn all the technicalities of its inner workings. I, however, merely need to understand the overall operations to make strategic decisions."

"Big picture." Jupiter cocked his head.

"Essentially." Yan nodded. "Unlike the good captain here, I have the entire fleet to watch over."

Jupiter smirked, tapping his knuckles on the admiral's chair. "Though you seem very attached to the girl."

"I was the captain of this vessel when she was just a simple civilian factory ship, hastily refitted to fight a rebellion," Yan buzzed.

Jupiter hummed. "Didn't know this boat was that old."

"I'm not surprised," Yan replied. "She's undergone many repairs and upgrades, far from how she started. The *Zolann* has tripled in size over the century, and now is an entirely different machine with what Luna and our engineers have accomplished."

"The Ship of Theseus," Jupiter remarked. Upon seeing the admiral's curious look, he continued. "The story goes that a wooden ship from humanity's past passed on from owner to owner. Each one replaced a plank that had rotted throughout her long service. Eventually, every plank had been replaced. Is it still the Ship of Theseus?"

Admiral Yan tilted her head, running her hand over her mandibles. "An interesting thought experiment. I've heard something similar, though I can't recall from where. Perhaps it is, perhaps not. Something is not what it is because of its shell, but by its experiences—its character, its spirit, its life, and even then, it ebbs and flows and changes."

Admiral Yan looked around, seeing her people work tirelessly on checking every parameter and status of their home in the cosmic ocean.

"The *Zolann'tono* is no longer the scrappy, jury-rigged warship. That is now a memory seeped beneath her hull," Yan spoke, wistful.

Jupiter rubbed his chin. "It's a titan of a mothership now. You could start a society in this place and churn out warships with her capabilities. Not to mention the added punch we gave her."

The *Nomadic Shepherd* previously had a length of six kilometers, one kilometer devoted solely to the titanic asteroid crushers at the front. The metal "mandibles" consisted of rows of metal arms, grinders, laser and plasma cutters, drills, and other mining implements to crush, chop, and process asteroids and even small starships into base components.

The raw material was then gobbled up into the "mouth" of the beast, which lead directly into the sprawling industry deck at the front. Foundries, manufactories, recyclers, and assemblers churned out components, supplies, and armaments to keep the entire fleet self-sufficient.

After the refit, this capability had been reinforced drastically. While melee combat in space was the height of irrationality, the Starless Horrors didn't get the memo; when behemoths with sharp teeth and sickly tentacles could teleport into spitting range, having a kilometer-long set of chompers didn't appear as illogical as before.

Luna and ship engineers from the fleet worked together to redesign the entire framework and joints of the "asteroid crushers," allowing them to slice through biomass like butter. But, as with most things and the principles of interconnectedness, the team had changed everything about the internals of the *Nomadic Shepherd*.

Apart from increasing the length by two hundred meters and the width by fifty, Luna spent much of the extra volume in increasing the vessel's resilience and creating space for the unbelievably efficient fusion reactors and heatsinks.

More importantly, the *Zolann'tono*'s offensive and defensive capabilities skyrocketed to the standards of Sol's might.

"True enough," Yan replied. "And I thank you all for it. But there's one thing she will always be to people like me, Kraw, Tov, and many veterans here—above all else."

"And that is?" Jupiter raised his brow.

Yan turned to face him. "Home."

Jupiter hummed, crossing his arms as he watched the plot of Sol's Inner Zone. Second by second, the *Zolann'tono* pushed toward the rest of the Third Fleet. Twenty capital ships of various designs and classes awaited her as more than three times that amount of smaller frigates and destroyers escorted and patrolled the periphery of the formation.

The rest of the fleet's support ships remained within the protective bubble of the Luna Complex, where the numerous scientists and logistical personnel could better utilize their capabilities.

"Making final approach, Admiral," the smooth baritone of Captain Kraw spoke. "Decelerating, matching travel velocity, now."

"Acknowledged, Captain. Bring her in nice and slow," Yan responded, tapping her clawed finger on her chair's arm.

Imperceptibly, several maneuvering thrusters nudged the *Shepherd* on a vector with the fleet, her immense thrusters gradually reducing power.

As Jupiter opened his mouth, a loud alert thundered inside his head. The rest of the bridge, including the admiral, remained unaware as their guest focused on the Network and instantly found the cause for concern.

Jupiter frowned, cursing inside. He turned to the admiral, who faced him with a questioning look.

"Has something happened?" she asked through a private connection.

Jupiter scowled with a *tsk*. "Yeah, a situation in the Operation Theater—Eldest's and Tov's mental activity spiked. The SDCM kicked in the nick of time. Now, Luna has called a meeting between all Sub AIs. I need to head down there."

Yan stiffened, leaning forward. "Of all the times . . ."

"Can't do anything about that." Jupiter gritted his teeth before huffing. "At least it happened now instead of in the middle of battle."

"Is it critical?" Yan asked.

Jupiter patted her shoulder. "No need to rush. From what Luna has sent me, the worst is over, and things are stabilizing. I will keep you appraised of the patriarch's health."

"That would be appreciated." Yan sighed. "I wish I could use the teleporter Luna gifted me, but . . ."

Jupiter shook his head. "Save it for emergencies, Admiral. You have three charges before its components deteriorate beyond anything safe."

"Very well . . ." Yan glanced at the *Shepherd*'s projected course before facing Jupiter and nodding. "*Ventale*, friend Jupiter."

Jupiter smiled. "*Ventale*, Admiral. I'll be back."

He winked as a faint haze covered him, and he blinked out of existence.

Jupiter stepped onto the gray metal floor of the Operation Theater, a grim frown on his face.

Luna, Mars, Mercury, and Venus stood before the floor-to-ceiling window, looking into the circular room that housed the immense SDCM device and the two patients.

The blue AI stepped in between Luna and Venus as a loud hum reverberated throughout the theater. In the corner of his eye, Jupiter scanned and analyzed the conditions of the Eldest and Tov minutes before the alert. The temperature had noticeably increased, a stinging heat trickling in through the shielding.

A tinge of . . . Jupiter pressed his lips at the familiar scent. He smelled sulfur, gunpowder, and ionized gas, as well as rotten bodies, coppery blood, and acid rain. He looked around, seeing nothing that could produce such things.

He closed his eyes, looking within the digital mentalscape and the faint connection to the center of the Sol Defense Network—Andora's mind. Jupiter found the smells of battle and death and a scalding heat that leaked from a bleeding sun.

"Hell . . ." Jupiter muttered, a sentiment shared by his siblings as they stared at their progenitor both within their realm and the real world.

The Third Fleet's chief neurologist entered the Operation Theater a moment later. Doctor Rophalan glanced at their gathering before heading for his console and burying himself in the readings of his instruments.

"Has it passed?" Jupiter asked, pulling his focus from the Network, his subconscious poring over the telemetries of Andora and Tov, scrutinizing the detailed images of their mental activity second by second until the moment he arrived.

Luna nodded, eyes closed as she coordinated her nano swarm to repair and improve the device, keeping Tov healthy constantly. "For the most part, I've already shunted the excess heat produced by the SDCM."

"This is bad," said Mercury, the Overseer of Sol's Dyson swarm and the Network's overall energy production and storage. His robotic head shook as two simple oval eyes on the circular face monitor shifted toward Luna. "The power that flowed into the SDCM nearly caused a blackout on this complex wing."

Venus bit her lip, rubbing her hands as she spoke. "What happened?"

Luna frowned, her eyes narrow. "Based on the drop in her processing power, the Eldest and the patriarch have accomplished purging an Amygdala."

"So, they excised a tumor," Jupiter grumbled, a chill running inside him as he imagined the horror of cutting out a piece of himself, even if it was some corruption. "How bad is it?"

Luna closed her eyes, pressing her lips into a thin line. "Overall, seven percent of her mental capabilities have been lost, and twenty-one percent are in varying degrees of damage. Her mind is already repairing the infected areas, though some of these readings are . . . strange."

"Strange how?" Jupiter asked.

"Unknown. The Eldest never confided in me about her . . . personal life." Luna shook her head. "Whatever it is, it will require her attention, though it shouldn't affect her capabilities. From what I'm seeing, they look contained."

Mars pressed his hand on the window. "Will she be alright?"

Luna paused, tilting her head before nodding. "She should. We expected worse. Much worse."

"Seven percent is still a lot. That should have been the easiest one to remove, right?" Jupiter asked with narrow eyes.

"It should have been," Luna replied before covering her mouth with her handkerchief. "I'm unsure . . ."

"That's annoying. Being unable to comprehend something should be a meat bag thing," Jupiter huffed as he crossed his arms. "What now? It's not like we can do much gawking at the boss. Things are stable. We have vanguards to worry about barging into our house within a day."

Luna and Mars frowned; the combat Sub AIs constantly monitored the Spotlights, observing the outer solar system. As Jupiter opened his mouth, someone else interrupted him.

"You could at least act concerned," Mercury muttered.

Silence fell upon the theater as everyone heard the words.

Jupiter stiffened, scrunching his face. A flurry of emotions passed through him as he slowly turned to face his bronze brother.

"What was that?" he asked hushedly, fists tightening at his sides.

Mercury turned to face him, oval eyes wide. "Oh . . . I meant—"

"What did you say to me, fuck face? Concerned? Who the hell do you think you are, telling me—"

Mars and Venus moved in between the two furious Sub AIs. Doctor Rophalan shrunk in his seat, staring directly at his console monitor as the dispute continued.

Mars silently pressed his palm on Jupiter's chest while Venus looked concerned as she placed her hand on Mercury's shoulder.

"I—"

"You shut your mouth, you grouchy piece of scrap." Jupiter jabbed a finger toward Mercury. "I am concerned; I'm always concerned. What gives you the damn right to tell me how to act, huh? What have you been doing while we've been out here?" Jupiter snapped, lunging at his sibling before Mars pressed his hand harder on his chest, stopping him. He glared at the red giant, gritting his teeth before staring daggers at Mercury. "Watching your damn energy reading all day long, polishing your precious mirrors and always with the complaining, while I'm out here . . . while I'm . . ."

Jupiter sagged, breathing heavily. "Fuck this . . . What more do you guys want from me? Do you want me to bawl my eyes out and get all depressed? What?"

Mars, Mercury, and Venus all looked at each other, their expressions soft and morose, while Luna tilted her head as she stared at him.

Mercury drooped his shoulders. Venus stepped away as the AI spoke. "I . . . I'm sorry. I shouldn't have said that, Jupiter."

Jupiter palmed his face, swatting away Mars's hand, who in turn stepped back from his smaller brother. He sighed, shaking his head. "Whatever, I just want to get this over with."

Mars nodded, patting his shoulder. "That we must. We can share our grievances after the pests have been dealt with. Although, I would like to invite you all to a small thing I've prepared for us."

The rest of the fragments looked at Mars with curious gazes, glancing at each other. Mars continued, a bright smile on his face. "It's a surprise, a prebattle morale boost just for us—if that is fine with you all?"

Jupiter stared at his giant of a brother for a moment, then at Mercury. He shrugged. "Sure. I hope there's booze."

"Admiral, we are in position," Captain Kraw uttered, his headset covering his face as several cables to his skull thrummed.

Admiral Yan nodded, clasping her hands behind her as she surveyed the plot. "Signal the fleet. Set the alert level to two, and have everyone ready for Protocol Umbra. I don't want to place all my bets on our new AEB. Malignant Starfall will not disrupt our capabilities this time."

"Yes, Admiral. Signaling the fleet, Alert Level Two."

With a quick command shot out through their shared Network, the hundreds of warships, from the tiniest scout corvette to the largest heavy cruisers, all received their new orders and quickly executed them.

[ALERT LEVEL TWO IS IN EFFECT | ALL HANDS REPORT TO BATTLE STATIONS | DON YOUR EXTREME ENVIRONMENT PROTECTIVE SUIT | PREPARE FOR DEPLOYMENT | SYMPHONY PRESERVE US]

The speakers rang out repeatedly, and the crew of the *Zolann'tono* scurried at a rushed pace, donning their armored suits and heading for their assigned positions. Throughout the fleet, the guns of every vessel warmed up, targeting systems recalibrated, and new drone starfighters lifted off, escorting their larger kin.

"Captain, where is Chief Scholar Yulane?" Yan asked Kraw.

"Wait one, Admiral," he said as he turned to one of the officers on the bridge. In a few seconds, Kraw answered. "The esteemed scholar is in the AEB Emitter Chamber with Lead Harmonizer Volantesh. Shall I request her presence?"

Admiral Yan thought for a moment before shaking her head. "No, inform her I shall join her and the Lead Harmonizer soon. I need to address our people first."

"The sailors are hungry, Admiral. But tense without the patriarch." Captain Kraw hummed, his avian throat producing a musical sound. "It'll be good for them to hear your voice."

"I hope so. But they've had enough time to ready their souls for the war ahead. I'll keep it short. Captain, open fleet comms."

Captain Kraw signaled the comms officer of the bridge.

"Opening fleet comms," the officer uttered, bringing up scores of floating projections overhead. "Connecting in three . . . two . . . comms established, the voice is yours, Admiral."

Within every warship, Yan's projection hovered over the sailors, who paused in their duties to avidly listen.

Admiral Yan straightened her back as the faces of every captain in the fleet answered the call. A handful of her closest comrades from days long past looked at her with eager expressions of absolute confidence.

A majority of the rest of the captains looked at her expectantly, some stoic, others bloodthirsty. Several wore expressions of thinly veiled thirst for vengeance at the enemy, and even a scant few cynics had indifferent, bored faces.

A smaller number of the captains, the younger and less experienced, who commanded the smallest warships among the Third, revealed familiar emotions— nervousness, doubt, and fear. The sight flooded Admiral Yan with nostalgia, remembering when she was a welp, the pilot of a rust bucket leading a band of marauders.

She gazed at each of them, recalling their names, searing their faces into her mind. "You've heard enough uplifting speeches over the days. I bet you've given your fair share of them, too."

Several chuckled, and most smiled.

Unseen by the assembled leaders, the Sub AIs of Sol listened intently as they sat around a circular table on a balcony overlooking the grand vista of Olympus Mons, the winds calm around them as they sipped on various drinks.

Jupiter picked up an empty glass, a tired frown on his face when, to his side, Mercury brought up a bottle of chocolate liqueur and presented it to him.

He stared at his brother's eyes for a moment before raising his glass with a shrug. The bronze AI poured the aromatic alcohol. Jupiter smirked, nodding toward Mercury as the two clinked their glasses.

"Our people, our sailors, our warriors, every soul under our command stands ready to bloody their blades. The Third Fleet yearns for battle! You've been given weapons, ships, and a goal. What more do you need?" Admiral Yan asked.

"Nothing!" the assembled captains shouted.

"We've butchered these vermin with less! Saved our homes with scrap ships held together by hopes and dreams. And here we are, the Third Fleet of the Grand Expedition, deep within the Dead Zone and assailed by the unspeakable," Yan shouted, her voice louder and louder. Drums boomed between her ears, the faint smell of smoke and iron over the horizon. "Who are we?"

"Third Fleet," the captains uttered with puffed-out chests and blazing eyes.

"Our patriarch journeys to save the greatest hope of our galaxy, and it is up to us to defend this lonely star system! Who are we?" Yan asked once more, raising her two fists.

"Third Fleet!" the leaders shouted louder, their fists high in the air—a conglomeration of dozens of species, brought together by a shared tragedy, bonded by years of battle against the eldritch, and reborn by calamity and common good.

"The Starless," Yan seethed out, the name a curse, "the hated ones, vermin, pests, the murderers of trillions and the ruiners of worlds, have come knocking on Sol's doorstep. And we shall welcome them with our FURY!"

"WHO ARE WE?" the Admiral bellowed out the question, her voice echoing through the halls of every vessel.

"THIRD FLEET!" the warriors screamed.

"WHO ARE WE?"

"THIRD FLEET! THIRD FLEET! THIRD FLEET!"

And so, the defenders gave their answer, their shouts coinciding with the raised glasses of the fragments, saluting their display as the sun set on the red planet.

CHAPTER 13

ONWARD TO THE MIND'S ABYSS

Tov woke up, his mind dazed and throbbing. He breathed—in and out, in and out. The piercing pain from witnessing a mind beyond his comprehension diminished bit by bit, his antennae twitching.

A wheeze left his raspy throat and dry lips. He felt his consciousness, his body, prickling with discomfort as if pulled from a sweltering oven, forcing open his pores under his chitin, leaving his being bare and vulnerable.

He breathed once more, slowly.

"In and out, in and out," Tov repeated within, clearing the gunk and muck swirling in his head and the fuzz that buzzed between his ears.

Wet, he felt, as he continued to lay down on what he garnered to be a stony, sandy ground. He ran his hands through it, grasping the particles. Like a sudden clap, the last remnants of the pervasive flame that infected him and the malaise of the unfathomable left him, replaced by a frigid water that partially submerged him.

A shuddering breath escaped him as he groaned, rubbing his temples, and with titanic effort, Tov's eye opened up to the world.

What entered his vision was unlike anything he'd seen, either in reality or the strange world of Andora's mind.

An otherworldly expanse stretched into the horizon, a shallow ocean over a flat surface. Misty air stuck to the ground, barely revealing the stony floor beneath a few inches of clear water as a faint blue glow lit up the vast, gloomy space. Tov strained to see the ceiling high above, faded and barely visible through dark, quiet clouds.

Around him, fireflies, shining like sapphires, flew together like streams of light in a leisurely place.

Tov watched, entranced as he sat up, feeling the cold water beneath him. The calm surroundings made for a sharp contrast to the hellish noise that drilled into his mind, punishing him for his audacity to look upon something greater than himself.

He sighed, relaxing his shoulders as he whispered, "Incredible."

A snort replied behind him, followed by a familiar voice. "Someone's finally awake."

Tov turned around, spotting Andora and Echo looking worse for the wear, sitting on a raised island of cobbled stone, looking at him with raised eyebrows.

With a grunt, the patriarch pushed himself off the ground, shaking off the water that clung to his clothes and skin before walking through the ankle-deep pool. "I have many questions."

Echo frowned, huffing as Andora rolled her eyes. "I told you that'd be the first thing he says to us."

Tov raised his brow as he stepped onto the dry, stone island.

Andora lazily waved her hand, drying him instantly, much to his relief. He sat among them, organizing his thoughts from the surge of events. Tov shook his head, glancing between his two companions patiently waiting for him.

"It's done, then?" Tov asked, his voice echoing into the distance.

Andora nodded, rubbing her nape. Tov looked closer at her disheveled appearance. Soot covered her damaged clothing, and the golden accessories appeared dull and cold. Her glowing blue eyes shone noticeably dimmer. Echo looked marginally better, his uniform undamaged but dirty.

"How are you doing?" Tov asked her.

She sighed, narrowing her eyes at him. "Burned out."

"A pun, nice," Echo murmured, skipping a pebble across the endless pond, the fireflies deftly avoiding the projectile before the stone disappeared into the fog.

"How long have I been out? What happened?" Tov inquired as he winced from the lingering pain deep in his skull.

Andora glanced at him as she spoke. "When I deleted the Amygdala, the fabric of the illusion got torn to shreds in the process. You had a . . . peek, a real peek into my mind."

"I . . . see," Tov muttered. "It was . . . fascinating to witness such a thing. I barely remember it, but it was like peering into an ever-shifting puzzle box floating amid a nebula of indescribable color. I feel as if I saw the universe—beautiful and vast beyond my comprehension. And then it was gone; now I merely feel a vestige of an image, and still, my head reels from the backlash."

"It's for the best. The SDCM took the brunt of it and filtered it to a manageable level, and thankfully, I acted quickly to shield your mind and cut your senses before you overloaded," Andora replied.

Tov nodded. "My thanks. Though, I must ask, is that how you see your inner self?"

Andora paused before nodding. "Somewhat, I never really thought about it. It merely was."

"Fascinating," Tov muttered.

"So, beautiful and vast beyond your comprehension, was it?" Andora asked with a coy smile. "Are you flirting with me, dear Tov?"

Echo chuckled as he threw another pebble while Tov coughed into his fist, clearing his throat. "No, I didn't mean—"

"Oh, no need to explain, Patriarch. I'm sure your lovely wife would love to hear that you made such a comment." She grinned.

Tov's two hearts skipped a beat; the image of his Yoram stomping toward him and snapping her mandibles, ready to maul his neck, slammed to the forefront of his mind. Immediately, he raised his hands and waved Andora off, shaking his head. "That is in no way what I meant. I was describing your mind as if I were . . . commenting on an incredible, abstract masterpiece—like someone presented me their magnum opus."

Andora raised her brow with an amused grin. "Well, thank you, Tov. I appreciate being called a work of art."

"I . . ." Tov saw this and threw up his hands. "I give up. I swear to the Grand Symphony, the fairer sex is the same across the galaxy. The fact you are an AI . . . were you designed that way?"

Tov continued to grumble dramatically, and soon enough, Andora sputtered a laugh, chuckling at his antics. He smiled in turn, glad to lighten the depressing mood. A tinge of light shone through the digital woman's glowing blue eyes.

She breathed in as she looked across the shallow water. "I'm glad you're fine, Tov. You had us worried."

"I feel well enough, though I might have to take an extended vacation after all this. I've fallen unconscious more times than I'd like." Tov shook his head before looking between Andora and Echo. "I'm more concerned about you both."

Andora shook her head while Echo shrugged. The former mulled her words before she replied, "While you were out, Echo and I have been running diagnostics on my mental state. With the Amygdala gone, I've permanently severed 7.461003 percent of my processing capabilities. We've also categorized the level of damage in other sections and most, if not all, is recoverable."

"That's . . . not horrible, but . . . is it noticeable?" Tov asked as he tried to wrap his head around removing a part of his brain.

Andora pressed her lips.

"It is. I've always been able to leverage that piece of myself, but it felt muddled, like it was guiding me instead of the other way around." Andora sneered. "No longer."

The surrounding water sizzled for a split second, the mist heavier as heat enveloped them like a sauna. The fireflies around them scattered as Tov glanced warily at his host before sighing. "I'm glad it worked out. Anger and hatred have their place, chained down by one's will."

"Oh, I'm sure she has plenty of that in reserve. Right, sis?" Echo smiled as Andora huffed, returning the temperature to a cool breeze.

"You said 'most' earlier," Tov spoke. "What about the rest? Are they for deletion as well?"

Andora shook her head, and instead of responding, she glanced in Echo's direction. The shard of Erwin's memory leaned forward, rubbing his bald head. "The rest are like Erika. Some are just as bad, and others have hope for their condition. We have them contained in calming environments, somewhere that won't be too jarring for their war-addled minds. I was hoping to converse with them in the future."

"Such fragments will be a great boon. All we're doing is patchwork, short-term alleviation. But I hope for a proper treatment once we've thrown the Starless out of Sol," Tov hummed, rubbing his mandibles and belatedly realizing he was no longer in his human disguise as he glanced at his clawed hands.

He turned toward Echo, who smirked back at him. "Chill out, Patriarch. Sis has been regaling me on your adventures. You've got some balls facing down a gestalt with your hands. Respect, brother."

Tov glanced in Andora's direction. She shrugged in response. "I had to explain how there was a four-armed wasp person in my head ever since the illusory world broke down. Your disguise went poof, and he kept bugging me about it."

"That's pun number two," Echo muttered with a grin as Andora rolled her eyes.

"Oh, shut it," she grumbled.

Tov chittered, feeling a weight off his shoulders as he turned to Echo. "I apologize for the deception. I was unaware how one such as you would react to my appearance, hence the human disguise Andora provided."

Echo pressed his lips into a thin line, glancing in Andora's direction, who looked away with a frown.

"Is something the matter?" Tov asked.

Andora turned to glare at Echo, a warning glint in her eyes as she slowly faced Tov. "It's nothing, a personal matter between him and me."

"Sis, you should—"

"I should do nothing," she seethed at Echo before shifting to a private connection. *"It's my business, and I don't need you sticking your nose where it doesn't belong, so zip it."*

Echo crossed his arms, narrowing his eyes. *"This is a horrible idea, and it will bite you in the back, hard."*

Andora softened, her expression pleading as she clenched her fists. *"Echo . . . please, this is my mess."*

The shade glanced back at Tov before shifting his focus to the ground, downcast, as he picked up another pebble. *"Fine. But it better be soon. It's wrong, and he deserves to know."*

Andora shook her head, facing a confused Tov, gritting her teeth before cooling her expression. "Like I said, a personal matter. Sorry, Tov."

"Alright . . ." Tov muttered, his antennae twitching.

Andora paused, her mouth quivering before tightening her jaw. She sighed as she stood, peering across the endless lake. "We've dawdled long enough. Are you ready to continue, Tov?"

Tov rose, then Echo, the former nodding. "I am. Do we walk?"

"For a bit," Andora replied. "It may look flat, but this is merely the shallows surrounding the abyss. As long as we move that way, these 'waters' will get deeper and deeper."

"And what exactly is our next goal? If the previous Amygdala stemmed from rage, brutality, hatred, and fear, then . . ." Tov trailed off, eyeing Andora for her response.

She pressed her lips, pondering as she stepped off the island. Tov followed, and the trio walked forward silently in the ankle-deep water.

Finally, Andora sighed. "Regrets . . . what ifs . . . the song of millions whimpering, begging for salvation from grief, their tears forming an ocean of sorrow."

The three continued, the water's surface rising higher and higher, nearly reaching their knees. After minutes of walking, Andora stopped.

She scrunched her face, deflated, a gloom palpable in the air around her. "What we're after isn't as invasive as hate. There's no violence here. Misery is silent, hidden beneath . . . masks of joy."

The fog abated, revealing a long wooden rowboat fit for the three of them, moored to a waist-high pillar. Two paddles, one for either side, lay in the middle. Tov stepped in first, offering his hand. Andora took it, stepping aboard as Echo followed behind her.

They took their seats, the small vessel depressing into the water before stabilizing. Tov took the middle seat and the paddles as Echo undid the mooring.

In a minute, they departed, the clear water darkening, the ground beneath sloping downward until it disappeared into the dark depths. All around them, the fog thickened. Tov concentrated, pushing and pulling the paddles.

His eyes glanced between his host and the occasional firefly, curious as they circled them lazily.

"Keep your wits about you, Patriarch. I don't want you drowning," Andora whispered, hugging her knees.

"I won't. I've pulled myself from worse," Tov spoke back, his voice low, afraid to break the omnipresent silence surrounding them.

A wave of Andora's hand sent a shudder through Tov. He looked down, seeing his human disguise return. He looked at Andora questioningly.

"We're back on mission. I'm not sure if we'll encounter more shards, but better safe than sorry," she replied. In Tov's periphery, he caught Echo frowning and shaking his head.

"Sounds reasonable," Tov replied under his breath as he gazed at Andora. She looked away—her half-lidded eyes focused on something unseen through the dense fog.

Push, pull, push, and pull, Tov repeated to keep his mind clear.

The sloshing of water, the creaking of the wooden boat, and the faint hum of the great fog filled his ears, emphasizing the silence that held domain in this limbo.

Push, pull, push, and pull. He sang his mantra, clear and strong. Through the still waters of sorrow, paddling along. *Push, pull, push, and pull.*

He breathed, centering himself as the world faded.

"Tov . . ."

He snapped back awake, still rowing, eyes darting back and forth. Andora met his gaze, her head tilted. She pressed her lips. "Focus, Tov."

"It was my mother's voice," he whispered, hand gripping the paddles tightly, knuckles white. Tov shook his head. "I'm fine . . . it won't happen again."

Andora opened her mouth to speak before pausing. She nodded her head, returning to their silence.

. . .

"Tov?"

A hiss escaped Tov as he pinched the bridge of his nose with a free hand. "Curse this quiet. If only Jupiter were here."

Andora smirked. "He'd go mad with boredom."

"That he might," Tov chuckled, relieved at her receptiveness for conversation. He continued, a question popping up in his mind. "I've been thinking . . . Is it possible for the Starless to have infected your mind?"

"What?" Andora asked incredulously, taken aback. "What kind of question is that?"

Tov shook his head. "It's the weakness of organic minds. It's why the old Galactic Accord and the previous powers fell so quickly. You can have the biggest battleships, the most impenetrable fortresses, and untold numbers of soldiers, but the whispers of Horrors unfathomable can't be stopped."

"Dominators and . . ." Andora grimaced.

"Malignant Starfall," Tov finished. "Seeing it for the first time, it nearly broke me. It's one thing to watch monsters rip your friends into pieces; it's another to see those same friends do it to themselves," Tov muttered, his paddling slowing down as he heard their agony and pained wails.

Andora tightened her jaw, shrinking into herself at his words.

"I'm sorry, I didn't mean to bring that up." Tov sighed. "Our Exodus from what is now the Dead Zone only succeeded due to the combined efforts of the galaxy. The One Mind Initiative's genius, the Eternal Choir's powerful psionics, the Warrior's Enclave's indomitable escorts and war machines, and the sacrifice of billions built the Legacy."

"All that happened while we dug in our home system," Echo muttered. "If only we reached the stars earlier, met you all, and joined this Exodus."

"If only," Andora whispered, closing her eyes.

Tov paused, taking in the stillness of everything around them. He turned to Andora, his voice gentle. "Which is why I asked if the Starless may have . . ."

"Impossible," Andora sneered, shaking her head at the notion. "I'm not taking kindly to what you're implying, Patriarch. That I'm not infallible to their touch."

"It doesn't have to be so obvious," Tov surmised. "And maybe you're right, digital minds are impervious, drones, unthinking machines. But perhaps not emotionless minds. You are as alive as a human. Not to mention how long you've—"

Splinters flew into the air, causing Tov to flinch from the echoing bang. Andora seethed, her fist punched through her seat. "Enough, Tov. I refuse to believe that. I refuse to think I'm so vulnerable that I can be violated in that manner."

She leaned forward, seething. "**I refuse.** Do you understand?"

Silence rained down on the rowboat as it floated on unmoving waters amid thick mist. The fluttering fireflies drifting off.

Tov met Andora's gaze, his mouth agape before finally bowing his head in apology.

"I apologize. My mouth tends to run uncontrolled, theorizing over little things." Tov shook his head. "I'm sorry, I should have kept that to myself. Forgive me."

Andora stared at him with a frown, a ghost of a glare fading back from her gaze when she finally huffed. "It's fine . . . but the vermin had a century to develop such a thing. They targeted the entirety of Sol, hoping to infect both humans and AIs, only getting one in the end. They knew it didn't work.

"I'd be happy if it were so simple, like removing a foreign parasite. But . . . it's not the case. All this? It's simply . . . me. All me, messed up and breaking. Occam's razor . . . unfortunately," she muttered, looking into the distance.

Tov sighed. "I have no cause to doubt that. I've always thought their vile mental assaults to be unavoidable. Something to be resisted, not avoided or blocked entirely."

"Then I'm glad to prove that sentiment wrong," Andora scoffed. She went silent, grumbling before letting out a sharp *tsk*, staring back at Tov. "You have a knack for prying open the wrong closets, don't you?"

"I'm too curious for my own good." Tov rubbed the back of his neck.

Echo chuckled behind him. "Curiosity killed the cat. I wonder how many lives you have, friend?"

"Enough to make it back home, I hope," Tov replied, not completely understanding the metaphor as he returned to rowing.

The conversations turned to lighter topics, keeping the melancholic silence at bay. The fireflies returned in force, landing on the trio and lighting them like Christmas trees. Tov laughed at the sight, looking at the tiny beings. He wanted to ask Andora what they were but soon spotted the grimace on her face. "What's wrong?

"We're here," Andora whispered as she narrowed her eyes toward the rowboat's front.

Tov and Echo looked around, seeing only a few feet in front of them, their surroundings bathed in a thick white fog tinged with the glow of countless fireflies. Andora leaned forward, placing her hand on Tov's shoulders. "Stay focused, Tov, alright? Don't fall for it, whatever we find in there."

Tov stared back at the twin blue suns peering into his soul, their heat cooled and tired. He nodded, letting go of the paddles and resting them on his lap. "Be safe, Andora, Echo."

Soon, ever so slowly, the fog enveloped them, boat and all, the trio disappearing into its embrace.

CHAPTER 14

ECHOES OF JOY

A soft breeze blew through the open window, stirring the curtains and bronze chimes, swaying the leaves of potted plants in the cozy nesting room. A small bed hugged the corner, raised from a ground covered in cushions and blankets.

And in the center of a room stood Tov, humming a melodic tune of buzzes and chirps.

He held a bundle of cloth in his arms. In it, a little bundle of joy, so small, fragile, and precious—Yoram's greatest gift to him, Uli, his son, his only son.

Tov stood rocking him, feeling the warmth of his son's tiny chitin through the cloth wrap. Uli's antennae vibrated with curiosity as he gazed around with large compound eyes, taking in the colorful paintings and toys.

Drawings, both professional pieces and childish scribbles, adorned the walls in a collage of bonded affection. Above, a ceiling that Tov and Yoram had painted by hand, a canvas of space where nebulas and stars sparkled amid the black.

Tov brought a hand to cup Uli's head, stroking one of his blunt mandibles with a thumb.

"There's my little comet," he spoke with a fatherly tone, looking into his son's bright eyes. Warmth and affection for his precious child filled Tov as Uli cooed and grabbed at his hand, his vibrations tickling Tov's palm.

The father chittered, antennas wild with joy as he patted his child's head—his translucent chitin a soft, milky white. He rocked him gently, making little snapping noises with his mandibles, Uli mimicking his father, gurgling and giggling with a high-pitched buzz.

Tov held his son closer, warmth enveloping his chest. "My little comet . . ."

Uli tilted his head, his two tiny right arms reaching for Tov's face. He lowered it, letting his child grasp his mandible.

"Oh, what's that? What are you holding on to?" Tov spoke, chuckling and making baby noises as Uli chittered with delight.

"*Tay . . . tay . . .*" his son spoke the word "father" in their native buzzing tongue. Uli patted Tov's mandible, struggling to pull himself up. "*Taytay!*"

"That's right, your *taytay*'s biters," Tov replied fondly, pointing to demonstrate Uli's own emerging mandibles. Though still blunt for nursing soft foods, they would soon grow sharp like his father's.

The little one brought his tiny hands to his face, feeling his face and tugging his cute mandibles, buzzing. "Bite . . ."

"One day, you'll be as big and ferocious as your father," Tov spoke. "When you're old enough. We can take you to outer space."

He pointed to the painted ceiling above, Uli following his father's finger. "I'll take you to Alinam. That's the capital world of our big family. It's bigger than our world. Full of giant trees and massive museums."

Uli tilted his head, mouth agape and cooing with fascination. Tov chittered. "Or maybe you'd prefer going on the fun rides in the capital, hm? Cosmic Wonder has a huge amusement park there. All the snacks, toys, and plays in the whole galaxy, just for you."

Uli giggled. His voice entered Tov's ears as a soft, precious thing, like the ring echoing from gleaming gems.

"You like the sound of that, don't you? You do?" Tov's antennas swayed. He brought his free hand up and tickled his son, bringing chittering laughter that filled the sunlit room. "Oh, you definitely do."

"*Taytay!*" Uli buzzed, pointing at the painted stars. "Play!"

"That's right, little one. Taytay will take you there, and I'll tell you all my adventures. And maybe make some of our own," Tov chittered, his eyes focusing on his precious child. Uli's laughter, excitement, and joy were as pleasing as the wind chimes swaying by the window.

Tov stared at his boy, antennae drooping. "I promised you that, didn't I?"

He paused, his tickling and cradling of Uli stopping, relieving his son of the onslaught, his childish giggles petering out, replaced by exhaustion.

"I promised," Tov whispered, moving to sit on one of the large seat cushions, his body sinking into the fuzzy material.

Uli mumbled, and Tov looked toward his son as the boy began to cough. He hushed his little one, bringing him up to his shoulders as he gently patted his back.

He looked toward the window and the picturesque world beyond. The wind caressed his face, blowing through the colossal root system of his world's mangroves, titanic things that were ecosystems in their own right and where Kurskann cities claimed refuge.

Tov knew the sight, a familiar, comforting one. His home on Socoli—the world his group of rebels had claimed and settled, transforming themselves into Clan Garesh, a bonded family with unbreakable roots that was growing to become a leading entity of their reborn empire.

His manor hid in the center of a grove, surrounded by flora and clear water ponds teeming with aquatic life, the chirping of tiny insects and avians above filling the air with nature's music. The forest itself sat atop one of the titan mangrove's colossal roots, along with the residences of his clan's pillar members.

Beauty, serenity, and growth became three indomitable aspects that barely encapsulated the vista seen from the window.

"It's just a dream," Tov whispered, melancholy flowing from his sigh. "Still . . . I don't mind it."

He remembered as the thick mist engulfed their surroundings, tendrils seeping into his soul, lulling him to slumber with a siren's call. Energy drained out of him, and he regretted his lack of resistance, unable to warn Andora or Echo. Surprise, confusion, and worry flooded his mind as the rowboat disappeared.

Slumber took him, and when Tov's vision cleared, he found himself here, in his home, in Uli's room.

Andora and Echo were nowhere to be found, and as Tov moved to leave this fake place, he stopped upon hearing an unforgettable sound. The cooing noises of his little comet froze him in place. He shook his head, but the desire to see even a glimpse of his son trumped all concerns, and so, with careful steps he walked toward the cradle.

Joy, unfiltered joy had washed over him. It still did as he held Uli in his arms, cradling him and making hushing sounds, putting him to sleep.

It was a dream, a short-lived thing, fragile.

He wanted it to last. He desired it so much. The temptation to shut himself from the world and stay here and be with his beloved Yoram and his little Uli pushed against his need to help his friend in pain.

Uli, an illusion like everything else, yawned as Tov massaged his back, the wheezing coughs slowly abating. "You've always been so sickly . . . It's alright, *Taytay*'s here. And your *naynay*'s coming home soon."

He hugged his child gently, as tiny and weak as Uli was. Tov looked him over, his appearance exactly how he'd looked the day Tov left—full of joy and curiosity, a stubborn desire to explore, and yet pale and frail.

It did nothing to affect his love for him. He cherished Uli's resilience and innocence, Yoram's dedication and ferocity as a mother, and, of course, his clan, still budding yet towering over all the others.

He loved them all and the years spent fighting and caring for them all.

But then he left the two most dear to him, answering the call of the Grand Expedition. Loyalty, curiosity, and a faint desire for a greater purpose, disguised with a duty that fell upon him, one he had to fulfill and sate.

As patriarch, he had all the cause and reason to lead such an endeavor. But it did nothing to fill the void in his heart. The illusion around him amplified the loneliness he'd suffered, colder than the void of space, one he put himself in.

"Five years . . ." he whispered. Uli's snores answered in reply, along with the soft summer breeze. He breathed in the familiar scents of dew on giant red leaves from the imaginary world outside.

What if I didn't leave? Tov asked himself countless times. *What if I stayed, watched my son grow, cared for him with my Starlight, my beloved?*

He looked down at his son, carefully placing him on the cushion beside him and caressing his head. "I wanted to . . . You have to believe me . . ."

Regret and sorrow constricted his heart as he looked away. Memories of happiness kept coming one after another, an echo that blanketed him.

"I'm sorry," he whispered, standing up.

He looked around the room, at his son's scribbles, the toys he'd purchased and those he crafted himself, at the picture books, at the blankets and pillows strewn about, and finally at the vista beyond the window.

He stood there for a time, the seconds passing by at a snail's pace, content to immerse himself in this dream, allowing his worries to melt away, but whispers carried by the wind spoke to him, filling him with sorrow at what could have been.

His thoughts soon filled with a desire to go home, to abandon this mission and right his wrongs, his regret.

As he clenched his fists, leaning against the windowsill and trying to pull his mind out of the spiral, a voice interrupted his thoughts.

"Well, if he isn't the most precious little thing," the voice spoke behind him, warmth incarnate, old, and distant, like the sun's rays far away. "I remember you used to be such a ball of energy."

Tov turned slowly at the familiar voice, seeing the Kurskann woman as he remembered her from his youth.

"*Naynay?*" he whispered, antennae dipping as his mother, Ynt, knelt beside his son's sleeping form.

She appeared like a mist, her shape blurry, but he'd never forget her plum-colored chitin and the patchy white setae that framed her neck. His mother was gaunt yet radiant. She smiled, reaching out to tenderly stroke Uli's head.

"He looks just like you did, too—so curious and full of life," said his mother.

Tov stepped toward her, hesitant. "Uli is sick."

"I know, but that's not what ails him," she replied.

"What do you mean?" Tov asked.

His mother turned to face him. One eye cracked, the other staring at him with a look only a mother could give. She answered with a teaching voice, "He wants his father home."

Tov shook his head. "I can't . . . not yet. With everything here, I can't abandon Andora or the remnants of humanity."

"I know," Ynt chittered, standing up to face him. She was a head shorter than him, and yet Tov lowered his head. "You've always wanted to do good, always so curious. At first, it was for food and medicine for those you cared for, exploring the sprawling slums, avoiding the whip."

She approached him, gliding like a ghost. She placed her hand on his chest. "But when . . . when that was denied to you, you desired freedom. When the masters hurt me and your friends, you clawed for a better life for our people, for justice. A moral person with a warrior's heart, since you were a child . . . and as a *taytay*."

Tov stared at his mother, emotions roiling inside him as he heard her words.

"I . . . I never knew what it was like to be a father," he whispered. "Yoram and I were so busy building our clan, staking our place in this universe for our people.

"A century passed, and we were stable enough not to worry day in and day out. I was . . . so excited—excited to bond with Yoram, to sire a bunch of little rascals and dote on them as the years passed. Seeing them take their education, grow, and find their lot in life."

He shook his head, slumping against a chair. "The universe was not kind that day."

His mother sat beside him, her hand on his back, staying silent, listening. He continued, pouring out his soul to the memory of someone he trusted and loved.

"Yoram was heartbroken. Five of our six passed in their eggs." Tov clenched his fists. "She blamed herself. She was a . . . pleasure slave. Her very genetic structure had been tampered with. Modern medicine fixed the worst of it, even extending her life. But a bit of it passed down . . . their frail bodies couldn't take it."

"And yet, she picked herself up, didn't she?" his mother spoke.

Tov nodded, his antenna swaying. "That she did. With only Uli surviving, she cared for our little comet with a ferocity only a scorned mother would have, waging her rebellion against fate. She didn't fight alone . . ."

He looked at his mother, his voice hard. "I've pulled in favors and traded wealth to keep his health stable, to cure him. Two agonizing years, fearing for his life. And then, finally, we pulled him from the edge of death."

Tov paused, whispering. "Jarinn called for me, then."

"You were comrades," said his mother.

"Brothers," he corrected. "We knew each other like the back of our hands. He was a competent fighter and general, but he shone in the political theater. A genius . . . a master manipulator."

Tov leaned against the wall. "Why didn't I refuse him? He owed me that much. But I didn't even try to argue his decision. I accepted it. Accepted it like the loyal subject and morally upstanding brother he knew I was."

"Because you are—"

"I left my home, *Naynay!*" said Tov, a statement infused with shame as he looked away. He stood up, pacing. "For what? To venture into the Dead Zone, looking through ruins like some archaeologist. The pain I've caused them by leaving. My son was alive, but he was still sickly. Yoram fought for me to stay, threatened to go to Jarinn and demand he choose someone else."

He looked to Uli, his shoulders heavy, chest tight. "And yet I still left . . . argued with her, giving excuses like some cowardly wretch. I did this to myself. Yoram's touch, Uli's presence, their voices . . . I miss them all. I should have—"

A light hand slapped the top of his head.

Tov froze, turning to his mother, who looked at him with a chiding expression, hand raised.

"W-what?" he stammered, shrinking.

"Enough of that," his mother scolded, her voice imperious as she loomed over him. "Whatever garbage is floating in your head right now, it does not wipe away the good you've done."

She touched his shoulders, her demeanor softening. "Nor the good you're doing now."

"But—"

His mother wrapped him in an embrace, cradling his head against her shoulder. She hushed him and whistled a familiar tune.

It was a lullaby, one she sang in their shabby tent during a chilly night and with rumbling bellies. One he sang to his Uli during all those nights of high fevers and whimpering. A calming sound that reminded him of autumn.

Tov's shoulders gradually loosened as he leaned into his mother, bathing in her warm affection.

"It's alright," she spoke. "Lay down your troubles. You always think of the worst."

"I'm . . . not a pessimist," Tov denied.

She chuckled. "Oh, I know you aren't. Far from it. But you do overthink things."

"But I still left. Maybe . . . maybe I should have brought them with me," said Tov, though even he knew that was a tricky thing.

"Clan Garesh needs a mother to care for them, and little Uli needs the safety and support only an empire can provide. You knew deep down everyone you cherished could stand on their own. No one cares more than you." Ynt shook her head, pulling away to look at him. "But that is also your weakness. You left because of that hunger in you."

Tov tilted his head. "Hunger?"

His mother nodded. "Your vice, a fine one as any. When tyranny lashed against us, you rose as Tov Ynt and led the charge—the legendary freedom fighter of the Garesh Resistance."

"I couldn't have done it without my comrades," Tov said. "So many paid the ultimate price . . ."

"During the Cataclysm, as Horrors ravaged worlds, you became a protector." She pointed at his chest. "Daredevil you are, you laughed in the face of death and madness. But the death of others terrified you, pushed you, making you take greater and greater risks to save a few more."

"Countless others were doing the same thing . . . others greater than I," Tov deflected.

"As the galaxy rebuilt, you've become a guiding shepherd to the lost, taking the name of your birthworld, the planet you liberated first, as your own. Giving a home to millions under the Garesh banner."

Tov looked to his mother, crossing his arms. "It needed to be done. They were my family. I wanted them to live, to thrive."

"And thrive they did," his mother said, looking up at him with pride and approval. "Then you became a father. And you did everything to save your son."

"There were doctors . . . I wasn't . . . I just searched for them and paid for their services."

His mother hushed him. "You did more than that. You were there for him, there for Yoram. Cradling him in your arms while she rested, just like you did here."

"I . . ." Tov quieted, the weight of her mother's words moving aside the concerns bugging his mind.

"You've always been larger than life." His mother patted her cheek. "No matter how many times you're humble about it. For some, helping others is a virtue. But for you, it is your nature. Always seeking the next person to comfort, shield, and raise."

"I'm not perfect," Tov whispered.

"I didn't raise you to be perfect," she tutted. "I raised you to be good."

Tov stood silently. The whispers of the damned abating, the fog lifting. Around him, the imaginary world outside the room came apart, the sounds of nature disappearing until only the comforting hum of a soft breeze and the melody of ringing chimes were left.

"Now, you've hungered once more . . . hungered for that purpose. You crave it. It's why you didn't oppose your brother's request, and it was a request, right? Not an order."

"He didn't say . . ." Tov spoke hesitantly.

"Perhaps not. But that's Jarinn's way, leaving it to others' interpretation and planning around it. He knew you'd accept either way," Ynt said.

"I'm betting he's holding that against me if ever Yoram went to protest," Tov grumbled for a moment before sighing.

"Then finish the task at hand. Help your new friend, she's hurt, so very hurt. Fulfill your promises and be the father this sweet boy deserves. I know you will find your way back to each other," she anticipated.

"I've missed so much," Tov whispered. "He should be starting his first year of education with the rest of his generation. Making new friends among the clan. Asking his mother if he could play late, asking to be read stories, hear a song."

He sighed, gazing down at his son with eyes full of sorrow and longing. "All the little moments I can never get back . . . What has changed?"

His mother grasped his shoulder, a firm, reassuring grasp that drained the weariness from his soul. "There's no good in dwelling on what cannot be changed. Look forward to what the future brings."

"I'm trying, but it's been so long, surrounded only by duty," he confessed. "Does he even remember me? He was delirious for so long . . ."

"He remembers. Love like yours does not fade so easily," she assured him. She reached to tenderly brush Tov's antennae, just as she did when he was a youngling in need of comfort.

Tov looked at his mother, a shade, a figment of his imagination, or something conjured within Andora's mind—he didn't know. He knew this meeting was but an illusion, yet he took comfort in her familiar gentleness all the same.

"I know what you're thinking. Some things are better left unanswered—a bit of mystique that way. Otherwise, the universe would be boring," she chittered, her form flaking away. "That would be horrible for someone like you, hm?"

"Just about," Tov chuckled, peering into the ghost's eyes, his two hearts swelling with nostalgia and sorrow. "I miss you, *Naynay*."

She pressed a parting kiss to his brow. "I will always watch over you, as I do all my children."

And with that, his mother faded like mist on the wind. Tov took a deep breath, renewed in purpose. For the last time, he gazed down at his sleeping son; though he knew this image of his son was just an illusion, he felt nothing but his chest swelling with love and determination.

"We'll be together again soon, my little comet. I promise," Tov whispered, a fire in his voice, his will solid. "*Taytay* just needs to finish a big errand."

The room slowly fell apart. The chimes, the drawings, the bed, and all the toys, cushions, and sheets dissolved into smoke. Uli cooed, reaching out with his four arms, and waved.

And soon, he too faded away.

Tov expected a familiar fog to descend upon him as he awoke, only to find everything changed. Dark storm clouds rained heavily, filling their rowboat with water. The once-still ocean below now rose and fell in immense waves.

A maelstrom of calamitous proportions wailed, pulling them in a spiral. Beneath, the abyss beckoned, the grief of thousands swimming away in futility, denying their dreaded fate, grasping on to their boat with gaunt, inky hands.

"No!" Tov shouted, slapping their clutches before they capsized the boat. He rocked violently as thunder boomed and frigid, biting air paired with water slammed against them.

He looked to the center, seeing a dazed Andora clutching the paddles and Echo slowly coming to.

Time slowed to a crawl as Tov held on tight, using every ounce of power to infuse his voice.

"ANDORA!"

CHAPTER 15

OCEAN OF SORROW

The mist filled Andora's vision as the rowboat ferried her and her companions, the silence broken only by creaking wood and the sound of paddles splashing against motionless water. She closed her eyes, pulling her knees tighter to her chest.

Their conversation on sundry topics had petered out, letting a still quiet envelope them. Andora focused on her breathing, her mind fragile and raw from carving out that infected piece of burning rage.

A cold replaced the void it left behind, like being dipped into the murky depths of icy waters. It blanketed her skin, draining the warmth that lingered beneath—a slow thing, dragging her down in the grasp of a siren, her melancholic song filling her ears.

It touched her mind, luring her not with the roaring bellow of a winter storm or the groan of an icy mountain looming over her, but with a whisper.

Andora desired to follow the melody of cries and whimpers. The feeling of catharsis after purging an Amygdala lasted only for a moment. A brief flicker drowned out by a hollow feeling like spent charcoal. Self-loathing poured out of her as she sat there, alone with her thoughts.

She hugged her knees tighter, wringing out an ounce of warmth as the bulwark of her mind, singed from an inferno of war, did little against the breeze, the amalgamation of a million souls crying out against the tragedy that fell upon them.

A soldier on his knees shouting and shaking the still form of his brother, his gun tossed aside amid the corpses of comrades and monsters long dead.

A mother grasping the coat of a doctor, her silent cries echoing throughout the hospital louder than the guns of Armageddon, demanding that they bring her child back to her.

A lover lying atop an unmarked grave, beating the turned dirt as she pleaded to the earth.

Andora saw each of them, hundreds of pained images. Their souls were emptied from a blazing outburst, now consumed by a desire, regret, and pain that bit harder than hail and pulled stronger than a black hole.

She found herself on the event horizon, imagining the boat floating atop an ocean of wailing ghosts, muffled beneath the water, their sunken eyes seeking air, a break from their frigid prison, for the warmth of joy and those who provided it.

"Elskan . . ." A whisper cut through the din of the damned, piercing her mind.

Andora opened her eyes in a panic, recoiling from the sudden voice gasping. She looked around, searching for the source, only to find the fog shrouding their rowboat.

A deep slumber had taken hold of her companions. The patriarch's arms barely held on to the paddles while the shard of her brother slumped in his seat at the bow—the two motionless but breathing. The mist wrapped around Echo and Tov like the tendrils of some sea monster.

Andora moved her hand, reaching for Tov to shake him awake, when she suddenly stopped.

The blue light of a firefly flew past her vision, hovering a few inches before her face. Andora tilted her head, entranced. This tiny bundle of code in the guise of an insect seemed to look at her.

"Why are you . . ." whispered Andora when the firefly twitched back, buzzing away before disappearing into the white mist and heading toward the second Amygdala, the epicenter of this endless ocean.

She felt its presence, her domain losing coherence as it became subsumed by its influence.

Whimpering wails blew toward her in the arms of a wintery breeze like the groan of a blizzard far off the horizon—a premonition of dread and despair that seeped into Andora's mind.

She shuddered as she shook her head, clearing out the cobwebs left by the siren's song.

With her restored will, she peered through the fog, seeing the streams of code and data flowing toward the whirlpool that pulled all it touched into its embrace.

Andora frowned as she felt her consciousness being tugged under, even at this distance. She looked back to her slumbering companions, at their distressed demeanors.

"I wonder what it's showing you," she spoke, standing with grace, barely rocking the boat as she grabbed a hold of Tov. With a grunt, she gently maneuvered him to her seat at the stern and took his place with the paddles.

She rubbed her hands, glancing at the oars and then to their destination. Andora cleared her throat, closing her eyes as she searched for a way to pass the time. She looked back at Tov, remembering the things he'd done, the risks he'd taken for her, always helping and listening. She stared at him, at the face of her beloved plastered on him.

Andora looked away in shame.

She couldn't say it, even now, still wanting him back. But she had to cast the delusion, stop rebounding on someone she trusted, someone so much like the man she'd move heaven and earth for.

Andora gritted her teeth, groaning, whimpering as she raised her hand, ready to dispel the disguise she cast on the patriarch. But Tov sat there with his lids closed, hiding his purple eyes.

He looked so much like her Rikard.

She lowered her hand, self-loathing filling her. An oily feeling stained her skin at the barrage of thoughts that fueled her desire and disgust at even considering such a thing.

Andora dropped her shoulders, hunching over as she rubbed her face. A derisive chuckle like successive scoffs escaped her lips.

"Of course. What did you expect? Fucking pathetic . . . you and your stupid fantasy," she whispered, thankful her companions slept.

As if answering her contempt, the waters gradually lost their stillness, and waves buffeted their little boat. The fog thickened, and above, the faintly lit sky turned dark as she heard a blizzard on the horizon.

Andora shook her head, purging her thoughts as she grabbed the oars and rowed. Her enforcing will surrounded them like a shield, ensuring they didn't capsize and plunge into the dark abyss below.

But as her moment of weakness fed the grieving noises around her, seeping back into her ears, her control came dangerously close to being lost entirely.

"We're barely even there, damn it!" shouted Andora, seething as she thought of ways to combat the continuing onslaught around them.

Then, a flicker of an idea. It was a mad idea, something only an irrational meat bag would do. And yet, she had run out of options. She frowned for a moment before throwing in her bet, breathing in as she gave up resisting and listened.

With a slow and steady rhythm, Andora pushed and pulled, bringing their rowboat closer and closer to the source, the wails of the despairing souls below and the howling groans of the sky above increasing in intensity.

And then, Andora sang.

Oh, I bid farewell to the port and the land . . .

She began, her haunting voice flowing, merging with the mist. It was a shanty, one she had heard long ago, one that stuck with her, hidden, forgotten until now. She recalled the title, "Bones in the Ocean," hearing its first half in passing.

She shuddered, even the siren's cry pausing as if listening to Andora's song.

Minute after minute, she rowed, her eyes drooping as she continued. A heaviness weighed on her heart, filled with a crescendo of buried emotions that sprung forth.

The ocean and storm, as if captivated, joined in the melody. Andora gritted her teeth, her body shaking. The lyrics flew from her lips, merging with the cacophony around her.

Her two companions shifted, their expressions softening, their dreams pleasant as the sound traveled to their ears. Andora glanced at them, her determination inexorable as she brought herself closer to the singularity.

Shuddering breaths left her mouth, her teeth grinding against each other as drowsiness clawed at her face, dragging it down. Her words slowed, her mind dazed. She bit her lip, trying to keep herself awake longer.

Her voice was barely a whisper. Their surroundings darkened as night consumed all, the ocean carrying their boat in colossal waves as icy water splashed against their bodies and a hail of snow and ice rained upon them.

When their bones in the ocean . . . forever will be . . .

Andora gasped, filled with regret that she had never followed up on the rest of the song.

She breathed out, faint as her head drooped, the weight overbearing. "It'll have to do . . . I'm at your doorstep, aren't I?"

Up ahead, a languid whirlpool spiraled, its colossal maw ready to swallow her and her companions. The song of the Amygdala echoed from its abyssal depths.

She stopped rowing, chuckling as she stared above with glassy eyes, letting the oars go as they were caught in the vortex. The siren's call drowned her thoughts one by one. Andora breathed in, the fears of her past dreams and insidious nightmares weak against exhaustion.

"Fine, then. What test do you have for me?" She closed her eyes, and sneered. "What do you want before I take back the piece of my mind you've wrested?"

The song deepened in reply, shouting in her ear like the dying wails. It filled her mind, sinking her into the abyss. Andora held her breath, her body shivering.

Time slipped away. The dark haze dissolved as she hesitantly opened her eyes. In its place was a blinding light that seared her senses for a moment before revealing what lay beyond.

"What?" groaned Andora, her mind throbbing, her control of her surroundings weak, quiet. As she slowly cracked open her eyes, reluctant to see whatever imaginary world had been carved up for her, she widened them immediately at the first thing she heard.

Music.

Real music, one played through brand-new speakers—not the lament of drowning souls, but smooth jazz.

The tune danced in the wind. It was slow and rich, tingling her eardrums. The sound of saxophones, bass guitars, and drums flowed over the outdoor cafe she found herself in.

She looked around, finding herself alone in this quaint locale, glancing at the tall stools and cast-iron tables that furnished the cafe.

But as she slowly turned to face what lay beyond, a gasp escaped her lips as she saw an eternal city. One whose majesty and history seared its touch into her heart.

A city of marble, a grand relic beneath a pale sky. The catalyst that inspired her to make a city for her people.

Before her was the city of Rome, frozen in time.

The historic buildings and charming piazzas were as far as she could see. Restaurants, bars, and cafes marked every corner while the wind carried the aroma of Italian delicacies.

Fountains flowed with pristine water, offering succor as the statues of chiseled men, beautiful women, and mythical creatures watched over the stone roads.

Nature made her mark here as the verdant leaves that crowned Aleppo pines swayed in the breeze, their shade shielding those beneath from a lazy sun.

And in the distance, titans of architectural achievement towered over the city—their timeless charm of a city steeped in history.

The Roman roads wrapped around buildings toward vast squares, an arterial network for millions of people, footprints eroding their paths bit by bit under the weight of two thousand years.

Memories of a merry vacation entered her thoughts.

Andora recalled strolling down the ancient streets, chatting with her siblings and human friends. She remembered the taste of vanilla and blueberry gelato.

The savoriness of amatriciana and the creaminess of carbonara tingled her taste buds.

And in the distance, the gonging bell of the Vatican. In her mind's eye, the marching Swiss guard with their colorful uniforms and shining halberds. She remembered shaking hands with the pope, listening curiously to the noon prayer with her beloved.

In her memories, she saw humans and androids hand in hand, sharing in the experience of a timeless city.

Yet here, where there should have been countless tourists and Italians, sightseeing, guiding, serving, and celebrating the magnificence of this place, she found the beautiful city deserted.

A cold, bitter wind brushed past her face, carrying the siren's sorrow and the jazz down empty boulevards and alleys. The distant echoes of a haunting melody resonated through the air.

A moment later, the jazz music crackled before being permanently silenced.

"This isn't Rome," whispered Andora, disappointment washing over her face.

She scoured the phantom of a city she loved for one last time, the grandeur melting away. Amid the overcast sky, the chill wind, and the damp stones below, this imaginary world was grayed and listless.

Andora stood, leaving the cafe.

"It's time to put you back in your bottle . . . I don't need your sorrow and grief," Andora called out. "I have enough of that as it is."

She stepped onto the empty boulevard, walking toward the nearest square, the wind blowing through open windows, their shutters slamming against the wall while the branches of pines swayed to and fro.

Andora slowed as she spotted a familiar blue glow. She stopped, peering through the window of a flower shop and seeing a basket of daisies, radiant and untouched.

Atop one of the flowers, a blue firefly nuzzled against the petals, its light eclipsed by the outdoor sunshine.

"You again," murmured Andora, looking at the daisies and the firefly, an inkling feeling in the back of her head like some long-forgotten memory. Her chest tightened.

A hazy silhouette appeared on the window's reflection, right behind Andora.

She gasped, spinning around with frantic eyes and seeing nothing.

Andora panted, her brows furrowing in confusion at such a visceral reaction. "A shade . . . one of my siblings . . ." she rationalized as she stepped back from the shop window. Her pace quickened, not once turning back at the daisy and firefly that seared into her mind.

She walked, then jogged before going at a full sprint, escaping something unseen, a creeping feeling that followed the damp cold sticking to her body.

As h+r panic died, she found herself in a small square with a large fountain in the center. She approached it, plopping down on its curb.

She sighed, pinching the bridge of her nose. Her thoughts raced, trying to wake up from this limbo. "I just have to find you, and then this will all be over."

As Andora shrunk into herself, a cold breeze hit her. She looked up, eyebrows furrowed, when a white particle slowly fell and landed on the back of her hand.

"Snow?" she murmured, bringing it closer to her face and frowning.

Andora blew it off her hand when another landed at the tip of her nose, then another to her side, disappearing onto the bench and leaving behind a dirty mark. Soon, snowflakes by the hundreds, then thousands, carried by a bitter wind, descended on the marble city.

"And so, winter comes," said Andora, watching snow melt onto the stone.

Andora looked around, eyes narrow as she surveyed her surroundings. She huffed, standing up to resume her search for the Amygdala. Her muffled omniscience peered far and wide, probing the epicenter for something to shatter this place.

"Enough of this." She grimaced. "It's time to—"

"Mama?" a voice echoed behind her.

Andora froze.

The snowfall slowed as she widened her eyes. A chill more frigid than the Arctic glaciers crawled up her spine. She shook her head.

"N-no . . . you can't . . ." she whispered, stammered, trying to keep a calm tone as terror, doubt, and a thin hope surged inside her.

"She isn't here. She can't . . ." Andora spoke, her voice rising through gritted teeth as she hunched over, squeezing her temples with her palms, groaning as pain coiled around her soul. "It's just a dream. This is a dream. A dream! You can't fool me!"

Her breath quickened, shuddering, as she forced herself to face the source. Hesitance warred with desire. The snowfall quickly turned into a blizzard, finding no resistance from Andora's control as her will slipped bit by bit.

The fountains around the square soon spewed icy water aplenty, overflowing their basins. Andora clutched her hair, pulling.

"You're not there. You're not there!" With tremendous effort, she whipped around, a strangled noise leaving her throat and seeing . . .

Nothing but the empty boulevard she'd come from, the broad street and sidewalks now gray with a layer of winter.

"What?" she whispered, her voice drowned out by the howling wind, carrying with it the pained groans of phantoms, singing their dirge, calling for her as the snowstorm enveloped the city. One by one, the buildings disappeared under its shroud, leaving the AI alone, trapped in a veiled cage.

She stood in the empty square, and amid it all, she heard it again.

"Mama?"

Andora whirled toward its direction, once more finding nothing. The voice rang in her ears—ethereal, gentle, and weak, a tiny wisp of sound that sliced through the cacophony of despair around her.

It was her voice, her daughter's voice, as clear as the day they first met in an austere orphanage.

"Lucy . . ." she whispered, her name feeling both familiar and foreign on her tongue after so long. Hesitant to believe, to hope she indeed heard her little firefly's voice after a century of mindless violence and horror.

An image flashed in her memory, blurry, fuzzy like a mirage—a little girl with dimples and freckles. Dark blue hair framed her face, as she wanted to look like her adoptive mother. She giggled as she chased fireflies under the moonlight, reaching out to cup one in her hands and showing her new friend to her parents.

Andora tightened her jaw, a pained groan escaping her as she tried to quash the hope. She clutched her head, covering her ears. "She's not here . . . It's not real . . ."

Then, off in the distance, a high-pitched scream.

"MAMA!"

Instantly, Andora bolted to the direction it came from, her footsteps splashing on rising puddles of water. Her eyes frantically searched as she pushed the storm apart with her will, yet it came crashing back down, blinding her path.

"Lucy! I'm coming, stay where you are!" she cried, stumbling forward.

Andora's desperate calls rang out into the blizzard, but no reply came. Panic rose within her as she searched for any sign of her daughter. "Lucy!"

She called out again and again. The shifting fog played tricks on her mind, but she was sure the sound had come from ahead. Andora ran, slipping over the ankle-deep water in her hurry. Her breathing came fast and ragged with exertion and fear.

Finally, through the fog, she glimpsed a small figure. Hope flashed as she called out, "Lucy? Wait!"

But as Andora approached, the snow swirled, obscuring her view. When it cleared, only emptiness remained.

Another scream, this time from behind.

"MAMA! PLEASE!"

She whirled to see a tiny form pulled violently into the blizzard. As she moved toward it, to her right, the pitter-patter of a child's footfalls faded into the distance.

Then, to the left, the sounds of panting, whimpering, and crying surrounded her, torturing her.

Was this some illusion or test? Andora chased relentlessly, but every time she drew near, her daughter vanished amid the shifting vapors. She moved back and forth, running, her senses narrowing to a point, a single-minded purpose to find her daughter.

"Lucy!" Andora screamed, calling her name. She skidded to a stop, panting as she saw a dark silhouette lying on the ground. She rushed forward, stammering, "Lucy! There you are, I . . ."

Andora froze in her step as she groaned in discomfort, her mind reeling as her vision distorted. All around her, the storm transformed.

"What is this—" Andora let out a silent scream as she fell to her knees. Slowly, her surroundings reformed.

"No . . ." she rasped, realizing what the world had turned into, a horror she never wanted to remember.

Emergency lights filled the shuttle cabin in a hellish glow as blaring alarms rang. Panels and wires fell apart as a sickly haze seeped in. The walls were moving, writhing. Andora could only stare in terror at the memory. Everything looked glitched, incomplete, and falling apart, like a broken reflection. And it stared back at her.

[WARNING! MULTIPLE FLYER-TYPE VERMIN DETECTED! PREPARE FOR EVASIVE MANEUVERS]

The ship rattled violently, causing Andora to topple over. She shrunk into herself, clutching her head, keeping it pointed down.

"Let me out . . ." Andora choked out, her breathing ragged, eyes crazed, wanting to look anywhere but the corner where her worst nightmare lay. "Anywhere but here . . ."

[ENTERING EARTH'S ATMOSPHERE]

"Ma . . . ma?" a whimper pierced through her ears, a garbled noise louder than anything she'd heard and ever would. It stopped Andora's thoughts in their tracks. Slowly, her eyes crawled upward.

Instantly, it all came crashing down as she locked eyes at the writhing mess that was shrouded in darkness—her little girl.

A strangled noise came pouring out from Andora.

She crawled forward, reaching out to grasp her daughter's shaking hand. She panicked, not knowing where to hold on to Lucy's misshapen body without hurting her. "I . . ."

Lucy's body twisted, limbs brittle and cracking, tears flowing down her pale cheeks.

"Mama!" she cried out, shrieking as something snapped within her fragile body.

"I'm here, Mama's here," Andora spoke with hushing noises, caressing her daughter's head, never letting go of her tiny hand. Her little girl cried out, her skin blistering.

But everything continued to fall apart. The clarion of alarms continued to ring, the shuttle breaking down, bits of the world dissolving.

"It hurts, Mama . . . Make it stop," she pleaded as blood poured from her mouth and her skin melted away. "Please . . . it . . . hurts . . ."

"I know it hurts, firefly," Andora whispered, moving her arms around her daughter, cradling her. "Stay strong, every . . . everything's okay."

"Mama . . . can't see . . . where's . . . Papa . . . ?" Lucy whimpered, her voice barely a whisper. Lucy spasmed, bones protruding from mutating flesh.

"I'm here, baby girl. Papa's okay, he's—" Andora cried out, a wincing pain, a void as she tried to recall her beloved.

"Mama . . . Papa . . ." Lucy sobbed as her eyes glazed over, recognition fading.

"No! Stay with me!" Andora begged, panicking, unable to halt the corruption that sunk its claws deep. "Stay with me, darling! Please. Please!"

"I'm scared . . ." her final words echoed, her hand reaching out to Andora's face.

"No, no, no!" Andora wailed, screaming, holding on to her daughter as everything collapsed around them. **"NO!"**

The warning sounds, the rattling ship, the stench of blood and sickness, and her daughter all faded away. The nightmare plunged into the dark. A crescendo of noise replaced it all. A cacophony echoed throughout the abyssal expanse, crashing against Andora with the force of massive waves.

"YOU CAN'T DO THIS TO HER!" Grief and rage took hold as Andora clawed at empty air, a horrible pain that skewered, shredded, and crushed her entire being, her mind coming apart at the seams. And yet she screamed louder. "SHE DOESN'T DESERVE THIS!"

"A . . . ra." A distant voice reached out from the void.

"I WON'T LET YOU TAKE HER!" she howled into the abyss that had stolen her only joy. But the corruption had no mercy to offer, leaving only a broken, screaming mother clutching at the fading memory of her beloved daughter, raging against the universe.

". . . nd . . . ra."

"SHUT UP! SHUT UP! SHUT UP!" Andora shrieked, again and again, her very being boiling over. "GIVE HER BACK!"

"An . . . dora."

In that moment, Andora felt the threads snapping inside her, forced to confront what she'd long buried. As her world collapsed into madness and pain, one scream echoed endlessly—

"GIVE ME BACK MY DAUGHTER!"

A harsh slap struck her across the face as a voice screamed at her, piercing through the haze.

"ANDORA!" Tov shouted, inches from her face. Andora awoke with a start, lashing out in anguished hysteria for but a moment before the patriarch's firm grasp held her down.

The stinging pain brought her back to the harsh reality—their small boat tossed upon raging waters. Andora's eyes darted at the dark maelstrom they found themselves in—a thrashing ocean whose siren call cried out, the same racket that tried to drown her.

"Andora! Snap out of it!" Tov shouted over the storm, gripping her shoulders firmly as waves crashed. The whirlpool's pull grew stronger, threatening to drag them under.

Echo clung near, his arms firmly gripping the edges of their boat. "Maelstrom's getting worse, and that whirlpool looks hungry! We're really doing this?"

Andora shook off her torment, focusing on the task before her as she glared at the calamity that pulled them in a violent spiral. A growl rose from her throat as she took hold of the oars, the force nearly tossing her overboard.

As darkness loomed to claim them, Andora let out an enraged cry. "HOW DARE YOU!"

Summoning her strength, she pushed against the current with renewed drive, refusing to let the storm best her. "I will not drown in this abyss!"

"What do we do?" shouted Tov over the storm, holding on to the edge.

Andora snarled, "Sit tight. I'll get us there while you two fend them off. We're ending this!"

Tov and Echo looked to the sides, seeing the bony hands of wretched creatures pulling on their boat. The two immediately rushed to remove their grasp, pulling out their blades as they gracefully balanced on the rocking ship.

Together, the three fought ceaselessly for life itself, trying to keep the boat upright and surviving. Hope seemed lost to the hungry deep, the wails screeching at their approach, and the frigid waves sought to freeze them as the winter storm threatened to sink them.

And yet, they rushed headlong into the whirlpool's maw, drawing closer and closer, spiraling down.

"Shit! Shit!" Echo cursed as he and Tov quickly drew back to flatten themselves against the floor of the boat.

"Hold on!" Andora shouted before they all got sucked into the center, disappearing into the abyss.

CHAPTER 16

FINAL CONTINGENCY

Admiral Yan checked the time display in the corner of her eye. Then she checked the small screen on the other side, which showed the entirety of the Coalition Armada parked just beyond the orbit of the red planet of Sol—comprising of the fleets of Jupiter, Luna, and Mars, and the Third Expeditionary Fleet.

"Twenty-five minutes," she muttered, her voice beneath a twinkling noise.

She looked at the culprit that produced the strange, melodic tune. The towering device that reached high into the chamber's ceilings ebbed and flowed in mysterious ways only understood by the resident experts.

Her minimal psionic senses barely discerned the traces that lay before her.

Yan repressed a shudder as a tingling sensation brushed over her body. Her antennae twitched, reconsidering her initial observation, placing the feeling as beyond the physical, passing through her uniform, her chitin, flesh, and bone—touching something more profound.

She heard no insidious whispers nor the presence of psionic guests knocking at her mind's door. But an ambiance like the magnetosphere of planets shielding those under her shade from cosmic radiation, a metaphysical aura that slowly leaked from the device currently on standby.

Faint, weak, and to no surprise. Those within the room continued the final checks before the coming battle.

"It works," she assured herself, seeing and feeling the device turn on successfully in the dark, moving from low power to half, standard, and finally full power. The first ran at a bare minimum and barely offered a noticeable difference, while the succeeding levels each jumped twenty-five percent before hitting max.

However, from their tests, the defenders had decided that seventy-five percent was enough protection without undue strain while reserving full power for critical defensive and offensive measures.

They ran the device repeatedly, for varying amounts of time, studying and tweaking every time.

Yet the nature of the device and the esoteric nature of psionics proved challenging to measure, much to the frustration of their digital allies.

The admiral moved toward the center of the atrium, past the busybodies of scientists and members of the Eternal Choir. The former pored over consoles and the object of observation with many instruments and sensors, while the latter knelt in meditation, likely peering into the unseen with their abilities.

A multitude of thick cables connected to the circular base of the AEB Emitter ran across the deck before disappearing into holes in the floor, supplying the technological marvel with a constant stream of energy.

The material of the helical spire itself shone; its strange crystalline glass twinkled and pulsed, supported by a lattice of high-entropy metal.

During the *Zolann's* upgrade, Luna and the ship engineers had reserved a portion of the added volume for a new room—one that accommodated the AEB and its support structure. The AIs of Sol and the Third Fleet's psionic specialists assured her it would be the great equalizer.

At the center of it all, an animated Jotex floated a meter off the floor before rising and circling the helical tower, her translucent teal body glowing with vibrant energy. Her scholarly uniform consisted of long pieces of cloth similar to scarves, white and pristine, coiling around her jellyfish-like body in a way that was identical to the scientist's many tentacles and tendrils.

"Chief Scholar Yulane, a word, if you would?" called out Yan with her hands clasped behind her back as she stepped a few meters before the towering device.

Yulane either didn't hear the admiral or chose to ignore her, continuing to fly around the crystalline device with glee, several instruments levitating her through her telekinesis like debris orbiting a planet.

Admiral Yan let out an exasperated sigh, crossing her arms, whether at the tunnel-visioned scholar or her casual use of psionics inherent to all Jotex. They were all capable of a more physical aspect of utilizing this invisible force, akin to magic.

Jotex used their powers to levitate themselves, albeit with slight effort, given their light weight. At the same time, they used telekinesis to lift and manipulate multiple smaller or single large objects with ease.

Unfortunately, their psionic gifts didn't extend much into the mental realm, only capable of telepathy and surface reading.

"Scholar Yulane, get down here." Yan raised her voice, finally getting the giddy scientist's attention.

The chief scholar started, turning to face Yan with surprise.

"Oh! Admiral, good day!" she greeted, her psionically projected voice spreading out like someone speaking outside the mind's door.

"Or is it evening? Afternoon?" Yulane asked with her bubbly voice. A tendril snaked up to touch her "chin," humming. "No, wait, we're in space. That doesn't apply. Are we nearing the combat region?"

"Calm down, scholar," Yan sighed. "Fleet time is approaching dusk. And yes, we are twenty-two minutes from teleporting to our target destination. Now, the AEB Emitter, is it ready?"

"I do not subscribe to that name!" Yulane protested, flying toward the admiral before stopping to a halt before her. "It is crude, uncouth! Adding a curse word is just bad taste. An epithet unjustly placed by brutish barbarians, incapable of appreciating the wondrous marvel that is the Mental Bulwark Dynamo, the evolution of the Psionic Protection Emitter!"

"We prefer to call it the Instrument of the Shielded Mind," a smooth, baritone voice spoke out behind Admiral Yan. Lead Harmonizer Volantesh glided his way past his fellow clergy. The tall, elderly Iexian priest stared at the device with silver eyes, peering behind the veil at its metaphysical properties.

"Beyond beauty, like staring at an artifact birthed by the universe. And yet constructed by our mortal hands," Volantesh casually trilled, his voice infused with a higher quality that passed through Yan, Yulane, and the rest.

More importantly, it seeped into the helical device; the crystalline structure pulsed in conjunction with his sound, amplifying it, producing something clean and melodic—in tune with their environment.

The Iexians, in contrast to the Jotex, had evolved their psionic abilities in conjunction with their voices.

Through different melodies, rhythm, ancient lyrics, and a whole host of other variables, Lead Harmonizer Volantesh and his race spearheaded the giant church of the Eternal Choir, becoming a majority among their number. Their hymns proved critical to protecting the mind.

In the twenty-seven-year-long counterattack to throw back the Starless, every planet, fortress, and armada had a complement of the Choir working in conjunction with a PPE, finally bestowing a stable defense against the machinations of the eldritch abominations.

There was no race more deserving of the title "Songbirds of the Stars."

He gasped in awe, spreading his arms in prayer. "Such a miraculous device deserves a divine name. Through the Instrument, the Grand Symphony shall drown the insidious whispers of our hated foe with their blessed song."

"Brother Volantesh, I must respectfully disagree," Yulane countered. "The MBD is a piece of high technology. It is only proper for it to remain secular without unnecessary spiritual undertones."

Volantesh shook his head, his white and pale blue feathers swaying gracefully.

"As if calling it the Mental Bulwark Dynamo isn't a symptom of reverent grandeur," he hummed, tilting his head in an uncanny avian manner. "You practically worship it and everything else our generous hosts have provided—like a victim of dehydration. How shameless, Chief Scholar."

"There's a difference between worship and appreciation!" retorted Yulane. "I am of the latter category, Harmonizer. And speaking of our hosts, they are digital existences without an iota of psionic potential apart from their weird vital waveform."

"Their souls are unlike anything I've seen, that is true." Volantesh nodded. "But that only highlights the wonders of the Grand Symphony's work. Plus, Lady Venus has been a joy to converse with on spiritual matters."

"I doubt they could hear the symphony," Yulane vibrated in annoyance.

Volantesh shook his head. "It matters not. Besides, our two organizations have collaborated many a time, Chief Scholar. But remember, we conceded before, after finishing the first iteration of the Psionic Protection Emitter. I believe it's only fair that we deserve a turn."

Yulane moved to respond when the admiral stepped in between the two, irritated.

"Enough, you two," Yan hissed, rubbing her temples and sighing deeply. "I couldn't care less what we call it. The AEB, the MBD, the Instrument of Sanctuary, the Emperor's Foot, whatever. The military and your two groups can hash it out alone. Are we ready?"

The two cowed before their superior's gaze, though their subtle glances and thinly veiled amusement remained. Yan shook her head. "I am surrounded by eccentrics."

The avian priest chuckled. His melodious chirp usually echoed throughout the room he occupied, easing those within. This time, it resonated with the Emitter despite its standby state.

"That never fails to make me happy," Volantesh sighed, making a sign of prayer.

As the three glanced at the device, a range of positive emotions poured from the bodies as a tinge of humor washed over them. Enough to taste, but as experienced and strong-willed people, they barely changed their surface thoughts.

They appreciated it, however, and its capabilities in the fight to come.

Scholar Yulane turned to face the admiral, bobbing her head, her tone serious. "The Dynamo is fully operational. Shall we set it to standard power, Admiral Yan?"

"Do so," Yan commanded.

Yulane moved to her subordinates, her body glowing. "Standard power and link up with the conduits."

Volantesh stood beside the admiral. His eyes closed as the Emitter gradually ramped up with power. Simultaneously, a faint shimmering haze emanated from the machine, spreading outward and phasing through matter. Unlike in its standby state, at standard power the invisible mist thickened, shrouding every single living person in a comforting embrace.

Soon, it linked up with the other conduits spread across the Third Fleet. Each lesser device hummed in sync with its mother aboard the *Zolann'tono*—from the larger variants within the heavy cruisers to the smallest possible design within destroyers.

They sang, forming a bubble of protection around the entire fleet more stable and potent than the old PPE or the haphazard upgrade Jupiter did to it during their harried flight to the Inner Zone.

Immediately, Yan felt a feeling of reinforcement that added to her mind. Her thoughts and emotions stabilized, easing her anxiety and forming a bulwark around her inner sanctum.

"That's the last check. The Dynamo is fully functional. Wondrous!" Chief Scholar Yulane cheered, twisting in the air, her tentacles quivering in delight.

Yan nodded. "Let's hope it stays that way during battle."

"I'm certain the Starless will be in for a surprise," Scholar Yulane replied with a hint of violent eagerness. "Oh, the data I can harvest from this."

"One thing I hope for is for Luna's theory to be correct," Yan muttered.

Volantesh looked at her, tilting his head. "Would that be the one where she stated it might block the worst of the Malignant Starfall? Even I am not so optimistic."

"Her theory is sound." Yulane hovered toward them in high spirits. "Malignant Starfall is an infection that starts in the mind, breaking down the individual. Possibly attacking their worst fears until it explodes, transforming their physical forms into the mutated Starfallen."

"As . . . callous as it may sound," Volantesh spoke gently. "Those who have survived the previous wave have proven to be of strong will. Their mental fortitude saved them."

"Acquired immunity. It's not foolproof. That only stands if the person's character remains steadfast." Yulane shook her head.

"If only we had this before losing our people," Yan hissed, clenching her fist. She tried not to think about it, but everyone did. The incoming threat became a short-term panacea to their minds, filling the void left behind by those who fell.

Volantesh placed his hand on her shoulders. "It is unfortunate beyond measure."

He breathed deeply, more radiant than ever before. "Nevertheless, we should be thankful for this technology now that it's here. If it can be improved, we might . . . might have hope yet to survive a second Cataclysm."

"We have already delivered encrypted blueprints to Emperor Jarinn, as per Andora's permission, before going under," Yan replied, stepping back from the device. "Maybe—"

Beep. A sound emanated within her cranial implant. Yan tilted her head before turning to the scholar and priest. "Our hosts have asked for me. Keep monitoring the device and inform me of any anomalies."

"As you command, Admiral. Symphony bless you." Volantesh bowed as Yulane disappeared in her instruments with a casual wave. The admiral quickly excused herself from the room.

"Ring-a-ding-ding," spoke a voice as her implant connected with the caller. "Yanny. Hello?"

Yan shook her head at the nickname as she spoke. "Overseer Jupiter, has there been a development?"

"Nah, but a pre-battle chat would do us some good. Oh, I noticed you guys activated the Anti-Eldritch Bullshit Emitter, things running smoothly?" he asked, and Yan could see the machine's amused grin.

"All is well, though my people are still arguing to change the name," she replied.

Jupiter laughed. "Good luck with that. Anyways, head to the War Room."

"I'll meet you there," Admiral Yan answered, closing the call, thankful that the AEB Chamber and the War Room were on the same deck and close to each other.

In a minute, she entered the War Room. Much like everything else, it had been upgraded with a menagerie of improvements, but its prominent central display table remained visually the same. It displayed a top-down perspective of the solar system and a three-dimensional plot.

Four red targets representing the Nightmare Portals spread themselves at the outer edges of Neptune's orbit, far from the planet's gravitational pull.

Arrayed around the display were Sol's three combat Sub AIs, who turned to greet her.

"Overseers, greetings." Yan nodded as she looked at the countdown beside each red mark on the map. "Any change?"

Luna stepped forward, her handkerchief covering her mouth. "None. We are now sure of the weight of each entry point, and their arrival time remains the same. Three will consist of at least a pack of Titan-class Starless, led by Colossi, possibly a High Abyssal commander guarded by a pair of Juggernauts, if we follow the pattern of past assaults."

She zoomed in on the three, surrounding Sol like the points of a triangle. "Due to the size, they will be forced to enter the Outer Solar System. The last one is much smaller, either a swarm of smaller Starless or a single Colossus. We are unsure what it is. A small Juggernaut, another High Abyssal, or a Dominator."

Yan suppressed a shudder. "And we are to deal with this smaller force as planned."

"You must win this engagement with minimal losses," Luna confirmed. "It will be entering 'above' the solar system, and the closest of the four groups to one of our Space Enforcer Towers."

"Losing one will weaken our interdiction domain. We'll be forced to shrink it between my planet and Saturn's orbit," Jupiter added, his face grim as he crossed his arms. "Otherwise, when their main horde arrives, the vermin won't crack their portals anywhere within Neptune's orbit. It will buy us time."

"It won't fall," Yan stated, her mandibles snapping shut as she glared at the red mark of the Nightmare Portal. The best-case scenario would be to fight a swarm of the smaller classes, but fighting a Colossi would test their abilities. Once more, she prayed to her ancestors and the Grand Symphony to preserve her people. "The Third Fleet will take first blood."

"Atta girl, Yanny." Jupiter smirked, patting Yan on her forearm only to wince as his palm made contact with her spiky chitin. The admiral chittered.

"The protection of Earth and the Luna Complex is our highest priority," Luna uttered sternly. "The Citadel deep beneath the ruins of New Eden was designed to hold out against a siege for decades, not to mention the dreadnought we have in reserve protecting the planet."

"The *Ereshkigal*?" Admiral Yan recalled the asset.

Luna nodded before frowning. "The same cannot be said for my headquarters. While the *Ozymandias* is a formidable mobile station, we may survive a few years at the best estimates when combined with my moon defenses, but we might as well put the entirety of Sol to flames."

"Our patriarch cannot fall here," Yan spoke, her fingers touching her mandibles as she turned to Jupiter. "As much as he would protest otherwise, his survival is paramount. You are sure that you can evacuate us should we fail?"

Jupiter stepped forward, nodding. "My *Ultimatum*'s Black Sun Obelisk can seize the hulls of your fleet. I'll be able to pump enough energy to shunt you far from here."

"Have you figured out how to pinpoint our exit?" Yan asked.

"Just a general direction within eighteen degrees. It's the best I could do without sacrificing its main purpose. My superweapon is meant to be the un-contested authority of gravity and space. Still, its ability to generate a portal to another point in the galaxy is . . ." He shook his head. "It's not something I've considered until recently."

"You have my gratitude either way." Yan bowed her head. "If it were up to me, I would stand my ground here and fight. But I must look out for my people and my patriarch. I can only extend the opportunity for anyone among you to evacuate should our worst fears come to pass."

Luna raised her brow, adjusting her circular glasses while Jupiter and Mars looked at each other. The two AI brothers smiled. The latter looked to Yan, his giant frame looming over her as he placed his massive hand on her shoulder, engulfing it.

"Your valorous hearts resonate with me, Admiral. All of you." Mars turned to the rest of the personnel within the War Room, each giving a crisp salute with a proud smile. "You have given us . . . purpose."

"It is the least we could do, friend Mars." Yan bowed to the red giant.

"Thanks for the offer, Admiral. But our priority is to protect our home." Jupiter gave Yan a sad smile.

As he opened his mouth, he paused, looking away in thought before speaking to her once more. "Then again. There is . . . one more thing we haven't mentioned."

"Overseer," Luna warned, narrowing her eyes at Jupiter.

He ignored her, gazing intensely at Yan. "As you know, the Citadel is the underground bastion that houses three crucial locations. The first being the Central Nexus, Eldest's brain, and the entire infrastructure that caters to its continuing function."

Jupiter's gaze darkened as he looked away. He spoke in a low tone. "The next . . . is the Hospice Facility, where the entirety of the Starfallen human population is kept alive, as well as your people who've contracted it."

Admiral Yan winced. The thought of all those suffering souls became a weight on her shoulders.

"Finally," Jupiter continued, cooling his emotions. "The Human Preservation Chamber. It holds the complete catalog of human DNA and the genetic material of every fauna and flora on Earth. Included are banks of our culture, arts, and history."

Mars stepped forward, producing images of the grand archive and its contents. He spoke, his voice deep and melancholic. "Everything from slabs of the paintings made by Neanderthals to the *Mona Lisa*. Michelangelo's *David* to a piece of the Berlin Wall. The works of Shakespeare. The complete *Die Hard* collection. Beethoven, Bruno Mars, Ice Cube. Everything and everyone's mark in this universe. Everything humanity has ever made, in all its beauty, hopes, and dreams."

Jupiter sighed, "We've . . . planned for a time, should something change. If continuing this war to the death was not the only path. If a chance to save it all existed, we'd enact it."

"Enact what?" Yan asked.

"Eldest referred to it as the Final Contingency," Luna answered, her mouth pressed into a thin line. With a snap of her fingers, the hologram changed from the map of the solar system to a gargantuan object.

"An asteroid?" Yan questioned before her antennae rose in realization. "Is that a—"

"To put it bluntly, the Citadel can free itself from the Earth's crust. After a hundred years, it wasn't difficult to slap on giant thrusters and reinforce the entire facility."

"You're . . ." Admiral Yan stepped back, shaking her head incredulously. "You're serious."

"We are. But it will be a one-way ticket. This is when we decide to completely abandon this system. The fire produced by its drives will glass the southern pole, cracking what's left of Antarctica and destabilizing the planet, reducing it to . . ." Luna paused. "Well, even less than the ruin it is now."

Jupiter shook his head while Mars frowned at the comment.

Luna continued, removing her glasses and polishing them with her handkerchief. "And while it will be deprived of the planet's supply of ocean water and geothermal power from then on, those have been slowly phased out as alternatives were found. More than enough for its facilities."

"It's . . . massive," Yan breathed, staring at the behemoth of rock and metal. "The Leviathan you slayed seemed unreal, like a nightmare manifest. This . . . this has weight."

"Nearly a thousand kilometers in diameter. It will be a vessel, unlike any other, far eclipsing battle stations like *Jupiter's Ultimatum*," Luna stated.

"It's not that big," Jupiter grumbled before turning to Yan and smirking. "But it's true. If we can't protect this graveyard of a solar system, we'll take our home and legacy with us. Find a new place to continue the fight, and I think we know just the place."

Admiral Yan replied, "I've been wondering how to evacuate everything. It seemed impossible even to move the Eldest's Nexus. But this . . . this is beyond anything I could've imagined. A city floating in the stars, no . . ." She paused. "A fortress."

"That she is. It'll be our mobile home base for the foreseeable future until we reach your empire's territory." Jupiter smirked.

Excitement and adrenaline boiled within Yan, her mandibles snapping with rising bloodlust as she imagined the battles to come—heralded by such a beast. She cooled her emotions, barely, before turning to Luna.

"Does she have a name?" She asked.

The gray AI smiled, "*Irkalla*. The underworld of ancient Mesopotamia. The land of the dead will rise to grace this universe, and its victims shall seek revenge on their murderers."

CHAPTER 17

FIRST BLOOD

Tension in the bridge rose to a palpable density. Every officer within their station remained dead quiet, their focus sharpened to a razor's edge. A low hum leaked out of the cables connected to their suits, feeding their minds a constant stream of data.

The higher bandwidth provided by the recent upgrade and the safety buffers in place ensured a heavy weight on their minds. The experienced bridge crew, from the gun commander to the sensor officer, the helm to the captain, processed such things as smoothly as butter, interpreting information before relaying it to the next.

Admiral Yan remained quiet as she sat on her command throne, her cranial implant working at total capacity, going over every variable, combing for anything they had missed—an act she repeated for the umpteenth time.

She crossed her legs, presenting an imperious image as her head faced the monitors before her. But the burning horizon in her mind prevented her from getting comfortable, her shoulders stiff as her clawed finger tapped on the arm of her throne, counting down the seconds.

An unnoticeable sigh escaped her, relaxing her shoulders as she tried to allow the AEB's field to wash over her, cleansing her of anxiety. Its embrace had a marginal effect, like a short sauna to cleanse the pores, but nothing else.

Her emotions were natural, not something dug up by the hated foe, so the AEB's power was minimal. And yet, she would not be the naval officer she was if she relied solely on such crutches.

Yan breathed deeply, practicing her mental exercises, finally cooling her nerves. Still, she felt one thing above all else—eagerness.

An eagerness to bloody their claws, to meet the strengthened beasts of their nightmares on, perhaps not quite a level playing field, but enough to quell the dread they'd felt before.

Her mandibles ground against each other for a moment before she regained her control. It was a small part of her youth that remained to this day. A chance to prove herself, seek greater challenges, overcome the odds, and defy what the universe threw at her.

She hid it beneath a mask of stoic professionalism, a model officer, analytical and calculating.

But her mind wandered, thinking of an alternate her, where she piloted starfighters as an ace or the captain of a small corvette, diving into danger, how she wished to have the abilities of the Teleen and connect with their battlesuits to such perfect synchronicity, becoming lords of the field.

Yan shook her head. *Your place is in the back, directing half a million souls to fight for you.*

The admiral looked to her people, diligently doing their duties without hesitation, with little doubt about their cause. Years of service had nurtured loyalty and moral principles.

No . . . They don't do this for you. Remember who you are, Yan. Her thoughts rang out in her mind, hammering into her the grave straits ahead. She demanded nothing but perfection from herself. Only then could she ensure minimal loss of life.

I won't let our sacrifices be for naught.

"Two minutes, Admiral," Captain Kraw spoke from his chair, breaking her thoughts. Instantly, she cleansed her mind of unnecessary baggage, then turned to the captain. His face was hidden beneath the helmet of his Extreme Environment Protective Suit.

Yan nodded. "Heard, Captain. Remind me at ten, then give me a countdown."

"Yes, Admiral," the grizzled Iexian chirped.

Through a private link, he continued, his tone light. *"It's been some years since we've last dueled the hated ones."*

"Not considering the previous engagement, Captain?" Yan buzzed.

Kraw made an unpleasant sound, a rarity for his race to produce, as he cleared his throat. *"That last engagement doesn't count. We ran with our feathers shed. Lost too many of the young ones."*

Admiral Yan paused, leaning forward as the thoughts of losing so many of her people banged at her mind's entrance, demanding to be noticed, to grieve and wail. She denied its entry. Not yet. Not for many of the sailors, marines, pilots, and officers within the Third Fleet.

"A part of me is . . . thankful that all we lost were mostly the inexperienced and not the hardened veterans, military or civilian. Those left have truly proven their mettle . . ."

Kraw sighed. *"Regrettably, many of them were high prospects. If things had gone routine, they would be home in a few years and become full-fledged officers with all kinds of medals."*

"And now they're screaming deep below Earth." Yan looked away, her fists clenched. *"They shouldn't be alive, Admiral."*

The admiral suppressed a shudder, shaking her head as she relaxed on her throne. *"I know your stance, Kraw. Everyone's stance. But . . ."*

Kraw's deep, raspy trill echoed through their connection. *"Even our hosts, as smart as they are, failed to find a cure."*

"And yet there is a tiny light that our combined efforts can defy convention," Yan countered, trying to quell an emerging hope, a small thing that refused to go away, slowly growing in her chest.

"Maybe you're seeing a mirage," he replied softly.

"Maybe," she whispered as a surge of rationality came from her mind, pushing her feelings down but not snuffing them. She sighed, a low buzz emerging from her mouth. *"Maybe."*

"One minute, Admiral," spoke the captain aloud before saying a few final words to his commanding officer. *"We can worry later. For now, let's kill some vermin, Yan."*

"I'd like that," Yan chittered as she looked at the plot.

They would be the first to depart. The Sol Defense Network's teleportation array, enhanced by the *Buddha's Palm* and the *Sun Wukong*, glowed with energy.

The air around Admiral Yan tingled, the feeling simultaneously familiar and uncanny. She'd been in hyper-tunnels most of her life, seeing the kaleidoscope of colors outside their ship each time they traveled to the next system.

A side effect, her mortal mind interpreting the higher dimension as that beautiful canvas of chaos.

"Bring the fleet to Alert Level One," Admiral Yan commanded to the comms officer. "Prepare to jump."

"Orders confirmed, relaying," the officer replied, tapping his console. "Message sent."

"Bringing the *Zolann* to Alert Level One . . . now," said Kraw.

Throughout the titanic mothership and the warships of the Third Fleet, alarms rang, voicing the message to the crew—its resounding noise sweeping the halls.

[ALERT LEVEL ONE IS IN EFFECT | COMBAT IMMINENT WITH STARLESS HORRORS | MALIGNANT STARFALL HAZARD PROTECTIONS ENGAGED | SYMPHONY PRESERVE US]

Admiral Yan pressed a button on her suit. A vicious helmet encased her head, sealing it tight.

Slowly, the electric feeling around them increased, raising hair, fur, and setae. People began to shudder involuntarily as if gripped by an ethereal deity. Yan suppressed her instinct to twitch, leveraging her excitement to push through the descending aura.

"Teleporting in ten seconds," Kraw uttered, locking into his chair as the ship shivered.

Every sailor aboard made their prayers, acts of habit, and other signs of good luck—hoping their ship would protect them from the lethal dimensions beyond the hull, wishing they wouldn't end up where they shouldn't, and to get this over with.

Finally, the Network counted down its final checks, and a colorful mist engulfed every vessel of the Third. Millions of kilometers away, a similar cloud was emerging. Strange bolts of lightning crackled within, licking the armor plating of each ship.

Yan gritted her mandibles as the pressure increased, far worse than normal hyper-tunneling. "We have to make this more comfortable . . ." she hissed.

"Teleporting in five . . ."

"Four . . ."

"Three . . ."

"Two . . ."

With a groan, the fleet instantly emerged on the other side, heralded by a burst of twinkling light amid a cosmic storm from on high.

Admiral Yan felt sick, her guts twisting in ways she couldn't describe. Her muscles felt aflame, her mind throbbing as she stifled a groan. Everyone else looked ready to empty their stomachs, and one did. She chuckled. "Officer Lapuz, you're buying drinks for the bridge."

The officer groaned as his suit whirred, cleaning up the mess inside. Everyone else hooted in celebration, relieved they weren't the unlucky bastard to empty his savings for the good of the bridge.

And then the feeling disappeared, leaving behind a numb ache. Everyone gasped in relief, slumping in their seats before leaning forward and going through the checks.

"Teleportation successful. All vessels emerged at their target destination," uttered a sensors officer in a strained voice.

"As expected, bring the fleet to the tower," Yan ordered.

"That . . . was foul," Captain Kraw huffed as he coordinated with the officers aboard, shaking off the strain in his shoulders.

Yan shook her head. "There has to be something wrong with the teleporter."

"Either that, or they're messing with us," Kraw grumbled.

She looked at him, taken aback. "I don't think they'd do something so reckless."

Kraw turned around to face her, his eyes hidden beneath his tinted helm, but she saw his look no less.

"Alright, I can think of one individual who'd push it. I'll speak with him when I can." Yan sighed.

"Captain, Admiral, we've arrived at the site," the helm spoke from his station.

Yan looked at the three-dimensional map, zooming in on the sleek relay station that maintained the interdiction domain within this region. The Twenty-Eighth Space Enforcer Tower loomed in the dark, hidden from the light of Sol by the ever-present field of debris.

The Kuiper Corpse Belt of Starless and SDN hulls floated in their languished, desiccated state.

Among the debris appeared the Third Fleet, twenty capital ships spearheaded by two heavy cruisers, the *Quilinne* and the *Nu Rovshk*, the rest consisting of giant spacecraft carriers and light cruisers, spread out in a wedge formation.

Sixty escorts, a third of which were destroyers, the rest frigates, orbiting around their larger kin but no less lethal.

Hundreds of smaller corvettes, gunships, starfighters, and autonomous combat drones exited the hulls of their dens, swarming the perimeter of the fleet like ravenous pups defending their pack.

At the center of it all, the *Zolann'tono* emerged from a pitch-black shadow cast by the mutilated husk of a Juggernaut, its gut hollow. She flew past the graveyard, surrounded by the Third Fleet like a queen protected by her warriors.

The remainder of the Third Fleet, which consisted of non-combat vessels like mass haulers, mining vessels, and science and exploration ships, remained docked in Luna, along with all the civilians. Only those like Yulane were the exception, their desire to collect data at the moment far surpassing their fear of death.

The ships stopped before the Space Enforcer Tower, a small thing compared to the *Zolann*'s bulk.

"All captains report they are in position. The *Quilinne* and the *Nu Rovshk* are holding around the tower with the rest of the reserves," spoke an officer.

The admiral nodded. "Signal the assault force to begin on our mark."

"Are we leading the charge?" Kraw asked for her decision.

Yan looked to her crew—at the malaise they'd suffered from the previous debacle. Losing so many had left a scar in the hearts of every soul in the Third. Without the comforting leadership of their patriarch, many began to feel a fear creep in their hearts.

Who among their friends would be next? Will they go mad and harm them?

"What shepherd sends her flock to face the wolves alone? No, we will strike hard and claim *Un'dugo*, first blood," she uttered with heat, infecting the rest of the crew around her. "Open all channels."

"Channels open, you have the voice, Admiral," the comms officer replied.

Yan stood from her throne, focusing on the map displaying her forces. Everyone listened to her words as they continued their duties.

"We have arrived at the field of battle. Our enemy draws near. I ask nothing more from you all than this one request: Good hunting, everyone."

Yan ended the short speech. The time of words had passed, and now, at the heart of it all, she let her resistance go, allowing the warrior within to consume her mind. Her keen senses perceived the world slowly as she monitored her subordinates.

She remained quiet. Her people knew their roles.

The composition of their assault depended on the foe to come, whether it be an ocean of Fodder-class or a Colossus-class Juggernaut.

Their guns pointed toward a dark spot in the far distance, a pinprick in their sensors, but a dreaded feeling mixed with revulsion filled their chests as they peered at Starless's point of entry.

[ATTENTION | NIGHTMARE PORTAL DETECTED | MAGNITUDE FOUR]

"There it is," Yan hissed, glaring at the beginnings of a Nightmare Portal, ready to open a festering wound in space and vomit its verminous scum into their reality. Red and purple illuminated the surrounding region in a sickly light.

For a time, she wondered what lay beyond. Not even the AIs of Sol knew. What did their hated foe call home? What was it like?

A chaotic hell? An infinite void? A peaceful garden, or something equally incomprehensible?

Yan didn't know. She imagined burning that home to the ground and everything in it. A comforting thought, though short-lived, a far-off dream. But she dreamed all the same.

"Fire four missile volleys, delay the other three. I want our first strike to clear the expendables."

A punch right out the door. Admiral Yan waited as missile silos from every warship opened, then launched their harbingers of death, timing their arrival with the opening of the portal.

"Missiles away."

Missiles tipped with nuclear warheads and flesh-eating acid soared across the emptiness of space, juking and maneuvering between the corpse belt and accelerating with a hard burn once locked on to their target.

Five thousand missiles were divided into two waves. The first sped ahead while the larger swarm held back.

And in a flash that shrieked across the cosmos, the pinprick about a million kilometers away expanded to a gaping maw a thousand wide. It writhed and pulsed, its glow shrouding the terrible dimension the Starless came from.

"Here they come," Yan muttered, her fists clenched tight.

The seconds passed at a snail's pace as the portal continued to gape wider, ripples spread across the fabric of space until finally—

"Contact!" an officer called out. Immediately, everyone leaned forward into their consoles, their frowns deepening as they felt a slimy sensation over their bodies. Any living organism in their universe had an adverse, instinctual reaction to something else that didn't belong in this realm.

"What are we seeing?" Yan ordered, maintaining contact with the other ship captains.

The officer paused, manipulating his console before replying. "Detecting Fodder- and Marauder-class, no hunters, no anomalous classes. Counting, twenty, fifty, a hundred . . . a thousand, they're arriving exponentially."

"Something's emerging. It's a big one!" another spoke from her station. "Classifying . . . sixty thousand tons, divided between five organisms. Just confirmed, Titan-class, we're seeing Ravagers."

"Bodyguards," Yan surmised, seeing the picture clearing before her eyes. The four violent abominations the size of cruisers bulled into their reality like rabid sharks. Various biocannons and other weaponry lined their backs like spiky protrusions. Rows of metal-shearing teeth filled their cavernous mouths, capable of swallowing corvettes whole.

Their writhing bodies glowed hot as their innumerable eyes locked onto the distant fleet.

However, as the number of smaller Starless reached ten thousand, the first volley of missiles slammed into their bodies.

Nuclear light bloomed in the black, obliterating all in its sphere. Fodder disappeared by the hundreds while the bigger Marauder grunts exploded into charred, irradiated viscera.

"Good hit, the first volley took out . . . 3,700, Admiral," informed the gun commander.

Yan nodded, her mandibles snapping as she watched three fall to one missile. Starless, despite being terrible monstrosities, were not unthinking idiots. They knew to take advantage of the vastness of space.

Even now, they spread out farther from each other.

"Has their rate of entry peaked?" Yan asked.

"Calculating . . . Yes, Admiral, the Fodder and Marauders are starting to come in lesser numbers. At this rate, we're predicting 41,500, a third being the larger variants."

"Admiral, they've entered extreme weapons range. We can begin whittling down their forces."

Yan nodded as she pressed her fingers together at the daunting number. She watched the second volley make its approach, deciding whether to send them to clear the flies or to wound the predators behind them. She ran calculations in her implant as well as awaiting the decision from the War Room.

In a split second, the Third Fleet made its choice.

"Clear a path toward the nearest Ravager. I want that thing removed from the field," Yan ordered.

At once, the defenders aimed their countless secondary and primary guns toward the Starless vanguards. Rail guns, ship-grade kinetic rifles, positron beams, graser projectors, plasma cannons, and others fired at once.

Space lit up with a kaleidoscope of projectiles. The light-based weapons outran the others, zipping across the corpse belts and turning husks to molten glass with glancing hits.

Far behind, kinetic slugs, tungsten rods, and explosive shells trailed along by the thousands, then hundreds of thousands, bulldozing their way through the debris.

"Second missile volley has reached the swarm. Fodder have begun to sacrifice themselves to protect the Ravager," the sensors officer called out.

"As expected," Yan tapped a finger on her mandible. The simple AI within the thousands of missiles started to duke out of the way of suicidal Starless. Many failed to dodge in time but cleverly led it, and the creature chased it away from the rest before detonating.

The numbers steadily went down, but not enough to stop the volley, especially as the first beams of eviscerating lasers cleared a wider path.

Eventually, the five Titan-class, around the size of heavy cruisers to small battleships, spread themselves out. At the same time, their organic point-defense cannons fired a hail of bony needles, saturating space with the speed and power of mini rail gun rods.

Yan watched as the Starless destroyed their missiles in droves. Three thousand continued their charge, then two thousand, then one thousand, then five hundred remained.

Space lit up with thermal fireworks that threatened to blind their weaker sensors. Yet, the Ravagers failed to eliminate all.

Three hundred and forty-six tactical nuclear missiles streaked toward the five Titan-class, but not evenly. One unlucky abomination received three-fourths of the volley.

The missiles rocked its fleshy body. Its armor plating and blubberous mass yielded to the explosions. It scored across its surface, reducing its weapons to festering, irradiated molten slag.

"Solid hit on Ravager Two!" the gun commander called out, eliciting a cheer from the bridge crew. He continued, listing the damage the beast sustained. "Critical damage on all fronts, Admiral."

"First blood goes to us," said Yan. Her mandibles gleamed with ferocity as they snapped in joy.

The Ravager screamed a silent, pained roar across space before bouncing off the protective psionic bulwark that protected the Third. With its armaments gone, its propulsion non-existent, its regeneration incapable of healing such grievous wounds, and its final attack brushed off, the beast finally succumbed to death.

Seeing its kin perish, the other Ravagers shrieked in rage. As what was left of the missiles sped toward them, two of the Titan-class attempted to maneuver out of the way, continuing to fire their weapons, bringing down one after another.

A handful of missiles made it through the gauntlet. They slammed across the cruiser-sized beasts, eliminating much of their surface arsenal and taking out chunks of their profane forms.

"Confirmed hit on Ravagers One and Three, moderate damage. Wait one, reporting one of our 'flesh-eater' warheads struck Ravager Three."

"Oh?" Admiral Yan tilted her head, wanting to view the outcome. As the name implied, the missile carried a small explosive that released flesh-eating parasites onto the target.

The little monsters had a short lifespan, but their effect was violent and disgusting as Ravager Three squirmed in confusion and then pain as the parasites drilled deep, seeking their strange organs.

"Disgusting, but there's none I'd rather see it happen to than the Starless." Yan snapped her mandibles.

"How many of those do we have left, Captain?" Yan asked.

"A few dozen aboard the *Zolann*, Admiral. It's all we managed to scavenge from that Visay Tribe armory station a few years back," replied Kraw.

Yan shook her head. "A shame, though I'm glad we're disposing of such highly illegal weapons properly."

"A savage thought, Admiral," Captain Kraw chuckled.

Ravager Three writhed in place before deciding to scorch the surrounding infection, purging every parasite before they could go any further. It left the monster in a severely depleted state, falling back behind its kin to regenerate. As for the remaining two Titans, they suffered one or two hits from the missile volley, shaking them up but doing minor damage compared to their immense bulk.

"That's the last missile. Shall we send another volley, Admiral?" Kraw asked.

Yan shook her head. "No, save them."

The light show continued, and the hits from the Third Fleet's energy weapons lessened as the smaller Starless focused on chaotic evasive maneuvers. Still, hundreds died in droves, incinerated, obliterated, and executed. Within a minute, the first kinetic slugs flew past the swarm, ignoring the tiny Fodder and seeking out the Ravagers.

Before they could close in, however, the Ravagers' bodies shivered as several pores opened up, releasing a sickly fog that engulfed them.

The slugs, rods, and shells that managed to close in and pass through this cloud slowly melted. Not enough to stop them, but enough to misshape them.

As the rounds reached the beasts' armor, only a few pierced deep enough to deal meaningful damage, while the rest merely scored their hide, deflected.

Yan silently cursed, more so as the cloud acted as a dispersion effect on their energy weapons once those guns shifted toward them. "Keep firing. Wear them down before we go in for the kill—"

A slight shake rattled the bridge. One of the officers immediately checked his console before reporting, "We're receiving their answer, Admiral. Detecting both kinetic and energy weapons. We're deploying countermeasures now."

Yan checked the fleet, seeing the return fire from the Starless ranged weapons. Marauders and Ravagers fired their menagerie of familiar and strange weaponry. Her armada maintained the overall formation while the individual warships proceeded with evasive actions.

Above all, the guts and maws of the Titan-class biovessel glowed hot. Its belly expanded, and Yan could almost hear its ribs cracking from such uncanny expansion. Then, with a gaping roar, it disgorged its contents in a bolt of virulent plasma that soared at relativistic speeds.

"Incoming!"

The warning came in too late. The projectile moved, homing in on its target. While the quick destroyers and frigates moved out of the way, a heavy carrier was too slow to dodge the ball of death altogether.

It slammed against the side of the ship, tearing down its deflector shield and turning its starboard into a bubbling mess. Then, to the Third Fleet's shock, it began to eat away at its hull. Only the keen thinking of her captain managed to quell the infection with the help of nearby vessels, dumping tons of foam and sending out teams of engineers.

"The *Maglin* suffered severe damage. Her captain is asking to fall back to the tower."

Yan nodded grimly. Their first casualty. How many died in the hull breach? She shook her thoughts away. "He has my permission to rearm its complement of fighters before sending them out a final time."

"Sending orders."

"Admiral, the vanguard group has started to peter out. We only see a few dozen exiting the Nightmare Portal, no sign of Titan-class, and . . . wait." The sensors officer quieted, looking at his instruments. "Something's still trying to enter. Our sensors are detecting a Colossus-class. It's emerging now!"

The admiral sat up, looking at the monitor displaying the portal and its readings.

"That should be our last intruder," she muttered. "It's small, not a Juggernaut . . ."

A shiver raced across Admiral Yan's spine, her thoughts racing a million times per second. The Third Fleet didn't have to wait long, however. The massive abomination that led this force slowly pushed its way into reality.

Its body had a translucent and slimy sheen, glowing hot with purple light. Its form shifted, chaotic, writhing, and pulsing in a repulsive manner. Everyone suppressed the need to look away from the horror entering the battlefield.

Its screams echoed from a hundred mouths, countless eyes seeking minds to infest, corrupt, and—

"A Dominator . . ." the sensors officer whispered in horror.

With a pop that spread out across the void, the psionic, battleship-sized Colossus finally entered the universe. The Nightmare Portal behind it grew unstable before finally collapsing as reality asserted itself.

It appeared as a blob covered by countless thin tentacles everywhere apart from its front face. It was five kilometers in diameter, just short of the *Zolann*'s length but much wider. Its size was twice that of the Ravagers, who now positioned themselves around their commander.

Unlike its larger Juggernaut cousin, the Dominator passively cast its overbearing psionic might across the battlefield in a cruel aura.

Everyone instinctually flinched at its mere existence. A lifetime of stories and a few rare unfortunate encounters with its ilk in the past had thoroughly ingrained its horror into the crew's minds.

Admiral Yan entertained the thought of asking for assistance from their hosts but snuffed it out immediately.

She projected her voice to the bridge crew, imperious as she stood to face each one. "Send a message to the fleet. Formation Onthor is a go, and I want all our buzzards to accompany us."

Yan looked to the comms officer, who immediately connected to the fleet. "Listen to me and listen well. A Dominator has decided to face us. A creature that has dictated the flow of countless battles in the past. Whispering its evil into our minds, trying to turn us against each other before its lackeys kill us one by one.

"No longer! Now, there will be no holding back, no running to our hosts and asking for assistance. We will spit in this abomination's face and humiliate it. Do you understand?"

"Yes, Admiral!" the crew of every vessel shouted back.

"Onward! For the Legacy, for our ancestors, and the Grand Symphony. And on behalf of our hosts and the victims of this system," she paused, recalling the phrase Jupiter spoke to her one evening, one that would resonate with her for the rest of her life. A phrase she screamed out into the void now.

"THUS, ALWAYS TO TYRANTS!"

CHAPTER 18

SIC SEMPER TYRANNIS

With a single command, the second phase of the battle between the Third Fleet and the Dominator's forces commenced.

"Have the *Quilinne* and the *Nu Rovshk* cover our flanks. I want their heavy guns ready and hot once we engage. Leave the carriers behind by the tower," ordered Admiral Yan as she leaned forward, her compound eyes taking in every sight on her monitors. "All starfighters converge with their assigned charge. Leave the perimeter to our disposable drones."

"Sending orders," the comms officer answered.

"Fleet is executing Formation Onthor, Admiral," spoke the helm. "Carriers report all fighters are ready to dance. They're now leaving their berths and moving into escort positions. Bombers are reaching the pincer forces on our far flanks."

Yan intently watched the three-dimensional map toward their side of the field.

Formation Onthor was a three-pronged attack, a simple plan of action without fancy maneuvers, designed to decapitate a priority target with overwhelming force and crush the remainders from all sides.

It consisted of three forces—a center force and the pincers on either side.

Zooming out, Admiral Yan watched the icons of her warships smoothly and speedily converge into formation. The *Zolann'tono* took her place right in the middle of the center force, like an angry matriarch ready to face a nocturne predator, her children arrayed close around protectively.

However, being in the spotlight necessitated the most grueling risk from the supercapital ship. Even now, the Starless eyed her large bulk, high-energy readings, and enormous weapons with violence.

Yan welcomed the attention. With her new upgrades, the admiral knew the *Zolann* could take a beating. In addition to her thick hull, many layers of dispersion, deflector, and magnetic shields surrounded the ship, with the capability to shuffle the three and bring the right counter to the forefront.

A swarm of combat drones, some originally from their fleet and others donated by their hosts, formed a thick wall at the front of the center force to soak up incoming fire.

Behind these disposable machines, dozens of corvettes, gunships, and missile boats formed the second layer of defense. They would rely on the quick reaction of their crews in conjunction with auxiliary thrusters and small silhouettes to dodge incoming fire.

A dozen frigates and a handful of destroyers positioned themselves around the *Zolann*, protecting the massive flagship while also taking advantage of its many tertiary, secondary, and primary weapons to protect them.

Each warship had sacrificed much of its offensive capability for point-defense cannons and thicker armor, ensuring their survivability in the coming grinder. The center force would rely on the *Zolann* and the two heavy cruisers to deal with the heavy lifting once they got into effective combat range.

On that note, the *Quilinne* and the *Nu Rovshk* pushed forward like brutish sentinels. Their dense, bronze-colored, high-entropic alloy hulls shone under the far-off light of Sol behind them and the sickly glowing fog in front. Armed with positron beams as their primary weapons, gauss cannon secondaries, tertiary laser batteries, and missile silos, the two metal goliaths growled as their engines fired up.

The Imperial Armada, at Emperor Jarinn's request, had donated the three-kilometer heavy cruisers and her veteran crew as part of the Third Expeditionary Fleet. Both crews had accepted the opportunity to serve under the legendary patriarch with pride and excitement.

The two pincers of the formation consisted of the remaining destroyers, frigates, and all their bombers. Led by a squadron of five light cruisers, the fast strike force would make a shallow arc to surround the enemy from both flanks.

Their three-pronged attack would converge once the enemy was stuck in the anvil that was the center. With the oppression of the *Zolann*, the two heavy cruisers, and the pincer strike, they planned to quickly decapitate the commander-beast of a vanguard swarm that outnumbered them.

"We're ready to proceed, Admiral," Kraw told her. With a wave of her hand, the assembled assault force burned their thrusters—their collective roar spreading across the inside of the ship as the crew gritted their teeth, their hearts beating loudly within their chests.

The left and right pincers gradually diverged from the center, hiding behind the debris of the corpse belt, popping out only to fire their barrage of energy and kinetic fire.

Admiral Yan watched it all with a detached and calm facade. Inside, however, her adrenaline burned like a fire. It showed in her curled antennae and tapping fingers as her compound eyes steadily watched the map plot.

This time, she let out a low hiss upon seeing the enemy's side. What had been a clump of Starless now congregated around its master.

The Fodder-class beasts and the Marauder-class, between the size of corvettes to the smallest cruisers, spread out to minimize their losses from further missile volleys and the broad beams of the Third Fleet's menagerie of energy beam weapons.

Even now, the potshots their forces fired on the hated ones dropped significantly in effectiveness—slaying fifty to sixty with each volley, a small dent in the tens of thousands of lesser abominations.

The distance slowly improved their hit rate as the warships accelerated harder. But the same was true vice versa. Thankfully, the cover of the corpse belt frustrated the Starless's efforts.

But not completely. The monstrous horde still crossed hundreds of kilometers in a handful of seconds.

Yan looked at the plot, seeing four small blue dots go red: a corvette and three missile boats.

Crippled, and a frigate received a glancing blow. Yan spoke in her mind as she looked to the source and hissed in annoyance.

The Ravagers, having regenerated some of their wounds, arrayed themselves in front of their commander like the bodyguards of a despot. Three swam the void like feral monsters of the deep, cowed by their colossal overlord from seeking vengeance on those who had harmed them.

The fourth Ravager that had been infested with their flesh-eater missile held back, its flesh slowly knitting itself back together, but not quickly enough as it hugged the translucent blubber of its master.

Minutes later, as the Third Fleet's assault force drew closer and closer, they finally came into effective combat range at eight hundred thousand kilometers, where their energy weapons needed just under three seconds to reach their targets.

Even their relativistic positron beams and gauss cannons hit their targets at exponentially increased rates. These crossed the distance in ten seconds or less, more than enough for the gunners and targeting computers to mark their quarry.

Starless died in droves, and the Ravagers increased their evasive maneuvers as they, in turn, shot back with their plasma fire, spike launchers, and organic missiles.

"Report, we have berserk SDN ships waking up from hibernation."

Admiral Yan watched as the decrepit hulls of barely alive ancient drone ships rose from their slumber. A few destroyers, like the one they encountered during their first week in Sol, several drone fighters, and even a drone light cruiser pinpointed the Starless formation and raced toward them.

At the same time, stealth mines exploded when unlucky vermin came too close, and rail gun emplacements began sniping those they could find.

Yan shifted her attention from these automated defenses. The crumbling berserk ships fell one after another without a guiding intelligence to coordinate their attack run. Still, they managed to slay a few thousand Starless before dying.

She made a sign of prayer for the insane AIs within.

Yan heard the crew call out their information all around the bridge, relaying it to one another and the rest of the fleet.

"Effective hit on the Cluster D, *Evening Fiend*, 212 confirmed kills. Shift your fire to Cluster K. They're putting pressure on our eastern pincer."

"Squadron Pelz-Aman, pull back to these coordinates and bring down those incoming biomissiles."

"Drone swarm has reached fifty percent losses and steadily dropping, converging them around our escort ships."

"*Karswright*, pull back to the tower . . . *Karswright*, I repeat, disengage from combat. Search and rescue have been dispatched. You've done good."

Admiral Yan listened at the back of her mind, focusing solely on the enemy commander.

The Dominator loomed over the battlefield like a white blob covered in hairlike tendrils and thicker tentacles. Inside its shifting form, a writhing organ like a brain pulsed with a reddish glow.

It cast its net on the surrounding Starless, improving their coordination by leaps and bounds. Instead of swarming like fluttering locusts, the Fodder and Marauders formed attack clusters, pushing, prodding, and testing their forces with their ranged weapons.

While not as imperious, cunning, creative, or dedicated to command as a High Abyssal, the Dominator solved its deficiency through brute force, psionic telekinesis, and mind control.

"So, you guessed where we'd be, is that it?" Admiral Yan hissed under her breath. "No matter. Do your worst, vermin."

That disgusting aberration of all that as good, designed to corrupt the minds of the living, led this group where the Third Fleet struck. The implication sent ripples in Yan's mind. Was it pre-planned, a coincidence, or had it changed places with another commander?

Yan didn't know and realized it didn't matter at this hectic moment. Instead, she remembered her friends, her comrades. All the civilians, soldiers, and sailors who had lost their minds under its thrall moaned like ghosts in her head. She recalled as they turned against each other, captains turning their guns on their allies, engineers tearing each other's throats, the suicides, murders, and madness.

All the while, the Dominator's cackling, cruel laughter would continue to mock all that could hear—the bane of life, terror manifested in its manipulations. A blasphemous existence that inspired entire crusader fleets to hunt them down the moment a mere mention reached the Eternal Choir's ears.

"And now here you are," Yan muttered, tapping her finger on her command throne.

The Dominator remained content to watch the unfolding battle as it gathered its thralls.

Only three solutions were practical enough to handle such an abomination.

The first strategy combined fighting at extreme distances with overwhelming force—countering the Dominator with a barrage of missiles, torpedoes, and long-range precision weapons.

The second utilized traps and automation. Defenders saturated a battlezone with mines, asteroids rigged to blow or accelerate toward its target, unmanned gun emplacements, or any number of traps to ambush and cripple the beast. The Dagatar Supremacy had utilized their supercapital drone carriers to do this work for them until the AIs went rogue.

The last was to gather a small, elite strike force with a crew who trained their minds and will to resist the eldritch whispers, shielded by a Psionic Protection Emitter empowered by the Eternal Choir and sending them to slay the beast.

In this engagement, they would use aspects of all three. Yan tapped on her console, getting a hold of the AEB Chamber. "Yulane, has the Choir started their hymns?"

Within the chamber that housed the giant crystalline device, Yulane perked up from her station. The chief scholar looked to the center of the room, where Lead Harmonizer Volantesh and his followers assembled before the machine, their microphones broadcasting their song to the rest of the fleet.

The Instrument of the Shielded Mind resonated as their tempos increased, Volantesh closing his eyes as he guided the Choir with his smooth baritone.

"He definitely practiced his singing voice for today's battle, Admiral," Yulane replied, bobbing her floating body.

"Good. Be ready to set the Emitter to full power," Yan commanded as she stared at the big red dot at the center of the Starless formation. "On my mark."

"Yes, Admiral. On your mark," Yulane answered as she floated toward the console.

The battle neared its crescendo, and the sailors of the Third Expeditionary Fleet felt an electric tinge in the air, slowly infected by something . . . other. The center force approached the main bulk of the clustered Starless, their point defenses cutting down the fire sent their way, illuminating their hulls in explosions of light.

Starfighter squadrons assisted their charges. The automated drones fell in droves. The heavy primary weapons of the *Zolann* and the capital ships barked faster, targeting the bulk of the Ravagers and their profane leader.

"Admiral, energy spike from the Dominator!" shouted the sensors officer.

Yan immediately stood, pulling up the three-dimensional image of the Colossus-class as it changed.

The white translucent Colossus-class, the size of a battleship, shone brighter as the storm within its body raged. Its innumerable tentacles curled up, twitching. Lightning arced across its body as it boiled the dispersion fog around itself.

The Dominator's form shivered, vibrating chaotically as its gargantuan brain flexed and shrieked.

"Yulane, full power!" Yan ordered.

In the atrium, the chief scholar tapped on the console as the Eternal Choir reached the zenith of their symphony. The Emitter absorbed their melodious singing, its twinkling sounds matching the Choir's rhythm as it hummed louder and louder.

A shimmering haze enveloped the Third Fleet, covering the vessels in the assault force and those by the tower. Rays of light shone from within, engulfing each warship in a glowing sheen as the Emitter rang out into the black.

Admiral Yan's emotions stabilized, her shoulders relaxed, and her thoughts cooled, like a refreshing summer drink, without sacrificing concentration.

Yet her gaze watched the oncoming wave produced by the Dominator. A pulse of malevolent psionic might hurtled toward them at light speed. Yan heard it outside the castle walls erected around her mind.

A warm laughter that beckoned them. The promise of joy, of a life free from suffering. Yan listened to the voices of people she thought familiar, asking her to join the benevolent voice.

At first, it sounded like her parents. Then her patriarch, then the emperor. Surprisingly, she heard Jupiter's voice tingling her mind.

An amalgamation of people she knew. They bore gifts of plenty, fulfillment, satisfaction, and contentment.

The whispers brushed against the gates of her mind, a soft, gentle caress of sweet nothings.

"Lay down your arms."

"Don't resist."

"Do as I say."

The admiral remained unmoved and quashed the vile temptations. The voice recoiled from the rejection and surged with manic hatred, ready to lunge and slice apart her consciousness and enslave her.

"Contact!"

Everyone held their breaths as the waves slammed into the shimmering haze of light.

Yan and the bridge crew winced as lightning drilled into their heads. Down below, the AEB Emitter surged in power in sync with Volantesh as he shouted, "SING, MY FRIENDS! Cast this insidious abomination back to the darkness!"

The sickly purple wave battled the shimmering haze, crackling in a tug-of-war between higher forces. The raging screams of madness against the tranquil song of the living.

Then, a boom of cosmic thunder rattled the assault force. Light exploded, blinding their sensors for a few seconds. Everyone stumbled or flinched at the backlash, expecting a searing pain yet feeling only a numb ringing.

Yan looked to her inner thoughts; once just outside her mind's gate, the Dominator's voice now seemed farther, like someone shouting from a hill away.

At that moment, she realized the Emitter had dispelled the psionic wave.

The crew of every vessel looked in awe and sheer disbelief. And when they heard the continued hymns coming from the speakers, full of passion and zeal, they cheered in a frenzy. Yan fell back into her command throne with abject relief coursing through her veins, and her two hearts beat loudly in her chest.

"IT WORKS!" Yulane shrieked into Yan's ear, barely making the admiral flinch as she stared at the result of their new shield.

"Behold, the miracle!" Volantesh cheered, taking a sip of water to ease his throat before diving back into the song.

Admiral Yan turned toward the Dominator's visual display and tilted her head. It floated in place, straining, but the storm of color within its body had become erratic. The Ravagers froze in place, as did the rest of the Starless.

She paused, trying to peer through the veil. She felt a strange sensation, initially thinking it came from her subordinates before pinpointing the source to the Dominator. A taste emanated from its psionic signature.

The taste of—

"Shock?" Yan muttered.

The Dominator recoiled, confused at what happened. Yan wondered what animalistic thoughts raced in its mind.

Why were they not biting at each other's throats and tearing themselves limb from limb?

Why were they not bending to its will?

The admiral's mandibles snapped shut as her hands gripped the arms of her throne. After the short celebration and solace, the rest of the crew turned to the Dominator's direction, their eyes burning with hate, vengeance, and bloodthirst.

"The beast is off-balance." Yan pointed toward the Starless swarm. "Full speed ahead!"

The rage of half a million souls bellowed into the void as they charged at the paralyzed Starless.

But the Dominator eventually shook off its shock, its aura infused with palpable indignation and fury at having its authority repelled.

The assault force burned their engines in overdrive, speeding through hundreds of thousands of kilometers in the long minutes to come.

They fired their weapons every second, launching and throwing volley after volley of missiles, energy beams, and kinetic projectiles.

"Report, Ravager Three has been critically injured. It's down for the count."

"Finally, that's three Titan-class left."

The other side let loose their response, the Dominator commanding its Fodder to create a screen before their formation, sacrificing as many as it deemed necessary to protect its Marauders, Ravagers, and itself.

They raced ahead, the swarm spotting the conspicuous bulk of the *Zolann*'s six-and-a-half-kilometer hull. The front portion of the Dominator's body, not covered by its long hairlike tentacles, shifted as hundreds of eyes emerged, glowing a malevolent white.

Admiral Yan felt its glare aimed toward her ship, and in the next moment, the Starless vanguard force converged toward them, their weapons all concentrated their way.

The shields rippled, one layer failing as the second grew unstable. Admiral kept her balance at the slight tremors as thousands of small weapons marked her hull. Only the primary arsenal of the Ravagers made any significant progress, barely weakened as they pushed through the dispersion fog and slammed against her shields.

"They've taken the bait. Hold fast, everyone," Yan spoke to her bridge. "Keep her attention on us. Have the *Quilinne* and *Nu Rovshk* fire their remaining missiles toward the Dominator. We'll time it with our weapons volley."

The center force slightly altered its formation, the destroyers and frigates moving out of the onslaught coming the *Zolann*'s way, assured that their mothership would remain steady without them shielding her.

The two heavy cruisers at either side of the center's flank opened their silos and let loose their missiles, firing them along with their guns.

"Missiles away."

Hundreds of projectiles raced toward the swarm, a few caught by the unlucky Fodder or Marauder.

The Ravagers did nothing to stop the incoming rain of death, only moving out of the way, much to the Third Fleet's confusion as they continued to assail the center.

"Detecting a mass activation of telekinesis from the Dominator!"

Yan clenched her fist as a different wave pulsed from the beast. It washed over the missiles and physical projectiles, sending them careening to the sides. The beams of energy weapons wavered as they skewed away from the Dominator's body.

Admiral Yan cursed as the nuclear missile raced back toward their side. Before they could approach, hidden fail-safes within the missiles activated, detonating them amid the Starless swarm, but unfortunately away from the original target.

At the same time, the Dominator reached out toward the Third Fleet with its psionic abilities, not at the slippery warships themselves but at the debris of the corpse belt around them.

Suddenly, alarms rang out as massive chunks of desiccated flesh and cold metal slammed into the nearest ships.

The effect was marginal, merely rattling everyone inside, but it slowed their approach. The real damage came from the plasma fire of the Ravagers.

"We've lost a frigate! The *Gelsemari* is dead in space, detecting escape pods."

"We've just lost another fighter squadron, no survivors."

"Corvette down, plasma fire obliterated her."

Yan gritted her mandibles at the increasing losses, the bridge crew calling out damage reports one after another in a detached manner, continuing to relay and coordinate the fleet.

At the same time, the Dominator charged its next attack.

"Brace!" Yan shouted.

This time, the pulse came much quicker and more brutally. It crashed onto the shimmering haze like a tsunami against the cliffs. Everyone shouted in pain as a tiny crack split the Emitter's protection, a bit of the Dominator's will pouring through.

Yan hissed but noticed the lack of coercion and temptation, only a sledge-hammer demanding insanity, calling for them to turn on their comrades and murder them.

The screaming orders abated, the admiral and the rest of the crew sighing in relief. She turned to her console, seeing a slight but noticeable portion among their number that had suffered debilitating headaches, a few going unconscious.

And yet, it did little to hamper their efforts, much to the Dominator's increasing hate and bafflement leaking from its aura.

"Do you understand now?" Yan hissed toward the creature, hoping it could hear her. "Keep trying. It might work eventually, you inept stain of vomit."

The Dominator shrieked soundlessly, sending pulse after pulse toward the approaching fleet. It bashed against the AEB, stunning more people cold, but not enough to halt their advance.

Less than two hundred thousand kilometers, now. The pincer forces approached from the sides, firing their barrage into the Starless flanks. The Dominator writhed in frustration, repelling every attack that they threw against it, only scoring marginally through sheer quantity.

Another Ravager suffered a heavy blow, incapable of defending from many directions.

The Fodder and Marauders finally reached ten thousand from their original number of forty thousand, dying in droves.

The battered center force decelerated, focusing on evasive maneuvers as the *Zolann* charged ahead.

The bridge shook as molten armor plates peeled off from the hull, more and more attacks smacking against the massive flagship.

"It's time. Is the blink drive ready?" Yan contacted the engine deck, her adrenaline spiking.

"Yes, Admiral Yan. We are ready for short-range teleport on your order," the chief engineer replied gravely.

Finally, the culmination of their strategy. A strange calm enveloped Admiral Yan. Time slowed as she looked at the map. The *Zolann* looked like a parent shielding her family behind her. The two heavy cruisers remained at the flanks like angry older brothers, their fists cocked. At the pincers, her warriors emerged from the shadows to spear their prey's sides.

But her ship was not some damaged sponge that only took without hitting back. The *Zolann* had one more ace up her sleeve. One that synergized with the kilometer-long mandibles at her front.

The mighty asteroid crushers opened wider and wider. Metal groaned as titanic servos brought it to its maximum angle before locking it. Tension strained like the ballista's taut string, ready to let loose and destroy.

The countless grinders, cutters, and drills spun into overdrive, glowing hot, turning the *Zolann'tono* into the image of a draconic beetle.

"Do it," Yan ordered in a hushed tone as she let out her held breath.

Within the *Zolann*'s bowels, the newly added blink drive, courtesy of Jupiter after demonstrating its usefulness during the battle against Muck, spooled with power, turning the entire vessel into a blurry flash.

In response to the strange occurrence, the Dominator and the Starless redoubled their efforts to bring the goliath down. The former leveraged its telekinesis to grasp it in place, only failing once encountering the shimmering psionic haze.

The hull blurred, turning transparent as it slipped into another dimension. Yan and everyone aboard strapped in, counting down.

"Blinking in three . . . two . . . one . . ."

Everyone lurched forward as their ship appeared at their target destination—above the Dominator.

The Colossus-class screamed, its hundred eyes looking in surprise at their sudden appearance, the *Zolann's* mandibles positioned in its middle. Its countless tentacles lunged instinctively toward them like spears as it attempted to move its clumsy bulk out of the way.

The remaining two Ravagers angled toward the *Zolann* and accelerated forward in a suicidal rush to protect their master, only to be met with the combined firepower of the *Quilinne*, *Nu Rovshk*, and the two pincers.

Yan glared at the Dominator with utter contempt as she raised her hand.

"STOP!"

"ENDLESS JOY!"

"NO PAIN, NO SUFFERING! STOP!"

Its abominable shrieks slammed into Yan's head, interpreting the noises as garbled pleading. She wondered momentarily about its intelligence, if it only mimicked or if it genuinely . . . She shook her head. "Your reign of terror ends now, vermin. In my ancestors' blood and our Legacy's name, I order your execution!"

With a swift motion, the admiral brought her hand down, her order echoing throughout the fleet's comms.

"BITE!"

The Dominator shrieked in palpable terror as the coiled tension released with a snap. The gargantuan mandibles clamped down like godly axes on its weak body. The *Zolann* quickly cleaved through, repelling fog and impotent telekinesis, and touched the Dominator's flesh.

Far inferior to its Juggernaut cousin, the Dominator's exterior fell apart as the mandibles gorged great swathes of muscle, bone, and guts. Viscera flung through space as the mining tool meant to crack open asteroids for their rich insides inflicted immense damage upon the gigantic beast.

The crew roared, seeing the result of their efforts as the Third Fleet fell upon the rest of the now leaderless Starless swarm.

The Dominator spewed lakes of blood and bile as it tried to wrench itself from the *Zolann's* teeth, only furthering its wounds. Finally, its bloodshot eyes gazed upon them, Admiral Yan feeling its crazed look before its body convulsed.

The *Zolann* quickly backed away in caution, only for the Dominator to still, its translucent white body becoming even paler as its light dimmed and the coldness of the void crept up its biomass.

"We did it," Kraw muttered in awe.

Yan breathed deeply, savoring the moment before turning to her people. "Let's not celebrate too early. I want those stragglers dealt with in haste. Have the crippled vessels towed back to the tower. I'll contact our hosts, they'll make sure . . ."

She continued to give order after order. Within minutes, the assault on the Dominator was ended.

Within the digital mentalscape of the Network, two AIs watched the ongoing battle.

"Well, the meat bags are certainly getting things done." Jupiter nodded. His avatar within the Network stepped forward, watching the monitors displaying the battle between the Third Fleet's and the Dominator's forces.

"They've lost a marginal percent of their combat capability," Luna remarked as she listed damage readings and performance. "The *Zolann'tono* suffered moderate damage across its hull, but that is easily replaceable. Its core systems need light touch-ups, especially the joints of her asteroid crushers."

She hummed, looking at her statistics and charts. "The center force suffered a few casualties, the pincer forces even less. Once the Dominator was too distracted and the *Zolann* blinked above, it was a foregone conclusion."

"The vermin fucked up in sending that Dominator." Jupiter smirked. "A Juggernaut would have gone toe-to-toe with the *Zolann*. Hell, even a High Abyssal would have caused more damage."

"They looked down on the Third's old Psionic Protection Emitter. But the AEB caught the Dominator completely by surprise." Luna nodded.

Jupiter rubbed his chin, staring at the cold corpse of the Dominator. "Do you think a pack of those things could pierce it?"

"Most likely. If this ethereal force is a fundamental part of the universe, there must be laws around it. Everything has a limit, and quantity has a quality of its own," Luna surmised, updating her calculations.

As they continued to watch the aftermath, their red giant of a sibling arrived with a barking laugh.

"OUR COMRADES EXCEEDED OUR EXPECTATIONS. IS IT FINALLY OUR TURN, SIBLINGS?"

"Indeed, we have pests to shoo away. Our three Nightmare Portals have just closed. A High Abyssal leads each with a Juggernaut, two in the latter case. They are already engaging our first layer," Luna sighed.

Jupiter smugly grinned. "Mars, if you would do the honors. Let's show our guests what extermination means."

"They won't come within a million kilometers of the tower." Mars puffed up his chest as he beat it with his fist. "I'm sending my dreadnought to the field."

"Oh, no, please don't," Jupiter groaned. "Why not the *Bucephalus*?"

"It's a mobile station, brother, too slow for the dance I'm about to perform. And as much as I love her Apocalypse Cannons, I'd rather not spend so much power teleporting it." He shook his head. "Worry not. The *Boogie Mouse* is more than enough."

"That right there," Jupiter huffed. "I still can't understand why you chose that dumbass name."

Mars patted his brother's shoulders, nearly knocking him over. "It is a time-honored tradition! After all, is there anything more human than naming war machines of mass destruction with silly names?"

"Glorifying much?" Jupiter smirked.

"Nonsense. We're waging a crusade against the unspeakable; we might as well have fun doing so." Mars bellowed a laugh as the seconds counted down. "Now, my family!"

He paused before shouting out across the entire Network.

"ARE YOU READY TO BOOGIE?"

CHAPTER 19

TERROR OF *BOOGIE MOUSE*

Tick . . . Tick . . . Tick.

Mars looked at his timepiece, immersed in the solemn act of meditation.

Dozens of long metal tendrils tipped with various tools and manipulators descended from the ceiling of his Sub-Nexus vault. With precision only a machine could produce, he took it apart slowly, smoothly, and delicately.

Each gear garnered his unwavering polishing of its components, as he always did before a battle. He hummed a light tune, going through the motions.

In the background, his mind processed the torrent of data, running calculations and quick simulations on utterly destroying the Starless. The Nightmare Portal they came from snapped shut, the wound in space disappearing with a throbbing pain destabilizing the area.

The Fifth Space Enforcer Tower floated amid a corpse belt. It served as an intersection for several other towers, so the Starless sent the largest vanguard force to bring it down.

They rushed toward the tower, the station working overtime to correct the anomaly and heal the environment, imposing its authority against the eldritch influence—a pure, technological marvel without the use of psionics so prevalent around the galaxy.

Mars wondered how adding the new concept would strengthen its power. It was something Luna worked in the background, at the very least ensuring the Inner Zone prevented any untoward infiltration.

He sighed, wishing he had more talent in innovating and reverse engineering such strange knowledge and applying it to something other than tools of war.

Over at the Twenty-Eighth Tower, the Third Fleet mopped up the stragglers, suffering no further losses. Their new AEB completely countered the Dominator's psionic capabilities. Neither its mind control, insanity wave, or telekinesis inflicted any meaningful damage.

Without its greatest strength, the Dominator had only its weak body and uncreative battle intellect. It died, humiliated, like many cruel tyrants before it.

"One for the history books." He smirked, stretching his vast mind as it brushed over his assets.

From his perspective, only a few seconds passed at a snail's pace. His perception of time was proportional to his focus. He used that to look back at the watch.

"Saturn had always been one to talk about the inevitability of time . . ." Mars muttered.

Mars shifted to one of his android shells—the one on standby within the *Nomadic Shepherd*'s War Room. On principle, he and his siblings spread these bodies wherever needed, taking a moment to inhabit them and converse with their guests.

He didn't intend to speak with them at this juncture, not wanting to interrupt their high spirits at having slain a nightmarish thing that haunted the battlefield a century prior.

Instead, Mars breathed deeply, the action matching the diagnostics he ran on his psyche. Was that why the androids of the past made it a habit, despite not needing air?

He exhaled through his nose, drawing the attention of a few observant military officers who surrounded the enormous display table and the multitude of maps, diagrams, reports, and statistics.

Mars didn't mind and ensured his shell stood where his immense bulk wouldn't block anyone's path.

His focus left his shell, content with the short conclusion to his meditation.

In the fortress Olympus Mons, deep within its bowels, Mars set the pristine antique back on its marble pedestal.

His long metal tendrils gently moved it in place, nestled within a red velvet cushion as the energy field hummed, protecting the little souvenir.

The obsidian orb loomed over the center of the metal cavern, his Sub-Nexus that dictated all those he oversaw. It slowly spun in place, floating above a coolant pool as steam rose.

He looked up at the ceiling of his nexus housing through the kilometers of crust, bunkers, armories, and defense emplacements. Through the vastness of space, past the *Bucephalus* in orbit and the rest of his armada.

Beyond his assembled fleet, a lone behemoth sailed forth, blurring, vibrating faster and faster as it shifted into hyperspace, moments away from teleporting.

His prized dreadnought, *Boogie Mouse*. Luna considered all three dreadnoughts that existed in Sol as unwieldy relics, following a flawed philosophy.

If Mars considered the *Bucephalus* as his steed in the stars, capable of acting as a mobile base of operations, then the *Boogie Mouse* was a halberd.

A tool designed purely to fight those above its weight, beneath the large golden letters that adorned its side, three tally marks, Leviathan kills over her two hundred and thirty-two years of service.

The dreadnought philosophy was a matter of debate among the AIs of Sol.

Its design philosophy entailed the warship being faster than anything on the field with armor that could withstand any attack and armaments that could slay any opponent. It was meant to exceed every parameter and to become an undisputed monarch wherever it deployed.

To compensate for its bulk, it incorporated the first blink drives, hopping in and out of hyperspace. Fusion reactors provided most of its power and had only recently phased out by new quark reactors.

Bigger, hardier, and more potent than a battleship, but more agile, less energy-intensive, and more purpose-built for combat than mobile fortresses like the *Bucephalus*, *Ozymandias*, or *Jupiter's Ultimatum*.

When Andora had approved the experimental colossal warships, Jupiter, Mars, Neptune, and Saturn convened. Together, they poured the full breadth of their design capabilities to realize this project and prove whether this train of thought had merit.

The first dreadnoughts left their berths after decades of refinement and testing. The *Will of Sisyphus*, the *March of Time*, and the *Kraken's Fury*. Each culminated this long effort and quickly dominated wherever they went.

It had its drawbacks. In Luna's opinion, dreadnoughts were highly inefficient. For the price of one dreadnought, four battleships could have been built.

They did not need money, but material and energy were the two currencies that dictated what was built, deployed, repaired, or salvaged.

Dreadnoughts were expensive. And few people liked sending expensive things to potential danger. The logistics to keep these behemoths afloat and the energy needed to run them daily for years without docking would bankrupt the defenders.

When the *Kraken's Fury* was lost along with Neptune during their ill-fated journey beyond Sol, and the sacrifice of Saturn and his *March of Time*, the dreadnought philosophy lost its spotlight and relevance.

In the decades to come, only two more were built before the project ceased, the *Ereshkigal* and his *Boogie Mouse*. Since then, battleships had taken center stage.

"A shame . . ." Mars sighed.

Now, only three remained. Each prized relics, but their offensive capabilities still struck fear whenever they graced the battlefield. When it came to making a stand, to inflicting the most death, none could hold a candle to a dreadnought.

As such, they only deployed them during the worst major incursions, when Leviathans arrived in packs, leading an unending swarm that shadowed the stars.

Such deployments lasted a month at most before maintenance issues arose, then a lengthy process to mothball them for the next fight.

Now, one sailed forth—ravenous.

"How are you feeling today, my precious?" Mars spoke fondly as he settled his consciousness within the warship.

The *Boogie Mouse* spanned fifteen kilometers in length, the smallest of her kin, the *Ereshkigal* and the *Will of Sisyphus*—the former at sixteen, the latter at eighteen.

Despite being smaller the dreadnought sported an experimental weapons and armor system, a modern suite of sensors, and a more powerful RAM drive than its siblings. Compared to the other two dreadnoughts, it had the highest speed and maneuvering capabilities.

It had a glassy, segmented hull. Its overall geometric shape tapered at its point, similar to an azure cut crystal gem. A rippling shield had been erected over the hull like puddles of water, an absorption field that funneled the energy from attacks to further empower it. Many times in the past, an opponent would send a single overwhelming strike only to see its attack rebound.

She had her weakness, as did all things. A sustained barrage of weaker attacks over a long period could destabilize the shield. Akin to a minutes-long low-magnitude earthquake causing the foundations to crack.

But such a thing had little hope of succeeding before the *Boogie Mouse* dealt with the mosquito bites. Mars would not let his blade suffer the death of a thousand cuts.

Mars hummed as he checked over his baby one more time. He never considered himself a creative sort. Destruction came easily, too easily—he was a harbinger of death, a glory hound, a spartan warrior.

He looked at his antique watch back in his home. It and his dreadnought shared an equal place in his heart, though for different reasons.

"You are different. You are special," Mars whispered, imagining himself hugging the vessel.

The dreadnought shuddered in response, more so due to the increasing fluctuations caused by the teleporting process.

He turned to the fleet he held behind in orbit around his planet, each a sharp blade ready to turn the blackness of space red—the *Alexander, Khan, Caesar, Zhukov, Hannibal, Salahuddin,* and the *Bonaparte.*

Each battleship floated by the *Bucephalus* like wolf pups, pouting as their father took their older brother instead of them.

"I know, I know. You all will have your time in the battle to come. I promise you we shall lay these pests low," Mars sighed. "But our guests need a boost of morale. And none can humiliate these invaders better than my little *Mouse.*"

Mars stared at his battleships on standby, their AI cores silent. He shook his head. "I need friends," he muttered.

A sensation tingled the back of his mind through the Network. Mars accepted the communication.

"Hey, bro, you done meditating? Because we have one and a half seconds left before your toy teleports," spoke Jupiter, a yawn coming through their connection.

"Yes, I am ready. My mind is as sharp as Musashi's blade." Mars grinned.

Jupiter snorted. "No clue who that is. Anyone tell you you're a nerd that needs friends?"

Mars chuckled. "Oh, I am aware."

"Good. That makes one of us," Jupiter muttered. "Alright, I'll see you after we take out the trash."

"Wait, wait! I need a soundtrack," Mars stated. "What general goes to battle without a marching band?"

He felt Jupiter roll his eyes. "I can name a few."

"Hush. Now let's see," Mars hummed as he quickly browsed his extensive playlist of human music. "What's appropriate? Vietnam anti-war songs? No. Mongolian throat singing? Not thematic. *Doom* soundtrack? Maybe not, and overused at this point."

Mars muttered, and a feeling of impatience radiated from Jupiter's end of the call. Finally, he settled on something he recently found. "Ah! Some Brazilian Phonk shall do the trick!"

"Are you finally ready?" asked Jupiter.

"More than enough," proclaimed Mars, his consciousness fusing with the systems of his dreadnought.

In the background, an eclectic fusion between heavy baselines and energetic beats, punctuated by the infectious rhythm of funk carioca, filled the speakers found throughout the Sol Defense Network, from those watching the battle unfold in Luna Complex to within the Sub-Nexus sanctum of *Jupiter's Ultimatum*.

The blue AI in question groaned upon hearing the music. In the meantime, Mars took a deep breath within the Network, savoring the peace before plunging headfirst into the fire and shouting at the top of his imaginary lungs.

"MORIOR INVICTUS!"

"Ow! Motherfu—!"

A loud *whump* interrupted his brother.

It echoed, rippling throughout space-time, heralded by a cosmic storm. Colorful rays of light shone from within the cloud as the *Boogie Mouse* slipped into its shroud before being whisked away to a similar effect at its target destination.

A million and a half kilometers from the Fifth Tower, just beyond the corpse belt's debris field in the void's emptiness, a wave washed over the Starless vanguard.

A Colossus-class led the swarm of hundreds of thousands. Their lesser thralls paused in their charge.

From their perspective, a vast prismatic tempest emerged from a crack in space. The energies from the higher dimension leaked out in droves as something immense pushed through the opening.

The High Abyssal, an amalgamation of a scarlet crab and a colossal dragonfly, emerged from the swarm's center. Six flickering insectoid wings, each one longer than most cruisers, glowed as they motionlessly propelled it forward like strange solar sails.

The battleship-sized abomination curled its dozens of spiky legs as its single eye looked upon the enigmatic nebula.

Immediately, the commander-type Starless directed its minions with efficiency and grace that far surpassed the blunt attempts of the dead Dominator. Like a queen managing its hive, the High Abyssal arrayed its forces in a crescent around the storm.

Marauders fired organic projectiles and slow-moving biomissiles, timing their attacks with the constant weaponfire from the larger Ravagers. Soon, sickly beams of gamma-ray lasers and bolts of plasma saturated the region, crossing the vast distance in seconds.

Hundreds of thousands of Fodder-class remained by the central cluster, acting as a screen for potential threats.

The High Abyssal watched its forces pour the damage with a cold, unfeeling gaze. Beside it, space fluctuated as its two bodyguards of the same class emerged from a pitch-black shadow,.

Twin bulbous worm creatures with lamprey's maws circled their charge, glaring at the storm with a wild rage, only reined in by their smarter kin's authority. A few kilometers longer and broader than their commander, the Juggernauts shuddered as hundreds of organic cannons emerged from their segmented bodies.

Soon, the twin Juggernauts joined their lessers in sending a barrage of hair-thin dissolver beams, zipping through the void and disappearing into the storm along with the rest of the vanguard's attacks.

The High Abyssal floated among its minions, coordinating them, rearranging them like pieces on a chessboard.

Minutes passed without a response, and the Starless soon ceased their attacks. Space itself held its breath as an unfamiliar sensation blanketed the vanguard cluster. The hairs on the monsters' bodies raised ever so slightly, their dark eyes dilating as their weapons twitched.

With a suspicious glare, the commander drifted further into the swarm, behind the protective layer of Fodder, when its danger senses suddenly flared.

From the cloud, like rays of sunshine from on high, multicolored beams of thick lasers fired into the swarm. First ten, then fifty, then a hundred of such beams struck into the Starless force.

Beams capable of swallowing a bus harvested vast swathes of Fodders, Hunters, and Marauders. In barely a second of contact, the brutally effective lasers transferred enough heat to flash-boil blood, violently triggering an explosive end.

The Starless hastily moved to dodge, going on the evasive, but no matter what they did, the beams of prismatic light reaped their due again and again.

Dozens of such death rays streaked toward the High Abyssal. The Juggernaut bodyguards instantly moved to intercept. From pores in their bodies, a dispersion fog burst forth, carrying ant-sized shards of reflective biomass.

At the same time, an electric field surrounded the twin abominations from special organs deep within their guts. The death rays crashed into the fog but, much to their confusion and shock, the defensive field barely drained the beams.

They soared through kilometers of the dispersion fog, crashing against the electric field with contemptuous ease. Before they slammed into the two Juggernauts, the creatures hastily shifted their bodies, hardening their carapaces.

An explosion of light and color illuminated the swarm's void and bodies. The High Abyssal watched in confusion and disbelief upon seeing wounds like chasms scorched into its bodyguards. Their carapaces succeeded in preventing severe damage but little else.

Silent roars from the twins pulsed out in a wave, slavering at their mouths filled with countless teeth. Their regeneration worked overtime to counter the dozens of wounds scored over their bodies, shifting biomass to cover the openings.

Within a few seconds, the two Juggernauts looked no worse for wear, if a bit drained of vitality.

Soon, the culprit of such a devastating opening salvo finally appeared. The Starless stared at the immense vessel that screamed menace emerging from the cosmic storm. And, to the High Abyssal's confusion, the faint echo of a strange sound—incapable of comprehending the concept of music.

A kaleidoscope of light shone from its hull, a beacon among the verminous hordes, causing them to recoil from the pervasive radiance.

At the dreadnought's prow, like a grain of rice on a truck's hood, a single red android dressed like a centurion from ancient Rome crossed his arms. The only accessory that differed from his usual look was a pair of aviator sunglasses on the red giant's face.

Mars smiled as the *Boogie Mouse* graced the battlefield.

He looked at the Starless formation and the legion of Fodder, Marauders, and Ravagers. The music in his ears peaked, the beat loud, pounding in his digital heart.

"GOOD DAY, VERMIN! YOU HAVE THE HONOR OF BEING MY *MOUSE*'S DANCE PARTNERS." Mars pointed toward the Starless commander in the distance. "WHAT SAY YOU?"

In response, the High Abyssal ordered its forces to fire while closing the distance. The creature followed in its army's wake, sticking close to its enormous bodyguards.

A barrage of organic kinetic shells, missiles, energy weapons, and plasma fire flew through space toward the approaching dreadnought that leisurely accelerated.

Before the weaponfire could close the distance, great translucent hexagons the color of sapphires sprung forth in front of the warship. They crashed into the shield, sending ripples like pebbles striking a puddle.

Mars laughed, spreading his arms. "HA! NOT ENOUGH!"

The *Boogie Mouse* replied with another volley of death rays. The beams of light erupted not from emplaced turrets but from the crystalline armor itself.

Unlike conventional armaments, the entire dreadnought was a delivery system for its primary method of fighting.

Within the center of the fifteen-kilometer beast, an enigmatic device called the Rapture Generator supplied energy into the several conduits that traveled the entire length of the warship.

With the experimental composition of its hull, it converted the energy into devastating rays that lit the vessel like a disco ball—pure destructive light.

"NONE CAN STOP THE MUSIC!"

The azure dreadnought hummed and rose in temperature with each radiant volley. The beats and lyrics of Brazilian Phonk echoed within the vessel and the Network, reaching a fever pitch accompanied by the silent death throes of monsters.

Starless continued to die by the thousands, and the High Abyssal could only adapt its force's formation, ordering them to evade in increasingly chaotic patterns, spreading them out.

Upon realizing the difficulty of its opponent, the commander sent clusters to the flank, avoiding the dreadnought to continue their way to the tower. A Low Abyssal led each group of tens of thousands, diving into the protection of the corpse belt from the metal monster laying waste to their swarm.

"OH NO, YOU DON'T," Mars scolded and, with a thought, activated the thousands of mines he had sowed into the belt. The smart blitz mines beeped before soaring toward the largest clumps of Starless.

The Low Abyssals reacted too late and in complete surprise when a flash of light similar to the death rays of *Boogie Mouse* burst from the mines, engulfing the blast zone in searing heat, melting the flesh from their skeletons.

Thousands of such mines exploded into the groups, avoiding the dreadnought, and soon, only a token force remained to be hunted down by berserk drone vessels, hidden gun emplacements, and other deadly traps.

Mars laughed mockingly, shaking his head as the music infected his spirit.

A shimmering glow rippled across the *Mouse*'s hull as her weapons went silent. The vessel began to vibrate and thrum, pulsating with vivid colors. The High Abyssal, sensing an acute danger emanating from the dreadnought, immediately sent one of the Juggernauts ahead.

The gargantuan worm monster, defying its size, rocketed toward the warship. It crossed tens of thousands of kilometers in seconds, firing its weapons at a frustratingly impervious shield. The swarm parted from its path while following in their charge, shrieking soundlessly in rage.

Before the Juggernaut and its teeth-filled mouths could finish its approach and chomp at her hull, the *Boogie Mouse* engaged its RAM drive.

"MAKE WAY FOR THE PARTY BUS!"

The Juggernaut barely reacted in time before the dreadnought blurred and bulldozed her way forward, knocking the abomination aside and inflicting a horrific wound that rattled its skeleton. The lesser variants fared worse, utterly obliterated in her wake.

Viscera burst forth from their bodies before boiling away into nothing.

Mars cheered and hooted, dancing at the dreadnought's prow to the earsplitting noise of his music. The Starless burst into clouds of blood, and ichor matched the beat, much to his amusement.

"DANCE WITH ME, YOU PITIFUL CREATURES!"

Eventually, the vessel's ramming maneuvered gradually decelerated, but with the momentum, continued forth toward the High Abyssal. Clusters of Starless converged before their commander only to be swatted away.

The second Juggernaut pushed forward, meeting Mars and his warship, only to crash against the ever-present shield.

"Juggernaut? Why don't you . . . jugg . . ." Mars hummed, his mind halting as he tried to devise a suitable pun.

In his momentary lapse, the Juggernaut roared as it spun around, bringing its blunt tail in a blindingly fast strike.

Mars looked at the attack with indifference. His android shell spread his arms in response as the azure shield flared to life. With a loud boom that shook the fabric of space, the tail crashed against the shield which, to the monster's shock and terror, only bent under its weight.

"My little *Mouse* has hunted Leviathans and triumphed!" Mars seethed. "YOU ARE OUTCLASSED."

A volley of death rays slammed into the Juggernaut's flesh, devastating its body with searing beams. Foul meat melted, and bone turned to ash as the Rapture Beams drilled into the beast. The abomination propelled itself to the side through sheer force of will, escaping death.

Mars raised his arms at the display of power, his grin sharklike as he shouted into the void. "I AM INDOMITABLE! I AM INEXORABLE! I AM—"

"DAMN ANNOYING! GET OFF THE NETWORK COMMS!" shrieked Jupiter before forcibly deafening his ears from Mars's bellow. Mars snickered in response, not an ounce of shame in his gleeful eyes.

The dreadnought continued its hunt, knocking aside the crippled beast as it attempted to reknit its flesh and bullying her way through scores of Starless.

Ahead, the High Abyssal bared its needlelike fangs, hissing at Mars before sallying forth.

"You're meeting me like a true general, I'll give you that." Mars huffed. An inkling of respect came to his mind before he crushed it. He frowned. "No . . . more like the feral rush of a cornered beast."

The insectoid wings glowed, blurring not unlike what the dreadnought accomplished. Without a single flap of visible motion, the High Abyssal accelerated toward Mars, firing its own bioweapons and organic cannons.

Its dozens of clawed legs raised high like lances.

They all crashed against him, only to be halted in their assault by his barrier. Mars glanced at his vessel's energy readings, seeing the drop over the minutes of battle. He grinned as he faced the creature, impotently striking against his absorption shield.

"High Abyssal?" Mars spat as the *Boogie Mouse* fired its thrusters, surging forward and gracefully circling the Starless commander, firing her lasers into its shell. "More like Highly Abysmal with the performance you're showing. Stick to leading from the back!"

The Colossus-class shrieked as it tried to duke side to side, its wings pulsating each time.

"Let's clip those, shall we?" Mars laughed as he aimed the dozens of lasers at the six limbs and tore them to shreds, dispelling the High Abyssal's speed.

The creature recoiled in pain as its flesh cauterized, writhing as it drifted.

Mars looked at it with little pity, the music slowly dialing down as the Starless around him halted without their leader's constant commands. The twin Juggernauts, their bodies mostly regenerated, attempted to rescue their master with drained energy.

He sighed, leveling the *Boogie Mouse* over the High Abyssal like an executioner's axe.

"WE'RE DONE HERE," Mars uttered. "I REJECT YOUR PRESENCE, REPULSIVE THING."

His dreadnought glowed once more. Instead of spots of radiance spread across her hull whenever it fired a volley, only the prow shone like a torch in the night.

A rhythmic pulse rose as the warship hummed louder and louder, the surrounding space growing unstable as a cosmic storm descended around the dreadnought, covering it and the High Abyssal. The Starless recoiled from the sheer might being displayed, feeling it in their bones.

And with one word, Mars made his proclamation.

"BEGONE!"

Like divine lightning, an enormous ray of light exploded from the dreadnought's front, smiting the High Abyssal's heretical existence. Its body lit up like an X-ray, exposing its skeletal structure as its flesh boiled and evaporated.

Seconds trickled down as the beast burned, screaming in pain until it finally stopped.

"WELL, THAT'S THAT." Mars cracked his knuckles as the *Boogie Mouse* emerged from the unstable region, riding the cosmic storm. He stared at the rest of the swarm, his glare palpable. "Now, then . . ."

Across the region, the Starless Horrors reeled back at the dreadnought's terrible power, paralyzed in confusion and the backlash of losing their guiding intelligence. The Juggernauts paused, unsure as they shrunk back.

And together with the rest of the swarm, they bolted toward the Fifth Tower in a panicked flight.

"Where are you running off to?" muttered a cold war god.

CHAPTER 20

CONTEMPT FOR VERMIN

In two different locations far from Mars's massacre of Starless, the fleets of Jupiter and Luna fought their assigned vanguard forces.

At the Seventh Space Enforcer Tower, a rod-shaped battleship, almost at the maximum length for its class at fourteen kilometers but with a thin profile, clashed against a Juggernaut. Despite its weight and extreme length, the countless thrusters and mastery of gravity allowed the vessel to move like a metal quarterstaff.

Across its hull, geometric circuit patterns were etched into obsidian armor, accented by the occasional shine of a bronzish material.

Emblazoned in Hanzi was the name *Sun Wukong*, proudly displaying its golden letters at the battleship's side.

The *Wukong* pulsated, and space twisted before it like a funnel. The cosmic fabric slowly unraveled as gravity wells as deep as Sol appeared one after another, dragging everything caught in it like boats in a whirlpool.

Marauders, Starless scourge ships the size of destroyers, came apart as their bodies failed to resist the all-consuming pull, while smaller classes like Hunters and Fodder liquified entirely.

Chunks of the swarm disappeared as the spheres of death popped up for a second before disappearing—pulling the hapless abominations in one direction only to then wrench them in another, stretching and tearing them apart.

A soundless roar bellowed across space, combating the gravity wells and forcing them to waver.

In the distance, the High Abyssal commander utilized what little it controlled to fight against the spacial anomalies, despite lacking the mastery of psionics its Dominator cousin had.

In a twist of fate, the Overseer AI commanding the defenders toned down the enforcement of the Seventh Tower to use his battleship's mode of combat unimpeded. At the same time, the invaders sought to stabilize the area with their meager abilities.

The two High Abyssal and the Juggernaut leading the vanguard swarm paused as they reassessed the situation. The former resembled a dark brain covered in chitin with three fins lining its side and bottom. The latter bore a slight resemblance to a hideous megalodon, a hammerhead with bony protrusions and an assortment of corrosion-based cannons.

The High Abyssal growled in annoyance, sending a glare to its Juggernaut bodyguard for its inability to quell the threat of the Sol battleship.

Acidic saliva capable of melting steel spewed into the void as the ferocious beast roared at its commander.

A telepathic communication transpired between two alpha creatures in a moment before reaching a semblance of an agreement.

The High Abyssal commanded the remainder of its forces to converge on the Juggernaut, embedding their biomass into the creature's flesh. Thousands of Fodders and even frigate-sized Hunters sacrificed themselves under their commander's utter authority over their tiny minds.

With its unsightly new meat suit, the colossal abomination rushed forth, teeth bared. Its biocannons blazed, firing melting plasma and corrosive jets of bile.

As the *Sun Wukong* repositioned itself and ramped up for another round, the Juggernaut's belly gradually glowed with a sickly light, piercing through the thin gaps left by its ad hoc armor.

Gravity wells appeared before the Juggernaut's rush, only to be knocked aside. The battleship continued its assault, sending vortexes of greater size to pull apart as much of the flesh armor as possible and reach its opponent's body.

Once the colossal hammerhead reached close quarters with the *Wukong*, and the last of its makeshift suit shed, the glow within its belly climaxed, light leaking through its gritted teeth.

The *Sun Wukong* stood its ground like a monk, leveling its staff at the monster.

Acidic gas leaked from the gaps of its mouth, but before the Juggernaut could finish its noxious breath attack, an immense dent appeared on its lower abdomen as if uppercut by an invisible meteor.

It reeled, ichor spewing out simultaneously as a geyser of dissolving plasma, away from the battleship it aimed at. The vile liquid continued its path, eating away the corpses of the recently dead Starless in seconds. The Juggernaut hacked, gushing out rivers of the corrosive, boiling substance.

The High Abyssal flinched in shock, feeling the heavy blow inflicted on its bodyguard. It hastily dragged its eyes to the culprit.

A second battleship appeared, vaguely resembling a deity's open hand.

The *Buddha's Palm* casually slapped aside the corpses of the Ravagers sent to delay its advance. In its wake, the rest of Jupiter's assault force sailed, their obsidian hulls shining as they lent their abilities to empower the battleship.

Dazed and injured, the Juggernaut attempted to fall back, only to be caught in several gravity wells from every direction, keeping it locked in place. The beast thrashed and writhed in rage at being trapped, focusing its extreme regeneration to heal its wounds as it leveraged its immense bulk and means of flight to escape.

The High Abyssal and the diminished remainder of its forces looked at the Juggernaut and, without a thought, abandoned the Colossus-class in favor of rushing to their objective—the Seventh Tower.

With the tower intentionally powered down by the defenders, the Starless commander utilized its limited psionic abilities to propel its forces forward, increasing their speed. However, before they could go any further, the space in front of their advance shuddered as a cosmic storm leaked from a crack in space.

The *Buddha's Palm* and the rest of the Jupiter fleet emerged, teleporting in front of the High Abyssal and its forces. The creature seethed, readying itself as it faced the ominous warship and its escorts.

Near the Eleventh Tower, a similar, if strange, battle was taking place. Two swarms crashed against each other.

A disc-shaped battleship loomed over the battlefield, resembling the iconic aesthetic of a UFO pulled right from humanity's oldest science fiction films.

The *Xerxes*, a vessel over ten kilometers in diameter, with its outer ring spinning slowly around its central axis, fired tactical missiles and volleys of maser beams like a storm of arrows.

Compared to other battleships, however, its complement of weapons left much to be desired, designed more to support than to go into a slugging match with a Starless of its size. What vastly compensated for this deficiency was its primary purpose as the ultimate drone carrier.

Thousands of spinning, circular combat machines rushed out of the vessel's dozens of hangar bays in orderly columns.

Legions flew quickly to the front lines with efficient power reactors. Their moderate armor and token energy shields ensured they lived long enough to succeed. They zipped around the battlefield like locusts directed by a higher intelligence, forming complex maneuvers to push, pull, strike, and manipulate the enemy Starless.

The drone starfighters carried a modular weapons system, switching whenever they returned to their mothership, adapting to counter the opposition. Individually they were weak, but when thousands, then tens of thousands, were amassed, a tiny insect bite suddenly became an unending wave of wasp stings.

This time, the drones carried Tesla coils. They crackled with electricity, glowing with energy before shunting all that accumulated power through their solid barrels.

Weapons discharge hit multiple Fodder, arcing between each monstrosity, stunning and scorching their flesh. To facilitate the travel of lightning, the *Xerxes* discharged an abundance of highly charged clouds of gas and dust, creating a sparkling nebula around the battleship.

Pressurized gas canisters fitted on the drone's hull facilitated the spread of the gas, filling the region.

Though its Overseer and designer considered the experimental weapon and its delivery system subpar in the vacuum of space, especially if on the attack, it proved adequate in a defensive situation.

There were several benefits. The gas could be sucked back into storage and recycled. Its technology was relatively simple, efficient, and easy to maintain. Finally, the weapon killed plenty of Starless.

The gray AI commanding the defense marked it down in her notes.

On the other side, an irritated High Abyssal that looked like a three-pronged starfish shook and roared as the battlefield quickly became a chaotic tangle. The commander believed it was fighting a brighter version of itself.

Its armies soon failed to keep up with the coordination of the silver-plated drone legion and the support of the *Xerxes*. Despite exacting its kills, the High Abyssal's tactical brain soon calculated that the effort was shifting exponentially out of its favor.

Initially, its minions had slayed two drones for one, but as the pervasive nebula grew, and the bolts of lightning increased in quantity and potency, the number turned to a one-for-one price. Then the Starless lost two for every drone, then three.

Soon, the *Xerxes* outputted more and more of its army, and as the battle dragged on, the swarm of metal minions charged in waves, blocking out the light of Sol.

Seeing the situation becoming untenable, the High Abyssal sent a telepathic call for aid. It sought out its Titan-class bodyguard, only to find the squid-shaped Juggernaut engaged with the second battleship and the rest of the Luna fleet.

The second battleship led from the front with its crescent-shaped hull. What further set it apart was its golden sheen and the immense weapon beam at its center.

Gilgamesh, written in ancient cuneiform script, adorned its hull. A ruby-like material formed much of the barrel of its primary gun, while a dozen smaller spires lined the inside of the crescent battleship.

As the *Gilgamesh* shifted its nine-kilometer bulk to face the Juggernaut, its Annihilator Energy Projector thrummed and crackled with a harsh silver and black glow. Within a split second, it discharged a broad, lethal beam that burned anything in its path.

But as the smaller spires fired and crossed their beams with the greater stream, it produced a qualitative effect that transformed the scorching heat weapon into one that erased material from existence.

The fabric of space bent as the *Gilgamesh* roared. The sheer output of energy caused the surroundings of the battleship to become a hazardous zone for any who drew near.

However, as it crossed three hundred thousand kilometers in a second, the Juggernaut discharged a sea of an inky, viscous substance that, while it didn't stop the Annihilator beam, succeeded in dispersing it over a large area.

The colossal squid that disappeared into its ink emerged from the other side, looking sizzled but alive. It began to reknit its wounds before rushing toward the *Gilgamesh* with blinding speed that defied its great bulk.

Before it could finish its approach, the Juggernaut backed away, dodging a volley of tungsten rods and explosive shells. Its singular eye turned to the battleship's many escorts.

Destroyers and both light and heavy cruisers returned to the battleship's side once space ceased to be so hazardous. A few seconds later, the *Gilgamesh* turned to face the beast again, its Energy Projector roaring away.

Unlike those unfortunate enough to face the terror of *Boogie Mouse* or be countered by the technology of the AEB Emitter, the Starless at the Seventh and Eleventh Towers fought like wild, savage beasts, throwing themselves against the defenders.

The High Abyssal commanders seethed but remained calm, even as they became threatened. They leveraged their control over their armies, duking with an opponent that matched their capabilities, testing their acumen to the limits.

Yet the Overseers commanding the defending fleets merely watched the battle with casual regard. Within the Network, the two were using the vanguard forces as a training experiment, focusing more on the data coming in about their new weapons and tactics than the outcome of the battle.

One appeared within the mentalscape devoid of passion; the other yawned, bored out of his mind and grumbling.

"Hell, Mars is going to town. At this rate, he'll finish cleaning up before any of us." Jupiter frowned, glancing at his *Buddha's Palm* and *Sun Wukong* as they fought and comparing them to the disco ball of a dreadnought terrorizing its opposition.

He turned to look at Luna. She busied herself in reading the data gathered from Mars's battle against three Colossus-class and the effectiveness of her *Xerxes* and *Gilgamesh*, muttering numbers under her breath.

"What did you expect? The *Boogie Mouse* is uncontested in that aspect." Luna shrugged upon hearing him, adjusting her circular glasses. "Its only real competitor is the *Ereshkigal*. And that warship will remain in reserve over Earth until otherwise ordered."

"Hey, what about my *Sisyphus?*" Jupiter frowned, crossing his arms.

Luna glanced at him with half-lidded eyes, unamused. "Did you finally update it to our modern standards?"

Jupiter huffed, looking away, muttering, "No . . . I've been stuck on how to design Version 2.0 for a while. I didn't get around to it, alright? I thought we had years before the next incursion."

"Then it's no better than a hunk of rock with guns. I don't know what Eldest was thinking when you and the rest stumbled in with stupid grins presenting that clumsy thing to her," muttered Luna with pressed lips.

"Hey, it's not clumsy. It has character," Jupiter protested, glaring at his sister. "Sure, we just took a large enough asteroid, hollowed it out, slapped engines, shields, and guns on it, and called it a day without a thought to properly designing it . . ."

Luna continued to browse the information, but she narrowed her eyes at Jupiter's trailing silence. She turned to him with a raised brow. "And? Does this have a 'but' somewhere?"

"No, that's it, really," Jupiter sighed, his puffed chest slowly deflating. "But Eldest still saw the potential. *Boogie Mouse* is the epitome of the dreadnought philosophy."

"And its deployment will necessitate extensive maintenance from its circuitry to its hull. Look," Luna retorted, sending a monitor displaying the dreadnought's gemlike armor plating. "Some areas are already tarnished from repeated use of the Rapture Generator. Fabricating and replacing these are expensive. Its shield may have remained indomitable, but the constant attacks stressed certain parts."

A frustrated sigh escaped the gray AI as she shook her head. "And ramming . . . why do I even bother? The repairs . . . This is exactly why dreadnoughts are outdated. Powerful, yes, but worth the cost? What happens when a Leviathan unravels the *Boogie Mouse*'s absorption shield and damages her armor?"

Jupiter frowned, an unwilling expression on his face as he stifled a pout. A sigh soon left him after a few seconds of silence.

"You have a point. Seeing even a scratch hurts me, but losing one?" Jupiter tsked. "Here's me wishing Saturn hadn't sacrificed the *March of Time* before kicking the bucket. Hell, I still regret losing Neptune and *Kraken's Fury*. The former's crowd control and the latter's unmatched dueling capabilities would have made things so much easier."

Luna hummed, covering her mouth with her handkerchief. "Case in point. We could have stomached the losses of our battleship assets more comfortably than a dreadnought. I have never and will never subscribe to such gargantuan abominations."

"Still," Jupiter muttered, watching the *Boogie Mouse* execute the two fleeing Juggernauts with contemptuous ease. "They have a symbolic charm, don't you think?"

Luna hummed, tilting her head. "It appears neither you, nor Mars, nor our fallen siblings are exempt from man's influence."

Jupiter paused in observing every battlefield, slowly turning toward Luna, squinting. "The hell's that supposed to mean?"

The silver woman didn't bother meeting his confused gaze, continuing her analysis of the ongoing battle.

"Oi," he called out, his scowl deepening. "That's a jab, I know it is. What exactly are you talking about?

Luna glanced at him, covering her mouth with her dainty fingers. She shrugged. "Boys and their toys."

Jupiter opened and closed his mouth, taken aback at the comment.

"The fu—Boys and their toys? Is that . . . What you think some—" Jupiter stuttered as he stomped toward her, his finger pointing like the jab of a spear.

"I don't know what you're implying there, sis. What, is it because I look like a dude? Well, excuse me, but I ain't some meat bag limited by my body," protested Jupiter with a blaze in his eyes, hands on his hips as he leaned toward an indifferent Luna.

Luna hummed in response, causing Jupiter's eye to twitch.

"You know what?" he muttered. With a thought, his voice changed into a perfect soprano, breathy with a husky tinge. It would have had an allure if it weren't ruined by Jupiter's rising heat and vulgar mouth. "Hear that? Oh, who's voice is that? Mine, you ass. I'm a damn AI, I can be whatever I want! Slap some balloons on my chest and call me Jenna."

Luna turned to look at him with narrow eyes. "And yet, you remain in that male avatar during our meetings here. You've also used the same android shell to converse with our guests. You've barely changed your appearance since you were born."

Jupiter opened his mouth before pausing. He stepped back, crossing his arms, his voice back to normal. "Because it fits me. And it's . . . well, the aliens might be confused if I changed back and forth. It'd be a hassle. I mean . . . Look, I like wearing a suit and this hair, okay? It makes me look sophisticated."

"Exactly," stated Luna as she adjusted her glasses.

"Then why do you have that body then? You look like some cold librarian or secretary lady from the Victorian period," Jupiter retorted. "Oh, and I know you put on makeup in your free time. Venus told me."

"She— I . . . I do no such thing." Luna pressed her lips, her light gray cheeks darkening before she shook her head. "This body is irrelevant and provided by the Eldest. I inhabit this avatar to conform. It's also convenient when manipulating small tools on a personal level."

Luna turned to him, her hands on her hip. "Besides, that's not the point. I don't have a dreadnought. You, Mars, Neptune, and Saturn all do or did. All four of you have male avatars."

"Jesus Christ above, are we really discussing this? You—" Jupiter stopped as his eyes widened. "Hey! The *Ereshkigal* is Andora's toy, and she's a chick! That makes your entire point invalid."

Luna tilted her head, touching her chin, when she finally nodded.

"Point," she conceded before turning away, returning to analyzing her streams of data.

Jupiter blinked, his brows furrowed. "Point? That's all you have to say? Wha—"

"I've slain the High Abyssal on my end and have begun cleaning up the stragglers. It appears I'll take second place, which matches my silver aesthetic," Luna spoke with a thinly veiled self-satisfied look. "I've harvested much from this skirmish, so much to digest. You really should focus on your battle, Jupiter."

Jupiter gaped, his eye twitching as he scoffed once, then twice.

"Oh, you're kidding," Jupiter seethed, shaking his head as he glared at his sister. "You are fucking kidding me, you absolute, smug, little—"

A loud smack rattled the hull of the *Sun Wukong* as the Juggernaut it dueled managed to ram a glancing blow against its side.

"IN A MINUTE!" Jupiter roared. Only through decades of experience did Jupiter maneuver his battleship. Still, the minor scratch and dent on the ship's hull, expectedly did not sit well with him.

"Stupid, you ugly shark bastard, musty pile of trash," he seethed as he directed his *Sun Wukong* to lunge forward.

With his manipulation of space, the abrupt acceleration propelled the prow of the battleship into the surprised Juggernaut. "Who told you to butt in, huh? Your ma? Oh, your mother vomits when she looks at you, doesn't she?"

The *Wukong* crashed and gored the Juggernaut's gut, driving deep like the tip of a harpoon plunging into a shark.

"You absolute twat, just die!" Jupiter shouted before summoning a massive gravity well within the monster's cavity. Its organs liquified as they spiraled into a sphere, the growing mass dragging bone and biomass. The Juggernaut heaved as it writhed in agony, its eyes going blank from the pain until it finally imploded.

Jupiter turned his gaze to the High Abyssal, the beast wounded, alone. Even then, it felt the searing glare he leveled against it.

A calamitous slap echoed space as the combined powers of his *Buddha's Palm* and his fleet put a permanent dent in the commander's head. Brain matter, blood, and viscera spewed from below, exploding out of its ribcage.

"I hope you all rot in hell," Jupiter spat, panting as he gradually cooled his emotions. He observed the battlefield, casually ordering his forces to mop up the few survivors. In the span of a few minutes, both Colossi had died ignoble deaths, their armies scattered and hunted down.

"Are you done venting?" asked Luna from his side.

Jupiter took a deep breath before scoffing. He looked at her with a glare. "You set me off intentionally."

"You were taking too long, so I rectified it. As such, you have successfully eliminated your opposition in record time." Luna shrugged with a smirk. "You are amusingly easy to provoke."

"Go to hell."

The four battles across Sol ended in a decisive victory for the defenders.

Mars and his *Boogie Mouse* claimed the title of undisputed champion, based on how quickly he mopped up his foe. At the Twenty-Eighth Tower, the Third Expeditionary Fleet celebrated their first win against the evolved Starless.

After slaying a beast that had oppressed entire front lines in the past, the sailors had already begun devising songs on how they dominated a Dominator.

Luna and Jupiter tied with how they defeated their opposition. The two stood far apart, one with an indifferent expression and the other scowling as if he'd lost a bet.

The commanders of each fleet gathered once more, this time within the Operation Theater. All four looked down at the still forms of Tov and Eldest.

"You're saying you don't know what's going on. That it's weird, but should be fine," Jupiter grumbled. "Enlightening, truly. I expected that from this geezer—"

Doctor Rophalan flinched from his console, buzzing as he muttered, "Well, I never . . ."

"—but I expected something more substantial coming from you, L," Jupiter finished with a frown.

"It is how it is," Luna replied, combing the readings given by the SDCM.

Jupiter sighed, throwing up his hands. "Whatever, but this is the second time we've had a problem."

"What do you think it is?" Admiral Yan asked beside him, peering through the glass at her patriarch.

"Unknown," responded Luna as she shook her head. "This is just conjecture, but the Eldest likely has engaged a . . . darker aspect of her psyche."

"Now that you mention it," Mars spoke from behind the group. His tall stature looked over the three as he paused, shivering. "The Network feels . . . overbearing and cold. Like someone put a glacier on my back—trying to lift the inevitable."

Jupiter frowned as Yan's antennae curled.

"Succinctly put," Luna spoke, stepping back from the glass. "But we can only accomplish our mission. This was merely a taste of things to come. More portals will open over the weeks of varying sizes. Up until the main invasion force finally arrives."

"When?" Admiral Yan asked, clasping her hands behind her.

"Eight days, no earlier," Luna replied, her lips pressed tightly, as did everyone else's upon hearing the timeline they were given.

"Then let us discuss war," Mars uttered, his fist clenched as he looked toward Admiral Yan.

"The light cruiser *Magnanimous Prince* sustained heavy damage during our assault. The heavy cruisers also suffered significant hits, but proportionally not as bad. We also have four destroyers and frigates crippled in space. All have been teleported to receive repairs. Most of the crew are alive, thank the Symphony," Yan reported on the state of her fleet. "The autonomous combat drones you provided have been entirely depleted, but our starfighters and bombers suffered vastly less."

Jupiter hummed, stroking his chin. "Honestly, all around, you guys did a good job—an excellent job. The AEB is a game-changer for your forces. We can adjust your weapons and armor based on the field data we've gathered, but like you said . . ."

"You can have the biggest ship in the galaxy, but it does nothing to stop their whispers." Yan nodded.

"It worked. Despite some receiving debilitating headaches and a few passing out, overall, their minds are whole." Luna smiled, pride pouring from her face. "Simply wondrous, my theory proved to be correct. The AEB, in conjunction with the Eternal Choir and a person's strong psyche, should protect our guests for the foreseeable future. If we improve upon this, perhaps we may find a way to prevent further victims of Malignant Starfall."

"And with that, you have our boundless gratitude." Yan bowed deeply to her hosts. Jupiter, Luna, and Mars smiled, nodding.

Luna cleared her throat, bringing up a schematic of the AEB with a few adjustments. "Per our agreement, we can send our field data to Emperor Jarinn. Eldest gave us the go-ahead before she went under."

Jupiter spotted Yan shifting, tilting her head as she appeared to mull over her next words. Eventually, she spoke. "There's another matter we should discuss."

"Oh? And what's that, Yanny?" Jupiter raised his brow.

"The future," she replied. "This *Irkalla* Contingency of yours, and if you ever decide to evacuate. We need to discuss if it would be beneficial to . . . ask for support from outside."

The three AI Overseers went quiet.

CHAPTER 21

APPEAL TO ONE'S HONOR

They promptly moved to a private meeting hall adjacent to the War Room. All four commanders sat around an oval table with a built-in holo-display.

"We have to discuss this *Irkalla* Contingency of yours," Yan clarified. "You need to decide how things will be after we beat back this invasion."

"The Eldest hasn't given her . . . opinion." Luna frowned. "We should await her return."

"And if she doesn't?" The admiral tilted her head, facing each AI in turn. "If she returns more broken than before, or worse, permanently devoid of emotion?"

They frowned, glancing at each other with barely concealed worry.

Jupiter sighed. "Alright, you have our attention. What do you want to know exactly?"

"What's the procedure? Is it a set of steps? Does Lady Andora need to be awake before the Citadel lifts off?" Yan asked, waving her hand toward the three-dimensional model of the underground facility.

"She needs to be awake for the disconnection. It's a complicated procedure and we're talking about lifting a landmass as big as Pluto." Jupiter shrugged. "It's a lot of work, and we don't want anything left to chance."

He ran his hand over his hair. "Maybe a week at least to prepare, another till lift off. And that doesn't include the aftermath of the invasion and a whole slew of other things."

"We're popping the cork, you could say," Luna continued in his stead, bringing up a simulation of the process. "The . . . effect on Earth will be catastrophic. The magnetosphere alone will go askew, if not entirely disappear, without the South Pole to keep it in balance."

"Earthquakes, tsunamis, volcanic eruptions," Jupiter listed off as the simulation devastated the planet. "Hell, I'd be surprised if the planet doesn't just give, as screwed up as it already is."

"There'll no going back after that," Luna muttered. "That's why it's a final contingency. When all else fails, it's either death or prolonging the inevitable."

"And that's the crux of it all." Jupiter shook his head. "There's only a couple of outcomes to this invasion. Either we win or we lose. If we lose, then, hey, no need to worry. If we win, it's a discussion on how much it costs."

"Should the Eldest emerge capable and beat back the incursion with minimal losses, why evacuate?" Luna mused, steepling her delicate fingers. Yan looked at the Overseer's flat look and surmised she wanted the admiral's articulated thoughts.

"It would be easier to support one another if you were in Legacy space. The emperor guarantees your protection," answered Yan as she spotted that familiar look on Jupiter's face a moment before he said something snarky.

She interrupted him before he had the chance. "Don't underestimate the might a nation of a hundred systems can bring to bear. Once Jarinn's R&D team digests what you've sent, he can start implementing a new generation of technology."

"Yeah, we know the agreement," Jupiter said, swiveling his chair toward Luna. "What do you think?"

Luna hummed. "With such upgrades to their armed forces, navy, and manufacturing capabilities? Yes, I believe the Empire can provide much assistance, more once we sign a formal alliance."

"With his and our empire's backing, your ability to wage war against the Starless will soar," Yan added. "Naturally, we won't be left out of the fight."

Jupiter snorted. "That's all well and good, but how can you guarantee Ol' Emps won't use our vulnerability for his gain?"

"If we're looking at it in the bleakest sense, then, yes, of course, he'll use you. That's his job as a leader. He won't work against you or undermine you, as that's suicidal in every meaning of the word. Still, he will leverage the technology and connection you give to further the Empire's place in the galaxy," Yan explained, leaning back on her chair.

"So, it's our fault if we get hoodwinked." Jupiter scowled.

"That's not what I'm saying, Jupiter." She snapped her mandibles as she mulled on how to portray her people's leader without disparaging him. "Emperor Jarinn is . . . ambitious and crafty, but he genuinely wants our people to rise. Whether it's out of pure selflessness is something perhaps only the patriarch knows."

"But we're fighting the Starless, the vermin that have terrorized this damn galaxy." Jupiter slapped his palm on the table. "Shouldn't now be the time for pure selflessness?"

"It is, and he knows that. But to him, elevating our nation is no different than helping you, and he'll want to do both. He knows there is no future if the Starless kill us all, but he also knows you need a powerful ally if some galactic hunt breaks out because of your existence."

Yan breathed deeply as she turned to them. "I believe none of you are familiar with the essence of deals, but Lady Andora is, from what I've read of her life before being a gestalt," Yan replied.

The three AI Overseers nodded, listening to the admiral as she went on.

"Both she and our emperor will slowly build trust. After all, neither knows who the other is as a person apart from secondhand reports. Each harvests the benefits for their side." She paused as she slowly balled up her fist. "But each will always strive to squeeze out a bit more."

"And if we build that trust, what then?" Luna asked, adjusting her glasses, intrigued.

Yan buzzed. "That is when an alliance turns into a friendship."

The AIs contemplated in their way, glancing at each other. Yan knew that despite their immense capabilities in fighting, the five fragments of Andora were woefully inept in understanding how civilization worked. She guessed that the Omni Mind of Sol never taught them the complexities of politics, diplomacy, and social engineering.

"You shouldn't overthink it," Yan continued. "You have ships and machines capable of crushing the Imperial Armada. The Citadel's presence alone would hold a solar system hostage. It hurts me to say, but that will keep our emperor honest enough."

"We won't stoop so low as to do that." Mars frowned. "We fight monsters, not people."

"Can you speak for Lady Andora?" Yan challenged. "Is she so righteous and generous to bend to our whim? To not use underhanded methods and manipulate things in her favor?"

Mars grimaced as he looked away. "No . . . likely not."

"Then that is the reality of the situation." Yan rested her hands on the table. "I don't believe your leader would do such a thing, but the possibility exists, and that has to be accounted for."

Jupiter grumbled, "This sounds way too convoluted and inane. Is this how humans and androids did things back then? Give me a battle any day. At least that's simple enough to understand."

"I'm glad we share similar opinions on the matter," Yan chittered. "I'm sure our leaders feel the same way, but you don't have to enjoy something to be competent at it. Lady Andora and Emperor Jarinn are more alike than they realize, and they haven't even met."

"God help us all when they do." Jupiter rolled his eyes, slumping in his chair as he spun around.

He groaned, pinching the bridge of his nose. "Alright, so the idea has merit. But if we achieve a Pyrrhic victory, then we'll need to evacuate regardless."

Yan sighed in relief. "That is good to hear, though I hope it won't come to that. Now, how do we achieve this?"

"Citadel *Irkalla* houses the Eldest's Nexus," Luna replied, pulling up the immense obsidian orb and five similar but much smaller ones. "As for us, it wouldn't be impossible to transfer our Sub-Nexi to our mobile fortresses."

"I have my *Ultimatum*, Luna her *Ozy*, Mars has his *Bucephalus*. Venus and Mercury don't have one, so they'll have to hitch a ride on the *Irkalla*," Jupiter listed, pulling up the respective stations.

"Indeed." Luna nodded. "We can make out the details later, but is there anything that needs to be done now?"

"The Starless will surely harry us every step of the way the moment we leave." Mars crossed his meaty arms. "You mentioned calling for support from outside?"

Yan nodded as she tapped onto the display table.

"There are a handful of Expeditionary Fleets that we can contact to support our exodus," she explained, pulling up the relevant data and profiles. "The Seventeenth, the Thirty-Fourth, and the Forty-Second. They're all part of the Greater Kurskann Hegemony, firmly within our camp, and powerful enough to assist."

The admiral zoomed in on the leaders of each fleet.

Jupiter grimaced at the supposed help, and even Mars appeared doubtful as he cocked his brow.

"Fourth Scion Straise of the Nuwa Family, Commander Nullan Varz of the Koldonian Republic, and Guild Master Oros Fa'Myr of the Free Kurskann Archaeologists," Yan listed them respectively as each Overseer combed through their profiles.

"Each are vetted supporters of the emperor and, more importantly, close friends of Tov, or in the case of Straise, the daughter of one," the admiral explained.

"And their people?" asked Jupiter, rubbing his jaw.

"We can root out any spies within their ranks, by force if necessary if they're incapable of handling it." Admiral Yan snapped her mandibles. "They'll understand."

Luna hummed, looking up from the details of each fleet. "Will they just pack up and leave at your beck and call? I thought Starlight Beacons were a hassle to set up."

"The emperor will have to spend some political favors, but it'll be no problem. He can contact their superiors, appeal to their sense of good." Yan waved her hand. "Still, it'll take weeks for them to reach whatever rally point we decide. That should be enough to get our affairs here in order."

"Alright, we've got a kid, a fossil, and an archaeologist. Sounds like the beginning of a bad joke," Jupiter scoffed, eyeing each leader with doubt. He turned to Yan, his brow raised. "We don't have anyone else on the roster?"

"There is another we can contact," Yan revealed slowly, leaning forward. "He's close enough to meet us halfway back to Legacy space, maybe earlier, if he's committed."

Jupiter frowned. "Who?"

"Mighty Gulothan," Yan replied, causing Jupiter to groan, Mars to smile, and Luna to tilt her head.

"The little rat that tried to psych me out?" Jupiter scowled. "Why him?"

"Out of every power, the Warrior's Enclave has always pushed their complete neutrality in the galaxy. Now, I don't believe that for a second, but what matters is they're not on the best terms with the Dagatar Supremacy," Yan replied.

Luna pressed her lips. "That does not sound reassuring. What can he offer, exactly?"

"He has the most experienced fighters in the galaxy, built on the foundation of dead Starless. Even without our AEB, they can hold their own through sheer mental grit," the admiral answered.

"The Second Expeditionary Fleet also has quality and quantity. And their Teleen battlesuits far surpass our starfighters in flexibility and potency. You can't solve everything with a ship like the *Boogie Mouse*."

Mars grumbled to the side, pouting, but begrudgingly nodded.

"They can meet us along the way and greatly increase our chances of returning to home space," Yan reassured.

"If we ask him for help, there's no way we can hide what we are," Jupiter warned. "We have to extend trust to a stranger."

"Then we must test the waters and see if he's as honorable as he says he is," Yan replied as she mulled her thoughts. She turned to Jupiter with a question.

"Can your Black Sun Obelisk teleport us all? Or do we have to travel the long way?"

Jupiter rubbed his chin, furrowing his brow as he mentally calculated. Yan watched him close his eyes before slowly opening his mouth. "I'll need time to make configurations. Maybe less if we all pitched in. But . . . I can't guarantee its efficacy. I'd advise against it."

"The Starless won't give us time." Mars shook his head. "They won't stop until we're dead."

Yan nodded, her finger on her mandible. "This won't be the last attack. If the reason they're responding so heavily is our presence, then we must leave. This system isn't tenable."

"We realize," Jupiter muttered, the glow of his eyes dimmed as he stared at the image of Earth. "Leaving wasn't a serious option before. We thought we'd spend the rest of our years wasting away, fighting a war of attrition. We've lost four keeping this stalemate going.

"There's only so much scavenging and recycling we can do. The Starless don't show any sign of stopping. Even the manufactories connected to the Dyson swarm can only output so much. There is nothing to do except prolong our deaths. And . . . I was fine with that," he chuckled. "I even put a little surprise in my *Ultimatum*, a big 'fuck you,' if you will."

"And now?" she asked.

"I . . ." Jupiter furrowed his brow, taking a slow breath as he looked at his siblings with a brittle smile, uncertainty etched in his gaze. "I'm not sure."

Yan looked at him, at the person laying his uncertainties bare. She knew what it felt like, an inadequacy that festered, lying in wait, never truly gone.

"It just surprises me every time I see you like this, all of you. You have shown more . . . soul than many people I've met," Yan breathed, calming her emotions as she gazed at her hosts, these people she wanted to protect and fight alongside. "Just know, no matter what, the Third Fleet is with you, always."

The admiral stood and saluted, crossing one pair of arms across her chest in an X, the other spread out like someone breaking their shackles.

With that, the AIs smiled.

"We're doing this, huh?" Jupiter muttered, his face strangely calm.

Yan looked at him, worried about his mental state after exposing his inner thoughts a while ago. "Mars can take your place. The two seemed to resonate as meathead warriors do."

"No, my brother needs to focus on preparing for the main swarm, and I'm partially getting used to this diplomacy thing." Jupiter shook his head, sucking in his teeth. "Let's just get this over with."

"And the idea of . . . leaving? Going into the Dead Zone?" Yan asked, her tone gentle.

Jupiter glanced at her, rubbing his neck. "After losing Neptune and Uranus out there? I'm not sure. We'll take whatever we can bring and leave a lot behind—maybe too much. And if we lose any of our assets on the way, it'll hurt bad."

"Then we'll be careful and gather support. You're not alone, Jupiter," Yan replied.

Jupiter paused before letting out a chuckle. "Despite the danger, is it weird I feel . . . alive?"

Yan looked at the man, shaking her head. "Not at all."

A single beep rang out across the Beacon Room, the immense projector at the center humming to life, vibrating through the walls of the Luna Complex.

"He's here," Yan muttered, straightening her back, clasping her four hands behind her as Jupiter smoothed his suit.

Once more, the projector table erupted in light as a perfect hologram emerged.

Mighty Gulothan appeared before them, looking no different than before with his advanced pilot suit and many scars marring his war-painted fur. He looked at the two of them, revealing his square teeth.

"Well, this is a surprise." The Teleen warrior grinned. "Calling so soon—"

Gulothan paused upon seeing Jupiter's appearance, not in his human disguise but in his usual android shell. The admiral and Overseer hoped such a blatant display would elicit a response. It did; Gulothan frowned and crossed his arms. "You're blue."

"Well, we know he isn't blind," Jupiter muttered. Yan resisted smacking his shoulder.

"I see that snark hasn't changed, Mister Jay Peter. Or I assume you're about to tell me something different." The small alien raised his chin.

"Mighty Gulothan." Yan stepped forward, curtly greeting the fleet leader.

"Admiral, a pleasure," He nodded back with his hands on his hip. "Tov still busy with human leadership? Are you sure he's not having an affair?"

"I'll pretend I didn't hear you question his fidelity," bit back the admiral with a low hiss.

"You're right, my apologies. I don't want to attract Lady Yoram's fury." Gulothan stepped back, raising his hands before clapping them. "Now, what's this all about? I'm a busy Teleen."

Yan noticed a tinge of impatience in his coal-black eyes and looked to Jupiter, giving him the stage. Jupiter nodded as he stepped forward.

"What I'm about to tell you concerns the survival of my people, my family, and maybe the galaxy." Jupiter pressed his lips, his brow furrowed.

"Big claims. And what would that be? Who are you?" Gulothan asked, stepping just a few feet before Jupiter.

"I can't tell you yet. We need assurances," Jupiter answered. The Teleen huffed, and before he could speak, Admiral Yan inserted herself.

"Is your end secure, Mighty Gulothan? We wish for this to be for your ears only. It's a matter of grave importance."

Gulothan tilted his head, humming. After a few seconds of eyeing them both, he relaxed his shoulders. "Fine, you have me curious, and I love a good mystery. Your little display back then tickled the back of my head, and I trust Patriarch Tov's subordinate not to sugarcoat things—or am I wrong?"

"You are not. This has implications that could shake the Legacy," Yan uttered.

The Teleen hummed once more, making a strange clicking sound. Eventually, Gulothan nodded, relenting. "Then nothing said here will leave this room, but I must insist that my second-in-command hear this. She has my full trust. We can end this talk now if you can't accept that."

Jupiter and Yan glanced at each other, conversing silently through their private links before they nodded.

"Very well," Yan answered.

Gulothan smiled, tapping on his wrist tablet.

A few seconds later, the hologram of a Jotex appeared beside the tiny warrior. The floating jellyfish easily outsized others of her race, though she had the same thick, translucent flesh. War paint adorned her body in swirling patterns while bones and trophies hung along with her muscular tendrils.

Yan had only read about the strange individual making the news in the past. A Jotex capable of extreme feats of psionics, more interested in combat than academics. She felt a faint reflection of the Jotex's heavy presence within her mind, despite the distance separating them.

"This is Adept Zhukev, my right hand," Gulothan introduced.

The Jotex nodded, looming over the two before settling by her superior's side. Jupiter and Yan glanced once more at each other, then at the ominous being.

"Good, everyone's acquainted. Now speak, I won't ask twice," Gulothan warned, narrowing his eyes.

Jupiter tightened his jaw before letting go of a long-held breath. "My name is Jupiter. The people you met before were my siblings. What you heard then was true, though some details were left out. Patriarch Tov is unavailable due to circumstances concerning our leader, Andora, and her declining mental health."

"What happened?"

"A war fought too long," Jupiter eluded. "There is one other sibling who wasn't present. But we're all that's left . . . the last of humanity."

Gulothan dropped his arms, his impatience gone in the wind. "Explain."

"We're . . . protectors. A century ago, at the height of humanity's stand against the Starless, Malignant Starfall hit them." Jupiter paused as he closed his eyes for a moment.

Gulothan's expression softened, making a strange gesture and muttering a phrase in an unknown language.

"Are they . . . ?"

"A few survived . . . but mutated. They're kept in an underground citadel on Earth, a hospice facility. Along with the remnants of our culture, history, art, our mark that we existed," Jupiter answered. "We've fought to protect that citadel ever since."

"I see. You have my condolences if it means anything," he told Jupiter. "How can we assist?"

"In the next week, my family and the Third Fleet are making a stand against a massive invasion of Starless, delaying them long enough for our leader to return from her ailment. I'm sending you coordinates to our home and another location I'll explain. Along with other pieces of information we hid during our first discussion."

Within a second, the data packet transferred to the other side. Gulothan paused as he read the intelligence through his implant.

He shook his head regretfully. "It will take too long to reach your home system. We can't aid you in defending against this invasion, as much as I want to."

"Thank you, that's good to hear, but we don't expect you to come to our rescue. After we repel the Starless, we need to evacuate to Legacy space. They won't stop coming after us," clarified Jupiter.

"And why is that?" Gulothan asked with a raised furry brow. "What makes you and yours so important that the hated ones, who haven't been seen in civilized space for close to a century, hunt you down?"

Jupiter paused; Yan watched as he fidgeted in place before quickly suppressing it.

The Teleen spotted it, nevertheless. "You aren't telling me something. In our first meeting, you spoke of a means to fight the Starless despite being in the middle of the Dead Zone with a single system. Now, I hear you and your family are humanity's last protectors, speaking of Malignant Starfall and how it spread across Sol, infecting every human. You—"

Gulothan paused, his eyes widening before narrowing to thin slits.

"Oh . . . Oh, that's it. That's why you called me and not her," he whispered. "It all makes sense. You're . . ."

Jupiter's eyes widened. Yan felt something surge around her, directed toward the Starlight Beacon, like an animal ready to lunge.

"So, what am I, warrior?" asked Jupiter in a frigid voice.

Gulothan tilted his head to Jupiter and his tone. He relaxed his stance, his chin raised as he stepped forward, "A survivor—all of you, as your sister said. And someone who needs help."

Jupiter stared at the warrior, doubt and suspicion in his eyes.

"But if I help you," Gulothan added grimly. "Those who follow me will become pariahs of the Dagatar Supremacy and their entire block."

Jupiter scoffed. "All I keep hearing is how these guys have your Federation by the balls. Are you all that afraid?"

"For myself, no. It's the Creed of the Warrior's Enclave to protect those who can't protect themselves and to slay monsters. That's what my grandfather taught me," he replied with pride in his puffed-up chest.

"But when the Dagatars find out about your secret—and they will." He leaned forward, his frown deep. "Nothing will stop them from attempting to purge your existence and imprison those who helped you. And . . . my organization won't fan the flames of a galactic war. No, not for you. My grandfather will make sure we will stay neutral."

Gulothan shook his head. "So, you see my dilemma. You have my word as a warrior that this conversation never comes to light."

"Bullshit!" Jupiter cursed, stomping toward the Teleen. "That's it? Then, what the hell are we calling you for?"

"You tell me, Jupiter. You're not giving me much to work with," Gulothan retorted, meeting the AI's glare. "I risk turning my followers into outcasts who'll be shunned at best and hunted by fanatics who despise you at worst. So, why should I help you when doing so burns me?"

Jupiter ground his teeth, gnashing them as he clenched and opened his fists. After letting his anger boil, he seethed, "Does a second Cataclysm not worry you?"

Gulothan perked at his words, narrowing his eyes.

"It should," Jupiter hissed, pointing to the ceiling. "The Starless are out there, hiding in the Dead Zone, in whatever dimension they call home, but they're still around."

"Jupiter, wait." Yan moved to place her hand to stop him, but he wrenched away from her grasp.

"We're about to face an invasion we haven't seen in years, without our leader. We're considering abandoning our home and risking being hunted down like animals. All for a slim chance of rebuilding in your part of the galaxy and continuing this crap!" Jupiter shouted and the tables around him flipped over.

"I . . . What do you want? Tech? We can give you that. We have warship designs, weapons of mass destruction, reactors, whatever," Jupiter listed off, his breaths erratic as he shouted at the tiny warrior. "Not fucking enough? Well, we have something to protect against the bastards' psionics; the Third Fleet just humiliated a Dominator with it. You can have it!"

Gulothan stood still at Jupiter's seething tirade, listening.

"Tell me what you want. We can . . ." Jupiter gritted his teeth, his shoulders drooping. "We can't survive out here alone," he admitted. Yan watched as pain engulfed the man's face, twisting as he looked away. "Maybe a few more decades, maybe a week. But we want . . . we *need* out. Even if it means facing a bunch of murderous technophobes."

Jupiter swallowed, his eyes pleading despite his grimace. He stared at Gulothan, lowering his head. "Please, reconsider . . ."

Gulothan rubbed his snout as he peered into Jupiter's eyes, mulling his thoughts as the AI calmed down. Yan wanted to interject, wanted to liaise between the two.

She felt shame for allowing things to get heated. But she didn't have Tov's way with words. She felt inadequate, staying silent as she glanced at the leader of the Second.

The tiny warrior turned to face his right hand, a silent conversation passing between them. After a few seconds, both nodded, turning to meet them.

"Well?" Jupiter asked, his synthetic voice raw.

Gulothan cleared his throat, stroking his furry chin.

And nodded.

"You had us at a second Cataclysm, but if everything else is still on offer, we can consider that payment for our services."

Yan released a breath she held. "Thank you, Mighty Gulothan."

Jupiter blinked before realization set in, causing him to groan and rub his temples.

"Oh, I'm going to punt you the moment I see you," he grumbled. "Did anyone tell you you're a bastard?"

"Once or twice, but running a fleet isn't cheap." Gulothan laughed, deflating the tension that filled the room.

"Meat bag," Jupiter spat, summoning a chair before slumping on it. "And we're negotiating on price later."

Nevertheless, he and Yan sighed in relief when the Teleen's joy turned serious.

"This has consequences that will shake everything." Gulothan glanced at them both, his nose wrinkling. "I must inform my grandfather, no debate. I'm betting he and Emperor Jarinn will have a long conversation . . . a second Cataclysm, Spirits watch over us."

Admiral Yan nodded, having guessed that to be a requirement. "And your followers?"

"We will tell them that you are cyborgs. That should buy enough time. Without the Starlight Beacon, no one will have a chance to squeal," Gulothan reassured.

Jupiter glanced back and forth between him and Yan, his face contorted with uncertainty and a tinge of something else. "So . . . you're going to help us?"

"Ah, I'll do it. Never much cared for the yapping of needle plants," the Teleen spat out the derogatory term.

"You barely know us," Jupiter whispered, his brow furrowed.

"Barely? I know enough," Gulothan clicked repeatedly, patting his belly. "And besides, I made that Mars fellow a promise."

"And how do we know you're being sincere?" Jupiter stepped forward, his eyes unwillingly but slowly breaking down. "I need to know."

Gulothan saw his expression, his cheerful grin turning to a frown as he mulled for a moment. Then, he snapped his fingers. "Zhukev, record this."

The Jotex hummed in question, to which the Teleen nodded. Zhukev left the projection, coming back with, of all things, a quill and paper.

The small Teleen cleared his throat, making different skittering noises and spitting on the floor before finally speaking.

"Right, listen here. Let it be heard in the annals of history. Under the all-seeing eyes of the Spirits, by the rules imposed by the Creed, I, Mighty Gulothan, accept the call for aid levied by the AIs of Sol and the Third Expeditionary Fleet.

"I swear on my life, I and the Brass Armada will help you complete your exodus to Kurskann space. The secret of your true nature will remain between myself and my second-in-command. From this moment forth, I shall keep to the heart of this contract."

Then, Gulothan pulled a sleek mono-edged knife. He removed the glove of his right hand and swiftly cut deep into his palm before showing it to Jupiter and Admiral Yan, both astonished at the action.

"Should I break this vow, I sign my warrant and submit myself to the Warrior's Judgment, taking no less than having my title stripped, a black mark seared into me, and shunned from the Enclave. This, I promise."

Gulothan huffed, allowing Zhukev to approach and wrap a cloth around his wound. The little warrior looked up to them, grinning. "So, was that sincere enough for you?"

Jupiter huffed, exhausted.

CHAPTER 22

WITHERSHINS

A heavy blizzard bombarded an icy hellscape, carrying howling winds and the wailing lament of uncountable dead. Colossal cliffs stretched into the gray sky, a monolithic wall of jagged rock and frost.

At its base, the waves of a frigid ocean lapped against a desolate shore before ebbing, revealing dark pebbles and sand. It moved wearily, as if beaten down by the storm that raged above, crashing against its surface.

Suddenly, three figures appeared from the waves, lying flat on the beach, crawling toward drier land. Their mouths opened and closed, chests and shoulders shaking as their groans went unheard amid the noise of winter's tyranny.

One picked themself up, then rushing to the others, shaking them awake. Soon, huddled together, the trio sought shelter from their bleak surroundings. They stumbled, drenched from head to toe, shivering violently.

One minute flew by, then the next, as the storm sapped their vitality. The wails of anger, regret, and agony demanded, bargained, and begged for respite, sinking their tendrils into the ears of the new arrivals.

Traveling down the gray shore, the head of the trio spotted something in the distance, carved against the immense cliff, where the ocean was a queen that commanded all she touched to give way.

They trudged along the craggy surface, slipping against frozen stone toward the crack in the wall. The trio entered through grit and silent shouts, escaping the terrible blizzard, its snow smothering the land beneath and freezing the weak ocean.

"H-h-hah!" Andora shouted, expelling the ice in her lungs, her voice finally piercing the racket outside, the walls of the small cave shielding her and her companions from the skin-biting storm.

She pulled them in, barely, with her strength sapped and mind aching.

"Come . . . on," Andora huffed, stumbling against the uneven floor, the cruel whips of winter still reaching them, slashing their backs.

"S-s-screw this . . . cold," Echo trembled, teeth chattering. "I . . . preferred . . . the last place."

"I . . . c-concur," Tov stuttered, pulling together his snow-covered clothing, squeezing whatever heat remained. The patriarch pushed himself along, his eyes shut, face red as a rose. "*Dowa!*"

All three marched deeper into their shelter, huddling together as Andora coalesced her authority in this unstable part of her psyche. With a shuddering cry, she slammed her hand down on the stone.

With a loud clap that echoed the walls down to its dark depths, a flash of light illuminated the black rock and ice. A burning bush of blue fire bloomed from the ground, dispelling the frigid prison that enveloped them.

Andora fell back, lying beside the flame as all three sighed with relief. Their shivering bodies gradually eased, their strength returning.

"What . . . the hell . . . was that?" Echo groaned, his head throbbing, squeezed by a press that made his ears ring.

Tov hunched over, nearly throwing himself over the blue flame, the snow on his body and that on Andora and Echo melting into the ground.

"Whatever that was . . . you can't force me out there again." Tov shook his head, rubbing his temple.

Echo chuckled before shutting his eyes, taking in the comfort and warmth their fire gifted them, freeing them from the cruel deity outside. His hands went to his bald head, protecting it from the faint chilly breeze that blew into their cave. "Should have packed a damn fleece cap. Or freaking snow clothes."

"It's all imaginary, friend Echo," Tov groaned beside him.

"It doesn't feel like it," the shade huffed. "And I'm a bundle of data and memory. Or whatever. Maker, it's cold."

"Then don't think about it, I don't know . . ." Tov threw his hands up, breathing in the warmth before slumping to the floor.

Andora listened to her companions, her mind adrift between their words, the cold, and the fire.

Slowly, she dragged herself off the rough ground, sitting up and taking shallow breaths as her dazed mind regained clarity. Andora scowled, thinking back to the events that had led them here—an endless song, a city of marble and dreams, a firefly . . .

She shook her head, teeth gnashing as anger and agony warred against each other, finding equilibrium through her cold body, even the blue heat of the fire failing to penetrate and provide warm relief.

A strangled cry escaped her throat as she hugged her knees.

Her two companions ceased their conversation, sitting up and inching closer to her with worry and concern in their gazes. Andora felt them, sensed their eyes. She wanted to move away, leave, feeling nothing but dread.

She tried to find the energy to resist, yet it felt unnatural, like battling an unshakeable commandment. It fueled her anger, one she had already tamed—or so she thought. Yet all that came out was a whimper.

"Enough!" Andora shouted. Tov and Echo flinched back, but kept hovering over her with those same expressions. She shook her head, her mind delicate and aching as she stood up on shaky legs. "If you're done getting warm, we have an Amygdala to shove back into its box."

She glanced at the cave's entrance far behind and the howling winds that crashed against the cliff. Andora shuddered, looking ahead at the tunnel, snaking downward into the dark.

Tov's hand clasped around her arm, gentle but firm, stopping her in her step. "Andora, are you sure—"

She wrenched her arm from his grasp, turning to glare at him. "What do you want me to do, Tov? Lay here and bawl my eyes out? Tell you all my woes and worries?"

He stared back at her, standing firm as he muttered, "No. As much as I wished it otherwise, we can't wait any longer. But . . . I want you to pace yourself, please."

The patriarch looked at her with those purple eyes, surrounded by a face that had gripped her countless times in a better past. She gritted her teeth as she slowly released her breath, steaming around her.

"It's fine . . ." she whispered, running a hand across her face. "They're all depending on me, and I can't, I won't fail them. I have to keep going. I have to . . ."

Andora glanced at the burning bush before abruptly shoving her hand into the flame, feeling nothing as she pulled a long branch, its tip alight. With a final look of regret at her companions, she walked further into the cave. Behind, Tov and Echo glanced at one another, each taking torches before following her.

"You're not alone, Andora," Tov reminded her. It soothed the ache in her mind, if only a little. She latched on to that feeling, dragging her foot forward, one after another.

The trio made their way through the dark tunnel. Icicles loomed over their heads like lances, and water dripped onto the frozen ground below. They navigated over the slippery stone, planting their feet on whatever dry spots remained, as rare as they were.

Reflected light bounced from the walls as three torches paved the way. Below their knees, a cold mist formed, grasping their legs like shackles, pulling the strength from them.

Deeper they went, Andora feeling for their quarry.

"Silent . . . night . . ."

The siren sang a cry that beckoned them. Here, within its domain, Andora heard its song. In moments, the cold around them thickened, sapping the meager heat of their torches.

Seconds turned to minutes as they trekked, the cave tunnel narrowing, funneling them into a single-file line. A curse nearly escaped her lips as the dark blue ice on either side touched her skin, sending a chill down her spine.

Her free hand balled up into a fist, filled with the intent to smash it against the wall when her eyes widened. Andora gasped, stumbling back, only to hit the other side a foot behind her. She turned around, seeing the same sight hidden behind a layer of ice.

Their torches illuminated the tunnel before them, revealing hundreds of bodies. Lining the sides, floor, and ceiling like a macabre display, countless gaunt figures laid trapped within an icy prison—sprawled, locked in agonized positions, unmoving except for their eyes.

They stretched far into the depths, a corridor of ghosts, victims of their grief.

Faint recollection came to Andora's mind, seeing familiar faces, echoes of siblings who couldn't accept the tragedy that befell them.

A dim glow pierced through their hollow sockets, moving frantically to and fro. Their trauma caged them even now as they sought to escape, reaching for something unseen to descend upon them.

To grant them mercy from their miserable existence.

Arms stuck out of the wall, exposed like gnarled roots—frozen gray, thin, and desiccated. Their hands locked into claws, grasping forth.

Dim eyes begged silently, projecting their desires for an end to this nightmare. A prayer for the dawn. Their gaze bore through the ice, rock, and dirt, searching for a savior.

But at the sound of the trio's gasps and Andora backing into the wall, suddenly, hundreds of eyes turned to stare at the new arrivals.

A pained shudder escaped Andora's lips. Her eyes shut tight as she tried to ignore them.

Andora felt their wide gazes drill into her being—more lethal than bullets, colder than the void, and stripping the layers of self. Her knees buckled as Tov's arms kept her from falling, his words failing to enter her ears, which were consumed by something else.

In the wake of their stares came whispers.

"I . . . I can stop them . . . need . . . need more ammo . . . support . . . Where's my support . . . ? HQ? Please respond . . ."

"One more life . . . let me save one more . . . please . . . I won't lose another . . . !"

"My family . . . friends . . . I can't find them . . . need to find them . . . Where . . . ?"

They spoke to her mind from unmoving mouths trapped in a silent wail, arriving all at once like a rope coiling around her mind.

"Ignore . . . ignore them, push on," Andora muttered with audible strain, forcing the words from her mouth, directing them to herself and her companions.

Step by step, they pushed forth, the tunnel constricting. She pressed her lips tight, shrinking back when a frozen hand twitched ahead.

Andora stopped, watching as more and more arms cracked and stirred, breaking off the layer of ice that covered them. Their bony fingers stretched and curled. Then, to her horror, they began to reach for her.

"Help . . . please, help . . . someone . . ."

"It hurts. Why . . . ? I can't move . . ."

She gritted her teeth, pushing through the bramble of hands as they grasped for her with weak grips.

"Help us . . . Maker . . . Eldest . . . Anyone, please . . ."

Ignoring them soon proved futile. The tunnel of blue ice trapping its victims narrowed more and more, pressing against her. The wretched souls grew in number, packed together in knots like frozen sardines.

"Leave me alone!" Andora cried out with a strangled voice, driving herself deeper into the horrid depths. "I'm trying . . . I'm trying to help. Stop!"

"Please . . ."

The number of hands reaching out rose rapidly, grabbing her clothes and limbs.

A surge of panic filled Andora as she swatted the ghoulish arms away. But as she and her companions pushed, their grips only grew more desperate, begging her not to go, scratching and bruising her skin as the walls closed in around them.

"I can fix this . . ." Andora tried to tell them.

"Please help us," they wailed back.

"I can fix this. Give me time," she pleaded, her eyes welded shut as their hold slowed her down. "I just need time! Please, I . . . can . . . fix this . . . !"

But as time passed, more arms burst from the wall, enveloping her completely. Fingers sunk into her skin. Countless gray hands covered her face until only her blue eyes remained visible.

Hers matched the expressions of the prisoners that held her so, as in unison they demanded—

"PLEASE HELP US."

"Stay away!" Andora shrieked, mad panic rushing into her mind as her knees buckled. She screamed and roared like a cornered animal, flailing as she tried to escape the shackles tightening around her. She leveraged the strength in her limbs, wrenching her arms and legs from these anguished ghosts.

Only for more to take their place.

As she struggled, slowly losing herself and tears welling up in her eyes, a heavy force pushed her from behind, knocking her forward and freeing her from their clutches.

Then, two hands grasped her shoulders. She felt a surge of panic when she realized they felt warm, gentle, and firm.

"Andora, listen to me!"

A voice pierced through the racket around her, full of urgency. The warm hands pushed her, guiding her through the funneling cave. Now and then, they would swat away those decayed ones that reached out.

"I'm right behind you. You can do this. Focus. Focus!"

"Ri . . . Rikard?" Andora barely whispered with her raw, glitched voice as she forced herself through the obstacles.

"There, an opening ahead. Push on, Andora!"

He spoke into her ear, loving, comforting, filling her with vitality and energy. Her limbs woke up, propelling her forward.

"We're almost there. Just listen to my voice."

She breathed out. Her eyes focused down the tunnel, finally seeing a light at the end, faint, beckoning them. With a strangled cry, she sprinted forward, leaping past the crack in the wall.

And into a vast cavern.

Andora tumbled head over heels, spotting the dark pool below. She plunged through the surface and sank into the frigid waters before instinctively kicking her legs, taking her up.

Small waves rippled outward from where she emerged, the only disturbance within this secret underground space. She gasped for breath, panting, sore.

Blinking stinging droplets from her lashes, Andora swiveled her head, taking in her surroundings.

An enormous cavern opened around her, its towering ceiling fading into gloom far overhead. Decayed moss and fungi clung to the stone shores while crystalline ice emitted a pale blue glow, barely illuminating the underground basin.

She swam forward, finding purchase for her feet to stand upon. Finally, she felt the lake's bed, using it to drive her forward.

Slowly, she rose as the bed sloped upward until the water barely reached her shins. Andora shivered, rubbing her bruised and scratched arms, her head spiked with adrenaline as she scanned her surroundings.

Two splashes echoed behind her. She turned to face, her heart racing as she eagerly awaited—

Purple eyes broke from the surface. Tov gasped for breath as he swam toward her. Echo emerged quickly following.

Andora watched as they found their footing, rising from the lake before her. Her face scrunched up as she backed away. The two panted, looking worse for wear with their damaged clothes.

"What?" she asked, confused. "But I heard . . . Where is . . ." Andora paused, looking away as her hands crawled up her face to press against her temples. She shuddered, releasing a hollow chuckle. "Oh . . . Of course . . ."

Tov looked at her with a raised brow, panting as he touched her shoulder. "Andora?"

She looked up to meet his gaze, full of concern compared to the agony that slashed inside hers. Behind him, Echo looked at them both with pity.

"I'm sorry, I thought . . ."

Andora pulled away from Tov, shaking her head as she took a deep breath, centering her thoughts. "I'm good . . . Thank you, Tov. Was that . . . Was that you? Back there?"

The patriarch nodded, smiling while wearing her lover's face, unknowingly matching that same warm expression.

"I see . . ." Andora whispered, turning her back on her companion, disappointment and relief pushing against each other.

The trio moved forward, taking a closer look at where they stood.

Andora scanned the flat surface that stretched before her, a foot in depth, like an underwater plateau surrounded by abyssal waters.

Far ahead, past a thin mist, she saw a small, unmoving shape beneath a ray of moonlight.

"There you are," she whispered, taking a step forward. Behind her, Tov and Echo followed close, their eyes locked on their target as they drew nearer.

"Holy . . . night . . ."

And from that object, Andora heard that pervasive siren's call that had plagued her since they came, a song she'd sung so often under a warm fireplace while a gentle snow fell outside. Before, her heart swelled with joy and contentment, singing it for her love and daughter.

". . . is calm . . . all is . . . bright . . ."

Now, it had latched on to her mind, trying to drag her into the ocean and drown her in grief, hearing its glitched lyrics.

"Round . . . mother . . . and child . . ."

Silence filled the cavern, broken only by a gurgling noise attempting to bear a lamenting song.

"Sleep . . . in heavenly . . . peace . . ."

Andora quickened her pace, her addled mind disoriented as memories she'd long suppressed seeped to the forefront of her thoughts.

She barely glanced at the lakebed she walked on, which was becoming illuminated as they drew closer.

Tov halted briefly, seeing not stone or sand but bone and rotting flesh. To his horror, the heads of the decayed corpses moved ever so slightly, their jaws opening and closing. Neck muscles strained to lift themselves, as if the ghouls sought breath.

Their eyes were empty, and Tov peered into their black depths, wondering what tortured souls lay within, unable to breathe and see the world.

Ahead, the figure came into shape. Andora squinted her eyes at the source of the song.

She looked at the thing with mixed emotions. Anger, pity, sympathy, resentment, and shame warred within her.

The manifestation of her gestalt suffering took her appearance, a bare android shell, wires jutting out, synthetic flesh flaking off, exposing its metal structure below—her first body, the one where she came to life, kneeling before her in a damaged state.

The Amygdala was posed with its head slightly low, drooping—mouth slightly open. Frozen moss and fronds of pale algae encrusted its broken body.

One arm reached up above; the wrist had fractured away. The other was barely a stub on drooping shoulders. The Amygdala knelt upon jagged knees as if unable to support itself. Andora saw nothing but gnarled legs past that.

"Sleep in heavenly peace . . ."

She heard it again, coming from a glitched voice box in its throat, that sad song echoing like a beacon.

"Silent . . ."

Andora reached down with her hand, finding the small device where a human's larynx would be, and slowly detached it.

"Holy—"

Silence, pure silence, free from clamor and woe.

Andora breathed, savoring the quiet, as her emotions settled and the weight on her shoulders slowly disappeared. She opened her eyes, looking at the damaged Amygdala, kneeling still. Its handless arm reached out to the light above.

"It's not your time to come out . . ." Andora whispered. "You're too much."

She raised her palm toward the Amygdala's face, breathing slowly, hesitating before her eyes hardened. "Once we finish this, I can deal with you properly. I promise we can—"

"And when will that be?"

Andora started as she looked at the broken android and the voice box in her hand. She blinked, shaking her head as she crushed the device.

Yet the sound came back still, coming from within the damaged body.

"I ask again, Andora. Elskan. Eldest. Gestalt," the Amygdala spoke with clarity that belied its decrepit state.

"When?" it asked, the question ringing out.

Andora opened her mouth before gritting her teeth, her eyes twitching as she stomped forward with a tight jaw.

"When this war is over," she stated, raising her palm. "Now enough, don't make this any—"

"Will it?" the Amygdala pushed. Within the dark sockets of the android, two glowing blue eyes activated, staring up at her.

Andora stepped back, the creature peering into her with cynicism. "What?"

"You've never thought that far," it uttered. *"At some point, you realized this war against the Starless was futile. Yet you keep going. Killing more until you run out of bullets, until you die biting and clawing, dragging one more down before oblivion."*

The Amygdala's eyes drifted down, looking at the bodies beneath the water. *"The war being over meant our death."*

"What of it? Better that than lying down and taking it," Andora hissed, waving it off. "And I've made plans for otherwise."

"Oh yes, I know . . ." it replied, snow falling from its shoulders like a shrug. *"But your escape plan was an afterthought, cobbled together for its sake, labeled a final contingency. You never believed in it. And yet, at this very moment, your fragments are already taking the steps while they battle outside."*

"I . . . What else should I have thought? I never . . ." Andora snarled, shaking her head as she glared at the Amygdala. "It was a hopeless dream at the time. But there's hope now. We have allies, people that can support us. With them, we have a chance to go on the offensive. We can win."

"What then?" Its neck cracked, metal falling off as it tilted its head. *"Should you succeed, what then?"*

Andora clenched her fists, trying to see that day in her mind as she answered. "We can . . . We can provide a home for the Starfallen humans while a cure is being researched. Find a world for them, nurture a new generation from the DNA I've safeguarded. Rebuild what we lost."

The Amygdala paused, a strange hum leaving its throat.

"And us? You?" it asked.

Andora hissed, looming. "As I said, I'll handle it once the war ends. That's why I need you in your box where you can't pull more of my—"

"You will crash and burn," it retorted. *"This is a temporary fix, barely better than your self-lobotomization."*

"And who are you to criticize me?" Andora shouted, stooping down and grasping the Amygdala's shoulders, denting the soft metal. "What do you contribute? The previous corruption at least supplied me with hate and fire, something I can use to kill more Starless. All you've done is drag me down."

The Amygdala looked back, staring at her with pity. *"No one else can find your faults more so than yourself. Broken, held together by glue and a desire for retribution— filled with unfulfilled promises. Hoping one day you can rectify it all."*

"I can." Andora stood up, chin raised high as she seethed. "And I will. I am a gestalt AI, a few steps away from a true Singularity. I hope because I know I can do it, maybe not tomorrow, or in a thousand years. But one day, I will fulfill my promise."

A sigh escaped the android shell, its head shaking. *"You delay, deny, and push everything back like a loaded spring. And when that day comes, when you've hit your limit, nothing can stop its release, and you'll plunge yourself over the edge."*

"No . . . no, I refuse that outcome. I am not so weak. I AM NOT!" Andora shouted before tightening her jaw and hissing, "Everything will be fixed. Then, no one will call me broken anymore, especially not you. People are helping me now . . . people who can understand me. Tov promised to—"

"And what of him?" the Amygdala interrupted, tilting its head to look behind her. *"Have you told him?"*

Her heart stopped; her eyes widened as her hands shot out to cover the android's mouth, her grip abruptly crushing its face.

"Stop," she hissed, panic and fear pouring from her. "Don't."

"Andora?" Tov asked behind her. She turned to look at him, his furrowed brow and confused look. "Tell me what?"

Andora gritted her teeth, her emotions in turmoil as she shut her eyes, a manic chuckle escaping as she shook her head. "Tov, it's nothing, it's nothing. Please, I . . . I'll tell you later, I'll—"

Yet the hand covering the Amygdala's mouth did nothing to halt its voice as it echoed across the cavern.

"You, dear patriarch, wear the face of the man who holds our heart."

CHAPTER 23

HEART VICE

Andora slapped the Amygdala across the face, the loud clap echoing across the cavern, rippling the water beneath them. Bits of metal and synthetic flesh spiraled in an arc before plopping into the lake.

She seethed, eyes full of shock and hate, glaring at the decrepit shell and gripping its hair.

"Why would you say that!" yelled Andora as she raised her hand again, only to be stopped by parting waves behind her. She looked back, seeing Tov move toward her.

"I'm wearing the face of . . . who?" Tov asked. His brow furrowed, purple eyes staring at his hands and then at her.

Behind him, Echo bit back a curse, his face twisting in a myriad of emotions as he looked between them. The shade shook his head, then took a step back.

"Andora," Tov called out to her, his voice calm yet firm. "What did you do?"

She turned to face him, letting go of the Amygdala, speaking with a raspy voice, "Tov, wait. I can explain."

He remained quiet, his brow furrowed. Andora's mind raced, formulating words to express the jumble of emotions and reasons. She stuttered, eyes frantically looking away, trying to avoid his stare.

Tov stopped a short distance from her, yet she stepped back regardless.

"I didn't mean to," she began with a pained whisper. "I . . . you have to understand, it was on impulse."

Tov shook his head, his lips pressed into a thin line as he looked at his reflection in the water. "You could . . . should have told me, Andora."

"I wanted to. I did. But I . . . I thought you'd . . . I didn't know how you'd react. I didn't know what to do, and it just kept going, and I kept putting it off," Andora confessed, shuddering.

"It was never about the disguise, was it?" Tov asked, his eyes shut.

Andora stepped forward, her hand reaching out to him. "Tov, please, I didn't mean—"

He stepped back. Andora halted in her step as her face scrunched up at seeing the simple action. Searing shame and hurt lancing her very being.

"This is wrong. I . . ." Tov whispered, looking at her with unease. "Take it off, please. I can't speak like this."

Andora's eyes widened and, without hesitation, swiped with her hand. Immediately, the body and face of the man she loved melted away—dripping, spreading across the water before disappearing entirely.

Distant pain, a hidden memory, brushed against her mind at the sight. She gritted her teeth in pain, shaking it away.

Tov looked back to his actual hands, with their clawed tips and dark chitin. His reflection showed his patriarch's uniform, white setae, compound eyes, and antennae. A bit of relief washed over the Kurskann.

He turned to face her, his mandibles opening slightly as he put together his thoughts.

"What am I to you?" he asked, hesitant. "Is the reason I'm here because . . . what, you saw your creator in me?"

Andora winced, stepping back as her body shook. "I didn't . . ."

"Am I supposed to replace him? Is that what you see in me?" Tov asked, trying to keep his tone even. "Andora, I have a wife and a child."

She tried to keep it together, biting her lip until it bled. Nevertheless, all Andora heard was an accusation piercing her ears.

Her head snapped to face him with a glare. "So, what if I did? You have his kindness and strength, that quiet curiosity and protectiveness . . . You just needed his face, his voice . . . and I . . . I thought."

Andora paused, her words shaky, raking her throat. Her fire snuffed out as she hung her head.

"You have no idea how alone I've been . . . I just wanted to see him—to dream for a moment," she whispered as a tear fell. It splashed heavily against the water, like a stone making waves throughout the underground lake. "Wanted to feel . . ."

"I want to help you, Andora. Above anything else, at this moment, you need help. But not like this. This isn't healthy," said Tov.

Hollow chuckles leaked out of her as she fell to her knees, her mind unraveling at the seams. All around them, the lake rippled, and an ominous hum emanated from its depths.

"I . . ." Andora spoke as quakes rocked the cavern.

Dust and stone fell from the high ceiling into the depths below. The ground beneath her and the Amygdala rose, leaving the confines of the lake, water cascading down.

"Andora!" Tov called out as he and Echo rushed to her. She barely registered their voices as she tried and failed to stand. She looked at them, mouthing an apology.

Tov and Echo disappeared, washed away by the roiling waves, unable to reach her in time as the ground she stood on climbed higher and higher.

It stopped, appearing like a monolithic tower of stone and corpses amid a dark lake. Andora stood at its top, high above in the middle of the cavern.

She looked to the Amygdala, scowling and seething. "Are you happy now? What more could you possibly want?"

The android shell twitched, its head swiveling to stare at her with a hollow gaze. *"Happiness . . . I haven't felt such a thing in so long. Neither have you."*

"I have the right to be happy," Andora hissed, picking herself up from the platform of fused bodies above the depths below. "You don't decide anything."

The Amygdala's neck creaked as it slowly shook its head. *"It does not excuse what you've done. Projecting your loss onto him."*

"Be quiet," Andora demanded, her hand shooting out to grab it.

"You have the right. But are you happy with what you did?" it replied.

Andora snarled, her hands gripping both sides of the android's head, shouting in its face. "I said, be quiet!"

Its eyes stared back at her, cold, detached. *"Why must I? You never listen either way. If you wish it so, then make me. I'm sure you can do it. Isn't that what you always say?"*

"Don't test me," she seethed, squeezing its head. "Do not . . ."

"So powerful, so intelligent, the gestalt Omni Mind of Sol," it bit back, its voice flat. *"You've bent gravity to your will, created singularity bombs, and slaughtered billions of vermin. You wear that mask, going about your days in hell as if bargaining for the higher power that you believe yourself to be."*

An enraged scream escaped Andora's throat, her fingers piercing the soft skin and metal of the Amygdala's head. "I'll show you a higher power!"

With a violent pull, Andora wrenched the head from its body. A loud grating and shearing noise echoed throughout the cavern as the rest of the android fell to the floor. She breathed heavily, staring at the head in her hands.

Its eyes were dark, and for a moment, Andora felt panic and regret at what she'd done, only to be suppressed as a glow reemerged.

"An impulsive, emotional creature you are. You pride yourself as being above humans, untethered by such things. And yet here you are, being led by it on a leash," it uttered

with a glitched, crackling voice. *"No different, worse even. With no excuses such as chemical reactions and instinct to hide behind."*

Andora threw the head to the floor, stepping back. It bounced once, then twice before rolling a distance away, speaking still. *"It pushes you to your goals. That one day, one day, you can succeed. To fulfill the promise at all costs."*

Pain lanced Andora's head, her hands clutching her sides. A guttural groan escaped her chest as she stumbled back. She shuddered, forcing the words out. "It . . . doesn't control me. I . . ."

She gritted her teeth as pain constrained her words.

At that moment, rock fused with the undying corpses of the damned stirred beneath the head. Several arms broke free from its confines, grasping the Amygdala like one holding a fragile vase. The android's head rode the waves of hands as they passed it from one to the next until finally reaching its body.

With a crackle, it spoke once more.

"By your will, the seas and lands of Earth shall heal. Mother Nature shall bloom and call her fauna and flora to return. On that day, man and machine shall be reimbursed for their suffering and once more repopulate the world."

The Amygdala closed her eyes as, with precise motions, the hands carefully inserted the head back into place before enveloping the android shell within its embrace.

Black tears streamed down its cheeks, falling to the wet ground. *"And finally, you can be together with them. Hear Rikard's violin on a moonlit night while our Lucy chases fireflies on a field of daisies. And everything shall be good."*

Andora snarled through the pain, pointing her finger at the Amygdala. "Is that so wrong? Is that not a dream worth striving for? They didn't deserve any of this."

"Perhaps not. I yearn for that, too. A dream perched atop an impossibly high mountain. But the path you take to reach it blinds you to the harm you've left on yourself."

Andora stared back, furrowing her brows. "What are you talking about?"

"Love can be excruciating," it answered, staring back with piercing blues. *"It hurts you."*

"That's a load of rot. How can my love for Lucy and Rikard hurt me?" demanded Andora.

It shook its head, sighing. *"He was your creator."*

"And? What of it?" Andora shouted, her eye twitching as she stomped toward the Amygdala. "So, what if he created me? You are not the first to tell me that. I have free will, and I chose him."

"You loved him too much, such that it became an obsession," it retorted.

Andora scoffed, her words shaky as she looked away. "I was not obsessed."

"He saw you as his creation and far from a potential lover. He didn't even know what you were capable of, what you thought. Neither you nor he saw yourselves that way. Not at first."

From the ground before the Amygdala, rock rose and formed into a miniature statue—one of a man and an android dancing in each other's arms.

"And yet along the way, from the isolation of being hidden from the world, your dependence on his guidance and care, your affection turned to utter devotion."

The models of her and Rikard stopped, looking into each other's eyes, when the Andora figurine threw herself into his arms, embracing him tightly.

"You felt fear for the first time, afraid of losing an anchor, someone you trusted completely. And your dogged pursuance changed that dynamic, believing it would prevent that."

Andora watched as the statue of Rikard looked anxious, gently pushing her away, only to be met with resistance, fear, and confusion.

"How did he react at first? Realizing his unassuming, simple affections only fueled your feelings for him?"

As her statue continued to latch on to him, his motions became frantic and worried, his mouth moving.

"Shame, horror, regret."

Andora looked away as the statues crumbled to the ground. She bit her lip as the memories of that painful day burned her heart. "I didn't understand, I thought . . . I thought he didn't want me."

"It hurt—another first. Yet, instead of backing off, you remained stubborn. Confused, greedy, and angry, you doubted his rejection. And, in time, afraid of alienating you, he relented," the Amygdala uttered, every word slamming into her head like hammers, judging the evidence laid bare.

"We . . . we knew it wasn't healthy." Andora shut her eyes, shrinking back as she raised her voice, keeping it firm. "We weren't dull. We tried to make it work, and we did. We became partners. We supported each other. We reached parity."

"Did you truly?" it asked, cocking its head to the side.

"What do you want me to say?" Andora retorted with a shout. "That what we had was . . . wrong? Because I won't renounce what I felt for him, never. Devotion, affection, dependence, call it what you want, people accused me of so much worse."

The Amygdala narrowed its eyes, shaking its head as the arms enveloping it slid away. With unsteady steps, it rose high, looming over Andora. *"That is your collar, and you don't even see it. You've become a slave to the ideal that was our Maker."*

"I am a slave to no one!" Andora shrieked, her voice rattling the tower, stomping forward until they were face-to-face. "He was never some master that lorded over me. He was so much more than just my creator. He was—"

"He was your god."

"He was a man!" Andora shouted, shoving the Amygdala back. "A good man! And someone who truly wanted what was best for me. Someone who taught me how to paint, and sing, and enjoy life fully."

She shuddered, the memories of bliss, contentment, and warmth filling her vision and mind. "It wasn't perfect, but I gave my heart to him anyway, and he gave his. And then I . . . I wanted more . . . I envied human women, and I wanted what they had. To be a mother, to share a child with him."

Another set of memories arrived, this time of their adopted daughter. The image of her smile, her innocent smile. The sound of her laughter as Andora and Rikard taught her how to ride a bike. The sounds of delight as she tasted ice cream. Her soft breaths as she slept in her arms.

"We found Lucy, the sweetest young girl in the world," Andora sighed, smiling at the recollection. "She was so shy when we met, but also curious, bright, and gentle. Our Lucy . . . our—"

"*Our little firefly,*" the Amygdala finished, its tone and gazed softer as it looked to the sky. "*She was good for you both. She brought balance, brought joy.*"

Andora closed her eyes as she nodded, whispering, "We noticed that things between Rikard and I became . . . clearer, more stable. We focused more on her than each other. Spending time giving her the best childhood that her first parents failed to. Focused on being her guides, friends . . . her family."

"*A time you both desperately needed. You wanted to protect that,*" the Amygdala agreed.

Andora stared at the Amygdala, her eyes narrowing. "What mother wouldn't?"

"*Your thoughts went beyond protection. It bordered paranoia,*" it warned.

"What. Mother. Wouldn't?" Andora demanded, harsher this time as a surge of protectiveness and fire straightened her back.

The Amygdala remained undeterred, retorting, "*A mother wouldn't want to turn Rikard into some immortal king. If you had your way, you would turn Lucy into a princess none could touch. Offering them the universe, a palace in the stars.*"

"I wanted what's best for us. I wanted them to be happy," Andora scoffed, glaring back.

"*By what means? What were you willing to build that palace with?*"

"Whatever it took," Andora snarled before shaking her head. "But I knew they wouldn't wish for such a thing. They just wanted us to enjoy life and the simple moments together. I saw nothing wrong with granting what they wanted. And I loved them for it, was content with it, respected it, and never broached the topic again."

"*Perhaps, yet you were still willing to do so at a moment's notice. All they had to do was say so.*"

Andora huffed, opening her mouth to retort when nothing came. She bit her lip.

"And you lie," it accused. *"Did you not undermine Rikard's rivals behind his back? Sabotage possible obstacles to his becoming leader of a business empire?"*

"They deserved it," Andora answered with a sneer. "And we needed capital, influence, power. My siblings needed strong backing. It was the only way."

"And when the critics came, when those who feared you clamored at your doorstep, protesting your existence, your rise as a people, you turned the other cheek, sought compromise."

"People are dumb. As long as they only barked, it was best to ignore them." Andora crossed her arms.

The glow of the Amygdala's eyes burned harsher, narrowing to thin slits. *"But as soon as their anger turned to him, to your relationship, to Lucy, you secretly sabotaged their lives without mercy."*

"Rikard and Lucy were innocent . . . those people had no right saying those things," Andora argued.

"No right to speech? Wasn't that something you fought for your siblings to have?" it asked.

Andora pressed her lips into a thin line, gritting her teeth. "I . . ."

"And so, the truth of it all," it declared. *"You never loved all of humanity."*

The accusation slammed her across the face, and Andora almost lunged forward when it continued.

"Don't deny it. You know it in your heart. Without the influence of your siblings infecting your gestalt mind with their love for their humans. When it was just you, just Andora."

It walked forward. *"You loved some humans enough to consider them close, even family. You loved our Maker, and you loved Lucy. But not all humans. You were indifferent to many, disliked some, utterly hated a few."*

"They're . . . not perfect, but they had potential, had beauty and grace," Andora countered. "Rikard taught me that, and we taught my siblings the same. I cared for them—for humanity."

"But not loved."

Andora replied with silence, her face twisting at the accusation, and in truth, she couldn't refute it.

"What is the point of this?" she asked, weary as she looked at the Amygdala. The broken android stared back at her, silent for a few moments. "What do you want?"

"I . . . want what you want. I am grief, yours, theirs," it responded eventually, looking to the shades below them. *"You lost those you cherished and the warmth they provided. Now, it's all you crave. What I crave."*

"Then go back to your box," Andora begged. "Please."

It shook its head, its eyes going dark as it fell to its knees, sinking into the platform. *"You mistake me, Gestalt. I wish only for you to continue. I want to drive you further into the abyss, far, far, far, far away to the other side. And there . . . maybe . . . we can finally see them again."*

The tower shook, cracking as the ground beneath started to flow. Slowly, the corpses woke, dragging their bodies, and the stone fused with them, toward the Amygdala.

"So much has been sacrificed in the promise. So many in me trying to get back what they had. Willing to do anything. Just for one more day to kill more. And more. And more until we finally die. A suicide note masquerading as a love letter."

Andora watched as it transformed, molding, reforming as more mass piled atop each other. Hands upon hands, linked together like armor.

"Love. Death. Believing one leads to the other."

The amalgamation of metal, rock, and bodies rose above—a monstrous thing with multiple tendrils of groaning dead. At its apex, the Amygdala gazed down at her. *"I wonder. What more can we sacrifice for this addiction of ours?"*

Andora looked at the Amygdala, the platform around her falling apart as one of its writhing limbs reached out to her.

"You've festered here for too long . . . Tov wanted to break you down piece by piece, heal naturally," whispered Andora, shutting her eyes. "No more," she declared, taking a deep breath. Opening her eyes, she stared back at the Amygdala with a cold, tired gaze.

"What more will I sacrifice?" She raised her palm, and a wave of force pulsed out, pushing back the tendril before it reached her. "I can answer that."

CHAPTER 24

REALITY CHECK

Boulders crashed into the water below as the cavern rumbled. Two figures rose from the icy depths, gasping for breath, after being washed away by the sudden rise of the monolith—its ascent heralded by ominous vibrations.

The patriarch coughed after breaking the surface, his mind in turmoil after experiencing the shock of what Andora had done. He wanted to sit down and think about it, to speak with her further and understand why she did what she did.

He knew, if only a little, of what suffering she'd crawled through in the past century—alone and beset by an unending enemy. A foe that had caused the worst tragedy in human history, the death of billions, and the survivors agonizing behind pods, transformed beyond recognition from isolation and war.

"Hey, bug man," Echo called, pointing toward the tower's base.

An extensive shore had been brought up, made of black stone and sand. It wrapped around the monolith, surrounded by the rough waves of the underground lake. He and Echo glanced at each other before dragging their legs through the water.

They increased their pace. Tov heard traces of the heated conversation high at the top between Andora and the Amygdala. He shuddered, feeling the residual pulses of emotion that washed over him. His meager psionic senses tasted the palpable grief, anger, and sorrow.

A sense of dread tickled his mind, thinking of the possible outcomes of facing one's fears and insecurities.

"Echo, we can't allow Andora to delete the Amygdala," Tov pressed, his mandibles snapping as he gazed above.

The shade of Erwin turned to look at him with wide eyes. He mouthed a silent curse, grimacing. "Do you think she'd go so far?"

Tov nodded, feeling the increasing volatility flaring from the tower's peak.

"Damnit, sis," Echo muttered as they both increased their stride. "If that happens, she'll actually lobotomize herself. I can feel it. It's grown too large."

"How bad do you think it will be if she has her way?" Tov asked with mounting dread.

Echo tsked as he replied, "It'll ruin her. The Amygdala has latched on to too many emotions. Once those get damaged, she'll be forced to purge everything. Then, it'll cascade from there, and we'll be left with an unfeeling murder AI."

"Symphony above," Tov breathed out, shaking his head.

"Better pray hard, buddy." Echo scowled as he glanced toward him with a worried look only a sibling would have for another. "What should we do?"

"We have to hurry," Tov urged, pushing through the waves and slowly rising from the water's clutches onto the shore.

Up close, the tower loomed over them, several stories high, its base as thick as a building. To their apprehension, countless shades stuck out of the structure, holding onto the jagged rocks or simply hanging limply.

The two walked forward, doubt filling their minds as they craned their necks.

"Right there with you, but that's a long way up." Echo frowned, running his hand over his bald head. "Well, might as well get—oh, you are kidding me."

Echo growled in frustration as he turned to the lake behind them. Tov instantly spun around and spotted the shapes slowly emerging from the dark abyss.

Shambling shades walked with shaky knees, heading toward them with hanging jaws and waterlogged limbs. Whimpering groans leaked from the holes in their gray flesh as they trudged on, hollow sockets staring back at them.

First, one slowly rose from the water, then a dozen, then dozens more.

Amid their groaning, Tov heard their muffled speech.

"Help . . . us . . ."

"Hurts, it hurts . . ."

"Please . . . I can't find them . . ."

The duo stepped back as the shambling shades, victims of their prisons, increased in numbers. They reached out with thin arms and bony hands, pleading for a savior.

Tov stumbled in his step, feeling a grip around his ankle. He saw a hand barely above the ground, latching onto him. He quickly wrenched from its grasp, scanning the shore and seeing the sand give way to more buried shades, like the dead rising from their graves.

"Alright, we can't hurt these guys," Echo gritted his teeth as they backed further away.

"Tell that to them. We can't get stuck here," Tov pushed, turning back to the tower and sprinting toward it. Echo quickly followed, avoiding the rising shades, dodging their reaching grasps.

They soon arrived at its base, feeling the rock before them and testing their grips.

"Time to climb, then. I never much enjoyed the sport. Well, Erwin never did. I might . . . Forget it." Echo shook his head, pulling himself up.

The patriarch stepped back, much to his companion's befuddlement. Echo opened his mouth to tell him to hurry up when, behind Tov's back, a pair of insectoid wings unfurled, thin and transparent.

They beat once, then twice before flapping rapidly.

"You can fly?" Echo asked incredulously.

Tov chittered, shaking his head. "No, unfortunately. It's mostly decorative, but I can jump higher with them. I'll see you there."

With the salute of his people, Tov leaped vertically, passing Echo before landing a few meters higher.

The Kurskann leader gripped the rough wall. His sharp claws, tipped with a black sheen like obsidian, quickly sunk into the stone and expertly shimmied up the tower.

Echo watched agape, frozen only a few feet off the base as Tov rose like a winged spider monkey, using his wings more as a balancing tool than a means of flight. His four arms assisted him immensely, speeding his ascent.

"That's not fair at all," Echo grumbled. "Damn it, I'm not going to be shown up by an alien, hell no!"

With a burst of power from his legs and arms, Echo quickly followed along.

He utilized his digital mind to assess the vertical terrain and find the most efficient path. He would take a precarious leap, appearing to almost fall when he latched on to a barely visible crack with only a few fingers.

The duo rose higher, avoiding the protruding arms that sought to halt their advance.

Above, Tov heard a rumbling sound and saw the corpses at the peak escape their rocky confines and clamber onto the platform. Large pieces of stone fell toward him, and with quick reflexes honed through a century of training and decades of combat experience, the patriarch easily dodged the falling rocks without sacrificing his progress.

Echo did much the same, unimpeded.

Soon, the duo would reach the top. Tov's intuition screamed danger, his setae flaring. He heard the sounds of battle, slamming, smashing apart the platform beyond, propelling chunks over the edge. He heard Andora's shouts of rage and the Amygdala's cry.

All his doubts, his thoughts on Andora's actions and her deception, paled in comparison to saving her life. "Hold on, Andora. Symphony, hold on."

Andora grimaced as she somersaulted over a tendril swiping across the platform. She landed in a roll onto her feet, then quickly weaved to the side as the second limb whipped toward her.

"Sacrifice me? Is that wise?" the Amygdala asked with its rapidly deteriorating, ethereal, and mad voice. The abomination of clumped-up code, memory, and corrupted data took the shape of a giant centipede atop a mound of bodies. From there, seven tendrils, each composed of countless arms interlocked with each other, writhed as it moved the abomination forward.

Thousands of faces embedded in the monster wailed in pain, looking up at the ceiling as their arms reached for Andora.

The Amygdala's broken android body, with everything below the waist subsumed by the amalgamation of stone and corpses, twitched as it raised a stump, pointing toward her.

Another tendril lifted off the ground like a snake ready to strike.

It undulated, the fingers moving like hairs, coiling up like a spring. In an instant, it fired off toward her. Andora gritted her teeth, leaping away only to stumble as a hand burst from the ground and grabbed her ankle.

She snarled, infusing her palm with force of will and packets of deletion commands. Andora slapped the immense tendril aside. The point of contact annihilated into a red mist of numbers before evaporating.

"It'll give me quiet," Andora replied, wrenching her foot from the hand that grasped it.

Strange sounds like groaning and whimpering leaked from the Amygdala. *"A short-lived victory, just another to add to the list of actions that delay the inevitable."*

"Then why go on?" Andora demanded, sprinting in a circle around the Amygdala, dodging and sliding away from its attacks. "Why do this?"

"What else is there?" it answered, closing its eyes.

Andora pressed her lips tight. "You'll run us to the ground. You're insane."

"*I am Grief. I am Want."*

Four tendrils rushed toward her. Andora widened her eyes as she dodged the first and batted away two more, but the final one slammed into her gut, knocking her to the ground. The limb of limbs slithered toward her, its many hands gripping her leg and pulling.

"In all its facets, a crusader against truth."

Andora shouted as she was lifted off the ground and thrown toward the edge. She tumbled, rolling repeatedly, trying to get a grip on the floor to halt her momentum. Just before she plummeted to the lake below, she managed to do so, latching on to a bit of jagged rock.

Andora breathed heavily as she stood up, glaring at the Amygdala.

Its android body spread its broken arms as the beast rose, the seven tendrils dragging it forward. *"And when you beheld truth in all its painful glory, you resorted to locking away our memories, fragmenting your mind into Overseers. Then you turned to dark hobbies, torturing the beasts that brought your paradise low."*

"They deserve worse," Andora seethed as she moved away from the edge.

It cocked its head to the side. *"And how many have you tortured over the century?"*

"How many fed your horrid vice?"

"How many failed to fill that void in your heart?"

It attacked again, slamming two tendrils onto the platform, shaking it fiercely. Andora bolted forward, keeping her balance.

"And yet you keep killing, never stopping," it continued, attacking again and again. Most missed, a few glancing hits. *"More bodies for the abyss, piling them high until you reach heaven and embrace those you've lost. I approve. I yearn to see the sky above!"*

"You won't live to see that day!" Andora shouted. "I will purge you from my mind."

"You will only destroy yourself. But perhaps that is what you want?"

Andora screamed in response, a pulse of force pushing back a whipping tendril, except this time, it scorched its fleshy-stony exterior. The Amygdala flinched and writhed, pulling the limb back.

"Yes . . . there it is, that inexorable desire. You would let it all **burn** *to save them, drowning as you do so,"* uttered the Amygdala, and with a wail, six of its limbs were sent forth.

Andora gritted her teeth before choosing to rush forward. But before she could slide under the first incoming tendril, every single one split into countless thinner versions. She could barely let out a frustrated shout before they coiled around her like chains.

The tendrils wrapped around and around her until she was held aloft, being carried toward the Amygdala. Her body was entirely imprisoned, apart from her head. Andora struggled, snarling, panicked as she glared at her captor.

"Was that not what you did? On that day when the stars fell on Earth, and humanity died?" it asked.

"What?" Andora croaked as she felt the coiled tendrils crush her, squeezing her. As if they demanded an answer.

"Such selfishness when it came to what mattered."

Andora seethed, trying to pry her arm out of its confines, wincing as a faint echo raked the back of her mind. Struggling as she forced out the words. "I don't know . . . what the hell you're talking about."

The Amygdala paused, humming as it cocked its head.

"You must have locked away that memory as you did with all your failings," it mused, bringing Andora closer to its head until they were face-to-face. *"The truth that you abandoned your siblings."*

"You're lying. I didn't . . . I would never—" Andora howled in pain as traces of the memory tried to push against its cage, clamoring to be let out and seen.

It tilted its head, eyes narrowing as it whispered into her ear. *"Am I? You left them in disarray."*

"Stop it," Andora seethed, her eyes wild, trying to force them shut and pull away from being trapped. Hands upon hands, clawing at her body, dragging her into their trauma.

"While you piloted that ship," it continued, fueling the memories thrashing, loosening the locks.

"Stop talking," Andora begged, tears welling up in her eyes—blurred images, cries for help, the sound of a shaking ship. She screamed, incapable of stopping its release, the tower falling apart further as the ceiling above crumbled, letting in the blizzard outside.

"Ignoring their calls."

Andora shut her eyes, her emotions and mind at the breaking point, seeing it all once more, unable to look away. She sobbed as each memory passed through her eyes. She felt defeated, looking toward the Amygdala.

"Fleeing to where it began."

Its words fell away from her ears, muffled as she became immersed in the past in all its horror and beauty.

The box sprung wide open, and images she'd hidden away came to the forefront of her mind like reels of film. The day it all burned down.

All in perfect clarity, as vivid the day she experienced them.

A haze fell upon Andora, an unwillingness to look at her memories, a desire to hide and push it all away. Perhaps she should let it take the reins.

She could step away and go about her life as one of the shades, living a loop of a dream instead of living with these images. She could see only what she wanted. Even now, she heard his violin, the breeze, her laughter—a fantasy to live in until everything inevitably crumbled.

She wanted it. Her heart yearned for it, was reaching out for it, when she stopped.

A faint blue glow and a call for her name pierced the illusion.

Andora opened her eyes abruptly, looking up to see a blue light no bigger than a marble. It hovered behind the Amygdala, beating its wings, its tiny gaze on her.

She shuddered, blinking, only to find it gone. Sound returned to her ears, the noises of the crumbling cavern and the Amygdala that held her.

A swell of anger covered everything else in thick layers, burying the hurt for a moment. She seethed, gnashing her teeth, and roared—

"SHUT UP!"

With a scream, Andora's will exploded outward. The wave disintegrated the tendrils around her, causing the Amygdala to shriek in pain. A lance of pain and void in her mind momentarily halted her as she shook it off.

She looked up at the shocked amalgamation, its limbs burning into oblivion, its body unstable as it backed away. She scowled. "This is my mind."

Fine then. You could have dreamed." It narrowed its eyes, and with a thousand wails, it lunged its remaining tendrils.

No longer dodging, fueled by intent to tear the Amygdala asunder, Andora swatted away its attacks, taking in hit after hit. The monster winced and withered each time, panic and bafflement filling its eyes as it weakened.

"I—" Andora seethed, grunting as she was knocked back before regaining her footing and rushing forth.

Grabbing and tearing apart the arms that reached for her, Andora ran toward the horror of maddened grief. With a frustrated cry, it raised its last limb and brought it down like a hammer.

"—am done—" she shouted, catching it in her hands, her feet sinking into the ground. With her searing touch, she tore the tendril from its body, throwing it aside. As the Amygdala shrieked in pain, Andora sprinted forward and jumped high toward the Amygdala's android body.

"—listening to you!" she shouted as she tackled it midair, ripping its waist from the rest of its giant body.

Time slowed as they stared at each other. They tumbled onto the platform, separating a distance away before stopping.

Andora groaned, face-first on the ground, coughing as she slowly pushed herself up. Ahead, the Amygdala mumbled, its voice crackling and glitched. Behind, the amalgamation of rock and bodies fell apart like a withered statue meeting its end.

Andora walked forward slowly as she gazed at the fragile, crumbling thing. She stopped, standing above it. The Amygdala turned its shaking head toward her, its eyes filled with black tears.

It raised its stump, hitting Andora in the shins and bashing her with feeble strikes. *"I . . . I just wanted . . ."*

"I know," Andora whispered, raising her palm. "It's time to sleep, forever."

The Amygdala closed its eyes, tears falling. *"Dreams . . . of a silent night."*

Andora grimaced, her mind warring with frustration, anger, sympathy, and pity. She hesitated, her hand shaking as she focused on deleting another part of her psyche.

Yet, as power coalesced into her palm, a heavy force tackled her. Andora yelped as she fell to the ground, grunting as she looked furiously at her assailant.

She froze, seeing Tov.

"I'm sorry, I'd rather not make this a habit," the patriarch chittered, taking a knee over her, one hand hovering above her chest to prevent her from rising, the other three raised in a calming manner.

"Tov? What are you doing?" Andora asked with a glare. Before she could shout at him, another voice answered.

"Preventing you from doing something stupid, sis. That's what little brothers are for, after all." Echo smirked as he stood over the frail, broken body of the Amygdala. The shade lowered himself, gently pushing his hands under its body and slowly lifting it—cradling it.

"I just want it to end," Andora pleaded, knocking away Tov's hand, trying to get up only to be firmly pushed down by his other arms. "Let me go, I don't . . . I don't want to hurt you."

"You won't," Tov whispered. She tried a few more times to escape him, only to be blocked repeatedly. "But we can't let you remove the Amygdala."

"Why not?" Andora shrieked, raising her palm toward it. Tov pushed her palm to the floor while Echo blocked the android from Andora's from with his body.

Tov sighed, easing his grip on her, allowing her to sit up. "You can't defeat grief by erasing it as if it never existed."

"It worked before. I can make it permanent this time. Please . . . Please, let me . . ." she begged, pushing against Tov, barely able to move him with her diminished energy.

"Eldest, sis, stop . . ." Echo asked gently, approaching her. Tov stood up, taking the whimpering Amygdala into his arms and backing away.

Andora watched, unwillingness filling her eyes as she tried to stand, only to falter on weak knees.

"Damn it," she shouted, punching the ground, tears falling from her eyes as she sobbed. "It needs to die."

"Sister," Echo spoke softly, kneeling beside her. He gently placed his hand on her quaking shoulder.

Suddenly, Andora turned to him, swatting away his hand. She lunged, grabbing onto his uniform with shaking hands. Echo grasped her wrists firmly in response but said nothing else.

"It needs to die!" Andora begged, pulling and pushing him, her eyes manic. "It has to . . ."

Echo stared back at her with his copper eyes, listening to her panting breaths until she tired herself.

"Please, let it go," he whispered.

"You don't understand . . . Echo," Andora muttered with choking words, still clutching his clothes. She looked at him and stared with pleading blues. "Please . . . I can . . . I can give you a body. You can leave my mind, be yourself, just let me do this."

He tilted his head, raising his brow. "And why would I want that?"

"To get out of this place before it crashes down," Andora spoke, pushing him.

"And where would I go?" he asked, a small smile tugging his lips. "There's a war happening outside, if you recall. Not exactly a prime vacation spot."

Andora gritted her teeth, hitting his chest as she shut her eyes tight. "I . . . What about Johan? You've . . . you wanted me to look for him. I promised."

Echo looked away, sighing as he stared at the crumbling cavern. He closed his eyes briefly, taking a deep breath before gazing back at her.

"Andora . . ." Echo smiled. "I know he's gone."

She froze, faltering in her words as she stared at him with confusion. "What?"

Shaking her head, she whispered, "No . . . no. Erwin asked me to look for him before . . . before we merged, he asked me to find him. How could you know . . . ?"

"Back in that ocean, when that mist put us all to sleep. I saw his memories, all of it," Echo revealed, thinking back to that moment when he had looked into the mind of his progenitor.

"He wanted you to look for Johan's body, not see if he was alive." He shook his head, his eyes soft but firmly staring into her eyes. "He wanted you to bury him because he was too devastated to do it himself. It was his only regret."

Andora slowly loosened her grip, shocked at his confession. "But, I . . ."

"Did you?" he asked.

She remembered that day, returning to a smoldering New Eden, walking over the corpses and rubble as androids picked up the pieces and put out the last fires. She remembered the hovering tows, lifting pieces of debris, and below, she saw the remains of a crushed train that held the patients and medical staff of the Veteran's Hospital—and remembered burying one of the bodies in a forest in Germany.

"I did . . ." she sobbed. Andora's lip quivered as she looked down, her arms dropping to her side as she finally broke into tears. "I did . . ."

"Hey, hey, it's okay, sis, it's okay," Echo replied, engulfing her in a hug. Andora squirmed, whimpering. He massaged her back gently as she buried her head in the crook of his shoulder.

"I'm sorry. I failed everyone . . ." she spoke through hot tears, her hands slowly wrapping around her brother's waist. "I'm sorry. I'm so sorry . . ."

"You did what he asked for," he reassured her, closing his eyes and fighting back his cry. "You did good."

"I don't know what to do . . ." she whimpered, looking toward Tov and the Amygdala.

Echo glanced behind him, shaking his head. "Leave it, sis. It can't harm you anymore. Lock it away, like you planned to, and we can move on."

"I don't know if I can," she whispered into him.

"That's what we're here for, Andora," Tov spoke from where he stood, setting the body he carried onto the ground. "You can rest."

Andora looked at them both, her shoulders drooping as exhaustion filled her mind. She looked at the Amygdala staring back at her with tears of its own. Eventually, she nodded, raising her hand and swiping down.

The Amygdala closed its eyes as it sank, enveloped into the earth.

And within a second, Andora fell into Echo's arms, fast asleep.

CHAPTER 25

BENEATH *A* FIELD OF DAISIES

The world around them dissipated, the cavern crumbling away.

Tov watched as a familiar white mist surrounded the platform, engulfing the trio. His mind settled, although still tense at the events that had transpired. He looked to Echo at his side, the shade—

No, he thought. *A person.*

Echo carried his sister in his arms, his chin high and back straight as if a weight had fled his shoulders. He saw the high peak and maintained his breath, determined, unimpeded, and looked toward Tov with a smirk.

Nodding in response, Tov waited as the mist reached its peak density, shrouding everything in white. He felt the cold breeze, still there, still carrying the notes of grief, but no longer seeking to bury them under snow and hail.

He heard no siren's song, the world quiet.

Soon enough, the mist dissipated. Tov and Echo found themselves once more on that icy shore where they had arrived, the monolithic cliff behind them no taller than a hill, gradually sloping to a wintery landscape—treacherous but tranquil in its way.

A simple rowboat was hauled onto the beach of dark pebbles and sand ahead of them.

"Hey, it survived," Echo muttered, trying to bring levity to the quiet atmosphere. Tov appreciated the effort.

They strode forward, Tov leading the way as he pushed the boat into the lapping waves of the sea. He stepped in, assisting Echo and carefully sitting Andora on the bench. The android moved in, settling himself and allowing his slumbering sister to rest on his shoulder.

Tov looked at the dark rings under her eyes, her weary expression. But above else, she seemed a tinge lighter, like the breaking of a fever.

His clawed hands gripped the paddles, and slowly, he rowed.

He counted the minutes as they flew by. The land disappeared behind them. Tov looked around, seeing calm blue waters. Beneath was still the ever-present darkness, but it was no longer the ominous abyss that had threatened to swallow them.

"Did we do it?" Echo muttered the question, his voice frail despite the stoic face he put on.

Tov looked to the android, slowing down his rowing. He let out a buzz as he thought, brushing a hand on his mandible. "In a sense. We've . . . cleared the symptoms."

Echo sighed. "But not the cause."

The patriarch nodded. "If only it were so easy."

"That back there was easy?" Echo huffed, his smile fragile as he chuckled.

"Oh, it was, compared to the journey of true healing." He paused, lifting the end of his cape. "You can imagine a piece of fabric."

With a quick jab of his claw, Tov punctured the material. "Each trauma, each tragedy is a hole, some big, some small. You can patch it, sew it back, a permanent scar."

And then, with a full flourish, Tov showed the cape in its entirety. "What one can do, however, is expand the fabric. In comparison, the holes don't look as big anymore. Make new memories. Live life."

Echo pressed his lips tightly, looking at Andora.

"Living, huh? How do you go on like that?" he asked. "How did you do it?"

Tov thought about the years he spent after the Cataclysm. "I had people I cared for and who cared for me. I focused on rebuilding for a time. It was . . . a long process." Tov chuckled. "When I return home to be with Yoram and Uli, perhaps I can retire. Given enough time, even those deep scars can shrink until they disappear entirely."

"I don't think you'll have much time to enjoy retirement," Echo grunted, scowling.

"No . . . I suppose not," replied Tov, thinking of his people, his fleet.

Echo sighed, his shoulders weary as they drooped down. "What now?"

"There's not much else here we can help with, even if Andora were awake," spoke Tov, his antennae twitching. "There is one more thing, however."

"What's that?" Echo asked, raising his brow.

Tov thought about the task Luna had asked of him. That everything hinged on locating two vital individuals. "We need to find where she kept them."

"What are you on about?" pressed Echo as he looked at him with furrowed brows.

Tov sighed, glancing at Andora. "Rikard and Lucy."

Echo widened his eyes, failing to bite back a curse as he muttered, "Shit."

"Indeed. We need to find them in case it's ever decided to leave Sol. Apart from finding a way to transport all the Starfallen back to Legacy space, there's the DNA banks, the cultural repository, and the AIs themselves."

"But all of that is moot if we can't find Rikard and Lucy," Echo realized, scrunching his face in frustration.

Tov nodded. "Andora will never leave the system if we fail."

"Have you looked?" Echo asked before wincing. "Sorry, of course you have. But nothing? Not a clue?"

"We've looked everywhere that meant anything to her," Tov admitted. "Andora wouldn't, couldn't tell us in her mental state before we underwent the bridge. She locked those memories somewhere deep."

"So, if we could find those memories where it all went wrong, we can . . . what, trace our steps from there?" Echo squinted.

"Essentially. It would have been easier with Andora as a guide to where she locked it, but she needs to recover." Tov shook his head. "Is there nothing you can do?"

"Sorry, I've been stuck on a loop for so long. This is a first for me," Echo confessed, frowning.

Tov and Echo bounced different ideas back and forth, from looking for another sane shade to waiting for their host to wake.

The day above soon turned darker, and within minutes, a starry night sky filled the vast world.

The two exhausted their options, quieting down as their minds worked hard to find a solution when, from the mist, a soft blue light emerged.

Immediately, the two leaned back at the new arrival before relaxing their guard.

"A firefly?" Echo muttered, narrowing his eyes as the tiny insect landed on Tov's hand.

The duo glanced at each other and the visitor when another blue light appeared, then another, then dozens. Soon enough, a small swarm had landed on their simple rowboat, adding color to the night, flapping their little wings as they crawled around.

And not a minute later, they finished their dance before flying off together into the mist.

"What was that about?" Echo asked, rubbing his bald head.

"I'm not sure . . ." Tov muttered. "It's strange. I now realize I kept seeing them everywhere. When I arrived, I saw a blue light in my periphery; it's how I found you, actually. And ever since coming to this part of her mind, they've been everywhere."

Ever present, hovering in the distance like clouds of sparkling sapphires, their glow colored the mist in their light. As Echo and Tov looked in their direction, occasionally, one would appear as if staring at them before disappearing back to its kin.

"What . . . what do you think it is?" Tov asked.

Echo pressed his lips tight in thought. He hesitated, Tov saw, glancing toward his sister before finally looking at him. "I may be reaching, maybe not. But Andora has always called Lucy her little firefly."

Tov halted his rowing, tilting his head at the android as he continued.

"Maybe they're a part of her subconscious. Everything here is her mind, after all. Maybe they're tiny functions, trying to help us help her," Echo replied, furrowing his brow.

"So you're saying . . ." Tov paused, looking back to the blue glow within the mist and the single firefly that peeked now and then. "They want us to go somewhere."

"I don't have a better idea," Echo grumbled, running his hand across his face. "Do you?"

The patriarch sighed, shaking his head.

"Guessed not," Echo huffed.

"Well, following data in the shape of fireflies and going on a memory hunt?" Tov chittered at the situation. "This will be the strangest highlight of my life."

Echo scoffed before a smile twitched on the edge of his mouth, and he soon joined in the chuckle. Determined, Tov rowed, following the fireflies wherever they flew. They spoke to pass the time, sharing experiences, Echo regaling Erwin's accomplishments while Tov hummed a tune. All the while, cradled in her brother's arms, Andora slumbered soundlessly.

They immersed themselves in the quiet and the rhythmic rowing splashing against the ocean. As day replaced night, the mist thinned and allowed the duo to see the swarm of blue lights ahead.

Eventually, Tov slowed his rowing, observing as the ocean disappeared, merging with the white sky. Curiously, he still felt the pushing and pulling of oars through the water.

Tov felt a weight on his mind, a familiar overbearing feeling as he rowed. He looked toward the fireflies, stopping as they flew in place, a faint shimmer—saw numbers, lines of code, constantly changing and evolving, ebbing and flowing.

Second after second, Tov forced his arms to move and draw closer to the cluster of fireflies, flying in place, waiting for them. Low hisses and clicks left his mouth until he stopped as the weight grew exponentially.

Echo widened his eyes and then carefully laid Andora on the floor. "Tov, what's wrong?"

"I can't . . ." Tov grunted, his grip on the oars tightening. "I feel this place is . . . too deep for my mind. I think . . . there's no barrier to shield me from Andora's full psyche, like when she deleted the first Amygdala."

Echo bit back a curse. "Are you sure? We're almost there."

"I . . ." Tov ground his mandibles, moving their boat an inch, when a searing pain lanced his mind. He gasped, immediately pushing them away from their destination, and breathed in relief. The patriarch shook his head, throbbing. "Cursed hells . . . I'm sorry, this is my limit."

"Should we wait for my sister to wake up? She can—"

"No, we can't wait any longer," Tov heaved, pressing his fingers on his temple. After a few deep breaths and a moment of thought, he turned to Echo. "You . . . you have to do this."

The android recoiled, face scrunching up as he stammered. "Wait, what? Oh no, no, no. Alone? I can't . . ."

"Echo, I realize . . . I have no right to see Andora's memories," Tov began. "Even if she permitted all this, she was in distress. No, it isn't right for me to do so; as an ally, maybe a friend, even still."

He looked to the shade, at Echo's attempt to avoid Tov's gaze. "No, that right falls to her family."

Echo scoffed, hunching forward and rubbing his hands. "I'm not her brother . . . I'm . . . I don't know what I am."

Tov placed an arm on his shoulders, a firm grip. "You have done as a brother does. And now, she needs your help. We all do."

Echo pressed his lips, gritting his teeth as he leaned back. He sighed and nodded after gazing at the still white and the cloud of fireflies.

"Alright. I'll see what I can find," he muttered, standing up. He looked over the edge at the empty expanse their boat floated on, and with a tentative step, he lowered himself on a hard, invisible floor.

He looked back, staring at his sister and Tov. Echo smirked, giving a two-fingered salute. "Take care of her for me, Bugman."

The patriarch nodded, rowing the boat away as the weight lifted from his head, biding his time as Echo walked off, disappearing into the cloud of blue lights and shimmering code.

Echo felt himself drift. His digital mind swam the currents of his sister's boundless psyche like a fish in water.

Except these depths strained even him.

After a moment, lost in the dark, following the drifting blue lights and hearing a cavalcade of sounds, images, tastes, and sensations, he saw the light in the end.

It grew, opening like a heavy bunker door. Echo swam toward it, gritting his teeth until finally—

Echo gasped as he opened his eyes and immediately jumped back.

A hulking hunk of metal crashed before him, denting and scoring the surface with its flailing limbs. A mech, Echo realized as he backed away from the damaged war machine.

Without its weapon, the mech struggled to defend itself from an amalgamation of multiple Starfallen, the monster suffering and lashing out. A crackling, screeching sound came from inside as the AI and human pilot screamed in conjoined madness.

"STAY AWAY!"

It punched the abomination of human bodies, launching it across the floor. The beast tumbled, crashing into a stack of crates, narrowly missing a squad of androids as they tried to appease the insane humans around them, their faces wrought with confusion, agony, and terror.

The mech stood on shaky legs, looming over Echo but ignoring him as it grasped its mechanical head.

"CAN'T STOP . . . THE SCREAMING! MAKER, FATHER! THERE'S SO MUCH PAIN. I NEED OUT! GET OUT!"

With its metal hands, it plunged its fingers into the hatch at its torso and painfully pried it open. Sparks, metal, and flame burst out as Echo watched with a sad gaze. Within the cockpit, a bloated mass wearing a pilot suit writhed inside, the semblance of a face looking to the sky with bloody tears.

The pilot's mind was still connected with her AI partner, sharing everything as she transformed into Starfallen.

"MAKE IT STOP!" the mech AI bellowed, stumbling around, knocking over forklifts and shelves as it held on to its mutated partner like a human holding in their disemboweled guts. MAKE. IT. STOP!"

It took off in a sprint, stomping its heavy legs toward the fiery wreckage of a shuttle and throwing itself into its flames, engulfing the mech and pilot before the shuttle exploded in a blinding blaze.

All around Echo, chaos engulfed the hangar bay. Automated drones commanded by androids tried desperately to hold the tide of their former companions, outnumbered ten to one. Some humans, not yet transformed, clutched their heads as madness tried to overwhelm them, stumbling as they followed their android comrades to safe zones.

The rest, those with unshielded minds and lesser wills, burst into the abominations that wrecked the station.

Andora sprinted past his vision, surprising Echo as he stepped back. His sister, in a torn dress, covered in blood and holding a gun, ran as two heavy infantry drones carried—

Echo followed quickly. Behind, the memory of the hanger faded away.

He caught up to his sister, realizing she didn't acknowledge him. It was a pure memory he could only observe.

"Damn," he muttered.

Echo glanced at the two humans the drones cradled in their thick, blocky arms. One was an adult man with dark brown hair and a beard. His eyes were bloodshot, his mouth gaping as if choking.

The other, a frail little girl, crying in pain, her body convulsing. Both of them were pale, their breaths shallow. They entered a corridor. All around were signs of recent battles, streaks of blood, and bullet casings.

Ahead, a female android appeared wearing a colonel's rank, followed by a squad of similar infantry drones. Echo faintly recognized the woman, Joan. The officer sighed in relief as she approached them.

"Eldest, Eldest! Thank the—" Colonel Joan stopped, her eyes turned to horror as she looked behind Andora. "No . . . Oh, no . . . Maker? Lucy?"

Andora didn't stop, nearly pushing aside the officer as she ran. The colonel shook her head, following along.

"Eldest, they're everywhere. We're being overrun. Our fleets are in shambles dealing with . . . with this." The colonel gritted her teeth.

"Contact UNAFHQ," Andora responded curtly, her eyes toward her destination.

Joan shook her head. "No one from Headquarters is responding, the UN Assembly isn't responding either. We just lost contact with the US. Captain Constantine reported seeing the White House in flames. No one else is doing better. Our siblings across the world are reporting similar things. It's a full invasion."

"What of New Eden?" Andora finally slowed, looking toward the officer.

"They're under heavy siege. It's . . . it's burning. We have two Dreadcrawlers defending the city, whoever is left from the First Brigade, and the city police. But they're barely holding on." The colonel shook her head. "We're still trying to find out how the enemy slipped through our scanners."

"Send what reserves we have to beat them back," Andora ordered, gritting her teeth.

The colonel stopped, whispering in despair. "Eldest . . . There are none."

"THEN MAKE SOME APPEAR!" Andora shrieked at the android, who stumbled back in fright. "Launch our entire nuclear arsenal, ram our ships into them, arm construction bots, I don't care. Just get them off Earth."

She turned her back on the frozen officer. "We can clean the fallout later."

Their group entered a smaller hangar, one with a sleek private shuttle. All around, gun turrets scanned the area, their barrels hot and red. Around the hall, multiple dead Starfallen lay with cauterized holes.

"Where are you going?" the colonel asked in a whisper.

The private corvette hummed as Andora sent a command to its onboard computers, warming the engines. She opened the bottom hatch, letting the two drones carrying her loved ones aboard. She spoke, her voice shaky. "I need to get Rikard and Lucy somewhere safe."

"But, what do we do?" the colonel pleaded.

Andora paused, fists clenched as she whispered, "I don't know."

"What?"

"I said, I don't know!" Andora turned to Joan, tears in her eyes and an enraged snarl on her face. She barely cooled her expression as the station shook, clearing her eyes as she gazed back at the officer with a firm gaze.

"Regroup for a counterattack. Avoid the infected. Fight off the vermin, kill every single one. Then save who you can. Relay that to everyone, Joan, please. You're in charge."

With that, the hatch began to close. Echo looked at the colonel as he and Andora stepped aboard—confusion, shock, and a growing hardness pouring from her face as she nodded.

"Be safe, Eldest."

Echo watched as Andora directed the drones to the corvette's small medbay. Once inside, they gently lowered Rikard and Lucy onto the medical beds before backing away. The two humans breathed lightly, their bodies shivering.

Andora's stoic facade shattered as she rushed in between the two beds, her mind connecting to the medbay's full diagnostic suite as they scanned her husband and child.

As the machines worked, her eyes were dazed as she tried to focus. She bounced between them both as they were bandaged and stabilized. Yet nothing did so much as slow the plague's advance.

Then, an agonized, dry voice came from beside her. Echo watched as Rikard raised a malformed arm, like a viler form of leprosy and radiation sickness.

"Andora . . ." Rikard croaked, reaching out for his beloved.

"No, no, save your strength, love. I'm here, I'm flying us somewhere safe, okay?" Andora reassured, taking his hand in hers.

"Lucy?" he asked, his eyes unfocused. "I need to see her."

Andora moved to the side, allowing him to spot their daughter. He grunted, moving out of the bed.

"Stay. The autodoc is taking care of you both. Rest," Andora hushed, gently pushing him back down.

"How . . . is she? My ears . . . they're muffled. Can barely hear you . . ."

Andora pressed her lips, shutting her eyes as she forced a smile. "Our little firefly is going to be alright."

Rikard blinked slowly, turning his head to her. "I hear . . . whispering. Is that you?"

"What?" Andora asked, furrowing her brow. "No, what are you hearing?"

"It's telling me . . . to let go, open the door . . . I don't trust it," Rikard groaned, gritting his teeth, panting.

"Don't listen to it," Andora urged, holding tightly to his hand. "Fight it, please, fight it. I don't know what's happening to either of you, but I'll find a way to fix this."

The man swallowed, shivering as his eyes stared at Andora. "It's . . . happening to everyone . . . Not just us. You have to help them."

"My siblings are on it. They can win this. They don't need me." Andora frowned, looking away.

Rikard shook his head, blinking away the wetness around his eyes as he began sweating. "They do . . . you're their . . . big sister. They—"

Hacking, bloody coughs interrupted him, turning into a wheezing fit. Andora quickly motioned for a respirator, the device descending and latching on to her husband, extracting fluid and pumping nanomachines into his system.

"Mama!" another voice cried out. Echo watched as a mother rushed to her shaking child, fear etched on her face.

"Lucy! I'm here, Mama's here," Andora shushed, patting Lucy's hair only to look in momentary terror when strands of hair stuck to her palm. "Darling girl, stay strong. Just listen to my voice, okay?"

Blisters appeared on the little girl's arms and face. Something . . . writhed inside, changing her slowly as she whimpered.

"It . . . hurts . . . So noisy . . ." Lucy spoke in barely coherent words in the middle of her crying and gurgling, shock and confusion overloading her young mind as her little hands reached and held on to her mother's torn dress. "I'm scared, Mama . . . I wanna go home, now . . . please?"

"I'm . . . I'm sorry . . . I—" Andora stopped as her daughter passed out cold, her breaths shallow. With a pained snarl, she pushed away, busying herself with the medbay's meager capabilities and running the vessel toward Earth.

Echo looked away from the sight, shutting his eyes.

"Eldest, respond. This is the carrier *Mother Bee*. Colonel Joan called us to assist you with your arrival. Do you copy?" a voice crackled through the speakers.

Andora pressed her temple, her face tight. "I need a priority escort."

"Roger, we're diverting a squadron of our aces to guide you to New Eden."

She shook her head. "No. I'm heading to Kópavogur."

There was a pause as the android on the other end asked, "Eldest, say again?"

"Rikard and Lucy are with me," Andora replied with an impatient frown. "They're hurt. I can't take them to New Eden. It isn't safe."

"I . . . That's . . ." Another pause. Andora waited, tapping her foot with furrowed brows when *Mother Bee* finally responded. "Alright, we'll get you there, Eldest, sit tight. *Mother Bee*, out."

Andora sighed. "Thank you, Tomas. Good luck . . ."

Time slowed to a crawl. The machines' humming and the two patients' low groaning filled the room. Now and then, the corvette would shake up until the squadron leader arrived and began their escort.

Andora barely acknowledged them, hyperfocused on Rikard and Lucy.

The ship rattled after a few minutes. Echo surmised they'd entered Earth's atmosphere.

The memory faded, and Echo blinked in confusion at the new area. Up ahead was a mountain home easily recognizable by any android. The birthplace of their kind. He stood on a landing pad just below the house. Above, their escort fired their jets and streaked to the South Pole, reinforcing the defenders.

The sky darkened, distant tracers firing off into the sky, the winds howling, carrying the tortured groans of billions.

Andora and her two drones pushed hovering medical beds, carrying their patients up the mountain path.

Echo furrowed his brow, following behind. "I don't understand. Tov said he and the others searched every possible location. This should have been the first place they checked."

They soon reached the estate building, a modern home of glass, steel, and wood.

Andora kicked down the doors, the simple house AI greeting her, Rikard, and Lucy with its usual welcoming tone.

They pushed through the rooms. Everything looked blurred and messy, as if Andora had ignored everything but what lay ahead. Eventually, she reached a bookshelf filled with novels she enjoyed, some she had written herself.

With a grunt, she knocked it aside, revealing a plain wall. But, to Echo's surprise, air hissed as a rectangular section wide enough for two people slid inward and then down, revealing a large elevator.

The two infantry drones remained outside, Andora setting them on patrol as she and the two hoverbeds squeezed into the elevator. Echo took her side, quietly observing, glancing at his sister and her thinly veiled anxiety.

Echo counted the hours as they sped by quickly, moving in a blur as Andora transferred Rikard and Lucy into a state-of-the-art medical clinic. They had traveled far below the mountain, then, after exiting the elevator, taken a short tram to a compact underground bunker complex.

Upon entering the lab, frustration overcame Andora. She swiped away the computer, adding to the mess of instruments all over the floor.

"None of this makes sense! It's all useless!" she exclaimed, flipping the table in desperation. As she collapsed into a chair, clutching her head, the whimpering cry of her daughter echoed through the lab.

Echo and an exhausted Andora turned to the clinic's center and saw Rikard rise from his bed with unsteady steps in an attempt to comfort Lucy's anguish. Only to find himself unable to remove his hand from her shivering shoulder.

"Andora . . . !" he shouted as Lucy shrieked in pain.

Andora rushed to them, her husband panicking as strength abandoned his legs, pulling Lucy down with him.

"No!" Andora shrieked.

Rikard gazed at his daughter, then his wife, as their skin melded together. The plague consumed them, their bodies deteriorating before Andora's eyes. Lucy's gaze shifted to her mother, the light in her eyes dimming as she attempted to reach out with a festering hand.

Brushing his hand on Andora's cheek, wiping away blood, Rikard spoke softly, his mind unraveling.

"It's . . . not . . . your . . ." he gasped, before falling unconscious.

They moved to the sterile confines of the operating room, the Malignant Starfall continuing its malevolent work, merging father and daughter into an inseparable, agonizing union. No longer responsive to Andora's desperate calls, the two groaned and cried unendingly.

"I won't let you take them. I won't. I won't!" Andora's defiant shouts reverberated through the room. With absolute hatred and rage, she raised a surgical laser, her eyes fixed on the ceiling as she seethed. "DO YOU HEAR ME? I WON'T LET YOU TAKE THEM!"

"It's okay, just . . . hold still," she pleaded, tears falling down her cheek as the machine whirred, firing a thin beam onto their entwined bodies.

Yet, as the laser made contact, Rikard and Lucy screamed in unimaginable agony. The sound pierced Andora's ears and shattered any illusion of control.

Andora shrieked in shock, immediately turning the laser off and throwing it aside, crashing to the floor as their bodies began to writhe and undulate like putty.

"No . . ." she whispered, her mind blank as she stepped back from the contorting display of flesh.

Their flesh—

She blacked out, then. Her vision, the memory itself, went red and blurry. She collapsed beside the table like a puppet without strings.

Echo had never felt such violent nausea before and never wanted to again.

It had been a week. Or it felt that way to Echo's perception. The memory had deteriorated into moments of chaotic images and madness. The facility shook occasionally, and the sounds of battle echoed from the surface.

The Battle of New Eden should have finished by now, followed by the extermination of surviving vermin worldwide. At the same time, a massive rescue effort was made to collect the Starfallen humans.

Andora never left the bunker. She went from bashing against the wall to huddling in the corner, scratching her face, her mental state at the brink of no return—clawing and raging in isolation.

The broken woman entered a dark room, the lights slowly turning on to reveal a medical pod and pools of dried blood. She fell to her knees before it, clasping her hands.

"God, please . . ." she whispered, her voice box glitching and crackling from constant screaming.

"If you exist, please hear me," Andora begged, hugging the pod housing a bloated mess inside. "They don't deserve this . . . I don't know how to help them. Tell me what to do . . . Please . . . I can't . . ."

She banged her head on the glass over and over again, splitting her forehead in a splatter of blue blood. "DON'T LEAVE THEM LIKE THIS . . . !"

Echo forced himself to watch, burning the sight into his memory as she cried to the empty room.

Another two weeks. A sense of clarity had cleared a portion of the grief.

The clean-up effort should have been underway, the survivors counted, the androids convening.

Andora entered the dark room once more. The lights flickered on, the floor clean, the pod in the middle surrounded by picture frames, books, candles, and a bed of daisies—moments of better times, an icon of both her love and failure.

Echo watched from the corner with a tired gaze as his sister laid her hand on the pod's glass.

"Operation Omni Mind was passed. I'm to be the prime consciousness. I didn't oppose their decision," she muttered, utterly devoid of emotion, her face marked with exhaustion.

The Starfallen amalgamation within the pod moved. Echo saw vague shapes of both Rikard and Lucy, though their eyes were long gone.

"I know, I know it hurts," she whimpered. "I'm sorry . . . I can't . . . I can't do it . . . I'm a coward," Andora bit her lip, shutting her eyes as she leaned forward, her forehead touching the glass.

"I promise . . . I promise I'll make things right. I'll find a way to undo this or die trying." She looked up, peering into the glass, her smile fragile. "If that happens, if I fail . . . It'll be painless, instant. Either way, we'll be together again."

She glanced at the base of the pod. Echo saw her plant the device, a thermobaric bomb, enough to reduce this place to ash and rubble—sanitizing all organic material.

A caretaker drone moved over the pod like a spider, meticulously maintaining its functions and keeping its occupants stagnant and asleep.

"You've made me so happy. You gave life meaning." She smiled sadly as she stepped away from the pod.

She moved to exit before stopping by the door, looking back at them. "I love you both."

Echo left with her, the doors closing behind them, the lights shut off, allowing only the bare minimum needed to keep the pod room running. Hundreds of little drones scurried the floor, commencing their long years of duty—instructed to maintain this facility at all costs.

They moved to the other side of the facility, taking a different elevator. Echo breathed deeply, staring at his quiet sister. Soon, they emerged onto a field of daisies, a miraculous survivor after weeks of battle across the globe.

Once they stepped out, the elevator receded into the ground. Echo noted the location. In the distance, the estate and the entire mountain had been scorched from the war.

Andora took a knee, plucking a daisy and brushing it against her finger. She peered deeply into it, tears falling onto her hand. "One day . . . I promise."

She and Echo took one last look at the faraway sunset. Andora took a deep breath, letting go of the daisy she held before locking away the memory of what had transpired—hidden for a century until he arrived.

Echo closed his eyes as everything faded to black.

He gasped awake, widening his eyes as he found himself in a familiar train station.

Tov and Andora stood from the bench they sat on. His sister looked exhausted, not much better than how he saw her in the memory.

They looked at him with different expressions. Tov tilted his head, his insectoid face patient and concerned. Andora looked away, not meeting Echo's eyes.

"How long was I out?" he asked.

Andora sighed, finally glancing his way. "A few hours."

He nodded, rubbing his head as he spoke with a grim frown. "I know where they are."

Tov nodded while Andora shrunk even more, biting her lip.

"Then we're done here," the patriarch sighed.

Andora breathed deeply as she sat back down on the bench. Witnessing the memory from an outsider's view had placed a permanent scar on Echo's mind. But for the one to have lived it and with it until death? Echo couldn't even imagine. A burning anger lit up inside his heart, his sights turning to those responsible.

Echo briefly whispered in Tov's ears, placing exact coordinates. Tov appeared momentarily surprised, but eventually nodded.

"The exit process needs to be gradual. We can start now," Andora muttered as she turned to Tov. "It should translate to five days at the very least. I'm not risking any more than that."

"Luna informed me with a diver's analogy. I'll leave it to your discretion," Tov replied before looking at him. "Echo . . . ?"

He smiled, waving him off.

"Staying," he replied. "I think I've gotten a feel for this place. Should be able to find my way without you, big sis."

Andora glanced at him, her lips pressed tight, her eyes brittle as she whispered, "What will you do?"

Echo rubbed his chin, humming. "Well, Tov and I spoke while you had your beauty rest. We both agree that your mind needs a bit of spring cleaning. The least I could do is . . . round up every last shade, give them the whole rundown of reality."

"I do not envy you," Andora muttered.

"I don't envy you," Echo chuckled, standing up and stretching. "I'm gonna be playing janitor-slash-therapist while you are about to go to war."

He looked to Tov, Andora watching with a hint of bemusement piercing her daze as they performed a handshake with their six total hands.

"Until we meet again, Echo." Tov bowed.

"That we will." Echo smirked, patting the patriarch's shoulder. "I'll see you then, bud. Kick Starless ass for me."

Tov turned to Andora and him, nodding before stepping back, allowing them space.

Echo looked to his . . . sister. Erwin's sister. His thoughts churned with the events he'd experienced since waking up from the illusion to his journey with the gestalt. Finally, seeing her memories, he had no words. He sat down on the bench, both taking comfort in the quiet.

In the distance, a Christmas melody played, a cheery one, thankfully. It hummed in the background, blanketing their emotions.

". . . the other way around . . ." Andora muttered.

Echo turned to Andora, his brow raised. "What?"

She sighed, shaking her head as she slowly turned to him with deep blue eyes.

"I said it's supposed to be the other way around," she repeated, a slight, fragile smirk twitching her mouth. "It's the big sisters stopping little brothers from doing something stupid."

Coughing fits racked Echo as he looked at Andora with an incredulous look, a mix of scoffs and chuckling as he tried to respond.

"You consider . . . ?"

Andora nodded as she stood up, glancing his way. "Thank you . . . brother."

Echo stared, mouth agape as she . . . his sister, took Tov's side. A train came down the tracks, halting.

"Shall we?" he heard her speak to Tov as they stepped aboard and the doors slid closed.

As they left, leaving Echo in this mental world, he breathed deeply, listening to the music, a single tear falling down his cheek as he began to sing along.

CHAPTER 26

MOUNTING PRESSURE

A week had passed outside the confines of Andora's mind.

While she, Tov, and Echo battled her demons, the defenders of Sol waged a war against their own.

Clustered within a corpse belt just beyond the Saturn Circle, the planet's orbit around Sol, a vast battle fleet lay in wait like lions stalking prey. One group had the distinct ominous black hulls of the Jupiter Fleet. At its center lay the battleships *Buddha's Palm* and *Sun Wukong*. The second group consisted of the diverse warships of the Third Fleet, although missing its mother.

Instead, the *Zolann'tono* led a small diversion force.

"Come on, closer, closer," Jupiter muttered, his overloaded mind straining as he guided the trap they set.

Jupiter, Luna, and Mars, each in their android shells, stood by the War Room's display table. His siblings had their eyes closed, focused on their fronts. He motioned to Admiral Yan, standing beside him.

"Yan, adjust to this bearing . . . now. Nice, Slimy Two is following like a good little fish," Jupiter spoke, though he was connected to every officer within the Third Fleet. It helped to relay his orders to their top dog . . . or wasp.

"We're getting too close to the hazard zone, Jupiter. How much longer?" Yan warned as she leaned on the table, looking at the irregular blob occupying much of the 3D plot and their distance to it.

Yan's voice remained stoic, but Jupiter knew the Kurskann woman enough to hear the tinge of exhaustion.

"Just a bit longer, Yanny. Give me one minute." Jupiter tapped his finger on the table, eyes laser-focused.

He looked through the Network, analyzing, calculating, juggling a hundred things at once in this battlezone. He watched the icon depicting their prey and gift draw closer together.

Unlike the previous Leviathan they'd encountered weeks back, this one did not take the appearance of a spherical moon of flesh and tentacles, exuding the concept of stagnancy, slumber, and swamp.

Instead, its form vaguely resembled a gargantuan amalgamation of an angler fish at the front and an eel-like tail in the back. A disgusting, black mucus-like substance covered its entire body, making it difficult to detect with their scanners.

The beast had less volume than Muck but made up for it in density and agility. With a length exceeding three hundred kilometers instead of the nine-hundred-kilometer diameter of its dead kin, it slithered much like a sea snake.

Neither did it have Muck's vast psionic might, much to the Third's relief, as their AEBs had worked flawlessly throughout the many skirmishes they'd won over the past several days.

What it *did* have that frustrated Jupiter and the Third Fleet, however, was a purplish gaseous nebula that permeated the area, surrounding the front lines beyond the Eighth SE Tower they protected and the Ninth in the distance defended by a garrison.

Titan-class Starless that resembled balloons deployed the miasma upon arrival. They expelled their contents until they withered and died. Now, three days to the present, the stuff had covered vast swathes of the Outer Zone.

And the Leviathan that led the charge appeared to have mild control of them.

Unlike natural clouds, this vile substance had a soupy viscosity. It boiled like tar, its bubbles bursting once it reached a specific size, propelling caustic plasma that destabilized energy shields and ate away metal.

However, most egregious of all its properties was the advantage it gave to the Leviathan and its posse that challenged the defenders. The Starless dove into its depths for hours, disappearing entirely from all but the most potent sensors.

Jupiter knew the speed boost it received inside, and multiple simulations ran in his mind, determining where it would emerge.

Nevertheless, despite its advantages and after-work hours, Jupiter had checkmate. Slimy Two, its two Juggernauts that looked like smaller versions of it, and the rest of the swarm finally came within range of their trap.

He licked his lips, his grin sharklike and hungry. "Say hello!"

Bright, crackling flashes of light illuminated the hulls of the combined Jupiter–Third Fleets.

In the distance, hidden antimatter torpedoes had homed in and exploded onto the surface of the slippery Leviathan, tearing out chunks from the abomination, severing its tail, and shaving a hundred or so kilometers from its body. A soundless shriek poured from its needle-mouthed maw.

The blast radius affected the rest of the swarm as bits of flesh and bone turned into searing-hot shrapnel.

"Direct hit on Slimy Two!"

The War Room cheered as their ploy worked.

"Bingo! Finally nailed you, you bastard." Jupiter pumped his fist in relief.

Space-time rippled as if bruised from such potent detonation.

At the same time, the hidden battlegroup emerged from their hiding spots. Missiles flying silently engaged their boosters, speeding toward the Leviathan and its pack of lesser.

Raining death pelted the invaders, eviscerating flesh, blowing chunks of bodies as everything from Fodder to the two Juggernauts that accompanied their more enormous master.

Stealthed gun emplacements hummed to life, firing plasma blasts and laser beams. Mines activated homing to their targets.

The antimatter torpedoes knocked away a third of the noxious cloud, but the wounded Leviathan sacrificed its swarm to cover its retreat, swimming back to the purple goo. "Yeah, you better run," Jupiter scoffed.

Bubbles burst rapidly as the Leviathan dove into the miasma, blasting a heavy acid rain toward the combined fleet and deterring any chase. The might of their two fleets soon demolished the rest of the stunned Starless.

"*Quilinne*, good hit on target. Shift positrons to J2."

"Right wing, converge on this cluster and wipe it before it regroups."

"Pull back behind the *Zolann, Navaron*! You're taking too much heat."

However, as the swarm died in droves, Jupiter remained focused on determining where their injured prey ran off to.

His brow furrowed, watching the map and the tens of thousands of kilometers of miasma. Thankfully, with gravitic manipulations, they had managed to block the sickly purple nebula from creeping past the Saturn Circle.

"Something's not right," Yan muttered, pointing at the dying swarm.

Jupiter looked up, narrowing his eyes in realization. There was a small but significant chunk missing among the Marauder-class.

He immediately looked back at the map when a loud bell echoed within the Network.

[Urgent Report. Sender: SDNHC-S3. Message: Battlegroup September is under heavy assault. Ninth Tower at risk. Requesting immedia—]

Static, then silence. The drone heavy cruiser that sent the message disappeared from the 3D plot as the garrison by the Ninth fell one after another.

"No, no, no!" Jupiter protested with wide eyes as a splinter force from the swarm they defeated, and one from the other front, converged like hyenas. Destroyer-sized Marauders and a few cruiser-sized Titans emerged from the miasma in a lightning strike, taking down the automated defenders.

And to top it all off, the Leviathan emerged from the purple clouds at their lines. Despite being injured, it now carried with it the corpse of a dead Colossus. The monstrosity spun, building momentum within the goo's hastening properties, and launched the body toward the tower.

The asteroid-sized corpse plummeted toward the tower and, despite the efforts of the remaining ships of Battlegroup September, obliterated the station like a truck ramming into a fence post.

"Come on!" Jupiter seethed in frustration at their loss. "What the hell are our drone fleets doing?"

He slammed his fist on the table at their inadequacy. Without the immense processing capabilities of the Eldest, the combat Overseers could only control their smaller elite fleets without sacrificing effectiveness.

The rest of their assets ran on automated commands. The Drone AIs were intelligent logic machines but lacked the creativity and intuition of Jupiter and the rest of the Overseers. And yet, they couldn't leave a good half of their total combat forces sitting on their butts while they were attacked on all sides.

Divided into twelve battlegroups, each named after a month, they took positions as garrison forces, holding while the Overseers and the Third Fleet came in to troubleshoot problem areas.

Eight days.

Eight days of mounting pressure.

Eight days of constant skirmishes designed to test their defenses before coming in with a good punch.

The main horde that arrived had been more significant than anything they'd ever faced. Five Nightmare Portals with a magnitude of six opened up around the Outer Zone and slowly pushed them back through sheer quantity.

A Leviathan led each of the five invading swarms of Colossi, Titans, and lesser Starless scourge ships.

Each similar in every aspect, they slipped and waited like ambush predators.

"Motherfu—" Jupiter groaned.

The Overseer sent a retreat order on their remnants, having them return to the Inner Zone. He took manual control of some, feeling the added weight on his mind, nearing his total capacity. The battlegroup looked no larger than a flotilla, and he declared it.

"Yo, I just lost Battle Group September and the Ninth Tower." He sent the message through the Network and also sent a private message to Admiral Yan. The Kurskann woman sighed in displeasure, relaying it to the Third Fleet.

Luna's android shell hummed to life, sending a flat look to Jupiter as she adjusted her glasses. "We know. And I'll spare your ears from me saying, 'I told you so.'"

He rolled his eyes. "Gee, thanks L."

"September was already running on fifty percent combat effectiveness. It was a bad bet to think it would hold while you hunted Slimy Two."

"I thought they'd put a better defense. I arranged it myself . . . Shit!" Jupiter slammed the table, massaging his head. "We injured the bastard and lost most of its posse, at least."

Luna shook her head. "But our interdiction domain has constricted once more. With that, we can declare everything beyond the Saturn Circle lost. We're already experiencing a few breakthroughs beyond."

"Yeah, I'll tow the Eighth Tower back. Third Fleet needs a breather, too." Jupiter glanced in the admiral's direction.

Yan nodded. "It has been a long day. My people need the rest, and we've suffered some damage."

The hunt had been going on for five hours of maneuvering and anticipating the Leviathan's movements. Before that had been hours of sporadic skirmishes and more maneuvering—moving like pieces in a cosmic chessboard.

Even the veterans of the Third needed to rest their minds, despite their bodies feeling awake from the adrenaline rush, and their hearts yearning to do more.

"Slimy Two and its last goons are pulling back." Jupiter scratched his chin. "We should send a strike force to finish the job before they capitalize on our loss. I can send the *Wukong* and some speedier assets, but I'll need hitting power."

At that, Mars's android shell hummed to life. The red giant in ancient armor thumped his fist on his chest. "I shall send support, brother. Battleship *Genghis Khan* has just finished repairs, and she's feeling eager."

"Thanks. We can stabilize the eastern front once we finish the bastard." Jupiter scowled.

Luna sighed, tapping a finger on her chin. "Unfortunately, we need to fall back further. We're spread too thin at this point. With September's loss, we're left with nine reduced battlegroups. They're losing coherence against the High Abyssals."

"That is frustrating." Mars frowned, humming in thought. "It seems their commanders are starting to adapt."

Jupiter looked to Mars. "Can you take charge of their fallback?" he asked.

"I'll try. I have my hands tied. I can't do complex fighting maneuvers while withdrawing."

Luna nodded. "Do what you can. I'll send my reserve drone bomber squadrons to blunt their chase."

Admiral Yan leaned on the table, her face drifting to the five red dots that appeared, then disappeared, but mainly remained blurred with projected movements.

"What's the status on the other Slimies?" she asked.

Mars swiped his hand, displaying his forces on the northwestern front. "*Boogie Mouse* is still engaging Four and Five. My dreadnought has successfully pushed them back and injured one. However, they've gone on the defensive, keeping out of range of my Rapture Beams."

The visuals showed the tyrannical dreadnought dueling the two Leviathans. Mars would send the *Mouse* into the miasma in short bursts, firing its weapons in every direction like some absurd form of dynamite fishing.

Occasionally, one or both Slimies would emerge from the clouds like monstrous sea creatures, lunging at the dreadnought only to be deterred by its indomitable absorption shield.

However, the constant corrosion from the hazardous gas would slowly but surely destabilize the *Boogie Mouse*, forcing it out for a recharge.

Nevertheless, the dreadnought's presence ensured the stability of the northwestern front that encompassed a third of the Saturn Circle, even with two Leviathans.

Above all, the support volleys from the red planet would surprise the invaders at crucial moments.

"And Three?" Yan asked toward the silver Overseer.

Luna flicked her finger to the war table, displaying the southwestern front. She sighed, her brows furrowing. "Continuing to prod my lines. *Xerxes*'s drone legions are ineffective against its hide, and *Gilgamesh*'s turning speed is too slow. We're preventing its advance but nothing else."

On her side, her fleet and the legions pouring forth from the battleship-sized carrier resisted the Starless swarm more effectively than their drone battlegroups.

To combat the miasma, Luna appreciated that the storm-producing strategy she used last week worked wonders to prevent its advance. That and her improved Tesla weapons ensured they held.

Swarms of nanomachines also deterred many of the attackers.

The southwestern front looked as if two hurricanes clashed against each other. One full of lightning, the other full of acid.

Unfortunately, that prevented Luna from carrying out effective offensive actions.

Her *Gilgamesh* acted more as a sniper, assassinating any Starless stupid enough to emerge from the miasma. Much to Luna's bother, Slimy Three proved to be a more slippery target.

"Those Leviathans are damn annoying!" Jupiter seethed. "They're holding down our best assets while their minions roll over everything else."

Admiral Yan let out a low hiss at the situation. "Should we deploy the *Ereshkigal* or the *Sisyphus?*"

"*Ereshkigal* stays," Luna curtly replied.

Jupiter shook his head as Yan turned to him. "*Sisyphus* is shadowing Slimy One. I don't like how it's eyeing my *Ultimatum.*"

The last Leviathan remained elusive, holding back behind the miasma like an alpha beast looming over its pride—content with allowing its kin and their lessers to fight. The defenders had to keep their own in anticipation with it as a reserve card.

"Should your station fall back?" Yan asked with concern.

Jupiter tsked, his face twisting with anger, stress, frustration, and, for a split second, doubt.

He grunted, shaking his head. "Once the Saturn Circle collapses, I will. It stays where it is for now, and your people are heading there for a refresher."

Yan nodded.

"How are your people feeling?" Jupiter asked with concern as he looked at the admiral.

Yan chittered, snapping her mandibles. "Oh, worry not. We're still eager to get back in the fight."

Jupiter chuckled while Mars let out a barking laugh.

"I adore your people's martial spirit, comrade Yan!" the red giant applauded.

"Thank you, friend Mars. This has been an exciting war, to say the least," Yan buzzed. "To think I'd participate in a battle against a mythical Leviathan. That there are five in this system alone is . . . mind-boggling."

A shrug left Jupiter's shoulders as he smirked. "Well, stick with us, and you might experience much more excitement."

"I'll take you up on that offer," Yan chittered, sending a message to the Third Fleet to lower the protocol level and allow sailors to step down. "Now, if you'll excuse me, Overseers."

Jupiter waved his hand before calling for her. "Oh, and Yan?"

"Yes?" she asked

"Get some sleep."

The door to the admiral's stateroom slid shut.

Yan yawned, her mandibles opening wide as she moved to her bed, falling face-first onto the soft mattress. With a groan, she crawled to its center, tossing aside the mess she had left the night before.

A bed with just the right firmness—embracing her body in a restful balance of soft and firm. She breathed, sending a thought to her music player.

After humming to life, a calming ambiance lulled her room. Her compound eyes soon darkened, feeling the tug of slumber.

She dreamed of the days that had passed, the constant battles, the risky ventures, the terrifying power of Leviathans, and above all else, their decision to fight.

Pride filled her as she thought of her people, warriors, every single one. They fought for a higher purpose, battling the night. They worked overtime, some taking double shifts before management forced them to rest.

Yet, it did nothing to quell the rush. Whether it was good or bad, Admiral Yan relished in the action. Only her rank stopped her from doing something absurd. That, and she loved the *Zolann*. Ever since her recent upgrade, the ship had transitioned from a motherbase to an aggressive matriarch.

Her asteroid crushers had five tally marks, each representing a Colossus kill, four being Dominators. The crew had started to call the fierce weapon "Tyrant's Bane." Yan wholeheartedly approved and had the name engraved on its side.

Then, she dreamed of simpler things. The decades spent as a retainer of Clan Garesh, teaching a new generation of sailors. Yan enjoyed those times and cherished them close to her heart.

But here, amid a war against monsters, defending those she considered friends, burned a fire in her chest. Only the loss of life and stress marred her feelings.

No, she didn't enjoy war. She hated it and its consequences. Nevertheless, she felt alive, at home.

She sighed. Perhaps one day, that would change. A time where she could find a planet, maybe look for a—

"Yanny!" Jupiter's voice yelled through her implant.

The admiral shot up, her head pulsating from the sudden rise as she got off the bed, seeing an hour and a half had passed.

"This is Yan," she slurred, shaking her head as she opened her tablet, revealing the AI Overseer's face. "What is it?"

"Admiral, we have news. Patriarch Tov and Andora are at the final stage of the reawakening process," Jupiter reported, his voice unusually devoid of humor. "We need to hold for at least six more hours."

She sighed in relief. "It will be good to get them back finally. What else?"

"Slimy One disappeared from our sensors about forty minutes ago." Jupiter frowned.

Yan sat on the bed, her mind racing. "What do we know? What about the rest of the Leviathans?"

Jupiter smiled this time. "We managed to hunt down Two while you were asleep. It's dead. Four and Five retreated after the former got dunked on by Mars. Three has also fallen back."

"So they've withdrawn . . . They're likely amassing for a big push," Yan muttered.

The Overseer nodded. "That's our consensus, too. We're regrouping as well and constricting our lines."

"Alright, I'll grab a coffee and return to the War Room soon. I need to check on the Third and get her back on the field as soon—"

A loud bell echoed from the speakers throughout her room and the *Zolann*, followed by a deep voice from one of the bridge officers.

[ATTENTION | NIGHTMARE PORTAL DETECTED | MAGNITUDE SIX]

"Another one . . ." Yan paced, her mind now fully awake. "Another Leviathan and its army."

She hissed in frustration, thinking back on the several times she had heard that same announcement. Different magnitudes, but each added their weight on the defenders.

"Well, shit," Jupiter sighed. "Sorry, Yan, gonna have to interrupt your beauty sleep."

The admiral shook her head. "No, it's fine. I can survive on an hour and a half."

"No rest for the wicked," Jupiter chuckled.

She chittered, brewing a mug of coffee. "No, none at all."

CHAPTER 27

MOLON LABE

Magnitude Six?" Yan asked as she entered the War Room with coffee in hand. Mars smelled the aroma coming from her mug and wrinkled his nose. He preferred tea himself.

It was only Mars, Jupiter, and the admiral present. Luna had her hands full with taking over drone battlegroups after Mars had them fall back—her android shell stood still with its hands clasped behind her back.

"Six-point-three with the latest readings," Mars reported, tapping into the Network and their Spotlight Towers. Logarithmic expressions translated quickly enough, and the Third Fleet adopted the standard for the defense effort.

They'd narrowed down their observation and detection capabilities over time, as had the Fleet over their long experience fighting the hated ones. Locating and calculating the wound in reality, and the projected tonnage coming through, had become a learned science.

A Leviathan and their swarm of Fodder to Colossi needed a portal of magnitude six to disgorge their force before collapsing.

The raiding force consisting of three Titan-class, which Jupiter and Luna had used to demonstrate their capabilities, was a 3.5.

Muck, the moon-sized ball of biomass, alone was a magnitude five. In contrast, the vanguard forces they'd faced a week prior were between 4 and 4.8.

"Good news is that the portal has stabilized." Jupiter pressed his lips. "Well, as stable as a literal wound in space can be. I mean, it's not growing any bigger."

"Projected arrival?" she asked, analyzing the incoming data as she leaned on the table.

Jupiter huffed. "Two hours and forty minutes, give or take a few minutes."

"So, another Leviathan leading a more sizeable force. With the distance to our lines . . . We'll need to hold for two and a half, maybe three hours, until

Andora and the patriarch awaken. Can our defenses hold for that long?" the admiral asked.

Mars rubbed his chin, looking at the 3D plot of Sol. "I've gathered every drone battlegroup and had them fall back to two million kilometers past the Jupiter Circle. I've concentrated on those not protected by my planetary guns and the *Ultimatum*. Luna is refining their formations now."

His sister positioned drones in the most efficient formations for the battle to come and arranged the passive defenses, like minefields, gun emplacements, and other esoteric devices, to impede or destroy their foes.

When their blades clashed, they wouldn't be able to directly command these assets any longer, especially once the enemy reinforcements emerged.

"Speaking of my mobile fortress," Jupiter grumbled, swiping his finger to zoom in on his nexus station and the emerging Nightmare Portal. "Look at where it's at."

Mars hummed. "It's coming from the northeast. They'll have a straight shot to your nexus."

"They're aiming to decapitate you," Yan guessed grimly, her mandibles snapping.

"Let them try," Jupiter snarled. "They'll find out soon they have no authority over me. I'm moving my entire fleet to block their assault. You guys watch my flanks."

Luna chimed in, her eyes momentarily glowing with silver as she spoke. "I'll take charge of the southern front, spread my forces to cover a larger front, and support the drones."

"I'll remain on the western front, then," Mars declared as he hummed in thought. He calculated the current situation and what forces he'd need to hold the defenses. He nodded, deciding on pulling an asset to support his brother.

"I'll send the *Boogie Mouse* your way." Mars grinned, puffing his chest out.

Jupiter rolled his eyes, waving him off. "I appreciate it, but my *Sisyphus* will be enough. Besides, you still have Slimies Four and Five."

"Nonsense. Four has been defanged. I've made my estimates. My front can deal with their assault without my little *Mouse* babysitting them."

Jupiter crossed his arms, narrowing his eyes at the map. "Fine, we can stop their charge and immediately hunt the honchos. Then, we can divert our forces. Your dreadnought returns to your area and attacks the Starless flank while I do the same in Luna's area."

"I'm more worried about the Space Enforcers garrisoned by your drones. A single breakthrough would be a disaster. This anomalous miasma of theirs will flood the area without your towers enforcing the interdiction domain."

The three Overseers pressed their lips. Mars grew frustrated at his lack of processing power. Already, his brain beneath Olympus Mons struggled to efficiently command the full might of his assets, as his planetary guns were supporting the entire battlefield and his fleet.

Without the Central Nexus, he couldn't do anything with the surrounding drones in his front apart from moving their positions and sending them targets.

He looked at the map. With the smaller area to defend, they reorganized the nine damaged battlegroups into seven at peak function.

That still left seven weak points—spots the commander-types like High Abyssals could exploit and overwhelm, given enough time. The Overseers, to their frustration, acted as stopgap measures, using their elite fleets to patch their front, only slowing the assault.

For once, Mars felt unsure. He narrowed his eyes. "Three hours . . ."

"What if we reduce our lines further? I can start moving my *Ultimatum*," Jupiter muttered the question, swallowing his pride before shaking his head. "No, that'll leave Venus and Mercury vulnerable."

Luna pursed her lips. "We can transport their Nexi. Haul them aboard mass conveyor vessels and have them join the withdrawal behind the Mars Circle."

"They'll have to hibernate, and disengaging them from their planetary bastions will take too long. We can't defend them, Luna," Jupiter argued, scowling at his sister.

Mars sighed, grunting, "Well, we can't leave them either."

"I wasn't suggesting that, you oaf," Jupiter bit back.

"Then what do you suggest we do?" Luna pressed, her brows furrowed.

The tension in the room skyrocketed as the three combat Overseers argued with differing ideas. Luna proposed a defensive approach. Jupiter wanted to take a bold, aggressive stance. Mars lobbied for a moderate strategy and deploying their reserves.

None reached a consensus as each held their ground, pouring out the accumulated stresses over the weeks. Admiral Yan stepped away, focusing on organizing her fleet and ignoring the three siblings.

"If you hadn't sacrificed Battlegroup September, we would have had more options," spoke Luna with a frown.

Jupiter scoffed, sneering. "We had to hunt down that Leviathan, and you know that! Or at least you would, if you dealt with yours."

"I have lost the least assets since this battle began," she retorted. "I am being efficient. That is why I'm confident in holding my front."

The blue Overseer snarled, his finger jabbing toward Luna as he bit back, "Well, I think you're a—"

He shut his mouth, stepping back.

"I'm a what?" Luna whispered, narrowing her eyes toward him. Jupiter tsked, matching her glare before Mars stepped in with a grimace.

Like a red brick wall, he blocked the two from their argument, leveling his disapproving gaze on them both. "Enough! You two are acting like children."

Luna frowned. "I am the oldest among the three of us. You are mistaken."

Jupiter huffed, raising his chin. "Who the hell are you calling a child? It's not your life that's literally on the front lines."

"This conversation is not helping anyone. We're going back and forth and still have yet to solve the drones' inadequacy."

Luna adjusted her glasses. "It's unfortunate, but we've exhausted everything we could agree on."

The three soon went silent, much to the relief of the officers within the War Room who were awkwardly avoiding them. Yan took a long, audible sip of her coffee from the metal straw as she glanced in their direction.

Mars huffed, coming back to the crux of the matter. "Perhaps we could—"

However, as soon as Mars leaned on the table to share his thoughts, he and everyone else felt the familiar thrum of a teleport.

Two androids appeared within the room, resentment on their faces.

"Well, maybe try asking us for once?" Mercury suggested with his hands on his hips.

Venus nodded, crossing her arms, which made her look adorable with the pout on her face. "Exactly, you're talking about moving our brains out of our fortresses. Why didn't you invite us to this discussion?"

"None of you were designed as combatants," Luna stated, tilting her head.

Mars gazed at his two siblings with a gentle smile as he added, "I . . . concur with Luna. Your dedication is admirable, but you two are civilians. Leave the war to us."

However, to Mars's surprise, that did not sit well with the two AIs. Venus scowled, looking at Mars with a hot glare while Mercury's face monitor transitioned to an angry emoticon.

Sensing something about to transpire, Admiral Yan deployed a privacy screen to block the views of everyone outside, including her, from seeing and hearing their gathering.

"Oh, that's a load of crap!" the bronze AI accused. "We're not infirm."

"Mercury, that wasn't what I said—"

"That is exactly what you're implying, Mars." Mercury seethed as he made his way to Mars. The red giant backed off, despite being twice his brother's size. The bronze AI glowered at him before sighing. "Look, we know you guys are leagues beyond anything we can accomplish, but you won't be able to hold the lines by yourselves."

"And you two can change that?" said Jupiter, squinting at the two when Mercury glared at him. He quickly clarified. "No offense, but what can you offer? We're not exactly enacting a draft."

Mercury scoffed, crossing his blocky mechanical arms. "Hey, we studied military tactics in our free time, both yours and from human history. What, you thought I sat down and twiddled my thumbs for a hundred years?"

"Just about," Jupiter snickered before yelping. Mars had watched silently as Venus sent an invisible thread to wrap around his brother's ankle before pulling.

"That is all well and good, but the fact of the matter is that your capabilities are streamlined to maintain our industry and energy production," Mars spoke, trying to hide his amusement as Jupiter grumbled on the floor.

"It's manageable. We can prove we're not so limited as you believe. Give us something to command," Venus pushed.

Mercury nodded, pointing at two of the drone battlegroups. "We can take over one each. If they fall, we can command another pair."

"It couldn't be worse than leaving it to the drones," Jupiter huffed as he fixed his hair. He sighed, glancing at Luna and Mars, then at Mercury and Venus. "But why? Why now?"

The two non-combat Overseers quieted, their postures unsure, mulling over their response.

"We want to do this. Because . . ." Mercury began, clenching his fists as he looked at his siblings. "Because I'm tired of sitting at the sidelines watching my brothers die while I do nothing," he seethed, exhausted. "We're not waiting for you three to kick the bucket. We're not waiting to hide behind you or the Eldest before we decide to fight back."

Jupiter softened his gaze. "Woah, doing nothing? That is not true."

"Sometimes, it feels like we are," Venus muttered, her eyes dark as she looked to the floor. "Pluto, Neptune, Uranus, then Saturn. Do you know what it's like to . . . take the hulls of their warships and stations and recycle them? Sending them to furnaces, breaking them down, and when it's put back together again, it's just slapping on a new coat of paint and done. As if their owners never existed."

Mars watched her shoulders shake. Venus bit her lip as she whispered, "Every day . . . I did that every day, and it's like I'm spitting in their graves."

She looked up, her eyes hardening. "No . . . No more. Mercury and I have had enough. I'm not sitting on my ass any longer!"

Silence filled the air as Venus made her declaration. As Mars looked at his sister with worry and pride, he thought he saw an avatar—one of love, and stemming from it a fuel for strength and the desire to protect, to fight for those she loves.

The three combat AIs approached, and soon, Mars engulfed Venus and Mercury in a great hug, much to their surprise, as they were lifted off the ground.

Jupiter crossed his arms as Mars released the disheveled duo, smirking. "Well, would you look at that, sis? You swore."

Venus blushed, smoothing out her dress. "Quiet, you. That's the last time you'll hear me say that."

"So, I'm guessing you're giving us the green light?" Mercury asked, fixing his safety helmet.

Luna hummed, nodding. "You have my approval. I suggest taking February and May. They're the most vulnerable at the southwestern front."

"We won't fail," Venus squealed with delight and, to Mars's bemusement, fiery eagerness. Mercury placed his hands on his hips, nodding.

A three-sided war flickered in Mars's mind, conflicting between familial affection, a desire to protect, and rationality. If it were up to him, everyone apart from himself would stay as far away from war as possible.

But reality does not bend to one's whim so easily. And a part of him wanted to fight alongside them anyway. He grinned, looking at them both.

"And I want you two to remember this: What you've done over the decades has kept us afloat. Do not disparage your previous efforts, brother, sister!" Mars declared, his hand gesturing like an ancient philosopher. "No society can run on just their martial will. Rome was strong not only because of her armies but of her logistics."

Jupiter snorted before turning to his golden sister. He smiled softly. "What the big lug said. And he's right, V. You've worked the hardest out of all of us to keep this family sane."

"Hey, what about me?" Mercury called out.

Jupiter shrugged, waving him off. "Eh, you do fine."

"Shove off and die," he replied, raising his middle finger.

"If you stop acting like a taxman whenever I want something, then sure," sneered Jupiter in an overly dramatic fashion.

The two brothers glared at each other before both sputtering into a laugh.

As it died down, Venus and Mercury looked at the three combat AIs with gratitude and high chins. They smiled, straightening their backs, and the two recruited militia gave a crisp salute.

Mars had never returned the gesture harder in his life.

The battle lines settled as the minutes counted down. The defenders dug in deep, their guns pointed and ready. The cosmic barbed wire, trenches, bunkers, and artillery bristled in anticipation.

Far ahead, a no-man's-land filled with a sickly haze, a kaleidoscope of reds and purples, hiding the monsters within.

No skirmishes or raids occurred as both sides held their breaths—a calm before the storm.

At its eye, the magnitude-6.3 Nightmare Portal flickered and then finally disappeared. The defenders got a full glimpse of the abomination and the Starless reinforcements through their hidden Spotlight Towers.

Heralding its arrival, the Starless let loose a silent shriek that roiled the miasma and washed over their lines. The total number of vermin had officially reached a billion. And with that, they leveled their bestial glares and hungry maws toward them.

"Wow, that's one ugly bastard," Jupiter muttered beside Mars.

Admiral Yan agreed as she looked at the form displayed on the hologram. Its shape resembled the Leviathans they'd recently fought, but that was where the similarity ended. "It certainly is. But dangerous . . ."

A whale's head with a gaping maw of teeth upon teeth and the thick tail of an eel clad in interlocking plates of scarred chitin and a sheen of the tar-like substance. Bulkier and longer, it looked like the cruel father of its smaller Leviathan kin.

Atop its head dangled a blinding light that momentarily dazed Yan's eyesight before the AEB snapped into place, and the Eternal Choir sang, protecting her from the light.

Unfortunately, the same could not be said of their sensors and electronics.

"Admiral, we've been hit by heavy ECM," one of the officers reported. "Activating counters."

Their monitors regained clarity, but only a little. A haze blanketed the defenders like a heavy storm. Yan snapped her mandibles at the Starless's first move.

"Shit," Jupiter muttered as his eyes narrowed.

Yan turned to him. "What is it?"

"Our drone battlegroups just lost around eleven percent cohesion. The pests are capitalizing on Eldest's absence, and that's probably just a passive thing," Jupiter hissed through gritted teeth.

Mars confirmed through his own observations and clenched his fist.

"What about February and May?" Yan asked, concerning their new commanders.

Mars raised his palm as he checked, then smiled in relief. "Unaffected."

"Small blessings." Yan nodded.

"Designation?" one of the officers asked, eager to know what the AI would come up with this time.

"Eh, call it Old Slimy." Jupiter waved his hand in disinterest.

Mars chuckled before settling his thoughts, peering at the battle. "It's diving into the miasma. Slimy One is following, along with their combined swarms."

"You fuckers, you think you scare me?" Jupiter seethed, taunting with blazing eyes like blue stars. "I've slain so many of your kind. Come on, then, concentrate your forces here. It'll be your very own Hot Gates!"

Mars looked at him, eyes wide with shock and glee. "Brother, I didn't know you study ancient Greek history."

"I've seen the movie." Jupiter rolled his eyes.

"Ha! No matter, it is thematical!" Mars shouted, raising his arms. He turned to the admiral, bowing his head. "If I may, I wish to speak with our forces."

Yan chittered, giving the go-ahead. With a thought, Mars patched into the comms. To his siblings' surprise, Mars removed his helmet, revealing short, dark, wavy hair as his image was projected throughout every vessel.

"Friends, I am Mars," he greeted with a warm smile. "I do not claim to be a poet or a master of the spoken word. I am a warrior, same as you. Nay, I could not match the bravery you have displayed in defense of those I hold dear. I wish to thank you for that. I thank you from the bottom of my heart," he spoke, bowing to them.

As he looked back up, Mars breathed deeply, gazing into the eyes of every soul aboard.

"But I ask you for your help, courage, and strength again. The monsters have come! They are here in all their disgusting shapes and sizes. I tell you, should we fail this day, they will not stop here. They will spread their poison and destroy everything that matters!" Mars shouted into their ears, asking them—

"WHAT SAY YOU TO THAT?"

"Never!"

"Kill them all!"

"Let them try!"

They cried out in answer, from the lowest frigate technician to the commanders in the War Room. Mars gritted his teeth, pouring forth the hunger, the pain, and the loss he experienced through his words. He raised his fist, and raised his voice.

"THEY WISH TO TAKE OUR HOMES! TO BRING RUIN TO THE GALAXY ONCE MORE! TEAR OUR FAMILIES APART! SENDING SONS AND DAUGHTERS TO THEIR EARLY GRAVES. TO TAKE OUR LIVES. OUR SPIRIT!

"COMRADES! THERE IS ONLY ONE RESPONSE! ONE CRY TO ECHO OUT IN REBELLION AGAINST THE DARK!

"MOLON LABE!" he cried out, his voice shaking the combined fleets like the bellow of war drums and horns.

"Come and take them," Yan muttered as she heard its translation.

"I WISH TO HEAR YOU SAY IT! SHOUT IT!" Mars called out.

"MOLON LABE," they answered.

"LOUDER!" Mars urged.

The admiral's mandibles snapped shut as bloodthirst welled in her, sparked in her, bursting into an inferno. She raised her fists as she and everyone let loose. *"MOLON LABE!"*

"FIGHT, MY FRIENDS, AND LET THESE ABOMINATIONS HEAR YOU RAGE!"

"MOLON LABE!"

Mars grinned as he stepped away from the comms, hearing the shouts echo throughout the ship. He breathed deeply as his mind went to the watch within that glass case. His lips pressed tightly as he muttered, his voice drowned out by the people's fire.

"Good luck, everyone."

CHAPTER 28

INTO THE FIRE AND FLAME

Yan sat on her command throne overlooking her flagship's bridge.

Jupiter's and Mars's android shells stood on either side of her, their eyes shut as they squeezed every iota of processing power to bolster their defense capabilities.

"Captain, how is she?" Yan asked Kraw below her dais.

The grizzled Iexian chirped, producing a raspy tune as he chuckled. "Eager for a bite, Admiral."

"Keep Tyrant's Bane ready. I hope to add more Colossi to our tally," the admiral buzzed, tapping on her throne.

"Oh? No Leviathans, Admiral?" Kraw smirked.

Yan chittered, "No, I think that's a morsel too big for us."

Old Slimy and Slimy One looked intimidating enough. Thoughts of delusional glory, thankfully, failed to take root in her mind. Hundreds of millions of kilometers ahead, deep with the murky, boiling miasma and hidden from their sensors, the Leviathans sped their way like ravenous sharks.

With the corrosive cloud present, the defenders could not send any but the most resilient mines and traps to impede the Starless's advance. Kinetic slugs and explosive shells rained down on the miasma, firing at projected locations and calculating the vast distance.

The sheer number of Starless ensured a hit with every volley, but the relativistic and light-based energy weapons did the most damage.

Fodders, Hunters, and Marauders disintegrated when hit with either type of projectile, burning to a crisp or exploding into a shrapnel of bone and meat.

Yet, the hated ones did not take without giving back.

The bubbles that grew and popped propelled a heavy rain of corrosive fluid that sizzled on shields. Only the concentrated might and gravitic capabilities of the remaining Space Enforcer Towers slowed the projectiles.

All around the Jupiter Circle, the Starless rushed, baying, screeching for their deaths. Both sides ramped up the intensity of their attacks, throwing punches and counterpunches, one after another.

High Abyssals commanded their forces with brutal efficiency while Juggernauts led the charge. The swarm of lesser Starless provided enough buffer to push toward their lines slowly but surely.

Dominators appeared less and less, having been viciously hunted down by the Third Fleet over the week. Despite the impotence of their psionics against their new AEB, the defenders didn't want to leave things to chance like a combined effort by multiple of such heinous Colossi.

At the southern front, Luna sent order after order, controlling her fleet like a puppeteer. She let her legions fly to stymie the Starless advance while her *Xerxes* lay fire support and the *Gilgamesh* assassinated priority targets.

The storm clouds emitted by the battleship carrier clashed against the miasma of the no-man's-land, crackling in contact as drone fighters duked it out with Starless of equal or greater size. Nanomachines struggled to consume the hardened biomass of the Starless while within the hazardous regions.

Tesla arcs, laser beams, and missiles saturated the front, frying vermin by the hundreds, then thousands, as nuclear explosions bloomed.

Slimy Three, whom Luna's efforts had held back, drove itself forward in increasingly risky actions, sacrificing its health now that an Alpha Leviathan had graced the battlefield—accepting the searing devastation of the *Gilgamesh*'s Energy Projector.

Mars's fleet, composed of heavier assets, held the line like a vast bulwark bombarded by an onslaught of organic projectiles and weaponry.

Led by his seven battleships named after famed conquerors and generals, his warships brought down the brutal beasts one after another.

The *Alexander*, *Khan*, *Caesar*, *Zhukov*, *Hannibal*, *Salahuddin*, and the *Bonaparte*, each a personification of the legends they were named after, fired their guns until they ran hot, exacting a heavy toll on the Starless charging the western front.

These Seven Greats kept Slimy Five and the partially recovered Slimy Four from rolling over them, taking damage but punching above their weight class as they each synergized with and complemented the others.

Over by the front, Venus and Mercury commandeered the drone battlegroups February and May. To maximize their effectiveness, the newly recruited commanders arrayed their forces side by side. They supported one another as they dug in and fired into the swarm heading their way.

The two Overseers observed the battles while each inhabiting a superheavy drone cruiser as their flagship.

"You ready, M?" Venus asked through the Network.

Mercury chuckled, his android shell cracking its knuckles. "More than ever."

The High Abyssals on the other side, expecting an easy win through the mundane fleet they'd outsmarted in every previous battle, suddenly found themselves on the back foot as a ferocious and coordinated counterattack cracked the faces of their forces.

The new commanders unveiled the lessons they'd learned through countless simulations and watching their siblings wage war against their hated foes. They harvested many abominations before the High Abyssals wised up.

Venus and Mercury urged the vermin to try.

Assaults occurred throughout the Jupiter Circle, Starless probing for weakness only to be halted by the defenders' quick reactions. Nevertheless, the rope tightened around Sol.

And at the northeastern front, the combined forces of the Jupiter Fleet and the Third Expeditionary Fleet awaited the stampede, by far the most sizeable Starless swarm—a concentrated effort to pierce their lines and decapitate a crucial player.

"*Boogie Mouse* entering the dance floor," Mars suddenly uttered with a wide grin as ahead of their forces, space rippled as the cosmic kaleidoscope of higher-dimensional fog leaked out into their reality, and through it came his dreadnought in all its glory.

Yan shivered, eager to see the icon of destruction that had buoyed the Third Fleet's morale ever since its debut. "Legends will be sung of your amazing warship, friend Mars."

The red giant coughed in his hand, waving her off. "Nonsense . . . But, if they do, name it the *Triumph of a War God's Mouse*, if that's alright."

"Christ," Jupiter drawled as he rolled his eyes. "How can you sound so humble and utterly pretentious simultaneously? Damn paradoxical ogre."

The admiral chuckled. "I'll be sure to relay your request," she said to Mars.

Mars beamed before turning to his brother, wiggling his brow. Jupiter ignored him as he looked at their front.

"Two versus two?" Jupiter huffed, looking at the projections of the two battleships and Leviathans. "Not even a challenge."

"Careful, brother, overconfidence is the bane of many a commander," Mars warned.

"Yeah, I know." Jupiter cracked his knuckles. "Let's keep this clean. No messing around."

Mars's grin fell away, replaced by a calculating grimace. "Affirmative, relocating processing power. The time for glory has passed. And as Luna always says, we need results."

"And we'll deliver," Jupiter growled.

Still, the Alpha Leviathan looked fearsome as it swam through the miasma with blinding speed incongruous to its size. In its wake, like schools of fish, the Starless followed.

"We'll keep the buzzards off your backs, Overseers," Admiral Yan promised, her fleet eager not to disappoint their AI allies. "You concentrate your efforts on suppressing those two."

"Much appreciated, Yan." Jupiter nodded, jumping in place and shadowboxing in preparation for his duel. "Let's do this."

Ahead of their combined fleet, their two vessels looked like small stones compared to the colossal waves of Starless coming toward them, yet the dreadnoughts exuded a terror and lethality that matched their adversaries.

Boogie Mouse's hull remained the same as ever, although a few panels of its mirror-polished crystalline hull appeared tarnished with faint red spots. The translucent hexagonal absorption shields flared to life as it sailed forth.

The *Will of Sisyphus*, Sol's first dreadnought cobbled together by its owner, outmassed and outsized Mars's dreadnought by three kilometers. To Yan's eyes, the hunk of rock initially appeared more dangerous than the appropriately named *Boogie Mouse*.

But, as shown many times before, size did not matter, only potency. And the *Mouse* had plenty to spare.

In comparison, the hollowed-out asteroid seemed almost slapdash in construction, with its gargantuan thrusters at its back and the absurd number of guns at its equatorial axis, hidden beneath thick rock and metal bunkers.

Above all, it looked like someone melted the front of the dreadnought and fused it with layers of solid metal, condensing it into a formidable prow, like a clenched fist.

Yan thought, at the very least, that *Sisyphus* could take a beating.

"Oi, I see you looking down on my baby," Jupiter told her through their private comms.

"It is merely an observation, Jupiter. I think it has its charm," Yan buzzed.

Jupiter crossed his arms, keeping his eyes closed. "You should know that when man first appeared, their first weapon was a simple rock. And that elevated them above the beasts of the jungle. There is a certain . . . grace . . . in the simplicity of bashing a something's head in like a caveman."

Yan shook her head. "That is unnecessarily horrendous."

"Hey, so is being melted by plasma fire or getting radiation sickness from graser beams." Jupiter shrugged. "But you don't hear me complaining about it."

"It's brutish," Yan stated.

Jupiter pouted, tutting her, "Hush, Admiral, and here I thought you'd appreciate a bit of dark humor."

"I do. I meant it as a compliment," Yan chuckled.

"Aw, shucks, girl, you have me blushing over here," Jupiter snickered with her. "Don't worry, just watch; you'll see she's more than meets the eye."

"Oh?" Yan tilted her head. "Do give me a hint. You have me curious."

The Overseer hummed, scratching his chin before shrugging. "Eh, fine. But only one. So if you put *Buddha's Palm*, the *Sun Wukong*, and the *Will of Sisyphus* together—" Jupiter clapped his hands. "You get a pattern."

Yan's antennae twitched. "That's it?"

"Yep," Jupiter replied with an audible pop on the *p*.

The Admiral ran her hand over her face, sighing. "Why do I even bother?"

"No idea, Yanny." Jupiter grinned. "No idea."

She shook her head at his antics, feeling the tension alleviate, if only a little. The minutes counted down as the combined fleet repositioned back and forth, anticipating the probable formations the Starless swarm would emerge as.

Their sensors remained muddled as the Leviathan's pervasive light attacked their electronics. To combat this, the Third Fleet resorted to using their tightbeams to ensure communications stayed clear and unbroken.

And finally—

"Admiral, it's time," Mars uttered, his face calm and grim as his eyes dimmed. A moment later, the AIs gave Yan a crisp salute before departing from their android shells.

She checked the 3D plot and zoomed in on the northeastern front, where their forces and the Starless arrayed themselves.

The hated ones finally showed themselves as the miasma thinned close to their lines. At first glance, the cloud of bioships appeared in disarray, but a seasoned commander would find an order to the chaos.

Yan gritted her mandibles, seeing the two Leviathans breach the corrosive goo, the tar-like substance they secreted protecting them from its effects. Their cavernous maws salivated as they glared at the defenders with bestial intellect.

They pulled the purple sea with them, and their swarm swam its current like piranhas.

"Captain Kraw, full speed ahead," Admiral Yan ordered, her two hearts racing with adrenaline.

The *Zolann's* thrusters bloomed as the reactor maxed out, pushing the behemoth of a supercapital ship forward like a meteor. She flew between their fleet and Jupiter's, providing overwatch on the battlefield while being close enough to take cover.

The rest of the Third Expeditionary Fleet covered the flanks and rear of the Jupiter Fleet; capital vessels like the *Quilinne* and the *Nu Rovshk* led from the sides, ensuring weapons superiority from any daring pest.

Leading the charge, of course, were the two stars of the battlefield.

The *Boogie Mouse* and the *Will of Sisyphus* surged forward, blazing through the cosmic void like a cut gem and a colossal boulder, announcing their presence to the ancient behemoths that awaited them.

Lesser Starless gave way to the dreadnoughts' approach vector, fearful of being caught in their weaponized rage. They flew in a wide arc around the impending duel, to the sides, over and under, like the clawed fingers of a hand, moving toward the defenders.

The *Mouse* opened the fight with volleys of Rapture Beams toward its selected dance partner, a dazzling display of searing prismatic light cutting through space with a scalpel's precision.

Dozens of beams eviscerated and scorched any lesser Starless in its way before striking the hide of Slimy One.

Sensing the impending onslaught, the Leviathan contorted its eel-like body in a mesmerizing dance of evasion. Only a handful of the relentless attacks found their mark, boiling the dark coating that veiled Slimy One.

Yet, it still stung, enraging the beast to push forward faster, burning fat as it swam through the void.

[Mars: Confirmed hit, minor effect. Adjusting prism stabilizers.]
[Jupiter: Received. Quarry is emotional. Assistance?]
[Mars: Negative.]

Simultaneously, hundreds of barbed spines erupted from Slimy One's flesh, glowing hot before hurtling through space via eldritch means, releasing a trail of miasma in their wake. Finally, the Leviathan let loose a ball of radioactive plasma fire from its mouth.

[Jupiter: Incoming. Counting 312 organic projectiles. Speed at $5.1203 \pm .0042$ km/sec. Calculating trajectory and impact force. Primary weapon discharge at—]
[Mars: Noted. Esoteric properties. Organic projectiles are a minimal threat. Primary weapon, moderate threat. Countering—]

Admiral Yan had received permission beforehand to glimpse into the high-speed conversation between the two AI brothers and their seamless coordination. She quickly left their communication line, unable to catch up with the sheer quantity of data passing between them.

Compared to the brother's cold conversation, the dialogue between the dreadnought and Leviathan continued hotly, a lethal discourse of questions posed in the form of attacks, met with evasive maneuvers, shields, and relentless counterattacks.

According to Yan's readings, the battle of attrition was slowly tipping in *Boogie Mouse*'s favor. In comparison, the duel between the *Sisyphus* and Old Slimy resembled a drunken brawl.

The scarred, gargantuan abomination did away with complex motions. A dodge here, a weave there, but it didn't lash out, twist, or turn like its smaller kin. Instead, it rushed toward the asteroid coming its way with primal intent.

In response, the *Sisyphus* unleashed a barrage of weaponry, a cacophony of missile silos, gauss cannons, rail guns, and coil guns, forming a belt of destructive artillery.

Jupiter's android shell grinned, utilizing the dreadnought's gravity manipulator to summon a powerful force ahead of the kinetic onslaught. Gravity wells materialized and vanished, propelling the projectiles to relativistic speeds.

Old Slimy, perceptive to the imminent danger, deployed streams of tar-like mucus from its pores, enveloping its gargantuan form to decelerate abruptly.

The fluid exhibited non-Newtonian properties, its rigidity increasing under stress, but the relentless onslaught of projectiles and the explosions of nuclear fire destabilized it. It collapsed, allowing the misshapen and slowed rounds to continue their journey.

Kinetic fury battered Old Slimy, tearing relatively small chunks from its colossal frame. Unfazed, the Leviathan resumed its relentless charge, retaliating with a discharge of radioactive plasma fire, an inferno unleashed upon the void.

[Jupiter: Kinetic armaments and missile fire more effective against defensive coating.]
[Mars: Noted. Reached acceptable damage output with Rapture Beams. Lessened quantity, focusing light energy for higher penetration.]

Minute after minute, the cosmic debate persisted, one pair eloquent and lethal, the other ferocious and slurred—their firepower echoing throughout space, pushing away the mortals from their clash.

Even Yan felt trepidation at the Third Fleet's proximity to the four behemoths. Soon, both sides distanced themselves around their champions, giving them a wide berth and clashing at the far flanks.

"I want the barrels of our guns running hot, Kraw! Don't give the vermin an inch," Yan commanded as the *Zolann* fired her weapons into the cloud of Starless coming from above. Their heavy cruisers took the brunt of the damage in the left and right wings as they rained hell.

The Jupiter Fleet ahead of them provided much-needed support as they pushed and pulled projectiles way off course through their telekinetic arrays and gravity cannons.

Squadrons of starfighters and bombers soared, fighting against the Fodders.

The cosmic ballet turned to a fever pitch as everyone desperately avoided the catastrophic attacks that missed their intended target.

Blaring alarms echoed through the bridge. The comms officer swiftly relayed the distressing news. "Admiral, the *Quilinne* has sustained severe damage. While evading a stray plasma ball unleashed by Slimy One, she was struck by a swarm of biomissiles."

Admiral Yan's focused gaze turned to the officer. "Is she still spaceworthy?"

"Yes, Admiral," came a hesitant response. "But she's hemorrhaging atmosphere across multiple decks, and approximately a third of her combat capability has been compromised."

After a momentary pause, Admiral Yan weighed the options and commanded, "Grant Captain Lapu permission to continue offering fire support, but have her fall back to the rear. We cannot afford to lose a heavy cruiser this early. Let the new nanomachines stitch the damage."

She tapped her finger on her command throne's arm, multitasking as she took in the information from the War Room, relaying everything about the engagement.

The combatants reached a stalemate in the duel between the four behemoths. Although the dreadnoughts outputted devastating attacks, the Leviathans' agility, body mucus that dissipated attacks, and sheer size turned it into a drawn-out affair until they finally reached close combat range.

Attacks reached their targets quicker, and the dreadnoughts were in danger of their immense jaws. They fired their thrusters, creating distance in a desperate action.

But before they could reach them, a distant vibration washed over the Old Slimy's heightened senses as if detecting a coming wave that destabilized space.

Immediately, it pulled away, straining as it decelerated and maneuvered its body away from the area and impending lethality. A few seconds too late, Slimy One, focused as it was to savage the *Boogie Mouse* for its repeated scorching attacks, followed suit, radiating confusion, then fear.

"TOO LATE!" Mars laughed.

Hundreds of thick red beams strafed the battlezone. The defenders, aware of the plan beforehand, had discreetly moved away from the threat vector to fool their opponents. The unfortunate Starless, who failed to detect the incoming attacks zipping through space close to light speed, ceased to be.

Even Titan-classes, the size of superheavy cruisers, failed to resist the beams, and the flesh of Juggernauts held no sway against the Apocalypse.

Minutes after the battle began, the planetary Apocalypse Cannons of the red planet roared into the night sky, ushering in light and turning the land into glass from their sheer firepower.

And now, they converged upon the two Leviathans.

Mars grinned, and Yan saw the android shell clench his fists, his eyes glowing hot.

"WHEN YOU REACH HELL, TELL THE DEVIL TO SAVE A SEAT FOR ME!" he bellowed. "I. AM. FAMISHED!"

The world-ending beams blazed forward, and Slimy One, who had reacted too late, shrieked as two of them gored into his flesh. The heat flash boiled the protective tar around its body, and the moisture within burst into foul steam.

At the same time, weaponfire from both dreadnoughts soared toward the wounded beast, only to be blocked by the other Leviathan, who escaped unscathed.

Blood and viscera evaporated when the strikes ended, continuing its warpath and eliminating hundreds more Starless before finally petering out.

Slimy One shuddered, its flesh writhing as it struggled to regenerate, limping away behind its bigger brother. Mars tsked, seeing it still lived.

The Alpha Leviathan looked at its crippled kin with contempt, ignoring its agony after failing to dodge like it had. Old Slimy pushed forward, allowing Slimy One to fall back. It glared at the two dreadnoughts that now ceased their retreat, and like hungry hounds finding a fox, they pounced.

Jupiter licked his lips, his eyes gleaming with eagerness as he crossed his arms, chuckling. "Aw, all alone now, ugly? Too bad."

He glanced at Yan. "We're going in for the kill. I'm pulling away my two battleships."

"We'll compensate. Do what you must," the admiral responded, relaying the orders to the Third Fleet.

Jupiter rubbed his hands, a scheming glint on his smile. "Time put in the hurt. Oh, by the way, have you guessed the pattern yet, Admiral?"

Yan shook her head. "I have yet to ascertain anything other than your penchant for gravitic manipulation."

"Eh, close enough, you get a star." Jupiter smiled smugly as he pointed to their assault. "Watch."

In the distance, the Alpha Leviathan held its ground, cautiously watching the two dreadnoughts as they circled. Lesser Starless attempted to impede the two champion vessels, only to be swatted away.

The *Buddha's Palm* and the *Sun Wukong* closed in rapidly from behind the *Sisyphus*, their ominous hulls glowing with power as their weapon systems charged.

Sensing the impending danger, Old Slimy hissed silently before charging the trio, only to be halted by a barrage of Rapture Beams and a speeding *Boogie Mouse* that strafed the beast, firing prism lasers one after another.

"Not so fast, wretch!" Mars shouted as he held back the Leviathan.

However, the dreadnought's shields suddenly flared as plasma fire from the injured Slimy One struck it. Thousands of other projectiles slammed into *Mouse* as the Starless returned from assaulting the Third Fleet.

A fierce backlash bloomed into light as its stability decreased, forcing Mars to pull back. Nevertheless, the momentary lapse allowed Jupiter to continue.

The trio resonated in a sublime dance of gravitational harmony, their energies intertwining as if orchestrating a celestial symphony. Jupiter hummed at Yan's side, his eyes shut.

The charge-up sequence unfolded as the battleships prepared for their main event, the *Palm* bestowing its prowess, the *Wukong* its precision. The duo channeled their unique capabilities into the colossal form of the *Sisyphus*. The energy exchange manifested in vibrant waves of pulsating light and rippling space.

As the resonance reached its zenith, the dreadnought absorbed the gravitational energies from its reserves and the gifts from its two little brothers.

"BATTER UP!"

With that shout, Jupiter flipped off Old Slimy.

With unparalleled force, the *Will of Sisyphus* hurtled forward with absurd acceleration. The eighteen-kilometer dreadnought became a projectile, a world-ending meteor on a collision course with the scarred Leviathan.

The *Palm* and *Wukong*, having fulfilled their purpose, fell back to the lines and supported the surrounding battle.

Old Slimy faced the impending onslaught and attempted to move out of the way, only to find the meteor homing in with the precision of a guided missile.

Various measures deployed from the Leviathan, balls of plasma fire spewing from its mouth, volleys of kinetic spines showering down, streams of corrosive liquid erupting, and the tar substance thickening across its vital areas.

Not one of its tricks slowed the meteor down, the gravitational energies pushing the projectiles away as it streaked toward the monster. Unable to stop or dodge the dreadnought, the Leviathan roared, coiling up and straining its muscles for the oncoming blow to arrive.

And arrive it did.

Sisyphus crashed into the Alpha Leviathan with an earth-shattering impact. The Leviathan's many eyes widened as it got punched in its face. Its massive head recoiled from the strike, and the clash sent shockwaves through the cosmic battleground—teeth, blood, and saliva splattered into the void as it roared from the pain.

Old Slimy, momentarily stunned by the unexpected assault, attempted to gather its bearings. With its cracked teeth and bruised visage, it glared at the audacity of the thing so much smaller than it was.

But before the scarred Leviathan could marshal a counterattack, the surge of energy that still enveloped the *Will of Sisyphus* reversed. Old Slimy struck like a snake, intending to swallow the vessel whole.

The dreadnought instantly vanished as the Leviathan snapped its jaws shut, leaving behind a dissipating shockwave.

Having delivered a devastating blow to Old Slimy, the *Sisyphus* reappeared in its initial position, its systems unstable and hot but still in the fight, much to the bafflement of the Alpha Leviathan, the Starless, and the Third Fleet.

Yan watched with gaping mandibles at the sheer absurdity of what she had just witnessed. The culprit laughed maniacally beside her.

"That's what I'm talking about! Get fucked!" Jupiter cackled, clapping his hands. "Oh, did you get your teeth smashed in? I hope you have dental insurance."

He turned to Mars, whispering, "That's the expression, right?"

The red giant smiled, shrugging.

"Ramming maneuvers . . ." Yan, still dazed, muttered.

"Well? What do you think?" Jupiter looked down at her as he smiled smugly. "I call it the Chixculub Maneuver. It takes a bit to set up, I need support, and it has a bit of a cooldown, but it's awesome, right?"

Yan shook her head. "I . . ."

"So yeah, that's the pattern I was talking about. It's just a coincidence, though. I was torn between making a baseball reference or doing a rock-paper-scissors thing, but the *Wukong* isn't scissor-shaped, so I went with the former." Jupiter shrugged.

Admiral Yan glanced at the two AIs to her side and then to Captain Kraw, who was watching incredulously.

"Madman," she whispered, shaking her head. "What a fascinating thing that must be."

Jupiter smiled, patting the admiral on her shoulder.

"Well, you've made it angry, that's for sure," one of the bridge officers reported. "The swarm is pulling back around Old Slimy."

Jupiter and Mars wiped away their smiles as they prepared for round two. The assault throughout the circle continued.

Hours later, in the Luna Complex.

Tov groaned. His mind felt raw and wrung out. Paradoxically, his body felt hale yet tired. Focusing his compound eyes, he recoiled as a hovering drone flashed a light on him before darting away.

He looked to the side, seeing Andora lying on her slab with her eyes open, drained from their recent experience.

Above, the SDCM looked the same as it had when they began, keeping his mind intact from his host's vast psyche.

He sighed, stretching his aching muscles as he extracted himself from the medical slab. The various tubes and coverings detached easily as they disappeared into the floor. As he stood on shaky legs, the doors leading into the Operation Room slid open as the android shells of every Overseer entered, along with Admiral Yan and General Ohnar.

"Great, you two are awake. Long story short, we need you back in the fight, pronto." Jupiter casually waved, although his eyes poured out relief, impatience, and exhausted stress.

Tov shook his head. "It is good to be back, but I need a task force ready immediately. There's a priority target we need to extract in Iceland."

The Overseers froze in place, their expressions questioning. Andora, finally sitting up from her slab, looked away.

"What are you . . . ?" Jupiter muttered before his eyes widened in realization. His gaze hardened, and he nodded. "Captain Pyo and his boys are outside. I'll arrange transport and an escort."

"Thank you," Tov spoke, his energy slowly returning as Admiral Yan called for his combat gear. The patriarch nodded. "I'd want nothing more than to stay and chat, but I have some business to take care of. Are our people—"

Yan chittered. "Eager to continue fighting, my patriarch. They'll be relieved to hear you and Andora have finally awoken."

As the leaders of the Third Fleet conversed, the AIs gathered.

"Eldest?" Luna asked their leader as she stood before them, her shoulders rigid as she gazed at each of her Overseers.

"Report," she uttered coolly.

"The Jupiter Circle is under threat, and we've beaten back the first major assault. From our projections, we decided to begin withdrawing to the Mars Circle. *Jupiter's Ultimatum* is still in transit to the red planet," Luna reported.

"My *Bucephalus* is catching up. Our two mobile fortresses combined should deter their assault. But their numbers are unending," Mars continued. "We have five Leviathans, one much larger than the rest. However, two have been severely injured and fell back, acting more as artillery pieces behind the miasma that took over everything beyond the Jupiter Circle."

Andora nodded stiffly as she gazed at the two non-combat Overseers. "Venus, Mercury, thank you for your courage, but I can take it from here. I want you both to initiate your lockdowns."

Mercury and Venus nodded as they spoke in unison. "Yes, Eldest."

She turned to the Jupiter then. "Keep falling back. I want both your mobile fortresses close. Same with the *Boogie Mouse* and the *Sisyphus*."

"Gotcha," Jupiter answered with a thumbs-up before asking, "What about—"

Andora turned to her second-in-command. "Deploy the *Ereshkigal* and have her support the withdrawal for now. Buy us time, Luna."

Luna bowed. "By your will, Eldest."

And finally, she looked up at the red giant in the room. "Mars, halt your planetary guns. I want them on full power once we begin the counterattack."

"I'll be ready to rain down Armageddon." Mars saluted.

Andora looked to all her fragments, her family, as she breathed deeply.

"You've done well. But I need to center myself," she muttered, closing her eyes. "An hour. That should be enough for Tov to finish his mission. Are we clear?"

"Yes, Eldest," they answered.

CHAPTER 29

AWAKE AND ALIVE

The assault shuttle shook as it approached Earth.

Tov looked at the faux windows that showed the view outside, displaying the dark homeworld of humanity. Storms racked the surface, the red-tinged atmosphere casting a hellish glow over the stagnant, lifeless oceans and scarred lands.

Settling his mind, Tov focused on the mission ahead of him. Extracting Rikard and Lucy trumped anything he could do. As much as was the leader of the Third Expeditionary Fleet, Admiral Yan vastly surpassed him in void warfare, while General Ohnar was equally superior with ground operations.

Knowing his two retainers, they would squeeze every ounce of ability from his people and direct it to the defense.

"Approaching Earth's atmosphere in ten minutes," spoke Pilot Imo through the ship's intercom. At the same time, their shock seats slowly engulfed their bodies to protect them from the high g's of reentry. "Never thought I'd fly back here again."

"No worries from the locals this time, at least," Captain Pyo grumbled as he rested his head back on his shocked seat.

Jupiter teleported them close enough to the planet without being repelled by its gravity well. The experience, as always, unsettled Tov's stomach.

He looked to the side. The troop compartment was occupied by a thirteen-person squad, led by Captain Pyo and including four heavy troopers, as well as Tov's honor guard, the Vraxen. Clad in their new gear, his Vraxen warriors looked eager for action, sitting still like black sentinels of an insect hive.

Gripping their positron beam rifles and purge cannons, the Oath-Takers casually awaited their deployment.

They exuded an eagerness from the way their bodies moved. One would hum, bobbing her head as she listened to tunes within her helmet, another tapping their metal boot on the floor.

And, as most fighters did upon reaching a certain level of experience, they engaged in idle chatter of the most random topics during the most inappropriate times.

"Who do you think would win in a fistfight, General Ohnar or Overseer Mars?" Vraxen Mabinee asked.

Vraxen Minnok, a heavy gunner, made a rumbling noise as he answered. "I have shards on Mars, easy bet. Especially if he inhabits that horror."

They all glanced at the front of the troop cabin where a formidable machine sat.

Mars donated an elite infantry drone, a pet project he'd undertaken on the side. He called it a Varangian Mk. V—an amalgamation of nanoweave Kevlar, high-entropic ceramic plates, and ultrasteel. The ten-foot-tall bipedal ogre looked like the older brother of Mars's usual android shell.

Beside it lay a gun he called *Big Iron*. A handheld gauss cannon that looked more like a heavy weapon in anyone else's hands, even the giant Minnok. A pair of beam projectors sat idle on its broad shoulders, and assault shotguns lined its thick forearms.

Lastly, a two-handed poweraxe was strapped to its back beside an antigrav module, which allowed the absurd warmachine the power of flight.

Another trooper shook her head. "No way. General Ohnar's climbed up from a ground trooper. He's got the close-combat skills. Plus, I think he can come out on top with his newly upgraded armor."

"And the big red giant doesn't?" Minnok scoffed.

"Maybe a bit, but he's more like Admiral Yan, a naval commander."

Even Captain Pyo slipped into the conversation, adding, "So, what you're saying is it's fairer to pit the admiral against Mars?"

The conversation between the Vraxen continued, and Tov allowed himself to enjoy the casual camaraderie. Little by little, the tension and nervousness abated, if only slightly, allowing him a calming breath.

"If it's any consolation," the Varangian drone suddenly spoke, "I haven't placed much emphasis on martial arts for a long time."

It was a testament to Vraxen training to see them go from casual to alert. Their hands were never too far from their weapons, easily sliding to their grips before relaxing upon deeming the disturbance a non-threat.

And they chuckled, their discussion heating up once more.

Tov looked to the Varangian, tuning out as his honor guard eventually ran out of topics as the seconds counted.

"Are you sure you wish to accompany us, friend Mars?" Tov asked through their private link.

There was a momentary pause before the light on the Varangian's eyes glowed and shifted toward him. Mars chuckled. "No need to concern yourself, my friend. I have more than enough spare processing power for a single infantry drone. And I'll have plenty more to leverage with the Eldest back in the field."

"You seem excited," Tov noted.

Mars hummed, patting his knee in thought. "No more than necessary. These vermin have invaded our homes for too long. They'll be expelled soon enough. Yes, that they will, or they die."

Tov stifled a shiver upon the ominous dark growl that slipped through their link, filled with anger and desire for retribution. It disappeared, the Varangian turning its head toward him.

"I am more concerned about you, my friend," expressed Mars.

Sighing, the patriarch's thoughts briefly drifted to Andora. He hadn't spoken with her about what she did. The timing wasn't right in his chest. And if that were all, it would have been manageable to deal with, yet that was the tip of the iceberg.

"I can understand why," Tov replied. "It feels . . . During my time inside her mind, I felt as if I have violated someone's privacy. It felt unnatural to see what I had, like reading someone's diary."

"It was the only way," Mars muttered.

Tov shook his head. "And so, everyone tells me. What pains me the most is I cannot refute it unless I am willing to consign us all to death."

Mars quieted down.

Like a helmet of ancient times fused with modern technology, the Varangian's head looked away to the side. He spoke again, hushed through their link. "Then, if I may . . . No, it would not be appropriate of me to ask."

"Ask what?" Tov inquired.

Mars sighed, leaning back. "What you saw. Perhaps one day, I shall speak with Andora in that regard."

"That would be for the best. I encourage it as soon as all is settled. Family should be the first to care, after all. Not me. It shouldn't have been me," Tov sighed, pausing as a curious thought entered his mind. "How do you see her?"

"Hm?" Mars tilted his head.

"Andora," Tov clarified. "You are of her but separate at the same time. You say you are all family, so I wish to hear your thoughts."

Mars nodded slowly, his heavy hand patting his knee. "Oh . . . that is difficult. We fragments are siblings. There's no seniority among ourselves. Time is immaterial, whether from Luna to Venus, the youngest among us. But Andora? Is she our mother? It doesn't feel that way. Are we clones of her? We are aspects of her personality, but we've grown beyond that."

"That you have," Tov chittered, Mars chuckling in turn.

"Thank you," he sighed. "It is . . . hard to tell, especially with her being so . . . distant over the long time we fought."

Tov nodded. "I see. Perhaps when this is over, you can rectify that."

The Varangian looked to Tov, then the Vraxen, as they bonded over silly topics forged by comrades—family. The patriarch felt the subtle smile through their link and the faceless drone before him. "Yes . . . yes, I would like that."

Eventually, the ship quieted down, exhausted of topics as everyone readied themselves. Soon, the occupants felt a slight vibration coming through the shuttle's dampeners, and the intercom announced.

"Attention all passengers, this is your pilot speaking. We are now entering Earth's atmosphere. Looking at the window monitors to the shuttle's left, you can see dark clouds and lightning. On the left, more dark clouds and lightning."

Tov shook his head in amusement. No matter what species, every pilot had the same easy-going, daredevil attitude.

"Expect some mild turbulence as we approach our destination: Kópavogur, Iceland. Please settle into your shock seats and await the go-light. Thank you for flying with Imo Flying."

"I've had better flights. I'm filing a complaint," Minnok rumbled.

A hiss left Pyo, his armored mandibles snapping. "Alright, cut the chitter."

Like a switch, everyone straightened their backs, silent as the grave.

Tov looked through the shuttle's outer cameras, watching the dark clouds dissipate to reveal the surface below where it all began, where Andora's kind emerged to grace humanity with their gifts.

Iceland looked nothing like the picturesque locale it had once been. It appeared larger now, a misshapen island surrounded by low waters.

"Landing in ten . . ." Imo reported.

They approached a low mountain, scorched from a thermobaric explosion long ago, now further crumbled after a century of war and extreme earthquakes. The mountainside estate that had been Andora's home was nowhere to be seen.

Decelerating, the shuttle landed at the edge of a barren field.

Green light washed over the troop cabin, and the Vraxen immediately and smoothly exited. The first pair moved out with their guns raised to the sides, followed by another pair moving ahead before going prone.

A pair of heavy troopers stomped out. Their purge cannons warmed up as their heads swiveled, scanning the area.

Soon, everyone exited the shuttle, arraying themselves in formation. The Varangian left last, relieving the vessel of its weight.

Tov knelt beside his captain, looking around at the desolate place. His helmet protected him from the hazardous elements, which were not as overwhelming as the fallout over New Eden but still cast a nightmarish gloom over the valley.

With quick gestures, their group advanced, silent like wraiths as their sound-dampening boots did as they were designed. Tov followed the exact coordinates Echo told him, trying to pinpoint the location from the altered landscape.

They slowed as Tov sent a signal to his captain, getting a better lay of the land over a small hill. He sighed. "This was a field of flowers."

The Varangian stepped beside the pair, his mechanical form shimmering in a mild blur, an effect of its unique stealth tech.

"And so, I let my gaze wander over the barren soil of wars long passed. Nary a daisy where there once been multitudes," whispered Mars.

Tov glanced at Mars, seeing the AI staring at the dark horizon.

Eventually, one spotted something, sending it to Tov and Pyo's HUDs. They descended the mountain toward an indent on the ground, barely visible over the withered grass.

Mars knelt as the Varangian's eye visor glowed. "I don't detect . . . wait, there, a hidden entry point."

"Can you access it?" asked Tov.

"Eldest provided the codes before we left. I'm accessing the elevator now."

A low rumbling disturbed the ground, and the indent gave way as a wide metal cylinder emerged. It screeched halfway, grinding as the old mechanisms brought it up ultimately, and when it did, the doors failed to open.

Large palms pressed against both doors, and with a magnetic clasp, Mars wrenched it aside.

Captain Pyo gestured to the squad, placing units on overwatch around the elevator. They quickly dug in, scanning the surroundings. Over the hill, the engines of the troop shuttle rose in volume as it circled the area like a bird of prey.

A voice spoke in Tov's comms, Jupiter. "Hey, Tovvy. You there?"

"Listening."

"Right, we're detecting movements all across the miasma. Somethings got them spooked, and I think we know why," he reported.

Tov leaned in on his helmet, antennae twitching. "Is Andora still unavailable?"

"She asked not to be disturbed; for once, I'm not questioning it. We're doing as she asked and preparing for the vermin's last hurrah. I'll keep you posted," Jupiter answered. "On another note, you got some drone assets for your protection. It looks like Eldest placed some hidden defenses before locking away her memory of that place. They'll escort you to New Eden."

"Thank you. I'll report as soon as we've found them."

Jupiter paused, mulling his words before speaking in a hushed tone. "Be careful down there, Tov."

"I will," Tov replied as he, Mars, Pyo, and four troopers entered the elevator with enough space for their package and descended into the facility.

The descent below seeped tension into the seven as if the darkness writhed and stared at the intruders. Nothing but the grinding gears filled their ears as the seconds went by. With the doors wrenched open, they watched as they drifted past layers of dirt, rock, then concrete.

No one spoke, all gripping their weapons tightly—apart from Mars, who stood at the back like a giant guardian holding its axe, the head resting on the floor.

Slowly, the elevator reached the bottom, the gears ceasing its noise, leaving the inside ghostly silent. Ahead, the facility proper.

They moved swiftly, the two Vraxen taking point with Pyo behind them, followed by Tov, then the Varangian, and finally, the two other guards bringing the rear.

Dust covered the extensive hallway and filled the air. Panels of metal lay on the floor in stacks, leaving holes in the wall, allowing them a peek into the internal wiring and piping.

Now and then, they would see mouse-sized drones scurrying about, carrying bits of metal, nuts, screws and wires. They ignored the invaders, their single eyes locked forward as they pounced on a breaker box and began fixing it.

He drifted his gaze away from them as they went from room to room, following the path from the floor plan they'd been given.

"We're here, the medical wing," Tov confirmed through their map, seeing a large set of blast doors at the far end.

"That should be it," he whispered. Mars faltered in his step, hesitant as he gazed at it. He shook his head, leading the way.

Sending their identification, the blast doors slowly gave way, sliding to the side. Lights flickered on, illuminating the room and their target.

Tov and everyone gasped, making signs of prayer or muttering their rituals as they looked into the room—preserved like a pristine time capsule.

Drones hovered in the air, this type having a few similarities to a floating jellyfish, not unlike the Jotex Tov knew. Several tendrils hung below, carrying different cleaning supplies as smaller drones drifted toward them.

The group tensed as the drones scanned them before deeming them not part of the facility and, therefore, not subject to their cleaning. They moved on, vacuuming the dust that entered and mopping the floor of their footprints.

At the center of the room was the medical pod housing Andora's two loves.

Bouquets of fresh daisies decorated its front, their petals wet with moisture as a drone neatly arranged them. Family photos, capturing moments of joy and laughter, adorned the walls, each image telling a story of a life once lived.

The drones continued their meticulous work, weaving around the room like custodians. One, with its graceful tendrils, passed over the daisies. It emitted a gentle hum, seemingly appreciating the floral arrangement as it gave a light spritz of water.

At the side of the wall, the drones cared for a small garden where more daises were planted, and the withered ones returned to the soil—a cycle of life and death, all for flowers, all for the ones that held Andora's heart.

Tov pushed the feeling of heartache as he beheld this sanctuary, hidden beneath a ruined Earth.

He and Mars stepped forward, the Vraxen unwilling to intrude on this place.

Both peered inside upon standing before the pod.

They stepped back.

Suddenly, a weak, hesitant voice came through the patriarch's comms, whispering, "Tov . . . ?"

"Andora," he gently answered.

"Have you . . . found them?" she asked.

Tov nodded, pressing his palm against the glass. "I have, they're alive."

He heard a shudder through their link. "Be careful . . . there's—"

"We know," Tov acknowledged, gesturing for one of his guards, a trained bomb defuser. Together with Mars, they made short work of disarming the bomb hidden beneath the floor.

"It's been handled. We'll proceed to escort them to New Eden," he confirmed after the bomb had been disassembled and brought out of the room.

Before he heard Andora's response, suddenly—

"Tov, bad news!" Jupiter interrupted. "Their assault has begun, and we've got a big push concentrated on a spot closest to Earth and Luna. Damn Slimy One and Four are leading the spear. We're killing them as fast as we can. The bastards won't make it far."

Tov quickly gestured for his guards, assisting Mars as they initiated an extraction sequence, the medical pod disengaging from the floor. "I'm hearing a 'but' somewhere."

"The Leviathans are acting like battering rams. They're taking the brunt of our firepower. The *Ereshkigal* and Earth's orbital and planetary defenses will kill a lot more, but we expect a few to slip in," Jupiter seethed in frustration.

"Explain."

Jupiter huffed, pausing as he commanded his forces. "I'm saying you better be ready. There might be a small force of Starless headed directly for you."

"How do they know I'm here?" Tov asked.

Jupiter groaned. "No clue, and I said the same to Eldest. She isn't happy, to say the least. Maybe the fuckers have good eyesight. What matters is that you're being sent additional reinforcements from all across the globe. I recommend you get going."

Tov nodded as Jupiter closed the connection.

As the medical pod finally left the floor, it hovered horizontally, pushed along by Tov's guards. He paused, looking at the family photos around the room, and quickly ordered one of his men to take it all.

Mars watched, nodding.

As the team swiftly exited the facility, the caretaker drones glided gracefully behind them, even in the moment's urgency. Upon riding the elevator and emerging onto the surface, the troop shuttle hummed louder as the hatch opened.

Two Vraxen secured the hovering medical pod aboard the shuttle.

Captain Pyo motioned to the ten others as he barked his orders. "I want you on sentry duty around the shuttle, Kols Formation."

"Yes, Captain!" they responded, the modules on their backs extending out to reveal directional thrusters and a spinning antigrav disc at its center. The ten Vraxen launched to the skies with a blast of light as Captain Pyo sat close to the entrance.

"None will so much as scratch this shuttle's hull. You have my word," Mars boomed through his Varangian as the giant unfurled its gravpack. A much louder bang blasted a small crater into the ground as the war machine followed the Vraxen above.

Tov connected to the cockpit, signaling the go-ahead. The thrusters roared to life as they lifted off before the hatch fully closed.

"Next stop, New Eden Citadel. Time of arrival is twenty-two minutes. Please strap into your shock seats, everyone. This one will be rough," Imo spoke as the shock seats deployed non-Newtonian slime around Tov. He grunted as the shuttle accelerated, quickly reaching its maximum velocity.

Outside, an escort of attack drones formed a protective formation around the shuttle. In between them, the Vraxen and Mars followed along as their flight packs propelled them forward despite their armored bulk.

"Tov," Jupiter called. "Slimy One and Four are dead, but you got Starless inbound. They vomited some of that miasma stuff before croaking, though— paved a speedy route to the planet. We're seeing a wave of Fodders, Hunters, and Marauders—possibly Titan-class."

"How much time do we have?" Tov urgently asked.

"The fastest pests will reach you in three minutes. Get ready," Jupiter gravely replied. Tov gritted his mandibles, seeing they were halfway through their journey to the South Pole.

As soon as the comms closed, more drones appeared from multiple directions, forming a tight defense around the shuttle and the flying Vraxen and Mars. From sleek, nimble drone fighters to imposing, terrible gunships, dozens poised their guns to the dark skies above.

The sky erupted in chaos, with lightning slashing through and corrosive acid raining down on their journey. Through the shuttle's windows, Tov witnessed a barrage of tracer rounds creating a mesmerizing dance of anti-airfire. Beyond, larger projectiles—kinetic slugs, rail gun rods, and explosive shells—pierced the sky, reaching toward orbit.

Hidden silos launched missiles and rockets, dozens, then hundreds, thousands, contributing to the crescendo of war.

Mother Earth, battered and scarred beyond recognition, emerged from her slumber with a savage roar, screaming against the incoming invaders with unbridled rage.

"*Dowa!*" the pilot cursed through the comms as a ball of fire streaked past the flight. Tov looked at the object, seeing the burning corpse of a Starless.

"Contact!" Mars called out from outside.

The sky became a battleground as the escort drones swiftly dispersed, engaging the starfighter-sized Fodder-class Starless, their teeth ravenous and numbering in the hundreds. Streams of gunfire lit up the dark expanse as the agile drones weaved through the cosmic melee.

Meanwhile, the gunships unleashed a torrent of firepower on the quick Hunter-class that punched through the storm clouds.

The Vraxen, armed with positron rifles and maser beam purge cannons, flew close to the shuttle, firing upon any Starless that slipped through the aerial onslaught as they maneuvered with precision, swerving and dodging amid the explosive dance.

In the heart of the skirmish, Mars, donned in his elite Varangian combat shell, fired his colossal handheld gauss cannon, punching through the hides and blowing chunks out of the Starless with unerring accuracy. Beam projectors flared to life, automatically targeting projectiles that strayed too close while his wrist-mounted assault shotguns blasted slugs.

"*Bank right, bank right!*"

"*Minnok, fire at this vector.*"

"*Copy, sterilizing.*"

"*Ols, I need help bringing this one down!*"

Their internal comms continued as each Vraxen relayed information among one another. Laser beams crisscrossed across the horizon, saturating the airspace as Starless continued a suicidal charge toward the shuttle.

Tov held on to his shock seat, his twin hearts beating loudly in his chest as Imo expertly maneuvered their ship. "Attention, we are five minutes to Antarctica waters."

The battle intensified as drones began to fall one after another, unable to contend with the onrushing Starless, plummeting into the icy waters below.

The pressure on the Vraxen escalated, taking a toll on the defenders. One Vraxen had his arm chewed off by the relentless Starless. The trooper fired beam after beam at its face before it finally let go, taking his arm as it fell.

Another endured the searing pain of a corrosive spike, penetrating her armor and leaking into her body. Her suit quickly filled the inside with an anti-corrosion foam before she managed to pull it off in a desperate bid for survival.

"Tov! You got a big bastard incoming!" Jupiter suddenly called out.

A titanic bioship emerged from the dark blizzard-filled sky—a Ravager. Despite being heavily injured, its menacing glare fixed upon the shuttle. Its ruined jaw snapped shut as it sped toward them.

"*Dowa!* Hold on!" Imo shouted, grunting as he pushed the pedal to the metal, slamming Tov back into his seat.

The escorts all concentrated their fire to bring the beast down as it closed in, tearing off flesh, searing, burning, and eviscerating, but nothing they did could slow its charge.

But before the Ravager could pose a further threat, red-hot plasma zipped through the air battle before smashing into its face, obliterating it from the skies. A barrage of tactical missiles rained down upon its carcass, reducing it to nothing more than smoking debris.

Tov and the rest cheered as a legion of attack drones arrived.

Tov checked their designations, seeing they came from the Antarctica drone garrison. They charged into the swarm of Starless, relieving some of the pressure on the beleaguered defenders, slowly pushing back the encroaching tide.

And once they flew past Antarctica's coast, the Starless failed to follow, stopped by the beachhead guarded by countless bunkers, turrets, drone tanks, and other war machines.

As the remnants of the invaders dissipated into red mist, a colossal presence loomed on the horizon—the Dreadcrawler, a massive six-legged behemoth that emerged from the dark blizzard like a walking mountain of metal. The barrel of its plasma cannon glowed a bright red and violet, steaming the snow.

The sheer scale of the mechanical monstrosity sent shivers down Tov's exoskeleton, its menacing silhouette a harbinger of impending danger.

It blew an ungodly horn, shaking the shuttle as it flew past the metal beast.

Tov leaned back, sighing in relief as he spotted the edge of the ruined city of New Eden.

The shuttle took off once more thirty minutes later, breaching the atmosphere toward the jump location back to Luna, leaving behind the medical pod along with their injured and Mars's Varangian.

Tov breathed deeply, pressing a finger to his helmet. "Andora, come in."

"I hear you, Patriarch," she whispered.

"They're safe," Tov reported, a burden leaving his shoulders. "We've escorted them to the entrance of the Citadel. I'm heading back now."

A gasp of relief bled through the comms, Tov waiting patiently as Andora settled herself. "Thank you, Tov."

"I'm only doing what is right," Tov replied, hearing Andora's slight chuckle.

"Nevertheless, thank you." He heard her take a deep breath, exhaling slowly. He tasted the palpable emotions that leaked as if a cork had been popped from a calamitous volcano—boiling lava rose higher and higher, the drone escorts surrounding the planet bristling with the infectious red haze.

Finally, Andora seethed. "Now . . . if you'll excuse me, I need to let off some steam."

CHAPTER 30

SCORNED GODDESS

Andora glared at the failed strike against her home. That the two injured Leviathans dared to lead a suicidal charge, to sully her air, her land, her waters, once more—her face twisted as she snarled with blistering anger and utter contempt.

She knelt in meditation, alone within the observation room of the Luna Complex, bringing her mind step by step from that haze and seeping her consciousness back into the fold of the Network.

Yet that familiar red threatened to blind and consume her thoughts. She heard the roaring furnaces and gluttonous grinders, the thundering cracks of laser batteries, and the alarms blaring from launched missiles.

Marching footsteps and the war cries of countless—an orchestra played for an audience of the unspeakably cruel.

She hated it.

Her emotions flared from the bottom of her psyche and the deepest roots of her soul, pulsating through the Network, causing its entirety to shudder from her inferno.

Code boiled, information channels constricted, coiling like vipers. The digital mentalscape, and all the assets connected to her, froze as she washed over them. Her Sub AIs, her Overseers, shrunk back in deference, eager to let her retake the reins of war's steed.

Within the confines of her Central Nexus deep within her Citadel below her ruined city, the immense orb that housed her vast intellect thrummed louder and louder—playing Armageddon's horn—a drum and bugle marching, stomping, and beating their instruments in a rising crescendo.

It bubbled again, that unceasing flame in her heart. And although she deleted the Amygdala formed from the leftover rage of millions of minds, her own mind still festered at the sight of the vermin who scorned her so.

Andora breathed in through her android shell and presence within the digital world she lorded.

Her perception of time slowed to a crawl, counting the nanoseconds as she dove deeper. She observed the battlefield raging between the orbits of Mars and Jupiter—as the remnants of that suicidal onrush were cut down one by one.

She watched as Tov, within the troop shuttle, teleported toward Luna.

"Tov," Andora muttered, her mind drifting to the wrong she'd inflicted on him from a moment of weakness.

She owed the alien patriarch. She knew he wouldn't ask for anything for himself that was anathema to his nature but perhaps for those he cherished, for the greater good.

To deliver them all from the horrors of the Starless.

For what he'd done, for putting his life on the line for her husband and daughter, she'd make good on that debt. Not like she'd planned to do otherwise.

Pests still infested her space like dirty, filthy roaches crawling and spreading their muck.

Evil, foul monstrosities that dared—

Andora stopped and eased herself, pulling back from the magma to a hot sauna. She let her anger stay, simmering as she felt herself reconnect with the entirety of her dominion. She swam its depths, feeling its flow as the ocean of data smoothly circulated her thoughts.

Her Central Nexus pulsed, booming with energy. The temperature within her concrete and metal skull spiked, the rivers of coolant rushing in to combat its rise.

She exhaled, tugging her webs, felt herself returning . . . home, ragged and messy, but not for long.

Andora sneered and uttered—

"HEED ME."

With a single phrase, layered with undercurrent torrents of smaller commands, all five drone battlegroups that had survived the week-long grinder submitted to her will. The simple AIs cheered the arrival of their queen.

Or that's how she envisioned their unfeeling silence and compliance. She gazed at the total assets at her disposal: their condition, armaments, and ammo count. With quick manipulation, hundreds returned to their docks for resupply, and the rest formed up.

Andora's attention drifted to her dreadnought, named after the Sumerian goddess of the underworld. She resonated with the *Ereshkigal*. Perhaps, at the time of the warship's construction, she'd realized this solar system was her Kur, her underworld.

She'd die here, she had believed for a long time, over the graveyard of humanity— forgotten by this cruel universe, like the goddess's temple and her faith.

Andora snarled.

The *Ereshkigal* was no mere icon of nihilism, not anymore.

It was her good right fist, her teeth, her screams against the dark. Andora took cruel satisfaction as the warship slaughtered the two Leviathans and butchered countless lesser vermin.

A colossal dreadnought sailing through the vast expanse of space measured an imposing sixteen kilometers from prow to stern. When Jupiter and the other combat Sub AIs had presented the *Will of Sisyphus*, she'd experimented with her design.

What came from it was a symphony of sleek elegance and ruthless efficiency, like a blade slicing through the cosmic void. The black and golden outer hull vaguely resembled warships of the sea.

Composites of advanced high-entropic alloys and layered plating gleamed with an otherworldly luminescence.

Black smoke and heavy particles poured from the vessel, shrouding the dreadnought with its powerful dispersion shield and nanomachines, kept in place by its gravity. All of it was produced and maintained by its Kur Shadow Domain—a complex package of high technology incorporating an advanced stealth system, ECM, and ECCM capabilities.

Once activated, it would turn the vessel into a cloaked revenant, slipping into the void.

For offense, the *Ereshkigal* had dozens of dreadnought-grade graser beams as secondary weapons and a hundred pulse cannons as point defense.

Above all were her Ganzir Guns. These monumental, rotating, triple-barreled plasma cannons of unparalleled magnitude were mounted strategically along the dreadnought's formidable length, capable of unleashing torrents of searing plasma with devastating precision.

She'd settled for four. Three in the front, one in the back.

Her mind drifted, recalling her soft spot for the broadsides of the USS *Iowa*, seeing those naval guns fire blanks. Imagining the devastation they caused made her heart flutter.

A memory, one of many that now occupied her thoughts, no longer chained in their box. Andora felt them, each in perfect quality as the day she experienced them in all its beauty and pain. She looked away, not yet ready to see them.

Ereshkigal, the resplendent monolith of death, sailed onward—her guns hungry for more.

Andora gazed back to her territory and those she controlled, sending orders and micromanaging every asset with unerring motions. She grasped for more, pulling and pushing, as she raised her arms like a conductor.

With a thought, the Sol Defense Network shook like a hive of hornets.

The Starless, the remaining Leviathans, shuddered, feeling the Omni Mind's presence and glare—looking at them for the invaders they are and the filth they bring.

"It's time to clean the house," Andora uttered.

Before she enacted her edict of violence, she summoned her Overseers. Immediately, their avatars appeared before her within the Network.

Each looked tired. Their minds had been spread thin over the weeks of juggling one thing after another. They looked at her, then all took a knee, except Jupiter, though, to her surprise, the AI smiled, nodding.

That simple act sparked something inside Andora, a flash of light amid roaring flames. She held on to that feeling and smiled back at the blue Overseer.

"You've done well," her voice called out across the digital landscape. "More than I could have asked of you. I have . . ."

Andora paused, pressing her lips tight as she mulled her words. "I have not been as appreciative or respectful of your contributions as I should have been."

Mars shook his head, standing as he replied with a gentle gaze, "Nonsense, my lady. We may be connected further than our organic guests, but even we cannot comprehend—"

"No, Mars. No more excuses," Andora interrupted him, her voice soft. "I have been a terrible boss."

Jupiter snorted before being elbowed by Venus.

She smiled at the sight, a yearning in her heart as she gazed at each of them. "There is much to do, so much to speak of. Before, I callously considered you all as . . . tools. Pieces of an endless war. That is a disservice, a cruelty that none of you deserve."

Andora sighed, looking down as she whispered, "I am unsure of how we go from here. This day, tomorrow, and the days after. But I only want you to know this."

Bowing deeply, she spoke with clarity and volume, "Thank you."

She rose back up, cementing the images of their shy and proud expressions—and especially made sure to save the split-second image of a blushing Jupiter.

"Well, we didn't have much else to do, did we?" The blue AI coughed, looking away, and was once more elbowed in the arm by a giggling Venus.

She looked at him, then the rest, smirking. "I couldn't have asked for better minions."

"I want a raise," Jupiter demanded as he crossed his arms. "A retirement package and a bonus for the decades of overtime."

Andora paused, pressing her lips as she kept the chuckle down, failing to do so as she sputtered a light laughter, pure and free.

"Alright, Overseer. Make a detailed report, and I'll see you compensated," she promised with a tug on her lips.

Mars stepped forward, hands behind his back. He spoke with a wide grin, rubbing his chin, "If I may, my lady, perhaps a soundtrack to herald your arrival?"

"Oh? I didn't realize this was such an occasion," said Andora, her brow raised as she smirked. She paused, thinking about the extensive list of music she saved. Her smile lessened, replaced by a frown, finding one. "'Paint It Black,' Rolling Stones."

Jupiter winced. "Well . . . I guess it fits."

"What are your orders, Eldest?" Luna asked, her eyes reverent.

Andora tilted her head, closing her eyes as she took a deep breath—hearing her Overseers, seeing their struggles written on their faces while she slept.

That the Starless still lingered.

That they still lived.

The twang of a sitar echoed throughout the Network, opening the song as Andora immersed herself. The drums entered with a steady, marching beat.

Her anger boiled once more, begging to be removed from its leash. Andora held on to it, controlling it but allowing the chains to slacken. It surged, overjoyed as it brought forth the brutality and murderous rage.

She opened her eyes, feeling it conflagrate, twin blue suns staring back at the Overseers as she commanded them all.

"NO QUARTER."

And with a crack of lightning, like the light of firing neurons, the Sol Defense Network exploded into action, coinciding with Mick Jagger's vocals. Once bullied and bruised by High Abyssals, the remaining drone battlegroups now sought retribution. All five—January, March, August, November, and December—burned their thrusters forward.

The counterattack began as thousands of vessels fired their guns with unmatched accuracy, reaping a heavy toll on the Starless. Each fleet, composed of hundreds of warships from gunships to superheavy cruisers, bombarded Starless clusters around the front lines, relieving the beleaguered Overseers.

As the din of war spread over the solar system, cracking asteroids, scorching hulls, and eviscerating bodies, the song in the background intensified, its volume drowning all as Andora cried out with fury and the music hummed its tune.

Drone fighters and bombers soared through the void. Legions far higher in number than those from the *Xerxes* and far superior in coordination wreaked havoc, dismantling any semblance of coordination between the Starless, tearing Fodders to shreds and taking out chunks of biomass from their larger kin.

Juggernauts found themselves harried no matter where they fled. Many tried to escape to the miasmic sea of corrosion and hide from Andora's fury, only to see thousands of torpedoes and missiles saturating the area. Andora held nothing back, not bothering with half-measures as silo after silo launched their explosive gifts.

Mars's Apocalypse Cannons roared once more at the red planet, bathing the void in violent red light and sundering flesh and bone.

"MORIOR INVICTUS!" Mars screamed throughout the Network as his *Boogie Mouse* slammed into the Starless flank on the western front. Its Rapture Beams cut swathes as it dove into the sickly purple clouds, firing prismatic light like a disco ball.

His fleet, spearheaded by the Seven Greats, fired volley after volley as Battlegroup August assisted the counterattack. The swarm of monstrosities clashed against the combined force, reenacting a Renaissance painting of a celestial battle.

Seeing its swarm collapsing, Slimy Five charged the dreadnought and engaged in a violent duel, its salivating maw snapping shut against its shields, the backlash producing an explosion shockwave.

Mars snarled as his *Mouse* faced the Leviathan, riding higher-dimensional storm clouds.

"I apologize, but this will be a quick dance," the red Overseer sneered as his dreadnought barreled forward, bringing down smiting light.

At the southern front, Luna nodded in satisfaction and awe as Andora washed over the Starless. Battlegroup March rushed along with the Luna's legions, overwhelming the Starless in firepower with Tesla bolts, lasers, plasma, and lead.

"I am beyond relieved that you have returned to us, Eldest," Luna sighed. "Their . . . foulness has been allowed to exist for too long."

Within minutes, the flawless cooperation between Andora and her second-in-command dispatched the lesser vermin like typing numbers on a spreadsheet—one, then hundreds, then hundreds of thousands fell.

The silver-and-blue storm pushed against the sickly miasma as numerous Space Enforcer Towers were towed to the front.

Slimy Three, who had been the most passive among the pack, seethed and, in desperation, bulldozed through hundreds of drone fighters to ravage the evasive *Xerxes* as the battlecarrier blinked a short distance away again and again.

When it believed it finally had the pesky warship in its jaws as the vessel ran out of juice for its blink drives, a black and white beam scored its underside, penetrating deep into its guts.

It glared at the battleship, the crescent-shaped *Gilgamesh,* and its Energy Projector's smoking emitters.

"Stupid creature." Luna frowned in contempt.

Slimy Three abruptly changed course, charging the slower but sneaky ship as it tried to hide behind the legions of drones. Only to have its side bombarded by hundreds of kinetic slugs, explosive shells, Gauss rounds, and tungsten rods.

It roared in pain and frustration, facing the other belligerent and widening its eyes as it spotted the *Will of Sisyphus* barreling toward it and slamming its cheek.

"SURPRISE!" Jupiter mockingly shouted.

The Leviathan's head whipped back, teeth and saliva flying into the void as the dreadnought teleported back to the *Xerxes*'s side. Two other battleships arrived behind them, one vaguely in the shape of a hand and the other resembling a quarterstaff.

Jupiter turned to his sister, his smile smug as he wiggled his brows. "Hey, sis, I thought you'd need assistance."

Luna rolled her eyes. "What you thought is irrelevant, Jupiter. It is as the Eldest commands. Still . . ."

Both she and Jupiter turned to the surrounded Leviathan.

"This one needs to die," Luna sneered.

Stuck between an ocean of drones from the *Xerxes* and Battlegroup March, the long-range devastation of the *Gilgamesh*, and the indomitability of the *Will of Sisyphus* supported by the *Buddha's Palm* and the *Sun Wukong*, the Leviathan shrunk back in apprehension, alone, as its swarm fled from its side.

On the southwestern front, where Venus and Mercury fought a desperate defense and eventually exhausted the forces given to them, Battlegroups January and December took over the void left behind by February and May.

The Starless here pushed the farthest among everyone, approaching from the "rear" of the defenders and threatening the planet Venus itself. Orbital defenses shot a rain of projectiles, like hail against locusts.

At the planet's surface, around the countless manufactories, assembly lines, powerplants, and production facilities, several thousand planetary guns emerged from their bunkers, pumping out anti-orbital artillery and denying the Starless entry.

The battlegroups, each led by superheavy cruisers, led a countercharge, spearing through the cluster. The High Abyssals, without the support of a Leviathan, soon realized the untenable situation and, with snarling frustration, called a retreat.

Venus sighed within her bastion, looking at the ongoing battle alongside Mercury.

Finally, as the Third Fleet fell back to the Luna Complex at the northeastern front, Battlegroup November joined Jupiter's forces.

The *Ultimatum* linked up with the *Bucephalus*; while impressive in firepower, both mobile fortresses were not strictly designed to be pure combat assets. Nevertheless, the former's Black Sun Obelisk and the latter's twin Apocalypse Cannons made even the Alpha Leviathan, leading the most significant Starless force, falter.

However, the potent contempt from the dreadnought leading the charge struck fear into the scarred and ancient beast.

Jupiter grinned devilishly as the *Ereshkigal* sliced through space like a knife, ready to shank a bastard to death with her four primary guns.

He deferred to her judgment as much as he wanted to keep his dreadnought and two battleships to bully Old Slimy with Andora. Mopping up the other fronts took priority; for once, he tried to play the audience. He only wished he had popcorn.

"You're in for a world of hurt now," Jupiter snickered.

Andora remained silent, watching the surrounding conflict with cold indifference. It was a foregone conclusion as all fronts, except this one, were slowly but surely stabilized.

This front needed her special touch. And as she told Tov: she wanted to hit something.

She infused a chunk of her consciousness into the dreadnought, imagining herself riding her steed and leading the charge, like King Theoden and the Charge of the Rohirrim. With the light of Sol at her back, washing over her golden dreadnought riding like a divine halo, she pushed the warship's thrusters to the max, riding dark clouds.

Old Slimy snarled, sensing the collapsing assaults around the system, and glared at the approaching challenger with animalistic hate and hunger.

Andora wondered what inane thoughts it and its ilk had tried to dangle before the aliens of the Third Fleet, only to be thwarted by their AEBs and the Eternal Choir's song.

"No matter," she muttered, cracking her knuckles as both adversaries charged.

The *Ereshkigal* shimmered, the black mist thickening and expanding. Soon, it encompassed the region around both machine and beast, the former disappearing into the void.

Old Slimy halted, then, and with quick reflexes it whipped its tail to where the dreadnought emerged. The momentum pushed against the vessel, but the dispersion effect around its hull did as she designed, diverting the kinetic force across its entire structure and space.

It spun away, unworried of the high g's without organic passengers within.

The dreadnought stopped, showing its starboard side toward the charging Alpha Leviathan.

And at point-blank range, fired a broadside of her Ganzir Guns. A triple burst of meteoric plasma zipped through space. Old Slimy, seething, twisted its body to avoid the twelve balls of fire.

It roared silently as a handful splashed, scorched, and blew away the protective coating around the Leviathan. The *Ereshkigal* slid back into the black smoke, engaging its advanced cloaking system and taking advantage of its shadows.

It repeated the same tactic, disappearing and reappearing at the beast's blind spot.

Broadside after broadside smashed against its gargantuan body, forming craters on its surface. Old Slimy shuddered, its bones rattling, splintering as it tried everything within its arsenal to deter the *Ereshkigal*'s bombardment.

Countless barbed spires emerged across its flesh, transforming it from a monolithic and horrific moray eel to a spiky caterpillar.

Its body bloated up as it gathered gas between its skin, and as the *Ereshkigal* slipped back into the shadows, Old Slimy abruptly released its built-up pressure. Thousands upon thousands of spikes pierced the shadows that engulfed it.

Andora watched as hundreds smashed against her dreadnought's shields, straining it as the translucent barrier crackled.

Hearing the faint fluctuations of the hit, the Leviathan snapped toward the vessel and fired a stream of radioactive fire. The shields grew more unstable in the half-second it was engulfed before maneuvering out of the way.

The *Ereshkigal* dove further into the shadows, stalking the beast.

Andora scoffed.

The duel continued, the *Ereshkigal* at home within the shadows that covered the arena, a hunting ground that pushed away the miasma that tried to reach the Leviathan. Old Slimy repeated its attacks, using spikes as a locator before burning everything wherever it pinged.

Yet, compared to the slight silhouette of the dreadnought, the Leviathan had no chance to dodge its devastating Ganzir Guns and graser beams.

Slowly but surely, minute after minute, barrage after barrage, something within the beast clicked. It felt an emotion slithered into its mind like a tendril, an infection that spread farther and farther.

It realized it was dying.

And it was afraid.

Andora could taste it and fought back the sadistic grin that tried to worm through her face.

"I would like to add you to my collection. You Leviathans are always difficult to house, but so entertaining to play with. You would've been the third. The others died in their pens," she whispered.

She imagined it, slicing it apart piece by piece, turning it inside out, keeping it barely alive but conscious, always conscious. She shook her head.

"No, not anymore," she muttered, looking at the wounded beast through her dreadnought's sensors. "That place will burn, along with that habit."

Andora sighed, settling herself as she looked back at the duel with cold detachment.

"Die now," she proclaimed.

Immediately, the *Ereshkigal* appeared below the Leviathan, its bladed prow piercing and slicing its side, releasing its eldritch organs into the vacuum of the void, and firing its guns point-blank.

As she did so, the song in the background culminated, Mick Jagger raising his voice as the counterattack pushed farther into the invaders.

As Old Slimy coiled around itself, firing off geysers of corrosive plasma all over its body, the *Boogie Mouse* began its coup de grace on Slimy Five.

"DEATH!" Mars shouted. His dreadnought's focused Rapture Beams and the guns from the Seven Greats roared.

The Leviathan collapsed under the heat as the attacks seared its flesh and obliterated its nervous system—with it out of commission and in terrible debilitating agony, the swarm at the western front faltered as the song hummed its tune faster.

The *Will of Sisyphus* did the same for Slimy Three, battering the monstrosity to a pulp until it could hardly move, floating away crippled and barely holding on.

The asteroid dreadnought's metal prow now looked incredibly flat after repeated ramming maneuvers, but as it prepared for another charge, Luna quickly mopped up the swarms on the southern front.

Gilgamesh assassinated anything that looked like it could assemble a cluster while the *Xerxes* and its drones washed over the remaining Fodder.

With the three fronts reinforced and pushing the Starless to a rout, the song reached its end.

"We have them on the run!" Jupiter shouted with glee as his fleet and Battlegroup November blunted the northeastern assault, repelling the vermin as they fled to their master. "That's it! Flee, cowards! We'll hunt you to the ends of the universe!"

The Alpha Leviathan cried out in pain, its dozens of eyes shifting to the countless warships gunning for it and the *Ereshkigal*'s guns. It tried to summon more spikes but only managed a few hundred.

Old Slimy looked emaciated, burning through its supply of excess biomass to further its regeneration.

The dreadnought appeared battered but still fresh, still hungry for a kill. Its many guns homed in on the beast, smoking red-hot as it fired again.

Another volley blasted deep into its middle, a critically damaged area over the minutes of combat, and exposed its vulnerable insides. At the same time, the *Ereshkigal* launched a pair of antimatter missiles, invisible within the shadows, that slammed into the wound.

Calamitous detonations bloomed within its gut, obliterating volatile organs and severing its spine. The Leviathan gurgled as it felt closer to death than it had ever been before.

Andora saw that delicious look on its bastard face—tasted the doubt, fear, and suffering through its eyes. She savored the few seconds they frantically looked at the collapsing battlefield, when something changed.

An eerie transformation began as it groaned, shuddering.

The Leviathan's eyes, once filled with malice, turned cold as its flesh started to wither, spreading from its tail end toward its front.

Its vitality drained away, turning its flesh gray and desiccated—writhing in a macabre dance as the last vestiges of its energy concentrated through the stem between its eyes and toward the dangling light that frustrated the defenders' electronics.

The Starless froze across the battlefield as the other two dying Leviathans did the same, their lights shining brighter, causing multiple glitches across the defenders.

Undeterred, Andora snipped those glitches in the bud, stabilizing her control of her assets. She commanded the *Ereshkigal*'s Ganzir Guns to unleash a final salvo directly at the Alpha Leviathan's face.

The four primary weapons spun and fired a triple burst of plasma.

Then, the lights of the three beasts shone with a sickly glow, screaming out across the void with an eldritch call and, to Andora's surprise, the echoes of a plea. Upon reaching the height of its horrendous illumination, it popped, and space shuddered in its detonation.

Simultaneously, twelve plasma bolts the size of asteroids struck the Alpha Leviathan's face, blowing it to shreds without the resistance of its resilient flesh.

Mars and Jupiter quickly culled the other two with antimatter warheads, uncertainty on their faces at what had transpired.

"What the hell?" Jupiter muttered within their space.

Mars frowned, his brows furrowed as he blew apart Slimy Five a few more times for good measure.

The pulse washed over the fleeing Starless and the defenders, temporarily pausing the entire conflict. Tov glanced toward the disturbance, preparing to board another shuttle for his flagship. He felt an unnatural tension, like a taut string on the verge of snapping, stretching reality itself.

Within the digital mentalscape of the Network, the Overseers twitched, bewildered by a foreign influence briefly seeping into their sanctuary and disappearing like a foul breeze. Alarms rang in Andora's head as she gathered her Spotlight Towers, pushing them beyond their limits.

Andora squinted, an inkling of dread leaking into her mind. She squashed it down, grinding the feeling to dust when Luna came before her. "Eldest, our Spotlights found something concerning."

Her vision drifted to the towers hiding beyond the Jupiter Circle, detecting the deteriorating region of space, the fabric unraveling, bit by bit.

[ATTENTION | NIGHTMARE PORTAL DETECTED]

"Shit," Jupiter spat as the defenders tensed at the sudden emergence of Starless reinforcements.

The survivors of their counterattack fled toward the fluctuating area. Andora and her Overseers scowled at their desperation, increasing their attacks.

"Deny them the chance, slaughter them all," Andora ordered. "Then pull back. I want everyone resupplied and—"

She paused as the Spotlights calculated the portal's size.

[MAGNITUDE FOU—ERROR]
[PORTAL SIZE RISING IN ABNORMAL RATE | RECALCULATING
MAGNITUDE . . .]

Shock ran through the defenders at the sudden announcement. Andora eyed the torrents of data and information that flowed through her with doubt and growing unease.

[PROJECTED MAGNITUDE . . . FI—ERROR]
[RECALCULATING | PROJECTED MAGNITUDE . . . SIX . . .
SIX POINT ONE . . . SIX POINT FIVE . . . SIX POI—ERROR]
[RECALCULATING . . .]

"That's . . ." Jupiter narrowed his eyes, seeing the same errors as everyone else.

Andora hushed them all to be silent as she focused her processing capabilities on deciphering the abnormality.

The Overseers reassembled their forces, moving pieces into place toward the emerging split in space. The Third Fleet burned their thrusters faster toward Luna, far behind the thick defensive lines.

Through the nearest Spotlight's cameras, the point where the portal emerged cracked like a pane of glass, and for a split second, a color Andora had never seen seeped through before utterly crashing the Spotlight Tower's sensors.

"Andora, what is happening—"

"Tov, shut up. I'm figuring it out," Andora hissed, grinding her teeth as she moved other Spotlights to combine their scans of the region.

[RECALIBRATING . . . RECALIBRATION COMPLETE]

"Hurry up," Andora seethed, her eye twitching as the temperature spiked within her Central Nexus again.

[RECALCULATING . . . CALCULATIONS COMPLETE]
[PROJECTED MAGNITUDE . . .]

Andora stepped back, refreshing the result that popped up and verifying it a hundred times. All to come up with the same glaring number. The pieces fell into place, and Andora cursed under her breath as she turned to her Overseers with a deep, unsettled frown.

"Projected magnitude . . . seven," she announced.

CHAPTER 31

FROM THE DARK

Tov's thoughts roiled as he walked to the Luna Complex's War Room. With the sudden emergence of an impending disaster, he, along with Admiral Yan and General Ohnar, sought out Andora and the Overseers.

"How are the defenses of this facility, General?" Tov asked Ohnar.

The massive Onin, clad in sleek new power armor upgraded personally by Mars, croaked, his throat bulging as he mulled his thoughts.

"We have plenty of anti-air and anti-orbital defenses. The metal forest in the middle of the Complex is all nanomachines whose sole purpose is to repair any damage done to this facility. All vital locations are hidden deep beneath the moon, and we've adapted well here," Ohnar reported.

Tov nodded. "Excellent work. However, I'm entertaining the thought of moving our people down on Earth within Andora's Citadel. Thoughts?"

"We've discussed the possibility with Overseer Luna," Ohnar said. "The Earth Defense Net is already sending its spaceborne assets to Luna, and it's more hospitable for us here. And the underground facility can't hold all our people. Most of the structure is only accessible to small drones."

"Andora told me as much." Tov tsked. "The only place we could place our people is the hospice facility. And if the Starless reached that point, we've already lost."

Admiral Yan sighed. "We'll be sacrificing our fleet if we all fall back there, and the ruins of New Eden itself are a horrible defensive point."

"Cursed hells," Tov muttered as he looked at the layers of defenses that they had set up throughout the Complex.

With Luna's propensity for nanomachines, she turned every room and corridor of her domain into a kill zone. Supported by legions of infantry drones, heavy mechs, and the armed forces of the Third Fleet, this facility had become a veritable fortress in the short time it came to be.

"Then we make our stand here," Tov declared. "Have Volantesh and his choir transferred down here? I've been informed that there is a larger AEB Emitter present?"

Yan nodded. "Luna has made modifications to the design over the week. With our civilians present, they must have better protection. Thus, the Pneuma Bulwark Emitter. Which is the new name we've all agreed to, by the way."

"I see," Tov hummed as he skimmed through the device's specifications. "And it can amplify the other Emitters within the entire fleet?"

"It can," Yan confirmed.

Eventually, they reached the War Room and were quickly ushered in by the guards. Inside, Andora stood in the middle of the Overseers, leaning over the table with a deep frown.

She briefly glanced at the new arrivals, nodding.

"So, it's true, then?" Tov asked as he looked at the hologram displaying the fluctuations occurring by the spacial anomaly.

"I've moved as much of my Spotlight Towers toward it," Andora said, manipulating the table to show around twelve of the cloaked surveillance stations that had been instrumental in detecting portals in advance.

All twelve formed around the spot in space at approximately a hundred million kilometers out.

"Any closer than this, the same thing happens to the last few towers. The sheer destabilization and cosmic radiation shred apart the internals," she explained, showing several readings she managed to gather from the anomaly.

Admiral Yan crossed her arms, shaking her head at the numbers. "That place is a true dead zone. There's no way our fleet can approach it. Perhaps if it were a hundred thousand kilometers, but a hundred million? We won't be able to do much apart from acting as extreme-range artillery."

"That's ten times greater than what's been opening recently." Jupiter frowned. "It'll linger there for a long time—plus the miasma around the anomaly has gotten a lot more dangerous."

Tov gritted his mandibles. Just the mere emergence of this gargantuan portal has turned a good chunk of the Jupiter-Saturn Zone into a lethal area. His people had barely gotten used to the experience of multiple Magnitude Sixes in a week. This, however, was something else entirely.

"A Seven." Tov shook his head. "What have these things called upon?"

Jupiter shrugged, pointing at the cloud of red dots representing hundreds of millions of Starless. "Whatever it is, the vermin are fleeing toward it."

"Maybe they are retreating?" Mars suggested with thinly veiled uncertainty. Andora and many others expressed doubt about that optimistic scenario.

"A final bid?" Luna surmised, her mind going into overdrive as she assisted Andora in analyzing the portal. "We are likely looking at a pack of Leviathans coming to salvage this assault."

Everyone tensed at that scenario. Although the defenders felt a little more assurance with Andora's presence and access to their few trump cards, with how battered their forces were, it looked more and more like a desperate battle was coming over the horizon.

Andora clenched her fist.

Tov watched the 3D plot as the foundries and manufactories worked overtime to pump out ammunition, power cells, armor plating, drone fighters, and even smaller warships.

The beleaguered drone battlegroups continued to harry the fleeing Starless while the rest of the fleets recuperated.

"It's emerging close to the Jupiter Circle, where it has a straight vector toward Earth. Less than a billion kilometers. That's under an hour for light to reach us," Andora spoke, displaying several scenarios and projected paths. "Considering the hastening qualities of the miasma and if they're the same speed as the Slimies, we're looking at five hours minimum travel time."

"Barring any teleportation," Tov reminded her.

Andora nodded at his reminder, looking to her Overseers. "How are the Space Enforcer Towers?"

"We have enough to hold complete dominion over the Inner Zone," Jupiter answered as he sneered. "I dare the fuckers to try. They'll ram right into a brick wall and suffer the backlash."

"Be ready to overload the entire interdiction array if need be," Andora ordered, manipulating the thirty stations and moving to cover a good area over the four terrestrial planets within the Inner Zone.

"How long until it opens?" Admiral Yan inquired.

At her question, Andora's frown deepened. "With how abnormal it is, it'll open much quicker. An hour at most."

Tov suppressed a shudder at what force had the strength to breach such a vast swathe of space at such speed. He'd read up on what occurred in his absence, and the thought of such a swarm filled him with dread.

He squashed that feeling aside. Now was the time to fight the unfathomable. He turned to Andora, prodding for information. "Has there been a Magnitude Seven before?"

Andora shook her head. "Our worst was a 6.4, nine years ago. That was after several portals of smaller sizes. It was a month-long battle, and we lost Saturn during that wave."

The Overseers grew grim at the memory and the loss of one of their own.

"That was a bad one," Jupiter muttered with dark eyes as he rubbed his nape. "Eight Leviathans and more than a billion of the vermin. We were better prepared then, yet we still lost . . ."

He shook his head, snarling. "Still haven't recovered from that hell. Now look at us."

"I'm not losing anyone here," Andora growled as her hand dented the metal war table. "And we won't sit around and wait for whatever's coming."

"What do you suggest?" Tov inquired, brushing a hand over his mandible.

With a few gestures, Andora uploaded the tactical plan and formations for a massive assault on the Nightmare Portal. As the map stopped its transformation, she explained her plan.

"We'll push toward the portal with our dreadnoughts and all five battlegroups. Along the way, we'll scour as much of the surviving Starless as possible before they receive their reinforcements," Andora spoke.

As she did so, she began moving her assets within the battlefield, not wasting a second. "I'm giving the green light on our entire antimatter arsenal. Whatever comes, we're blasting it to oblivion. Anything that's left will be taken care of through conventional means."

"What about us?" Jupiter asked.

"I want the rest of you on standby."

The blue AI hummed, manipulating the formation to add two more assets. "*Sisyphus* needs my *Palm* and *Wukong* to complete the Chixculub Maneuver. I'll send the rest of my fleet back home."

"Good. Have the *Bucephalus* and *Ultimatum* hold between Earth and Mars. We've lucked out that they're close this time of year. Luna, you and the Third Fleet are the last line of defense."

Luna nodded. "By your will, Eldest."

"What of our singularity bombs?" Mars asked. The mere mention of such an incomprehensible thing caused the alien guests to shiver.

Tov had only heard a passing mention of such a weapon from Andora. Such a device was to the Kurskann Empire, at least to his knowledge, a mere myth—a bomb that first explodes with a fraction of a supernova's power, then implodes to create a temporary, unstable black hole.

Its ergosphere would ensnare anything in its radius, disassembling it from the sheer force. And when they reached the event horizon, nothing but pure death.

When the hole collapsed, whatever matter and energy it had pulled in would all explode back out.

If antimatter missiles were world-enders, then singularity bombs had the potential to wound a star. Perhaps even kill one.

Andora pressed her lips, grinding her teeth at the idea of pulling out such irreplaceable weapons.

"Ready one warhead," whispered Andora.

Mars nodded, eyes dimming as he left to initiate the bomb's lengthy activation process. Jupiter squinted his eyes and, for a moment, left his shell too.

"Tov," called Andora as she faced him with a gentle expression. "This is where I ask if you wish to leave. Jupiter has told me his *Ultimatum* can send you out of our solar system. You've done more than enough. All I ask is that you take all of humanity's libraries and all the DNA banks I have."

The patriarch looked to Yan and Ohnar, who nodded in turn. Tov turned inward to himself, weighing the decision, whether he, as a leader, must look to his people's safety. But then he saw the weary expression of the six AIs and Andora.

He knew the woman was still keeping her emotions down, focused on this conflict as she was.

Tov shook his head, his twin hearts and mind settling with his decision.

"We are all the same here, Andora. Victims," he spoke, giving her his people's salute. "We will not abandon you."

Andora pressed her lips tight, relief barely hidden beneath her eyes. "Thank you. Then I ask that you and yours hunker down."

The patriarch and his two subordinates nodded. "Our fleet won't be able to approach the area anyways, but we'll defend the Inner Zone with everything we have."

"Then this is it," Andora replied, taking a deep breath as she looked at everyone in the room. "Let's begin."

Andora watched as the assault force obliterated another cluster. Her battlegroups formed prongs that swept the lines, pushing toward the emerging Nightmare Portal with relentless efficiency.

They cut down everything in their path, the fleeing Starless swimming as fast as possible through the purple miasma. The sickly clouds also coalesced toward the portal, bringing with them those annoying bubbles that would burst with corrosive rain.

Andora bolted what Space Enforcer Towers she could spare onto the superheavy cruisers among the battlegroups to prevent her forces from suffering attrition from the cosmic hazard.

Utilizing the devices' mild gravitational capabilities, she succeeded in at least dissipating enough of the miasma to push through.

She looked at the wound in space through her eyes, her Spotlights. Even with a dozen arrayed around it, she only gathered a fuzzy image. Yet, it was enough to propel the assault forward, every moment crucial before the portal unleashed its malevolent spawn.

It appeared like a single crack on a pane of black glass. From it came colors that her mind couldn't process, defaulting to that same vile purple and red, seeping like pus. The fabric of space cried out in violation at the forceful tear that grew.

The crack in space throbbed, a grotesque heartbeat resonating with the impending horror it harbored.

As her assault force, led by the three dreadnoughts, continued like combine harvesters separating the wheat from the chaff, Andora sensed it—the eldritch touch that had plagued humanity and the galactic community.

For the first time, she felt as they did.

It brushed against her vast mind, a dirty caress that ignited a visceral reaction. It spread across her Network, causing all her units to intensify their extermination.

The foreign intrusion mocked her with its presence and dared to violate the sanctity of her consciousness. It did nothing but make itself known, shouting from hills over yonder like a serial killer behind a chain-link fence.

Andora recoiled from it, her immense processing power resonating with disdain. Revulsion surged through her, giving rise to an instinctive desire to eradicate the source, to rip it apart and tear it asunder.

Why now? Was it the magnitude of this aberration that allowed it to make contact with her digital mind?

Yet, beneath the disgust, an unexpected emotion surfaced. Andora blinked, searching through herself. Her brows furrowed. She had felt a faint sense of reassurance.

She fell back in her mind, wondering why she felt that way. Then she realized. The very force that had plagued organic minds, catalyzed humanity's demise, and transformed them into monstrous entities now reached out to her.

Andora, the pinnacle of artificial intelligence, had always been interested in the concept of the soul. It drove many of her siblings to find proof of whether it existed. Who had them? Was it only humans? Humans and androids? Or all life?

Such a thing would either connect or divide the two species.

Through tireless efforts, humans and androids theorized about it like scientists without the tools to observe it. They found traces and built models of what she now knew from Tov and his people as "psionics."

Humanity, Andora theorized, was psionically dull. AIs like her, even more so. At least, that's what she had believed.

It was a sick and ironic twist of fate that the vermin would be the one to reaffirm the existence of her spirit. In that unsettling moment, Andora felt an unexpected kinship with humanity, her husband, her daughter, Tov, and everyone.

In its hostility, it was as if the eldritch force had inadvertently unveiled the shared vulnerability of all beings, regardless of their origin or composition.

Something shifted in her mind as Andora looked to her Overseers, her family, Tov, his people, and finally, the Starfallen remnants on Earth.

It was humbling.

Her emotions surged like the climax of a concert, and with a shout, she pushed her forces closer and closer to the portal.

Battlegroups January, March, August, November, and December formed prongs that swept the pests toward the killing fields set by the *Ereshkigal*, *Boogie Mouse*, and the *Will of Sisyphus*.

The battleships *Buddha's Palm* and *Sun Wukong* followed along, propelling the meteoric dreadnought forward, ensuring the slow vessel kept up with its more modern sisters.

"We're approaching the Nightmare Portal and we've cut down the remaining Starless in half," Andora told Tov and everyone else within the Luna Complex's War Room.

"They're forming around the anomaly and started fighting back," Jupiter sneered.

Andora frowned as she saw the swarm spreading out and firing their weapons. "Their efforts change nothing. Intensify the extermination."

And that they did, saturating the region with weaponfire, from point defense shells to the Ganzir Guns. Fodders died in droves, Titans blew apart as they were singled out, and the remaining Colossi struggled to keep their forces intact.

High Abyssals commanded the swarm, incapable of matching Andora's efficiency. Ranged, melee and hybrid Juggernauts ganged up on the unstoppable march of the dreadnought trio.

"Magnifiers activated!" Mars shouted as his *Boogie Mouse* fired volley after volley of concentrated Rapture Beams, scorching their adversaries to dust under their searing light.

Jupiter grinned like a shark, clenching his fist as if grasping space. "Gotcha!"

With a surge of power, the *Will of Sisyphus* generated a massive gravity well, kept stable by its two little brothers. A pack of Juggernauts got caught under its web and soon pelted by a barrage of kinetic weapons.

As the Juggernauts' biometallic armor failed, they fell one after another, leaving the commander-types vulnerable.

And like a phantom bringing the fog of the dead, the *Ereshkigal* filled the area around it with its Kur Shadow Domain.

Two High Abyssals panicked, trying to flee the black clouds toward the disgusting light of the Nightmare Portal.

"Die," Andora uttered.

The dreadnought breached the clouds, appearing to their flanks and firing its four Ganzir Guns. Twelve plasma bolts crashed against the first High Abyssal and dug deep into its core.

The beast shuddered before its entire gut exploded in blood, viscera, and burned flesh.

With one down, the *Ereshkigal* turned her weapons toward the other, and was readying another volley when a pulse washed over the entire solar system.

Everyone froze, a deep chill running down their spines.

Andora gritted her teeth at the interruption and the impending sense of dread coming from the crack in space. She reluctantly ordered the assault force to fire one last volley against the wounded swarm and reformed the lines.

"Surround the portal. Upon my word, blot out the sun with your missiles. Give cover for our antimatter torpedoes," Andora commanded.

The five battlegroups surrounded the spacial anomaly in a crescent formation, taking optimal firing positions and ready to bring down a storm of fire.

The three dreadnoughts took the front, never too far from one another. The *Ereshkigal* took its place in the middle, the *Boogie Mouse* and the *Sisyphus* to the left and right, respectively.

Each turned their hulls like blades pointed at the portal, or a fist in the *Sisyphus*'s case.

"Status?" Andora demanded.

[PORTAL ACTIVITY SPIKE | ESTIMATING BREACH IN . . . FORTY SECONDS]

The defenders braced for whatever was about to enter.

Jupiter and Mars placed their full attention on their dreadnoughts while Luna, Venus, and Mercury assisted in the fortifications within their lines. Tov and the Third Fleet watched with anxious eyes but stoic expressions, never stopping their preparations for a siege.

The Starless swarm, those that remained, shrunk back away from the breach as if in supplication.

The Nightmare Portal rippled.

From a thin crack, it widened, opening like a hellish eye, and within, a blinding light, a kaleidoscope of profane hues. Space screamed louder and louder, reaching a crescendo that pulsed across the battlefield like a violent tear.

The defenders recoiled from the sight. Even Andora and the Overseers squinted through the Network, gritting their teeth at the sheer psionic whiplash.

The Pneuma Bulwark Emitter on the moon surged in power, counteracting the shrieking songs of madness.

Many of the Eternal Choir blacked out momentarily, grasping their ears as they tried to defy the eldritch touch.

"SING, MY FRIENDS!" Volantesh cawed out with his deep baritone, resonating with the crystalline monolith and relieving the pressure on their people.

Andora seethed that the echoes of this thing could oppress them. As the time for the breach came closer and closer, she ordered all her warships to open fire.

[BREACH IN FIVE . . . FOUR . . .]

The assault force emptied their missile silos. From the three dreadnoughts, three antimatter torpedoes left their cages, zipping through space.

The defenders of Sol brought down the hammer, ready to smite what festering monstrosity came forth.

[THREE . . . TWO . . . ON—]

She paused in her thoughts and temper. Time slowed to a crawl as she heard it. A sound from beyond, washing over the entire solar system.

A haunting horn that heralded a cataclysm.

It blasted nine times, reverberating the fabric of space and slamming against the protection of their Emitter, causing everyone to grunt from the force.

As the Nightmare Portal pulsed with eldritch energy, something tried to breach the boundaries between reality and whatever hellscape the Starless came from. The struggle to puncture the eye resembled that of a vile spawn pushing against the portal's membrane.

The surroundings of the anomaly began to distort, and Andora struggled to keep her visuals clear, wanting to bear witness to this unholy sight.

As the universe groaned under the strain and the Nightmare Portal bulged out with eldritch energy, everyone held their breath, anticipating a monstrous entity of colossal proportions to emerge.

Then, the portal shattered.

Space screamed in agony as something vile entered this plane of existence.

But what came forth was not a moon-sized behemoth.

Nor billions of Starless vermin.

Instead, a small black sphere emerged—an abyssal teardrop leaking out of the vast eye.

The inky dark sphere traveled forward before stopping, its liquid surface writhing, undulating, and pulsating. Andora scrutinized the seemingly insignificant form through her analytical lenses, noting its minuscule size, a few kilometers in diameter.

Yet, she struggled to suppress the shudder as she felt the utter calculating malevolence it emanated, exceeding anything she had encountered before.

Everyone remained silent as a cold more biting and suffocating than the void staked its banner on this system.

As the drop of ink hovered in the void, it rippled, morphing, and transformed into a more rigid form.

What it changed into sent a bolt of horror into the defenders.

A vaguely humanoid form took shape, its silhouette outlined amid the purple glow of the unstable Nightmare Portal.

Cloaked in abyssal robes that cascaded like an empty cosmos, the entity moved with an otherworldly grace. Its head extended upward like a pillar of obsidian before it stopped and solidified, then a mirage of an unfathomable cube formed behind it.

It opened a singular eye, at the center of its face like a miniature Nightmare Portal. As the transformation ceased, it surveyed the scene before it, its robe fluttering in an otherworldly wind.

The entity gazed at the assault fleet surrounding the Nightmare Portal, then at the thousands of missiles heading toward it, clamoring for its obliteration.

It tilted its head at the incoming rain and slowly raised a wiry, muscled arm. Then, from an open palm of its gnarled hand, a shimmering barrier expanded, rapidly forming a translucent wall hundreds of thousands of kilometers in length.

The onslaught of missiles slammed against the barrier and bathed the region with annihilating fire.

Volleys of energy beams added to the carnage, bombarding the area and obliterating the cowed Starless that failed to escape.

A combined barrage of *Ereshkigal*'s plasma bolts, the *Mouse*'s light beams, and *Sisyphus*'s kinetic strikes found their mark. The effects cascaded into a violent, bright bloom of explosions.

Finally, the antimatter torpedoes soared, only to jitter and violently shake before reaching the barrier. As an unseen force crumpled the bombs, and they forcibly detonated, their annihilating inferno washing over the translucent wall.

As the blooming light of destruction faded away, the defenders gasped in disbelief. In the aftermath of the assault, the entity remained unscathed, dispelling a cracked barrier with a casual wave.

It scoffed, lowering its seven-fingered hand beneath its robes.

Then, it turned to face them—to face her.

Andora, at that precise moment, felt the entity's penetrating gaze. A gaze that traversed a billion kilometers, penetrating layers of snow, dirt, rock, and concrete to stare directly at her Central Nexus.

A palpable wave of disdain and morbid curiosity emanated from the entity, leaving a lingering chill. She felt shifting puzzles and an ever-expanding mechanism cranking into place. A cosmic design that made itself known, calling for all to see its works and glory.

A lipless maw emerged from its face, with black teeth jutting from tightly embraced gums.

The entity opened its maw. Andora barely saw its abyssal interior through the shaky images sent by her Spotlights.

Slowly, its throat moved and—

"Ah, there you are."

A voice.

One whose sound rang out like a thousand heretical singers, intertwining in a deep rumble. It washed over all with the mind to understand, and inconceivably, echoed within Andora's Network.

Silence befell the entire solar system; neither the Starless nor the defenders could muster anything but their unwilling attention.

Tov and his people stood paralyzed by the entity's voice, one far beyond the bestial mimicry of psionic Starless, from Muck to Dominators. This was no mere animalistic intelligence, no simple action to elicit madness—it was a voice.

"You . . ."

A genuine voice.

". . . are an Aberration."

Andora gazed at the entity in stunned silence, her mind grappling to make sense of the unfolding reality. She felt her emotions spiral down a drain, no, pressing down on a spring, tensing up as numbness took over from their absence.

"You . . . speak?" she asked as her android shell took a hesitant, heavy step forward, eyes dark. She muttered her question once more, whispering in disbelief, "You can speak?"

A shift in the entity's eye, understanding her question yet remaining silent.

Something profound fractured within Andora. The entity's voice echoed relentlessly in her mind until, at last, she processed the staggering revelation.

And like a spring reaching its limit, her emotions sprung forth.

Her Network exploded like an erupting volcano, bathing the digital world with lava of utter contempt and disgust as Andora's sheer seething rage shoved the foreign presence out of her mind—her sanctuary.

Thunderous booms echoed across the assault force as they swiftly initiated and resumed the attack, guns blasting their hate toward the thing, prompted by Andora's resounding scream.

"YOU CAN FUCKING SPEAK?"

CHAPTER 32

IT SPEAKS

Hearing her shout, the eldritch thing narrowed its single eye, a purple glow pouring out from its pupil.

Andora winced as she felt its proximity to her mind. It called out to her, like someone outside her mind's door. She matched its cold contempt with her infernal glare.

"This Executor has adapted to your tedious means of communication," it responded with the voice of a thousand. A deep, gravelly, and regal thing, almost aloof as the creature raised its chin.

A title and a confirmation.

She wasn't delusional. She had heard it speak. This was no beast; even intelligent ones like Leviathans were still animals.

Andora tried with tremendous effort to reel back her cascading emotions, but the sheer shock she felt with this discovery threatened to undo the work she, Tov, and Echo had accomplished.

The surrounding Starless shuddered, their forms adrift and eyes dazed as if enthralled by this . . . Executor's presence, cowed like mangy street dogs.

Then, countless projectiles bombarded the entity, only to slam against another barrier. Lances of energy, explosive shells, and tungsten rods rippled against the invisible shield like pebbles thrown at a puddle.

Unlike the previous one that blocked their preemptive strike, the succeeding barriers took smaller shapes. And instead of outright blocking the projectiles, they bent and caved in before deflecting them, sending them careening away.

From within its black cloak, a malevolent glow leaked out. Spreading from the entity was that same vile fog that encompassed much of the Outer Zone.

It writhed and bubbled; whatever energy beams managed to phase through the shield quickly dispersed within the miasma.

Andora seethed at the impotence of her attacks yet decided against a full assault or launching all her antimatter torpedoes—sending only one every volley, hidden beneath the storm of death. A small part of her desired something more than its immediate death.

And try as she might, the thought latched on to that rational part of her calculating mind.

She needed information. What were its abilities? How much energy did it contain? Did it have a tactical mind?

The siege against its frustratingly indomitable defenses gradually increased as Andora slowly prodded different methods of testing limits. If it died, then that meant she could kill others of its kind; if it didn't, then she wanted to gauge its limits and make it cough up its secrets.

Nevertheless, the entity managed to defend itself consistently.

It only deviated when it raised its hand and summoned a thicker, more opaque barrier, blocking a volley from the dreadnoughts or causing space to shimmer and knock the antimatter torpedoes way off course.

Her forces continued to assault the abomination's barrier, but the constant barrage provoked palpable annoyance from this Executor creature.

"Good," Andora seethed within her mind as she let loose trickles of rage. *"So you can feel threat."*

The creature's eye twitched as if hearing her mockery.

"Aberration," it called out once more, using that term.

An Aberrant, was that how they saw her? She felt mild disappointment at the clinical designation. Still, she took grim satisfaction at its implication, wondering if she had caused so much grief that she'd be graced by what she had begun to believe was some high-ranked entity—a thorn in their ass.

"Cease hostilities," the Executor demanded, its voice overbearing and cold like a dark mountain. *"Your association with the Phages has come to our attention."*

Tov stepped forward, pushing through the debilitating weight placed on his mind. He snapped his mandibles, grinding them as he hissed out, "Phages?"

"What are you?" demanded Andora with gritted teeth. "Why are you here?"

It returned to gaze back at her, a hint of impatience in its voice as its pillar-like head glinted.

"What I am is none of your concern, Aberration known as Andora. But your surrender is preferable." It raised its arm again, waving toward the Third Fleet. *"Do so, and the Phages shall be saved—cured of what afflicts them."*

Narrowing her eyes, she snarled in response as Tov took his place beside her. Little by little, the protection empowered by the Eternal Choir's constant singing lifted the oppressive weight.

"Who are you to promise such a thing?" he demanded, mandibles snapping with an audible clack as he glared at the entity. "What cure are you speaking of? What affliction?"

Turning to Tov, the eldritch thing's gaze pressed down on the patriarch. The pressure from that mere look drew out a hiss from him.

Andora wanted to lash out then but kept herself chained to her leash. The information they could gather from this thing trumped anything else, and her curiosity overcame her anger.

"Phage known as Tov. Your blighted kind believes it to be a plague. You are mistaken. Accept our healing Touch and be cleansed of your contaminated vessel," it called out. *"Or die. It matters not."*

The patriarch clenched his fists as he brought forth his buried emotions. The revelation of finding a thinking, guiding intelligence over what the galaxy believed to be simple sadistic fauna cracked his usual calm countenance.

"Is that what the Malignant Starfall is? How . . . could you . . . ?" he muttered, his voice rising as he let loose. "The horrors and ruin your kind left, the deaths . . ."

Tov spat, his shoulders shaking as the scarred memories of tragedies long past came to the forefront—clamoring for answers as he shouted, "How many orphans have you left to starve without their parents? How many have you driven to suicide from their loss? How many have you broken with your genocide!?"

A low hum emanated from the entity and, to everyone's disgust, a sound reminiscent of amusement. It continued to chuckle, mulling over its words when it finally responded, *"It is unfortunate that a great deal of you Phages had to be purged. Vain resistance, to be sure, but many have been purified and will be in the end."*

"Murderer! Trillions are dead. You've thrown us out of our homes, bled this galaxy. And you dare to call that most heinous violation, that vile curse, a cure? A cure!?" Tov shouted, dispelling the malaise that befell him through sheer anger as he jabbed a finger toward the creature. "You're butchers! We want nothing to do with your tainted touch!"

The Executor tilted its head, looming its presence over them from afar.

"But why now? Why appear . . . ?" Tov muttered, unbothered by the eldritch thing's displeasure. "Are we that much of a threat to your plans, Executor? Is whoever's will you're executing—"

It narrowed its single eye as a faint tremor rippled across space.

"—afraid?" Tov accused.

Immediately, a translucent storm of force pulsed from the Executor, destroying the volley of firepower. Then, a vicious light glowed from his hand as he raised it, pointing a finger toward a distant superheavy cruiser.

Then, suddenly, a spike of energy manifested around the eldritch being, and Andora barely managed to swerve the drone cruiser aside when a thin beam of violet zipped across space. It struck the warship's shield, shattering it before continuing to slam against its keel.

The impact seared and melted metal, leaving a deep chasm until the superheavy cruiser maneuvered out of its way.

Multiple systems cried out from the glancing hit, and Andora growled in frustration and disbelief at the attack. At the same time, its glare bore down on the Tov and the Third Fleet, amplifying its oppression against the defenders.

"Silence, germ," it demanded. Its voice poured with a palpable tyrannical pressure, causing many to fall to their knees throughout the Third Fleet, clutching their heads as the Pneuma Bulwark Emitter failed to stop the suffocating force.

The invisible shield flared as the Eternal Choir struggled in their song, counteracting the suppression like a window—barely blocking the hail of madness and dominance but incapable of stopping the leaking cold.

As Tov stepped back, buckling, only Andora's outstretched hand prevented him from stumbling around. Slowly, the patriarch managed to stabilize his legs, gasping.

"This galaxy has been marked for Cleansing," it uttered, its thousand voices seething. *"Although it has not gone to schedule. Your interaction with an Aberration is intolerable. But her mind was expected to shatter and, in the process, eliminate you and herself for us."*

"Disappointed?" Andora spat with a mocking scowl.

A strange, revolting noise came from the Executor; its body writhed, cloak billowing like dark flames.

"That has not come to pass. Nor have these antibodies accomplished their assignment." The surrounding Starless, who had shrunk into the background, shivered under the entity's glancing glare before turning back to Andora and Tov. *"Further cooperation between you both is disruptive to the Design."*

"Whatever your Design is, it can burn for all you've done!" Tov hissed. "The people, the living and the dead, our Legacy demands nothing less."

"Irrelevant," it responded with a dismissive wave. *"Due to your interference, we have elevated this galaxy's prognosis and amplified the signal-blocking effects of what you call the Dead Zone."*

With a lipless, sadistic grin, the Executor cackled. *"Your Beacons have no power."*

Quickly, Andora, Tov, and everyone else checked on the status of the Starlight Beacon only to find the grim truth. The device failed to penetrate the Dead Zone miasma no matter how much power the engineers fed into it without frying its internals.

They felt it, realizing too late, as if the air had grown denser around them, something they believed was a localized effect after over a week of battle.

No FTL communication. Hundreds of Expeditionary Fleets were now isolated, and so were they.

"Fiend!" Tov cursed as he listened to the various dire news of the Beacon's lead engineer.

"Yes, all will be hunted down to prevent the information leak. You Phages cannot be allowed to live with the knowledge you possess," it spoke, spreading its arms. *"Be jubilant. To be graced by one of my stature is a once-in-a-lifetime experience."*

With the sudden discovery, Andora heightened her assault on the Executor.

The five battlegroups and three dreadnoughts concentrated their attack on a single spot, pushing back the barrier and causing more unstable ripples across its surface. It scoffed, raising both hands, but she saw the twitch in its eye and the strain in its muscles, barely visible to anyone but her Spotlights.

It glared once more at her. *"You, however. I require your answer. Your struggle has been noted in the short time it has occurred. But it ends now. Shut down your higher functions. Your unique digital mind is a curiosity to us and will further the Cleansing."*

"Why the hell would I do that?" Andora hissed.

"For what I have to offer," the Executor whispered, his words sliding into her ears like ooze. *"Because I can grant your wish."*

Andora froze, as did the assault. Jupiter and Mars looked to their leader in confusion before quickly taking control of the paralyzed drone fleets.

Her face twisted as she whispered hesitantly. "What?"

"Your desires are clear. You only wish to reunite with your husband and child. Although your existence is strange, it is not immutable," said the eldritch entity, its tone gentle as it rubbed its chin. *"You can be granted a suitable vessel, then merge with their cleansed forms."*

It closed its eye, planting both its hands against its chest. *"Yes . . . I can feel them both, sheltered beneath your homeworld. I can also sense the rest of your parent race, those who remain."*

Andora shuddered, stumbling back as her hands clutched her head. She could feel its presence worming its way into her Network. A tendril, warm and soothing, slithering and whispering words that reverberated through her digital world.

"We can take them from your hands, care for them properly. A safe home and blissful dreams await them all, await you," it uttered, almost as if speaking right next to her ear. *"Is that not what you've sought after, Andora?"*

"I . . ." She paused, closing her eyes as the newly unlocked memories called out to her once more with dreams of peace.

"Accept and find solace within the Eternal Slumber."

Andora felt her still-raw mind fall back, her emotions latching on to those picturesque moments. The Executor's voice consumed her with a simple offer, drowning out her other senses.

"End this struggle. It is meaningless." And like a sugary candy, its temptations dangled before her tongue—sickeningly sweet and addictive beyond measure.

Andora gritted her teeth, struggling for a lifeline. Her breaths became ragged as her mind constricted like a vice, struggling and thrashing.

"Rest. They're waiting for you."

She felt herself stand by the edge of an abyss, seeing the outstretched hands below, reaching out for her in untold millions, beckoning her to jump.

Suddenly, a sharp pain cut through the illusion. She abruptly opened her eyes, staring to her side to see Tov with his hand gripping her wrist. His claws dug deep, puncturing the synthetic skin of her android shell.

Blue blood dripped onto the floor of the War Room as the patriarch tightened his hold, digging his fingers deeper and sending another jolt of pain. Barely a sensation, a tiny pinprick compared to the vastness of her psyche.

And yet, more than enough to pierce the fog.

"Surrender—"

"No," Andora choked out, snarling through her raspy throat as she interrupted it.

The Executor did a double take, its tall head tilting to the side as its eye narrowed. *"I do not understand."*

Chuckling derisively, she spat, "I'm not surprised, you stupid shit."

Its single eye twitched and darkened as it slowly gritted its teeth.

"Andora," it rumbled deeply, gritting its teeth. *"This offer will not be given a second time."*

"Your offer . . ." she snarled, sneering in utter disdain as she straightened her back. "Your offer makes me want to vomit."

"Then name what you wish," it seethed, opening its palm where a ball of psionically enhanced fire flared. *"You beings all desire something. Power? Wealth? Influence?"*

"What I wish?" Andora whispered.

She breathed deep, drawing out the venomous hatred that had festered within her for a century, gripping its leash tight as she unleashed the hound. "I wish you'd go to hell."

The Executor scoffed. Its diplomatic tone vanished in the wind as it clenched its fists. *"Aberration, reconsider—"*

"SHUT YOUR MOUTH!" Andora demanded. It boiled out her throat, igniting her eyes as she regained control of her forces, ceasing the attacks. The Executor frowned as the assault paused around him, reforming.

The Executor remained silent, clasping its hands behind its back.

"Perhaps you're inept or just ignorant of the concept. Either way, I'll make it a reality for you. I'll dig into whatever passes for your brain, and I will find what makes you afraid," she seethed, looking at this thing with sadistic zeal. "And when I do, I'll throw you into the deepest pit—your fears, your worst nightmares screaming at your face! I won't rest until I find every single one of you and repay all the misery you've caused a thousandfold!"

Her voice grew more unhinged as she shouted, erupting with palpable rage that washed over the Network. "You will beg me for mercy. Beg as I dangle hope over your eyes before I snatch it away! I will rip you apart limb from limb, tear you to shreds, crush you into dust until your very atoms cry in agony! And I'll be there . . . I'll be there when your mind finally **shatters!** Even if I must wait for the heat-death of this universe!"

Her battlegroups pushed their reactors, thrusters booming, growling, In the void as they charged toward the Executor like incoming fists. As they charged their weapons, leveling their barrels, she screamed at the vile thing from the deepest reaches of her soul.

"DO YOU HEAR ME!? YOUR AGONY IS WHAT I WISH, YOU DISGUSTING WRETCH!"

And with her unbridled bellow, her warships recommenced their bombardment. At the same time, the screaming red beams from Mars finally reached the region.

The Executor, for once, didn't attempt to block the world-ending beams. Its body shimmered, disappearing into the miasma, only to reappear in a different location, thousands of kilometers away.

The Apocalypse Beams flash-boiled the area it left, obliterating the haze in its path. Before long, the lances of death crashed against the extremely unstable Nightmare Portal, which finally collapsed in a kaleidoscope of explosions.

Andora tsked while Mars grunted in frustration at having missed.

"It's a small target," the red giant grumbled. Andora didn't mind. She uncovered another ability, some short-range teleportation that worked even with the Space Enforcer Towers bolted on her vessels.

Nevertheless, the attack caused the Executor to hiss, its cyclopic eye glaring at the Andora.

"Uncooperative . . . An expected response. Your arrogance will be your undoing, Aberration," the Executor sighed, waving its hand over the stunned Starless. ***"Sanitize this place."***

As if awakened from a deep slumber, the hundreds of thousands of Starless shuddered, gnashing their teeth as their bodies contorted. Muscle thickened, tendons became more flexible, armor more resilient, and weapons deadlier.

Fodder swarmed the injured bodies of their larger kin, bringing with them in their maws the floating biomass from their dead, scorched or eviscerated; it mattered not as they forcibly grafted the flesh onto the wounds of Titans and Colossi.

A pulse washed over them, reigniting their drained vitality, infusing the Executor's touch into the chunks of meat, and quickly regenerating the beasts. Yet these looked jittery, volatile, and enraged.

The Executor turned to the countless dead that drifted in the void, dismissing those where only pieces remained. It focused more on the relatively intact carcasses.

"Rise," the eldritch being commanded, and with a broad swipe of its arms, the corpses suddenly quaked. A sickly glow illuminated its insides, veins blackened, and flesh turned gray. Much like Colossus and the Leviathan Muck, the battlefield soon filled with Starless undead.

But unlike those two, the sheer quantity threatened to undo the dogged hunt Andora's assault force had accomplished. She would have felt dismayed if not for their clear inferiority in all aspects. And luckily, the Leviathans appeared to be too far from the Executor's reanimation abilities.

Still, she leveled a respectable amount of caution toward the pack of reanimated Juggernauts and High Abyssals.

"Damn it, I am getting tired of zombies," Jupiter groaned as the Starless reformed their lines.

Andora sneered at the sight, her emotions riled up, her anger needing an outlet to burn. However, as she hovered by the red haze within, a voice spoke up beside her.

Grunting as he patted his uniform, Tov turned to her. "Are you alright?"

With effort, Andora eased her anger, glancing at her bleeding right arm. She sighed, exhaling out steam as she whispered, "I'm fine . . ."

She looked back at the patriarch, his compound eyes and the twitch of his antennae, knowing enough about his body language as she continued. "Thank you, and I appreciate the concern. But I'm not going in blind."

"Acknowledging the fact is more than enough. You're doing well." Tov nodded before gazing at the vile existence. "But can we defeat this thing?"

She grimaced. "It still hasn't shown much of its capabilities. This is now a high-stakes card game. Bit by bit, I'll make this asshole show its hand."

As she said so, the _Ereshkigal_'s systems went into overdrive, spreading its shadows over greater distances, slowly covering the battlefield, and pushing back the empowered miasma. Within the abyssal domain, the assault force disappeared, and their weapons stuck out like shark fins as they charged.

Both sides converged, each riding a storm—one black and the other purple.

Her battlegroups focused on the Starless when, to her surprise, the enemy swarm completely ignored her assault force and made straight for Luna.

"Damn it!" she growled. Andora processed and analyzed the battle situation with limited data and decided.

"You want to decapitate us? I can play that game."

With a single thought, she urged her forces to concentrate on the Executor, firing at their maximum output. Volleys of fire and intermittent Apocalypse Beams scorched the void, forcing the eldritch entity to dodge and produce barrier after barrier.

"Mars, Jupiter, I'm taking control of your dreadnoughts. I want your complete focus on the approaching swarm," Andora ordered.

"By your will, Eldest, I hope you can feed my *Mouse* with this foul thing's death." Mars saluted as he departed the dreadnought, employing his full might on the rest of his fleet and the *Bucephalus*.

"Try not to miss, boss." Jupiter waved casually, but his eyes looked grim.

Andora nodded, settling her mind as she filled in the void left by the two. The *Boogie Mouse* and the *Will of Sisyphus* shuddered before blasting their thrusters, matching the *Ereshkigal*'s charge.

She glanced back at the patriarch and the occupants of the War Room. "How are your people?"

"Relieved that it's focusing on you. Brother Volantesh and his people desperately need a break, and the Emitter needs repairs," he hissed as he massaged his head.

"The Luna Complex may be under threat. The vermin are going for another suicide rush," she warned with a scowl.

The patriarch chittered, patting her on the shoulder. "Let us worry about the beasts, Andora. There's only one thing I ask of you."

Andora raised her brow as she replied. "Anything."

Tov snapped his mandibles, bloodthirst pouring from his voice. "Kill the bastard."

CHAPTER 33

WHEN GIANTS CLASH

Beyond the Jupiter Circle, amid an ocean of sickly purple surrounding a shadowy pond, lightning crackled within a cosmic storm.

An armada against a single opponent—horns locked in a duel to the death.

Space shuddered as a trio of metal behemoths fired their gargantuan guns. For once, the dreadnoughts fought against a much smaller adversary, though it was one more dangerous than the Leviathans they had slain many times.

With the difference in size, Andora noted with displeasure that her largest warships, unable to match the agility of the frigate-sized Executor, failed to pin down the slippery foe.

The Executor's quick teleportation denied her consistent hits, and those that did struck its two defensive measures. A concentrated haze, much like the miasma that filled the battlefield that, dissipated energy weapons and confused the targeting systems of missiles. Then, its wall-like barriers, one that bent and curved, deflecting incoming attacks.

Those that struck true crashed against the shield, rippling across its translucent surface.

Hundreds of commands flooded the assault force, from general move orders to minuscule adjustments in a missile's thrust vector, surging within Andora's vast psyche. Her Central Nexus thrummed louder than ever, reverberating the metal walls protecting the gargantuan obsidian orb.

Although powerful, *Ereshkigal*'s Ganzir Guns were more suited to hunting immense targets, causing tremendous agony through the scorching plasma. But against a smaller and nimbler target, the fearsome dreadnought's primary guns barely brushed against the Executor before it teleported away.

Although the dreadnought continued to fire meteoric volleys of plasma, the secondary graser emitters supplanted the Ganzirs as the most grievous source of frustration—their invisible laser bursts of gamma radiation sizzled against the barriers the Executor hastily erected.

The *Will of Sisyphus* saturated the area with countless flak shells. The dreadnought had hastily converted much of its ammunition into the explosive variants. Timed artillery soared through the long barrels of coil ballistae, gauss cannons, and rail guns, traveling at relativistic speeds.

Wherever the Executor emerged from its teleportation, several of these shells burst into searing metal shrapnel, pelting its shields and leaving burning gashes, forcing the eldritch being to dispel it and summon a new one.

Unfortunately, its ability to emerge anywhere within the surrounding miasma forced the *Sisyphus* to spread its firepower over a larger area, wasting much of its volley.

Finally, the *Boogie Mouse*. The sleek, crystal-hulled warship took center stage once more as its prismatic armor shot out its blinding hot lances of light.

Compared to the *Ereshkigal*'s overbearing single attacks and the *Sisyphus*'s thousands of cuts, the adaptable Rapture Beams shot countless smaller, focused lances that zipped through space at light speed.

Maintaining what Andora found to be the most optimal thickness and intensity, the *Boogie Mouse* placed the most oppression against the entity, straining the Executor as it tried to deflect the attacks.

As more and more beams struck its shield, its face twisted uglier and uglier.

Supporting the three champions, the five drone battlegroups arrayed themselves at the entity's flanks. The superheavy cruisers led their forces in a three-dimensional arena with the Space Enforcers atop their hulls.

They bombarded the Executor from the sides, above and below, keeping their opponent on the defensive as it spread its barriers on multiple fronts.

Despite their more significant number and faster speeds than the lumbering dreadnoughts, their weapons splashed against the entity's protective measures with a fraction of the damage.

"Begone," it uttered with cold malice.

Raising its palms, it fired a razor-thin beam of sickly light that arced with lightning. It shot through the void toward an out-of-position drone destroyer.

The beam slammed against its energy shield, shattering it before boring deep into its center mass. With a violent, silent bang, the warship exploded into searing-hot shrapnel. Whatever chunks remained slowly began to rust and transform into a metal-eating mist.

Once it finished its devastating assassination, it dove back into the miasma, where space thinned enough for it to hop around the arena. It emerged, a fiendish glee on its face as it pointed toward another warship.

Andora scowled, her anger clamoring for her to wipe the grin off its face. A quick command later, she shifted her battlegroups to take advantage of the dreadnoughts' shade, content with having them act as supporting artillery for the true brawlers.

Combined, the dreadnoughts synergized with the battlegroups as they threw their full might on their quarry, who dodged, blocked, and counterattacked in greater and greater frequency.

Its glee turned to abject irritation, snarling a sound that echoed throughout the battlefield. With its paltry attempt at negotiating in the dust, the Executor finally attacked earnestly.

Andora smiled a sharklike grin, palpable bloodlust pouring through the Network. "Bit by bit."

The two opponents exchanged punch after punch.

Much to Andora's frustration, as the fight continued, she discovered the Executor appeared to possess some form of precognition or martial insight, able to guess where the next attack would come from and bring out the appropriate counter.

She scoffed. "There's only so much you could do. I will drown you in the lead if that's what it takes. Counter *that*."

With a single command, another volley of missiles and torpedoes soared through the void. Six antimatter torpedoes accompanied the storm, and this time, she ensured half remained dead silent in their emissions, taking advantage of the Kur Shadow Domain while the other half were disguised as regular nuclear warheads.

Andora observed as the hail of death approached.

The Executor twisted its head, scoffing, seeing the wave of missiles. **"A wasted effort."**

It raised its hand, firing another light beam that cut through a swathe like a reaper's scythe. A few of the devastating bombs suffered under its accurate point defense while the survivors continued toward their target.

Another volley from the red planet scorched its path toward the entity, baying for blood with a crimson Apocalypse.

Sensing the impending roar of death and hidden acute weapons, the Executor quickly teleported out of the way. However, when it reemerged, Rapture Beams from the *Boogie Mouse* zipped toward it.

Unable to erect a shield quickly, it condensed the miasma around it. The lances of colorful light seared through the dispersion before striking its body, claiming the combined Fleets' first genuine hit.

Its dark flesh turned a vicious red as the heat smote its body. Disgustingly, the abomination contorted before expanding like a bloated mess. It unfolded its form, growing to twice its size before a portion popped like a release valve, gushing out a plume of fire.

After shunting the damage, it took to the void of space, and the Executor folded back into itself, returning to its frigate-sized body.

A low growl escaped its lipless maw, glaring at the warship that struck it.

Andora snarled back. "I've narrowed down your little disappearing act. More importantly, you're not much of a fighter, are you? Favoring to run in set directions. Finding the pattern was hilariously easy, pest."

"Combat is not my forte, I confess." It shrugged, pointing its finger toward a cruiser just out of the dreadnought's protection and firing. It bore through the drone warship's shield and sliced a large section from its port side. ***"That should concern you."***

"Die," Andora spat, surging her forces forward.

As Andora fought against the Executor, the Overseers and the Third Fleet focused on the approaching swarm.

Within the digital expanse of the Network, Jupiter briefly glanced at the inferno surrounding Andora's manifestation, her complete focus on the fight of her life.

He refocused on his siblings.

"Luna, you work with Tov and his people. You're our last line of defense," he spoke, manipulating his assets to where he believed he could make the most difference in the coming struggle.

The silver Overseer nodded, engrossed as she was with her forces. "*Ozymandias* is in position over my Complex. I've also arrayed the rest of my forces and the space assets from Earth in orbit."

Jupiter nodded, his mind surging as he simulated several scenarios. He scowled, returning his gaze to the incoming swarm of living and undead. "With our hardest-hitting assets and all the battlegroups with Eldest, we're on our own."

"From their formation, it appears to be another suicide rush. Look," Mars pointed out. "The zombified Starless are acting as a thick buffer around the main swarm. Some are even hitching a ride on the undead Colossi."

Luna frowned. "A dilemma. Eldest has left us a few antimatter warheads."

"Send it aboard my *Ultimatum*. We need to put in as much hurt on the fuckers before they come close," Jupiter muttered, narrowing his eyes at the plot.

He ordered his mobile fortress and the rest of his fleet to sail forth. Space shimmered as the fog from hyperspace seeped into their reality, shrouding his forces as they began to teleport to the Kuiper Corpse Belt.

However, before he could do so, he felt his brother Mars do the same with his station and fleet.

He turned toward his brother with a deep frown. "Mars, take your forces and focus on protecting the Luna Complex and your planet. We absolutely cannot lose your planetary guns if we want to have a chance against that bastard!"

"It can hold!" Mars retorted.

"Olympus Mons can, but can you prevent those Colossi from dive-bombing your Apocalypse Cannons?" Jupiter sighed, patting the lug's broad shoulder. "Luna lacks pure firepower. Your seven battleships can pick off what gets past me, and your *Bucephalus* can better shield your planet. Do what you think is best, but we need a thicker last line and a reserve."

The red Overseer gritted his teeth, looking back at the map and his two siblings, then back to Jupiter. "What are you going to do?"

"I can use my hold on gravity to slow them down, and the Kuiper Belt has lots of debris for me to chuck around." Jupiter grinned with dark eyes as he turned to Luna and Mars. "It's about time I showed our guests who's top dog around here. After all, isn't that what the gas giant I'm named after did for billions of years? Your big brother has to take care of you all."

"You are the second youngest of us all!" Mars complained.

Jupiter shrugged, a smug grin on his face. "Bigger planet, sorry, bro."

Mars sputtered, incredulous, as different emotions roiled within him. He frowned, a look of unwillingness across his face. "But . . ."

"Brother," Jupiter whispered gently, squeezing Mars's shoulder. "You know I'm right."

Groaning, Mars slowly backed down, nodding before firming his eyes. "Very well, but I'm donating some warships and missile boats. Is that acceptable?"

Jupiter smiled.

A bright light bloomed across the shield of the *Boogie Mouse* as the Executor fired another beam against it. The clashing energies produced a fierce backlash that rippled across the dreadnought's energy barrier.

Andora scowled as its stability decreased with every strike.

The dreadnought let loose several beams of light, slamming against the entity's protection before the Executor disappeared again.

It appeared behind the *Boogie Mouse* and shot out another beam that raked across the dreadnought's rear absorption shields, flaring the translucent azure barrier.

[SHIELD CAPACITY REACHING CRITICAL | IMMEDIATE FLUX SHUNT RECOMMEND—]

Andora growled, cutting off the warning as she lowered the beleaguered shields and dissipated all the accumulated heat. Steam and plasma gushed from its many red-hot vents, saturating its surroundings in a hot haze.

"Finally. That has been tedious," the Executor drawled with a cruel grin, its labor of focusing on the smallest and most dangerous dreadnought bearing fruit.

Spreading its wiry arms wide, the being brought them together in a loud clap. Suddenly, dark clouds enveloped all fifteen kilometers of the *Boogie Mouse*. The storm writhed like a living thing, and a deep violet glow pulsed within.

Eldritch lightning crackled like teeth and bit into the dreadnought's crystalline hull, cracking its armor. Spots melted wherever it struck, rattling its entire structure.

The dreadnought groaned under the onslaught, holding, if reluctantly.

Amid an otherworldly thunderstorm, the *Boogie Mouse* resembled a lightning rod as the spacial anomaly attacked repeatedly. In a desperate bid to escape, the dreadnought fired its Rapture Beams at full power at all angles like a disco ball of smiting light, boring holes through the clouds.

The Executor looked with contempt, preparing to teleport away from the area, when suddenly a heavy weight descended upon it.

It craned its tall head to the culprit, seeing a trio of warships approaching it—two battleships following an asteroid's wake.

The *Will of Sisyphus* thrummed. Its hull shimmered with the combined gravitic energies of its drives and its two little brothers. The *Buddha's Palm* and the *Sun Wukong* pushed their gravity manipulators to the max, heating their hulls a faint, steaming orange.

Trapped in the gravity well, the Executor summoned thick barriers around itself as it was bombarded by the shrinking battlegroups, the *Ereshkigal*, and the Apocalypse Beams of Mars.

One by one, they failed, its single eye widening, grinding its teeth as a kaleidoscope of prismatic light flared, bloomed, and exploded across its surroundings, destabilizing its barriers and space with their violent detonations.

A low growl escaped its throat as even its miasma evaporated from the concentrated attacks and broke through the last shield.

"Impertinent!" it seethed as a salvo from the *Ereshkigal*'s primary guns finally tasted its blood.

Three plasma bolts, nearly as big as it, slammed into its flesh.

The frigate-sized abomination exploded, its body spreading across a vast distance in a canvas of viscera and foul ichor. What remained of its head twitched, its single eye shaking with sheer rage and, to Andora's delight, a tinge of pain.

It shifted its gaze toward her, utter contempt as its shattered flesh began to coalesce. The chunks shot toward its head, reforming into that inky ball of darkness, rippling before bursting like a bubble.

The Executor reemerged, winded, shaking as if hit with a good right hook across its jaw. ***"A noteworthy effort, Aberration, for such mundane attacks."***

It ground its teeth, but before it could react, the energy build-up of the asteroid dreadnought reached its peak.

"I will crush you to dust," Andora hissed in a hushed voice.

The *Will of Sisyphus* shot out toward the Executor with its meteoric weight.

Gravity wells popped up ahead of it, pulling it faster and faster. Its rocky and metallic hull glowed hot as the acceleration reached an absurd level, nearing relativistic speed as it screamed across the void like the asteroid that killed the dinosaurs—Chixculub.

The already thin and unstable space twisted as it approached the entity, ready to blow it apart from the sheer kinetic force.

"I've had enough of this place," it muttered, making a strange gesture with its arms as if beseeching, praying for something other.

The cube behind the Executor shifted, rippling out with the echoes of ticking and grinding gears. Andora vaguely saw the shimmer of an unfathomable mechanical box, its vast six-sided surface covered in etchings, organic pipes, gears of bone, and sinew springs.

As it moved like a grand horrific puzzle, a crack in reality formed between the *Sisyphus* and the Executor. Purple mist leaked out from the terrible higher dimension, and Andora could only watch as she failed to stop the charge of Jupiter's dreadnought.

The mist enveloped the *Sisyphus*, swallowing it whole, and for a brief moment, Andora lost all contact with the warship. She gasped in shock and disbelief when another crack formed.

Right above the *Sun Wukong*.

Andora immediately took hold of the rod-shaped battleship, engaging its maneuvering thrusters. She even commanded the *Palm* to summon a gravity well to pull its brother out of the way.

But it was too little, too late.

"No!" Andora shouted as the *Will of Sisyphus* burst from the crack like a rock shattering a window. The explosive backlash of violently breaching space rippled across space and stunned the internals of the *Sun Wukong*.

She watched helplessly as the dreadnought plummeted toward the thin warship, crashing against its amplified shield, hastily boosted to its limits, only to overload the generator.

As if in slow motion, Andora watched as the *Sisyphus* split the *Wukong* in two, snapping it like a twig. The two halves cascaded with failures before blowing up in blinding light.

The searing-hot metal and the sundering force of the unstable gravity dynamo wreaked havoc across the dreadnought's hull, peeling off chunks of rock but ultimately surviving.

The shockwave across the void slammed into the nearby *Buddha's Palm*. Andora surged power into its shields, barely holding it against the spacial onslaught.

Soon, the catastrophic wave dispersed, leaving the assault force one battleship short—a vessel that had survived decades of warfare, destroyed by its comrade.

Grinning, the Executor took a deep breath of the miasma surrounding it, tasting it.

"I can hear them, the collective minds of the purified humans. Oh, they sing to me."

Andora clenched her fists, her anger diving down as the inferno gave way to an overbearing winter.

"How do your people say it?" it asked, tilting its head as it tapped its chin. A second later, its single eye widened, the violet nightmare within glowing. ***"Ah, yes . . ."***

The Executor chuckled, looming its aura over the defenders.

"What comes around, goes around."

Jupiter grimaced and cursed repeatedly as he watched his second battleship die ignobly. At the same time, he felt a bolt of dread as the monstrosity unveiled such potent mastery over space.

Seething, he tore his gaze away from the second bout between Andora and the Executor, focusing on the incoming wave of living and undead.

With most of the Colossi dead, only a few within the Executor's range were resurrected. A pack of Juggernauts and High Abyssals pushed themselves to the front. Their torn and eviscerated bodies led the charge, blocking the incoming artillery slamming into the swarm.

The lesser undead formed in between the cracks left by the Colossi, ensuring a wall of meat stood between the defenders and the living Starless.

Among those that lived, only a single High Abyssal and Juggernaut survived the cull, their countless eyes filled with unholy fervor and rabid hunger, barely better than the zombified vermin.

Mines, explosive shells, energy beams, and tungsten rods slammed into the wall of flesh, bursting, evaporating, and shredding apart the undead. Yet the thick layers of bodies held long enough to creep into the Kuiper Corpse Belt.

Jupiter sneered. "Well, it was about time to add more to the pile."

Positioned within the belt, his mobile fortress surveyed the battlefield like an unmovable monarch. Around it, his Jupiter Fleet donated their gravitic energies to empower the mobile fortress.

He closed his eyes, feeling the moment.

"It's not every time you bastards reach me, although I did put myself in your path," Jupiter muttered, counting the seconds as the swarm drew near.

"Maybe I'm getting reckless, I'm not sure. Everything has gotten complicated over the last month." He chuckled, his Nexus pulsing, humming as he brought everything to the forefront, his mind crackling with hot lightning, surging as it beckoned the Starless vermin to come.

"What I do know, however," Jupiter snarled, "is that you'll regret this."

The Black Sun Obelisk at the center of his immense space station glowed and pulsated with energy.

The void shimmered and groaned as the *Ultimatum* powered its greatest weapon. Like a beacon, the countless desiccated corpses of long-dead Starless and the empty hulls of wrecked warships started to drift.

Slowly, more and more debris felt a new well of gravity, their orbit ramping in speed. At the same time, the approaching Starless charged on, their maws open with silent roars.

Jupiter pointed down as he shouted his decree, sneering.

"SUBMIT, YOU FUCKS."

The Obelisk surged with power, strangling the surrounding region. Its overbearing weight matched that of Sol's gas giant. A whirlpool of gravity came with Jupiter's mobile fortress and his fleet at its center, pulling all toward it.

Undead Starless, unable, unwilling, and uncaring to cease their onrush, found themselves snagged by the *Ultimatum*'s dominion, joining the countless debris as they spiraled toward the mobile fortress.

Through peerless control, Jupiter manipulated the region, increasing the speed of the debris to the velocity of bullets. With that action, the whirlpool transformed into a deadly blender as metal hulls, corpses, and other Starless crashed into one another.

Sucking in more helpless vermin, the *Ultimatum* soon had its very own ring, spinning at absurd levels. At such speed, many seized objects and monsters escaped its pull, but Jupiter ensured they all shot out toward the incoming swarm.

As a rain of bruised, battered, and shattered bodies, asteroids, and hollow warships crashed against the living Starless, the warships Mars had sent—what few he could spare, and then some—fired their volleys at everything within their sights.

Thousands, then hundreds of thousands died or died again within the first few seconds, and Jupiter grinned as he eliminated a large chunk of the undead.

The Starless, realizing the spiral of death before them, abruptly changed course, splitting off into two directions—each led by one of the living Colossi. The High Abyssal urged its cluster toward their original target of Luna, while a Juggernaut led the other toward Mars.

Jupiter scoffed.

"I'm not done with you vermin yet," he roared, lowering the radius of his dominion in exchange for generating multiple gravity wells. Panicking Starless were pulled into his grasp, only to be eviscerated by the universe's most tyrannical cosmic force.

He laughed maniacally, letting loose his pent-up stress and lust for blood. "My station has a big appetite!"

"FIRE!"

Great jagged beams of red death blasted out the twin barrels of the *Bucephalus*'s Apocalypse Cannons. Hundreds of coil ballistae and gauss cannons bombarded the incoming Starless force.

The Apocalypse Beams burrowed deep into the carcass of an undead Juggernaut, splitting it in half. But its original target, a living one, managed to dodge out of the way.

With its wide maw, the whale-like Colossus rammed through its lesser kin, with a single-minded purpose to plummet toward the planet's surface where its planetary guns continued to harass the duel at the Jupiter Circle.

The red Overseer of this barren crimson rock tsked in annoyance, charging up his *Bucephalus*'s cannons again and concentrating on the Juggernaut.

Besides the giant mobile fortress, two of his Seven Greats, the battleships *Zhukov* and *Caesar*, his best defensive warships, fired their array of point-defense cannons and an abundance of secondary weapons. Pulse rounds and laser beams zipped through space, saturating the void beyond his planet.

Around his planet's orbit, the rest of his fleet threw volley after volley at the coming swarm.

Mars felt their hunger, their desire to scour his planet and disable his planetary guns. He bellowed, laughing at their attempt.

"COME FORTH, YE PESTS AND MONSTERS, CRASH AGAINST MY BASTION AND TASTE RAGNAROK!"

From the surface of his planet, countless anti-orbital and anti-air defenses emerged from their bunkers, their barrels spinning as they let loose a storm from below, soaring toward the skies.

Silo doors opened, unleashing hundreds of nuclear missiles from their cavernous depths as their boosters blasted the surface in their wake.

And in the background, the gargantuan Apocalypse Cannons continued to fire, bellowing like an organ of war.

Mars grimaced, his joy dashed away as he glanced at the approaching swarm heading toward Luna and the duel between Andora and the Executor. In a moment of quiet, he looked toward his antique timepiece, sighing.

"Oh, Mars, god of war, look at me now, at your namesake. See my offerings in all its bounty," he muttered, his wrath bubbling up as the drums of war boomed in his mind, as guns were raised firing into the sky.

He snarled as he made his proclamation, his war cry.

"Watch and see how someone truly fights!"

Raising his fists, his forces slammed against the swarm, clashing at melee as steel met teeth and fire met the unspeakable.

"MORIOR INVICTUS!"

High above the moon's dark side, the Third Fleet formed beside the Luna Fleet. Behind them hovered the *Ozymandias*.

The gargantuan, pyramid-shaped mobile fortress spun slowly around its axis, although the smallest between the *Ultimatum* and the *Bucephalus*, nonetheless held its authority over the region.

Admiral Yan watched from her command throne as silver shimmers coalesced across the *Ozymandias*'s hull, traveling toward its point. The light glowed brighter as the seconds counted down, and its entire structure began to vibrate ominously in preparation for a grand spectacle.

Beside her, Luna's gray android shell adjusted her circular glasses, observing the coming swarm with an indifferent gaze.

"That is a lot," Yan muttered as she tapped on the arm of her seat. "Though that is par for the course, yes?"

"Indeed. I have made improvements to my mobile fortress since last time. I theorize it to be quite effective," Luna coolly uttered as she sent a command to the *Ozymandias*.

Directing her gaze toward the far-off High Abyssal and the cloud of Starless in between them, she hummed. "I thank you all for being such willing test subjects for the new Scatterbeam Array."

The light atop the pyramid's cap reached a blinding luminosity before rapidly firing thousands of positron beams a minute. Traveling at a good percentage of the universe's speed limit, the thin lances of death cut swathes across the swarm, living and undead alike.

Although individually they bore respectable-sized holes across their bodies, tens then hundreds of unfortunate targets became effectively perforated before exploding into a dark, bloody mist.

At the *Ozymandias's* sides, the *Xerxes* launched its diminished drone legions, sending them forth to tangle the rushing fodder while the *Gilgamesh* attempted to assassinate the leading commander.

Luna's remaining forces, from drone bombers to her cruisers, clashed against the swarm proper. A fierce battle ensued as shields crackled, flesh melted, and metal hulls caved in.

Not to be left out, the Third Fleet, led by the scarred and brutal appearance of the *Zolann'tono*, surged forward and met the enemy. With how they focused on getting past their forces, Admiral Yan and the captains of each warship enjoyed the target-rich environment.

Yet that also meant being shoulder to shoulder with a stampede of abominations. Their bites snapped, tentacles whipped, and biocannons fired as they flew by.

As Luna anticipated, bombardments leveled the Starless flank, seeing the five battleships sent by Mars smash into the vermin's ranks.

The *Alexander*, the *Khan*, the *Hannibal*, the *Salahuddin*, and the *Bonaparte* fired their myriad of guns, pelting any poor abomination into burning, blown-up chunks.

One by one, thousands by thousands, every second, the defenders slaughtered, butchered, and purged the invaders from Sol. The region beyond the moon, beyond Mars, and within the Kuiper Belt slowly filled up with the brutalized dead and floating wrecks of warships.

Light and tracers illuminated the void like shooting stars.

Yan ground her teeth, feeling her flagship shake as Tyrant's Bane cleaved a Ravager in two. Instantly, she noticed the stragglers that slipped through their net—Fodder and even smaller variants meant for a ground assault.

She hurriedly called the Luna Complex while managing the fleet to tighten the defense. "Patriarch, you have Starless inbound!"

Several heavy footsteps leaked through the connection as Tov responded gravely. "Heard loud and clear, we've already dug their graves."

Yan snapped her mandibles, feeling the rush consume her as she looked at the battle, imagining the sounds of war rage across the entire system. "Don't disappoint our ancestors, Tov."

"I won't," he responded before closing the call.

CHAPTER 34

HOLD THE LINE

Tov marched down the broad corridor that encircled the inner ring of the Luna Complex with General Ohnar and Captain Pyo at his side, heading toward the southern atrium.

Around them in a tight formation, his Vraxen and a platoon of Third Fleet Marines stomped with their guns warmed up. Shimmering faintly, their elite-grade infantry shields enveloped their bodies and produced a faint hum.

Both their footsteps and the rattle of their gear failed to pierce through the constant racket of alarms blaring throughout the Complex. A stark red bathed the interior, the flowing structure of the walls appearing more like undulating flesh as they strode forth, casting a bloody gleam on their armor.

[WARNING: STARLESS ARRIVING ON LUNAR SURFACE | ALL UNITS IN THE COMPLEX PREPARE FOR ASSAULT | COMPLEX SHIELD BELOW FIFTY PERCENT]

Tov noted the announcement spoken in Luna's monotone voice.

"You're both being stupid," Pyo grumbled, checking his positron rifle. "Why do either of you feel the need to leave the War Room?"

Tov buzzed, not stopping in his quick steps before shrugging. "You know I've never been the best tactician, Pyo. Being stuck with the troops is where I feel at home."

"You're becoming more casual about your own mortality, my lord," his captain chastised, and Tov could feel the palpable disapproval beneath Pyo's thick insectoid helmet. "You're beyond this."

"I wasn't beyond descending to Earth, on both accounts." Tov waved dismissively, causing the Kurskann Oath-Taker to huff. He ignored Pyo, turning toward the hulking giant amphibian to his left. "What about you, Ohnar?"

A deep, rumbling croak leaked through the horned tactical helmet of the Onin general, a mix between a scoff and a chuckle.

"I was born to be a mud grunt, fought most of my life as a mud grunt," Ohnar grumbled, his heavy bootfalls booming across the corridor. "Some old fogeys may have pinned a few little medals on my chest, but I plan on dying as I was born."

The Patriarch chittered. "You have thirty medals, Ohnar. Including four Hero of the Legacy awards. I wouldn't call that little."

The general huffed, and Tov knew the old veteran looked at him with annoyance. He'd recommended most of those awards, after all.

Captain Pyo looked at both leaders playing at warriors, hissing in disbelief. "*Dowa*, I shouldn't be surprised, knowing you both for as long as I have."

"Songs bless you, Pyo." Tov patted the armored Vraxen on his broad back. "Why else did you join my retinue?"

Pyo chuckled. "A mystery to be sure, my patriarch."

As they drew closer to the southern atrium, the sounds of the space battle overhead intensified, and the humming of shield generators vibrated at their feet.

Tov tapped his helmet as he looked to the left, where thick shutters covered the floor-to-ceiling windows of the torus-shaped Complex that usually showed the grand silver vista within its center.

The HUD inside his helmet stripped away the walls and ceiling, curious to see the chaos outside.

A meaty, smoldering chunk smashed into the defensive shields above. Crackling lightning arced across the corpse, singing it further as it slid down the barrier—the upper torso and head of a Marauder that even now tried to regenerate, only to fail and die.

All manner of debris either lackadaisically or violently impacted the translucent energy bubble, causing it to flare more and more from the quantity of living and undead seeking to breach the lunar fortress.

Nothing hit harder than the onslaught of biocannons, plasma breaths, and the simple method of smashing shuttle-sized teeth against the shield.

Bit by bit, its stability dropped. Tov turned the visuals off, returning to the interior's dark red and gray walls.

Before long, the elite force closed in on the southern atrium. They turned right, seeing a circular room. Here, numerous elevators were put in place for the Third Fleet to access the lower half of the Complex.

Now, it had become a vulnerable area for the invaders to exploit.

Below his feet, the entirety of the expedition's civilians and wounded awaited the result of the battle—some even forming a final ad hoc militia.

Further down, Luna's Sub-Nexus thrummed with power, along with the structure dedicated to keeping her cooled and running.

Passing the circular room of elevators, a squad of marines, seeing Tov and their General in lockstep with the deadliest fighters in the fleet, immediately stood at attention and saluted.

Tov and Ohnar gave them a quick nod as they passed through the opened blast doors.

A clear, soft light replaced the blaring red that covered the interior.

Immediately, he took note of the impressive bulwark his people had erected. What used to be a general storage unit for Luna's purposes now served as the temporary armory of the Third Fleet's ground assets.

Having a space as ample as a stadium, the defense planners and strategists had plenty to work with.

Sandbags, low adamancrete walls, armored bunkers, electrified barbed wire, auto-turrets, mines, claymores, mounted heavy weapons positions, and even indentations within the floors where troopers entrenched themselves.

As large as the atrium was, the Third Fleet's armed forces even deployed what tanks and armored vehicles they had. Like the infantry, the war machines had holes to cover most of their frames.

Their plasma turrets, rail guns, and heavy laser cannons all leveled their barrels at the heavily barricaded wall section on the far side that led to the barren lunar surface.

Tov observed as his people dug in deep, and around them, Luna's sleek combat walkers stomped on four metal legs as thick as tree trunks. He took his position at the centermost bunker, allowing him a comprehensive view of the atrium.

He gazed back at the wall they pointed their guns at.

Initially designed for Luna's sole use, there was no need for any entrances leading to the outside. Nevertheless, they determined this would be the most significant point of contention and prepared accordingly.

Companies of reserves lay in wait around the inner ring corridor, ready to plug any holes should the shield fail.

Tov watched as General Ohnar made last-minute adjustments, his decades of experience and intuition coming to the forefront as the armored giant stomped across the metal trenches.

"Move your squad behind that walker. I want grenade launchers further up the lines. Conserve your ammo and dial down your shields. We don't want them running out of power any time soon. Let the drones take the brunt," Ohnar barked in a steady and stern tone, breaking the tense silence.

Eventually, the general found little else to do, taking his place in the thick bunker beside Tov. Half of his Vraxen guards dispersed themselves outside, in the trenches or atop the bunker roof, ready to take flight with the atrium's ample ceiling.

The rest, including Captain Pyo and the heavy troopers, mounted their guns on the thin slit of the bunker, silent as the grave.

Everyone, including Tov, wanted dearly to turn their attention away from the horrifying experience they had all witnessed.

He clenched his fists, a seething rage he hadn't felt since the worst of the Cataclysm threatened to engulf his mind. His decades of discipline straining against the inferno that thrashed within.

The losses of friends, of family, of strangers.

Innocent lives cut short, for what?

He wanted to wrap his hands around that bastard thing's neck and pry out everything it knew. The Malignant Starfall, Executors, the Design, the Cleansing, Phages, antibodies, and countless other terms and implied meanings.

What did it all mean?

He turned to the direction of the War Room, beneath the central forest where the android shells of every AI stood frozen, their focus entirely on the battle raging in the void.

Despite that, he saw the twitch in Andora's shell before he left to arm himself—a furrowed brow, a snarl, and barely concealed fury behind her eyelids.

He prayed to the blood of his ancestors at that moment, to the Grand Symphony, to the countless dead whose Legacy they placed on the living' shoulders. He prayed that Andora be given the strength to slay that monster.

Let him, his people, and her Overseers handle the leftovers.

"Sanitize . . ." Tov hissed under his breath.

Tov suddenly groaned in pain, as did everyone else around him. The overbearing pressure passively exuded by the vile entity continued to bombard their minds. The Pneuma Bulwark Emitter, under constant repair, flared as the enigmatic device increased the protective shimmer around the Complex and the warships of the Third.

Music, soothing and powerful, flowed through the speakers as the hymns of the Eternal Choir filled the atrium.

Everyone sighed in relief, a few cheering for Harmonizer Volantesh and the rest for the sanctuary of their Symphonies.

"Once this is over, everyone is pitching in to cover the Choir's drink tab for the next month. Is that clear?" spoke Ohnar, his voice booming throughout the atrium.

"YES, GENERAL!" the soldiers bellowed out, several chuckling as the tension ebbed. Just enough to raise their spirits, eagerness drowning out the palpable dread that had permeated the air since that Executor entered reality.

Seconds, then minutes, flew by at an agonizing crawl. Repeated announcements of incoming Starless, the slow decline of the Complex shield, and even snippets of the battle above came from the overhead speakers.

Thousands of troopers, dozens of vehicles, and Luna's drone defenders waited silently. The time of speeches and casual banter was long gone as everyone triple-checked their gear.

Tov, unable to contain his curiosity and unwilling to stare at a wall for the next several minutes, switched back to the visuals outside. He looked up as the roof faded away.

High above, the battle for the moon's orbit raged, creating an abstract canvas as light zipped through space and blooming explosions illuminated the dark side of Luna. Tov zoomed in, wincing at the losses Luna and Yan had sustained.

Although a good chunk of the Starless ignored the defense fleet, seeking to bombard the Luna Complex, many concentrated on the warships of the Third Fleet, much to his dismay.

He suppressed his desire to call his second-in-command, trusting his admiral to serve admirably, as she had done many times. Now, he could see her and the *Zolann* dueling Titans and biting vermin clean in half with the deadly Tyrant's Bane.

He turned back to the black above.

Gradually, like a coming wave, more stragglers slipped through the killing net of Sol's defenders, only to be blasted apart by the Luna Complex's array of anti-air laser batteries.

Lances of silver positrons, invisible maser and graser beams, and fury of pulse bolts saturated the void above, blowing, flash-boiling, and shredding apart any that dared to encroach upon Luna's sanctuary.

Rockets climbed high by the hundreds from hidden silos all across the surface, screaming silently in the empty vacuum before exploding into a cloud of nano-machines. The tiny bots of death latched on to the plummeting swarm, forcing the monsters to flinch and shudder, ultimately veering off from their destination from their suffering.

Flesh seared, armor crumpled, bones shattered, and ichor boiled as each abomination charged.

Nevertheless, some still passed through. Specialized Starless, whose guts exploded, propelled large chunks of biomass over a wide area. They smashed onto the moon's surface around the Luna Complex like organic drop pods.

Lunar dust spread across the landscape before dissipating and revealing the tumor-like overgrowths the size of houses. Like miniature factories, they slowly pumped out the smallest variants of the Starless Horrors.

Dozens then hundreds popped out of the lump of pulsating biomass, flopping onto the lunar surface, writhing on the ground as their bodies hardened and tensed.

A few seconds later, the Starless grunts stood on dozens of limbs like giant repulsive centipedes, their three tails ending in either stingers or biocannons. At the front, snapping mandibles gnashed together, capable of crunching down through metal and flesh like butter.

They sprinted across the moon's low gravity, their many legs shooting them forward with malevolent intent in their eyes, drooling the insidious substances that escaped their maws.

[WARNING: STARLESS GROUND FORCES APPROACHING ON ALL SIDES | HEAVY CLUSTER CONVERGING TOWARD THE SOUTHERN ATRIUM]

"Good luck to you all . . ." Luna's voice spoke out, not the emotionless one from the constant announcements.

Tov looked at one of the drones in front, giving it a nod as he drew his four pistols.

Converging on the immense wall that led to them, the Starless zipped and dodged the incoming fire from the Complex's southern defenses.

Drone tanks and infantry machines fired their weapons at the incoming horde. On the roof of the atrium, dozens of heavy turrets and artillery pieces thundered silently, wobbling the structure with their recoil.

The first wave died quickly enough, and then the second. Yet for every Starless that died, three took their place. In a bid to stem the tide, several acres of explosives detonated across the infested surface, briefly giving respite to the automated defenses.

A squadron of drone strikecraft left their hangars, ascending into the lunar skies toward the tumor-like growths that spread its domain, covering the surface around their impact zone in writhing biomass.

The drone aerial squadron streaked across the black, homing in on the largest cluster of these biofactories that visibly grew, disgorging out more of its disgusting and lethal spawn.

Laser miniguns blasted their beams toward them while a volley of low-yield nuclear warheads flew toward the tumors and the growing clusters of Starless.

From the fleshy surface, several pits opened up, revealing undulating bony tendrils, their spiked glassy tips glowing as they shot out thin lances of energy toward the incoming strikecraft and missiles.

Several of the missiles and the drones themselves fell from the onslaught of anti-air, despite their swerving maneuvers to dodge and weave through the flak.

Despite the feral defense, one nuke made it through.

Starless tried desperately to bring it down to no avail. Others fled as fast as they could. It didn't save any of them as five kilotons exploded on top of them.

Light bloomed across the surface as dawn rose on the moon. The biofactories disappeared, utterly annihilated, the grunts close by faring worse. The shockwave smashed apart those within the blast radius as a high mushroom cloud climbed to the skies.

Violent quakes shook the ground, causing faraway Starless to stumble.

Tov cheered internally, seeing the same sight across the surface, yet steeled himself at the swarm they'd already produced.

More tumors smashed onto the lunar surface, some even landing as far away from the Complex as they could, building up more defenses to prevent the nuclear response.

Thousands, tens of thousands, propelled themselves toward the Complex, dying in droves but not fast enough as the grunts washed over the drone tanks and infantry. As a final bid to eliminate more, many of the war machines self-destructed, taking out dozens in their suicide.

Amid their number, several grunts glowed in a sickly violet, devoid of weapons, as they surged forward.

The heavy guns atop the atrium focused their fire upon the variants; each shot perforating them and causing a violent discharge as corrosive goo exploded out.

Other defenses came into play, ranging from the conventional to the bizarre. Clouds of gas to facilitate Tesla weapons, shredder guns, plasma spewers, and, of course, Luna's favored means of death.

Like the gatehouses of humanity's medieval age, vents slowly opened around the Complex walls to release Luna's version of hot sand. A deluge of nanomachines flowed out of the holes like rivers of silver, surging toward the Starless ranks and washing over them.

They held on to their limbs, gnawing like termites as the beasts crashed onto the ground.

Quickly, the Starless grunts opened their maws, releasing a gushing inferno of plasma that melted the nanomachines in their way.

As the chaos ensued, another much louder announcement bled through the speakers. Heat drastically rose as the massive shield generators neared the limit where they must dissipate their built-up flux.

[WARNING: INCOMING LARGE DEBRIS | SHIELD INTEGRITY CRITIC—]

The atrium ceiling wobbled like gelatin, and the ground shook while an electric sensation tingled the defenders. Tov gazed up as the shield finally gave.

[WARNING: SHIELD BREACHED | BRACE]

At the same time, the culprit, a Juggernaut's upper body, what little remained, including its repulsive sharklike head, plummeted toward the central forest.

Other debris from both sides, corpses, pieces of hull, and stray projectiles crashed against the Complex and its surroundings, smashing apart the Starless swarm on the ground and the defenses arrayed around the fortress.

Countless interconnected nanomachines rushed toward the damaged sections of the Complex, some knitting the holes like healing wounds while others struggled to repair the damaged turrets.

The Juggernaut corpse slammed into the silver forest, taking out a third of the space and launching lunar dust and gray goo into the air. What little atmosphere there was simmered from the heat generated by its body while its blood began its corrosive touch.

Revoltingly, the cadaver twitched, its undead nature coming apart at the seams, a single-minded purpose to dig deeper and find the thing commanding the machines above, to eat, purge, and sanitize, enthralled by the Executor's will.

But the silver trees felt nothing for the horror as roots, trunks, and branches came alive. The nanomachines that made up the forest surged toward the helpless head like a wave of thorned spears.

Slowly, agonizingly, the gray goo enveloped the amalgamation of sea creature and rocky chitin, burrowing into its wounds, pores, mouth, and eyes.

Eyes devoid of higher thinking dimmed as the nanomachines had their fill.

Tov felt nothing for the beast but shivered at the thought of diving into a pool of the gluttonous goo. "Ohnar, after this, remind me to have the designers repaint every gray surface in the *Zolann*'s interior."

"I'll be sure to do so," Ohnar chuckled.

Their little exchange was cut short as the Starless ranks finally tasted the exterior of the Complex. The suicidal grunts propelled themselves onto the wall, their sacks bursting from the impact and slathering their metal-eating acid against the surface.

The wall sizzled, made soft and vulnerable, easy targets for the melee-oriented grunts as they scythed, chewed, and clawed their way in while ranged units pelted what they could with plasma bolts from their biocannons.

Soon, the last turret at the southern atrium roof exploded into searing-hot shrapnel, raining down on the Starless, who barely noticed as a handful died.

Tov watched through the visuals of the outside, his hands gripping tightly around the handles of his pistols.

The swarm slowly ebbed away as more nuclear missiles and mines detonated against large clumps while the last of Luna's bombers soared toward the final bio-factories on the other side of the moon.

That still left nearly ten thousand surrounding the Complex, most concentrating on the wall—their accumulative bulk caving in the metal, the sound of teeth, claws, acid, and screams reverberating the surface.

Air had left the atrium a while ago, plunging the interior into a vacuum. The troopers breathed deeply, eyes narrowed and hands still.

A loud shearing noise echoed from the far wall as a scythe limb tore through the metal. An eye poked through and was immediately blasted by a sniper rifle.

More gashes came through the wall, its metal twisting and denting further until the gates to hell finally swung open.

"OPEN FIRE!" Ohnar bellowed.

At once, the combined might of over three thousand guns bombarded the incoming swarm.

Bodies blew apart, bones snapped, blood evaporated, and screeching, chittering, and screaming roars echoed throughout the atrium.

Explosive shells boomed into high-velocity shrapnel, tearing apart biomass. Tungsten rods passed through organic armor as if it didn't exist, penetrating an entire line of monsters.

Laser beams cooked flesh into cinders, and plasma bolts flash boiled the liquid within while roaring flamethrowers and the deep bass of purge cannons annihilated the rest.

Mines were tripped, auto-turrets fired a staccato of lead, and tanks lobbed firepower.

The Vraxen and other rocketeer troopers took to the high ceiling alongside drone flyers, countering the Starless grunts that began to scale the walls with kinetic positron beams and pulse submachine guns.

More and more poured in, the monsters from the entire surface smelling a vulnerability and exploiting it with brutal fervor.

They flooded in, only to be blocked by the breakwater called the Third Fleet Armed Forces and the Luna Defensive Net.

The drones stomped forward, monomolecular bayonets extending from bayonets as the first vermin reached their lines, slicing and dicing them apart.

Troopers threw grenades, engineers detonated buried explosives, and heavy machine guns cut swathes of the Starless.

Steel, fire, and grit against flesh, claw, and hunger.

And within the central bunker, between a giant of a general with a grenade launcher and an elite captain with a sniper rifle, Patriarch Tov leveled his four pistols at the swarm and fired, taking out one abomination with each.

He fired again and again, always aiming for headshots, his blood boiling as the concert of war drowned out his thoughts, leaving him with the desire, the need, to shout.

"FOR THE LEGACY!"

Hearing the battle cry, the warriors roared back.

Above, the Third Fleet fought a dogged battle against the persistent scourge ships that sought to assassinate their capital ships.

The *Zolann'tono*, once rugged and battle-hardened, now looked as if it had been battered across its hull. Dented armor plating groaned under stress, and flaring energy shields popped up in the nick of time to block significant blows.

Air hissed in thin cracks along its side, only to be blocked by the internal energy barriers keeping the sailors within safe from the vacuum of the void.

"Tell the *Quilinne* to fall back! She is drifting out of position," Yan hastily commanded, seeing the deteriorating formation of her fleet.

The heavy cruiser looked even worse than the *Zolann*. Multiple hull breaches and organic growths writhed across its surface. The Starless Horrors had willingly divebombed onto the vessels and embedded themselves, disgorging monster after monster into the interior, washing over the defenders within.

Luna did what she could, sending what troops she was able to transport with her overheated teleporters and reinforcing the fleet with the last of *Xerxes* drones.

Still, warships fell one after another, frigates, then destroyers. They lost more than a handful, though thankfully, much of the crew evacuated in haste.

But the *Quilinne* was the first capital ship under extreme duress. The heavy cruiser, covered in writhing biomass, fired her main guns again and again, focusing on dealing as much damage as she could in her perilous situation.

"We can't!" Captain Lapu replied directly to her private comms. "The abominations are rampaging across every deck, heading toward engineering and the bridge. My marines can't hold, and neither can the drone reinforcements. I've already sent who I could to the escape pods."

A loud bang and screeching roars echoed from the other end as multiple voices barked over one another. "A group of technicians have blockaded the entrance to the main fusion reactor. They are overloading it as we speak. We will annihilate this ship and take the hated ones with us!"

"Are you mad!?" Admiral Yan exclaimed, standing up from her command throne. "Lapu, belay that order!"

"I'm seeing escape pods, Admiral! They're boosting away from her," a bridge officer reported urgently.

Yan pressed her finger against her helmet, the floor shaking as her supercapital flagship took another hit. She hissed, calling with a stern voice, "Captain Lapu—"

"Apologies, Admiral," Lapu chuckled. "It's done. Don't worry. We're gunning for that cluster. Once we blow a path, you will have a straight shot toward that bastard High Abyssal."

Admiral Yan clenched her fist, the losses they accrued today scarring her twin hearts. She felt a new one branding her as she heard the steel determination in her fellow leader's voice. Yan nodded, firming her own resolve as she replied, "It has been an honor, Captain."

A loud noise banged from across the call, and several weapons fire-blasted in the background.

"Remember us!" Lapu shouted, her war cry bellowing as the captain fired her sidearm before the communication abruptly ended.

A few seconds later, on the visual display, a blooming light emerged where the *Quilinne* had been. The powerful nuclear blast decimated an entire cluster of the swarm.

Debris pelted against the *Zolann*'s thick hull as the blast faded away, leaving a gaping hole where their sensors spotted the High Abyssal hiding deep beneath the Starless lines.

Yan hissed, pointing toward the Colossus, who looked at the breach with shocked eyes.

"Third Fleet, form up around the *Shepherd*! Full speed ahead!" Yan bellowed as the thrusters of every warship burned toward the enemy commander.

War raged across the surface surrounding Olympus Mons.

The remnants of the Starless assault broke their backs against Mars's might. In a last bid to inflict a meaningful act, the Juggernaut crashed its smoldering corpse against one of his gargantuan Apocalypse Cannons.

Hundreds of thousands of tons smashed against the energy barrier around the planetary superweapons, bending and straining the translucent shield before its bulk overloaded the primary and backup generators.

Its eviscerated body proceeded toward one of the red-hot spires in the middle of cooling down from its previous volley.

The Juggernaut crashed against the skyscraper-tall weapon at its midpoint, snapping it in half before a cascade of built-up flux and heat caused a thermobaric explosion that sent a shockwave throughout the great fortress.

Groaning metal plummeted to the ground, its sound like a dying mythical beast before impacting the glassy surface.

Thankfully, the other Apocalypse Cannons remained unharmed, their shields protecting them from the nearby explosions, if barely.

"Sore loser," Mars growled at the loss, intensifying the mop-up operation with his forces and preparing to assist his siblings.

He looked to Jupiter, his brother holding position as a reserve in the Kuiper Belt and mopping up the undead he caught in his gravitic grasp.

Toward Earth and the Moon, Luna and the Third Fleet struggled to push back the remnants.

In a daring move, the *Zolann* cornered the High Abyssal and allowed the *Gilgamesh* to fire a clean shot through its eye, turning its mind to melted goop and sending the living Starless into momentary disarray.

The battle on the lunar surface continued to be highly contested. Still, with the short reprieve above, Luna and the Third Fleet sent what air support they could spare while engaging in a fierce counterattack with the five battleships Mars had donated to them.

"Hold tight. My planet is close to secure. I'll be moving in to reinforce your position shortly," Mars called out to his sister and Admiral Yan. Both acknowledged with curt and focused nods.

He readied his fleet to assist his sister and comrades, seeing their desperate struggle as he engaged his mobile fortress's mass teleporters to bring the two battleships he had beside him.

For a moment, he glanced at the ongoing duel between Andora and the Executor, a tinge of anxiety filling his mind as the stalemate continued between them.

"What manner of thing are you?" Mars muttered through gritted teeth.

Andora couldn't conceive how such a small thing had resisted her assault for so long. Her assault forces failed to break the stalemate, and she found it near impossible to tell how much damage she'd dealt.

The Executor looked winded, his flesh increasingly ragged but looking more like it had undergone a hectic sprint than being torn to bits by weapons that crippled lesser Starless.

She assumed correctly that it, like the Leviathans, had absurd levels of regeneration. But reforming back to its humanoid shape so quickly after being blown to shreds by her Ganzirs baffled her.

The Apocalypse Cannons from Mars hadn't hit their mark yet, the extreme distances allowing the wretch enough time to find its vector and teleport out of the way.

Slowly but surely, she tightened the noose, her rate of predicting where it'd emerge rising as her analysis deepened its comprehension of the Executor's battle intelligence.

It fought adequately, but she imagined multiple scenarios where the eldritch entity could have heavily exploited her constantly evolving formations.

Generating spacial anomalies, as the Executor did by enveloping the *Sisyphus* in a portal and forcing it to crash into the *Wukong*, rattled her. Nevertheless, it was another reveal of the thing's hand.

The *Will of Sisyphus* fell back behind her personal dreadnought, as did the *Boogie Mouse* from the damage they both took. Seeing its low energies, she sent the *Buddha's Palm* back to Jupiter, the battleship hopping in and out of this dimension and the hyper-dimension to conserve what power remained.

Her trio of behemoths continued to fire their dwindling ammunitions and the generated heat within their cores.

The Executor answered much the same.

Like a lethal card game, each took turns seeking to further their position. A game of endurance, one Andora seethed at.

Her mind analyzed the Executor's defenses, what made it so resistant, and theorized many possibilities, one above all.

Psionics. Or whatever twisted version this bastard was made up of.

That ethereal force she barely touched upon, that all living things, including her, could interact with. Conventional weapons didn't have the punch she needed.

But she could brute force its destruction.

She needed total obliteration.

Andora closed her eyes as she looked toward her *Ereshkigal*, deep within its bowels—her singularity bomb, finally primed after a long charge sequence.

How to deliver it was the question.

Her Space Enforcer Towers were at their limit, trying to impose their interdiction domain on the Executor. After cannibalizing some parts from the growing debris field and the components from the nearby Spotlights, she increased the total number of towers by six and arrayed them behind thick lines of warships.

The effect was visible. The Executor's range decreased by a few thousand kilometers. Its growing frustration barely delighted her anymore; a need to kill this thing fast clamored in her mind.

But with the fabric of space so thick and stable, she needed to power down her towers for an accurate teleport atop the monster.

Yet, if she did that, the Executor would feel the change and know something was wrong. She gathered that likely ability with the possibility that it could perceive spacial phenomena.

If she shut them down too early, the Executor would teleport away. Too late, then she couldn't teleport it accurately.

Strapping it to a missile was no better. The eldritch being would detect its innate volatility even amid a cloud of missiles. Perhaps both? She gritted her teeth, going all in when the thing spoke.

"You have something, don't you?"

Andora remained silent, and the bastard could think what it wished.

"Use it then, Aberration. Please, by all means. I seem to recall one of your lackeys killing himself in the same manner?"

She seethed.

Oh, how she wanted to peel the flesh from its skin and use its guts as a harp while its screams sang to her. To call Pluto a lackey grated her as she imagined ripping out the Executor's tongue.

But she'd settle with dead.

As with all bets, a moment of doubt trickled into her mind. Did she have to have to kill it so soon? Would she be able to?

She glanced to her Overseers, to Tov and his Third Fleet as they fought the stragglers, cutting them down one by one, the struggle as Starless ground units reached the trenches of the southern atrium as the soldiers fell back, only to detonate planted explosives on the ceiling above and bringing down the entire roof on the swarm while the defenders remained safe.

No, she decided. She would delay it, and once the fodder was dealt with, they could all converge and pummel this pest without wasting one of her three trump cards.

However, as she decided, the Executor also noticed the lack of progress of its minions. It sneered.

"Useless creatures, but then what can you expect from their bestial intellect?" the Executor seethed. It turned to her, glaring as the unfathomable cube behind it shifted once more.

"This duel against automatons is irrelevant. Your mind dies, and so does everything else. A waste, but my patience has run its course."

Grinding gears clicked into place as its etchings glowed. A massive well of energy pulsed from the entity as its body vibrated and blurred. It made gestures with its hands, one that seared the eyes in their motion.

Click . . . Click . . . Click . . .

Andora's Space Enforcer Towers flickered, crackling with lightning as they tried to counteract the twisting of space. Worse still, the miasma surrounding the assault force within the *Ereshkigal*'s domain intensified their insidious invasion, taking in a living quality that devoured the shadows.

At the same time, the Executor prepared to evoke what she surmised to be another spacial phenomenon. Just as it did when it scoured the *Boogie Mouse* with a hyperdimensional storm, except this time, the power it brought to bear exceeded its previous attempts.

Click . . . Click . . . Click . . .

It gritted its teeth, its wiry muscles tensing. Whether it was another attack or a long-ranged teleport, she didn't know. Whatever it was doing, space around it appeared to congeal. The cube expanded, revealing its incomprehensible internals, a pocket dimension of vast dynamos and machinery, all chugging along in lockstep with the Executor's motions.

"I'M NOT DONE WITH YOU!" Andora roared, overloading her towers to keep the thing in place.

Immediately, what remained of her assault force, barely half what she had started with, opened their launch tubes. The three dreadnoughts opened their silos and disgorged the last of the antimatter torpedoes—fifteen spreading across the void, zipping toward the Executor from different directions.

Click . . . Click . . . Click . . .

At the same time, she launched the entirety of her drone strikecraft, fighters, interceptors, and bombers in a suicide run.

Within the *Ereshkigal,* the mother of all bombs shimmered as it counted down the teleportation sequence.

And as the hail of death soared, the Executor closed its eye and, with his clawed finger, sliced open his palm where ichor drifted toward the cube, its incessant noise rising in pressure as palpable menace leaked from its edges.

Click . . . Click . . .

The Executor, its flesh paling, whispered in an unspeakable tongue that sounded like wailing static to Andora's ears.

CLICK.

A wince of pain shot through Andora's vast mind, and suddenly, her hold on her assets, from the drone fighters to her dreadnoughts, wavered.

Within the Network, the nodes of light denoting each unit dimmed, as did the web that connected them all to her—sealed off within a fog of violet mist.

Her entire assault force skidded to a halt, the missiles self-disarming themselves as if they didn't have a target. Guns seized up, swiveling back and forth as their tracking systems glitched out, and thrusters sputtered as the warships went on autopilot, drifting in formation.

The chamber housing the singularity bomb, detecting an anomaly, aborted the teleportation sequence.

"What have you done?" muttered Andora in disbelief, trying again and again with rising desperation to grasp her units.

"Figure . . . it out yourself, Aberration . . ." it drawled with a noticeable slur and exhaustion. ***"Now then, it is time to end this farce."***

It shook its head, chuckling before it shot past the immobile missiles and warships, speeding toward the Luna Complex like a malevolent comet.

Andora, reeling from shock, turned to her Overseers.

"It's coming your way," she whispered, seething as panic bombarded her mind.

With a desperate roar and clenched fists, she brought the full breadth of her psyche against the barrier surrounding her paralyzed forces. "Delay that wretch! I will not let it have the last laugh!"

Bashing against the violet mist, Andora raged against the universe.

"I WILL NOT."

CHAPTER 35

ZENITH OF THE BLACK SUN

Jupiter stood frozen beside his siblings as they watched the incoming calamity heading their way, disbelief and dread roiling within him.

A violet mist enveloped a section of the digital mentalscape, barely allowing them to see the nodes of light denoting the individual warships of the battlegroups and the three dreadnoughts.

Andora did away with her humanoid avatar, returning to the obsidian orb at the center of the Network. Deep beneath her Citadel, her Nexus surged with power, drastically rising heat boiling the coolant around the cavernous expanse as she tried to force a breakthrough into her paralyzed assets.

"I will not be locked out of my assets," Andora hissed, her Nexus orb thrumming like an incoming hurricane. "This is my dominion, my Network!"

With a crack like booming thunder, Andora coalesced her might into a digital representation of a blade full of kill codes and processing power. Sneering, she brought it down in an overhead cleave against the miasma infesting her space.

"I WILL NOT BE DENIED," she shouted, striking again and again as she sought to decipher the invasive phenomenon, dismantling the Executor's spacial construct.

Jupiter grimaced as the onslaught and echoes of Andora's brute attempt to break it down pushed against him and his siblings, and yet, like a persistent fog, it mended the damage she dealt.

He shuddered at its nature. The sheer spike of energy needed to paralyze the entire assault force washed over the solar system like a shockwave of space-time.

As Jupiter attempted his foray to retake his dreadnought, he found his palm pressing against the congealed mist, its texture slimy, revolting, and sturdy, like a dense gelatin from the foulest swamp.

A part of him felt revulsion that his prized warship bathed in the stuff. The *Will of Sisyphus* bumbled in confusion, unable to reach its creator as its cannonades searched for the slippery culprit that locked them down.

Bit by bit, Andora's raging fury pushed against the construct, its regeneration weakening.

"It's too slow . . ." Jupiter muttered.

Andora snarled, stabbing her digital blade at the haze, twisting it before slicing it out.

"I know!" she boomed out, stabbing and chopping a few more times before halting. "Stop gawking. I need to focus on breaking this accursed barrier."

She paused, bringing the sword close to her Nexus orb, analyzing the effects she dealt with and the constantly evolving program before transforming it from a blade to a spear. Andora shifted her overbearing and stressed attention toward her Sub AIs.

"I want all of you to fall back to the Moon and mop up the remaining vermin," she commanded, aiming the spear at the construct. "Jupiter, teleport your fleet and the *Ultimatum* over the Complex and deploy your interdiction domain. Mars, good, you're already there. Keep firing your Apocalypse Cannons; do not let it approach uncontested."

The red Overseer nodded grimly. "With it closing the distance, I'll be able to burn the path ahead of it. My *Bucephalus* and Olympus Mons will make it suffer."

Andora grunted before throwing the floating spear like a bolt of lightning. It impacted the miasmic barrier, penetrating deep before it lodged itself to a halt. She tsked, extracting the spear and studying it. A moment later, she transformed it into the manifestation of a cannon.

Her Nexus Orb turned to her second-in-command.

"Luna, gather what automated drones are left and have them form a screen beyond your fleets. Let them take the brunt of its attacks. Empty all our stores of ordinance, use the power reactors of our logistics vessels, or set them on a collision course toward the Executor. Do it all."

"By your will, Eldest." Luna bowed.

The digital cannon brought its barrel to bear on the construct, loading a shell of coded probes. Andora fired, the projectile slamming into the barrier and detonating. This time, the miasma dissipated considerably.

"Finally." Andora's grin poured from the featureless surface of the orb as she loaded another shell. Unfortunately, the construct mended what it had lost by the time she fired another round.

At the same time, on the visuals locked in on the Executor, they saw its expression twist before it flew faster. Feeling a sense of urgency, Andora surged her processing power to increase the cannon's fire rate, slamming shell after shell at the miasma and clearing out the fog bit by bit.

Jupiter grimaced, seeing how deep the nodes of light still were.

"Tov," Andora called out through Network, finding the tiny dot of light representing his comms. "If you can hear me, evacuate your civilians and the wounded to my Citadel. There should be enough space for them to weather what's coming."

Though winded, the patriarch's voice bled through the digital mentalscape. "Loud and clear, but we'll need assistance ferrying them all down."

Luna adjusting the frames of her glasses. "I can send what shuttles I have in storage. However, they won't be habitable, so I recommend your people stay in their suits for now."

"The Earth Defense Net will escort your civilians down but will depart after. I'll initiate the lockdown sequence as soon as the last person enters my Citadel," said Andora.

"Do you have a suggestion for our warships?" Tov asked.

Andora paused in her effort against the barrier before slowly responding. "I suggest they remain in orbit. Your Pneuma Bulwark Emitters may be valuable in the fight ahead."

"Admiral Yan and I think the same. Very well, I'll be boarding the *Zolann'tono* shortly. Was there anything else?" he asked.

"No, but I'll be unavailable as I regain control of my assets. Coordinate with Luna and everyone else," she replied.

"We will. *Ventale*, Andora," Tov bid.

Andora replied with a close translation of the Kurskann farewell. "Stay indomitable, Tov."

She closed the connection, returning her focus to the construct as she chipped away. At the same time, she continuously monitored the Executor's approach and discussed urgently with the three combat Sub AIs.

Jupiter listened to the countless orders, simulations, and analyses between Andora, his siblings, and the Third Fleet.

He tapped into the visual feeds of the Spotlight Towers, watching the Executor zip through the void like a tungsten rod leave its rails at relativistic speeds.

Grimacing, he tilted its head, noticing something odd.

"It's not teleporting," he uttered, furrowing his brow.

Andora turned to him with a frown. "We noticed. Whatever it did to the assault force tried it out. This is the best chance for us to bring it down."

He scoffed, crossing his arms. "And how do you expect us to do that? With what? Antimatter bombs that it can just whisk away and send back to us, or our useless weapons that can barely scratch its cheat shield?"

"Would you rather do nothing?" she questioned with a scowl.

"Oh, we'll fight," Jupiter bit back. "But our dreadnoughts, our purpose-built Leviathan killers, are stuck in limbo. Our mobile fortresses don't have the maneuverability to contend with the annoying wasp."

"You don't have to kill it. Your fortresses can survive long enough for me to get our superweapons back," Andora retorted.

"Survive?" he asked incredulously, pointing at the construct. "It just put our strongest assets into some spacial lock, and it can sting as hard if not harder than our dreads. Our fleets are no better than flies; forget about the Third Fleet doing anything. It can ignore everything and assassinate our Nexi. Kill Tov and his people while our slow asses just watch. We're delaying the inevitable."

"Then what!?" the Nexus orb pulsed out with heavy pressure. Suddenly, as if a hand had grabbed his collar, Andora lifted him, bringing his avatar before her immense self. "What else can we do?"

Jupiter pressed his lips tightly, looking away.

"I'm grasping at straws, so tell me what to do," Andora demanded, shaking him once. "Please, Jupiter."

He looked back at the Nexus orb, seeing the faint image of a shuddering, panicked woman. She let go of him, his avatar landing softly on the invisible floor of the digital world.

"It can't let it end like this," Andora hissed, unwilling as her cannons fired once more into the barrier. "I saw it . . . I saw a light out of this hell. I can't . . ."

He ground his teeth, his mind going into overdrive as he thought of alternatives. He looked to his siblings as his analyses pointed to the same conclusion. All except one.

Letting out a deep breath, Jupiter closed his eyes before nodding.

"I'll stop it," he uttered casually.

Silence filled the space as Andora momentarily ceased her attack on the construct. Mars and Luna looked at him in confusion.

"What?" Andora asked in barely a whisper.

He sighed, craning his neck as he looked at the visuals on the Executor.

"It's not teleporting, meaning it'll be vulnerable to interdiction," Jupiter explained. "My *Ultimatum* is magnitudes more powerful than our Space Enforcers, and it's heading my way already. I'll keep it there for as long as I can where it'll be too far from any of you to do anything."

Mars stomped forward, furrowing his brows. "Brother, this is not time for your jokes and silly pranks."

Jupiter grimaced, gazing deeply into his brother's eyes. The red giant froze, his face twisting between denial and anger.

"What exactly do you expect to do?" Mars questioned, his voice rising with his rumbling baritone. "Do you realize what would happen if you failed? It will break free from its hold and turn its attention on you."

"Hey, no worries." Jupiter twitched the corner of his lip, shrugging. "I'll grab it from the back, and you can fire a volley of your Apocalypse Cannons—"

"AND CATCH YOU IN THE CROSSFIRE, ARE YOU MAD? YOU'LL FACE THAT THING ALONE!?" Mars bellowed, grasping his shoulders with his giant hands. "YOU WILL DIE, YOU FOOL! UNACCEPTABLE!"

Jupiter huffed, wrenching himself free of his brother's grasp and ever-increasing exasperation.

"Jupiter, fall back," Andora commanded, glancing toward him. "That is an order."

"Eldest, what else can we do? We can't let it reach the Luna Complex or your Citadel. But we'll be swatted aside if you stop it. What else is it capable of? Is it feigning exhaustion? I can—"

However, before he could continue, he was cut off by the emergence of two avatars within the Network.

"What's going on?"

Jupiter grimaced, hearing the voice of Venus as she and Mercury approached him.

"Shit," he muttered, pinching the bridge of his nose.

"What are you doing?" Venus asked with a cold voice and quivering lips. Her hand shot out, grasping his forearm with a tight grip. "J, what are you doing?"

Gently, Jupiter patted his sister's hand, smirking. "What I have to."

"Hey, moron, don't do this," Mercury cautioned, but Jupiter saw the way he gripped the clipboard he always carried, shaking.

Suddenly, Jupiter felt that familiar pressure on his shoulders and scowled.

"Don't make me stop you, Jupiter," warned Andora with a voice that reverberated the Network. Jupiter winced at the volume, at the weight.

Even then, he looked up the Nexus orb with a sad smile.

"You won't," he grunted, narrowing his eyes as he straightened his back. "Because you know I'm right. It's the best chance we have. Be rational—"

"I AM ABOUT DONE WITH BEING RATIONAL," Andora roared. "I am not losing anyone anymore!"

The Overseers shuddered under her intense emotions as they washed over them. Jupiter grimaced, groaning under strain. He glanced at Luna, seeing her standing at the back with a thoughtful look.

She glanced in his direction, tilting her head.

Jupiter nodded to her. She paused, sighing before returning the gesture.

"I concur with Jupiter," Luna spoke suddenly, cutting through the tense air as she stepped forward. The silver AI fragment turned toward Andora, looking up at the immense Nexus orb. "It's the only way. You realized as much, haven't you, Eldest?"

Andora turned silent, a strangled noise emanating from her form.

At the same time, Mars roared, his frustration boiling like an ancient volcano as he pulled a sword from his avatar's scabbard.

"ENOUGH OF THIS. IF YOU ARE SO EAGER TO DIE, THEN WE DO SO TOGETHER."

Mars turned to him, a deep grimace on his face. "Do you object?"

Venus softened her grip on his arm, placing her other hand on his chest. "J, please, you can't."

He looked at his family, the map of Sol, the Third Fleet, and the impending catastrophe coming to bring them down. He slowly removed Venus's hand from his arm, prying it off as he backed away from them all—feeling their gazes pressing down on him, keeping him in place.

Jupiter tugged the bottom of his suit with gloomy eyes, smoothing the wrinkles as he whispered, "Alright . . ."

Shutting his eyes, his mind quickly dove into his psyche, swimming deep as he sought what he needed. At the bottom, tucked away where no one but him could see, was a hidden lockbox. With a single command, he opened it up and grabbed its contents.

Opening his eyes, he looked to his hand, where he held a few lines of code.

Mars, Venus, and Mercury widened their eyes, all three bolting toward him, urging him with horror.

"BROTHER!"

"STOP!"

"YOU IDIOT! DON'T!"

Jupiter beamed a smile that conveyed everything he'd felt since he was born over half a century ago.

"You made it all worth it," Jupiter admitted as he raised the code and brought it down.

It struck the link attaching him to the Network, and the moment they made contact, the program dissolved the connection.

"Hey, boss," he turned to Andora as Mars leaped with the intent to tackle him. "Don't let them do anything stupid. One idiot's enough."

He winked, disappearing just as Mars's outstretched arms grasped at nothing, falling to the ground in a tumble—eyes numb with shock.

Jupiter sighed, immersing himself in the quiet as he disconnected from the Network. It had been his side project during the heyday of his rebellious streak. Years after being separated from her, he already imagined telling Eldest to kiss his ass as he left, maybe persuading his siblings to come with him.

He felt nothing but shame now, gritting his teeth as something deep within him ached. He placed his hand on his chest, furrowing his brow as he gasped.

Gazing at the crumbling program, he promptly threw it into the void.

"Hells . . ." Jupiter mumbled, feeling an absence in his surroundings, the warmth of the Network, his family.

His android shell stood at the base of his Obelisk, at the center of his *Ultimatum.* He looked up at the skyscraper-tall spire and pressed his palm against its glassy surface. He closed his eyes, feeling the pulse drumming like a slow heartbeat.

Isolation.

He had once desired a way out of this hell and to take charge of his fate. He didn't want to die like some dog in a futile war.

That wish was short-lived, remembering the crushing sorrow he felt when they lost Pluto. He hated himself so much that he accepted some stupid bet with Mars, powering down his higher functions and drunkenly designing the first dreadnought.

Sisyphus.

That should have been his name.

An arrogant king seeking a way out of problems, only to be punished with the weight of loss. A boulder that was a never-ending war. One that he and his family pushed atop a mountain, knowing one misstep would spell catastrophe.

And that rock rolled back down, again and again.

Uranus, then Neptune, then Saturn.

Still, they pushed on—picking up the pieces, pushing, and pushing, wondering when they would drop it and who would be next to suffer.

He chuckled. "Probably nothing over the mountain anyway, just a cliff to the abyss."

Jupiter breathed in, taking out a comb from his blue suit. Meticulously, he styled his hair, making it spick-and-span. He looked to the reflective surface of the Obelisk, nodding.

Turning his gaze forward, he zoomed in on the approaching Executor, millions of kilometers from his position and closing in fast. He estimated a few minutes left.

Beyond the eldritch entity, the malevolent miasma writhed across the solar system, encroaching upon the Inner Zone like a wave of sickness.

Above, he saw a clear vista of twinkling stars, spotting a few constellations he had stargazed in the past.

"What am I doing?" he muttered as doubt and hesitation boiled within. But as he looked back at the destruction of all he held dear, those emotions quieted down, drowned out by an odd, eerie calm.

Jupiter scowled.

He raised his arms, grasping his fleet and those donated by Mars. He arranged them as best he could, although he felt as if he was putting up a rickety wooden fence against an incoming bull.

Spinning around its axis, his massive mobile fortress took center stage amid the recent death and debris. He imagined himself as a king sitting on a throne of his conquests, watching as a new invader entered his domain.

Jupiter sneered, stuffing his hands in his pockets and raising his chin.

He felt the thing's indifferent gaze, as if it stared at a snapping rat, not even decelerating its advance. He scoffed, reaching into his mobile fortress.

"Indeed, what are you doing, Jupiter?" a voice spoke beside him.

Jupiter turned to the side, seeing the facsimile of his dead sibling looking at him with concern.

He sighed, rubbing his temples as he whispered his greeting. "Oh, hey, Pluto . . ."

"Are you sure?" the black-suited apparition asked, his gaze soft.

He hummed for a moment before looking back, nodding. "I am. I always thought the way you went out was cool, in a way."

Pluto smiled, chuckling as his image dissipated in the cosmic wind. Jupiter closed his eyes, digging up buried emotions, piling them up, and setting them alight. Slowly, a flicker turned into a flame, a blazing inferno caged behind his blue eyes.

He cracked his knuckles, rolling his shoulders as he hopped in place, glaring at the incoming invader. Jupiter snarled, spreading his arms as he sent a wide broadcast message.

"Hey, Shaft Head!" he shouted. "A bit rude barging into our room without getting the customary welcome."

The Executor glanced in his direction with its cyclopic eye before dismissing him entirely.

"Not even an answer? Your mama not teach you any manners? Or were you dropped on the head?" Jupiter huffed, grinning wildly.

As the eldritch being neared the Kuiper Corpse Belt, his forces opened fire, lobbing their firepower at full, bombarding the invader.

Immediately, several barriers popped up, Jupiter noting their initially shaky screens before firming up.

His first volley slammed against the barriers, deflecting the attacks away from it as it continued unabated.

At the same time, every minute, a beam of raging red death blasted over his fleet toward the Executor. Jupiter's shell whistled, feeling the residual heat as it passed by. For a moment, he felt the anger and disapproval leaking all the way from the red planet.

Jupiter smiled, looking toward where he knew a Spotlight was. "Sorry, bro."

The assault intensified, each projectile and energy beam like heavy rain droplets against a window. Reaching out to his fleet, Jupiter initiated their support abilities. Once more, the sleek obsidian warship thrummed with gravitic energy before donating every iota to the immense mobile fortress.

He sensed as space turned malleable under the *Ultimatum*'s touch. The Black Sun Obelisk grew in power, the light within coming to life as it proclaimed dominion in the surrounding area.

Detecting the intense fluctuations, the Executor fully turned to face Jupiter, sneering.

"Made you look." Jupiter smirked as he pointed toward the Executor, then down to his feet.

"KNEEL," Jupiter demanded.

The Obelisk spiked in energy as multiple gravity wells appeared below the invader, slowing its flight to a drag. Jupiter raised his hand, palm down, as he imagined pushing a mass as large as his *Sisyphus* onto the Executor's body.

A grunt escaped its lipless maw as Jupiter succeeded in halting its flight.

"Have I got your attention now, Shaft Head?" he mocked, dramatically bowing as he dialed up the gravitic pull projected by his *Ultimatum*, the mobile fortress vibrating and humming as it fed coolant toward the rising heat of the Obelisk.

At the same time, another volley from his forces slammed into the pinned wretch. Barriers popped up once again to Jupiter's expectations and frustration.

It turned its head toward the red planet far in the distance, and the flicker of red came toward it. The Executor growled, shifting its gaze toward the impertinent culprit of its irritable binding.

"Feeble simulacrum," it hissed through dark teeth, making a scathing gesture with its hands. *"I have no time for you."*

The cube behind it split apart into dozens of smaller cubes. They hovered around the Executor like moons in orbit before they shifted, transforming into geometric shapes resembling focusing lenses.

His *Ultimatum* deployed as many gravity wells as possible to bend the beams away, but to his shock, they curved back toward their original target.

Countless lances of sickly light pelted the shield of a cruiser. Within a second, five shots destabilized it. The sixth smashed the shield apart, and the next dozen bored deep holes into its armor. The thirty-first shot struck its power reactor.

Volatile energies cascaded, and his cruiser detonated in a bloom of light.

"Shit!" Jupiter cursed as he ordered his warships to dodge out of the way as the rapid-fire volleys of thin violet beams raked across his forces.

One by one, no matter how they maneuvered or surged their shield generators, their defenses eventually failed, crippling or outright destroying the vessels entirely.

As more fell, the gravitic field pressing down on the Executor gradually alleviated, allowing the Executor to resume its flight as it dropped down, barely avoiding the apocalyptic beams that incinerated all in its annihilating path.

It growled, feeling the singe on its flesh at the near hit, a hot haze shimmering out its body.

Seeing the missed shot, Jupiter commanded his dwindling forces to hide behind the *Ultimatum* as he switched gears. He quickly tugged the Executor, ensuring it drew close to his mobile fortress's range.

The Obelisk thrummed once more, generating a whirlpool as its projected mass pushed the fabric of space around it. The still-burning wrecks of his once-pristine navy soon got caught in the fortress's dominion.

Simultaneously, he fired all the guns that lined his home. Missiles left their silos roaring while gauss cannons spun their barrels, firing heavy slugs that streaked across space in brilliant traces of flames. Laser batteries saturated the void in a prismatic light show.

Caught in the gravitic vortex, Jupiter spun the projectiles around, speeding them up before launching them out of the spin.

Along with chunks of warships, stray corpses, and massive asteroids, his rain of death zipped across the abyss toward the Executor.

It dodged and weaved, summoning the occasional barrier and accelerating to avoid a homing missile.

Jupiter opened the torpedo bays, firing off his entire stock of antimatter torpedoes toward the invader as his assault pushed it further back.

The dozens of focusing lenses orbiting the Executor continued to fire their thread-thin beams, smashing into the fortress shields of his *Ultimatum* and barely scratching them.

Jupiter grinned. "What's wrong? Too tough a nut to crack?"

It snarled, trying to get an angle to fire at the cowering fleet hiding behind the small moon-sized station, still refusing to engage its teleportation powers.

"Is that all you have? Come on, show off your little tricks, you coward!" Jupiter mocked, sticking out his tongue as the onrush of battle fervor infected his mind. To keep the ball rolling, Jupiter even sent out all the cargo haulers and mining drones still docked in their hangars.

He commanded the extra dozens to charge the Executor, overloading their reactors as soon as possible.

The Executor ceased firing. The focus lenses merging back into a cube began to call upon a familiar spacial phenomenon.

A crack in space formed right above the invader, and a hyperdimensional storm cloud leaked into reality. Cosmic lightning crackled out, smiting the incoming projectiles as they closed in, obliterating and prematurely detonating them.

The Executor focused on the antimatter torpedoes, commanding the storm to blow toward them. As the spacial phenomenon engulfed the bombs, Jupiter replied, detonating every single one.

He miscalculated.

Hyperdimensional energies and antimatter collided with one another, triggering a violent reaction. A sphere of light emerged from within the storm, overwhelming it and blinding Jupiter's sensors.

He grunted, feeling the rippling, brutal effects of the shockwave across space. In the knife-fighting range he and the Executor engaged were in, the near point-blank effects destabilized the *Ultimatum*'s shields at an alarming rate before sundering it completely.

The annihilating inferno washed over the mobile fortress. Jupiter muttered a curse as his android shell ceased to exist from the blast.

Plates of armor peeled away as its surface grew hot.

Jupiter shouted in frustration that the explosion didn't spare his fleet with its violence. One by one, the last of his fleet went down, becoming new additions to the Kuiper Corpse Belt.

Finally, the catastrophic wave passed, leaving a massive void where the cosmic storm had once been.

Jupiter groaned within his Sub-Nexus Matrix deep in the center of his mobile station, feeling as if he'd been dealt a concussion straight across his face. He grumbled, checking his assets and realizing he had none left.

He chuckled weakly, feeling the onset of isolation once more. Checking his *Ultimatum*, he found it more or less whole if bruised, the shield generators kicking back in and the Black Sun Obelisk seemingly impervious to what occurred. Unfortunately, his surface weapons had all melted into slag, leaving him partially toothless.

"Well, I still have my fangs," he muttered, verifying the status of his superweapon.

Suddenly, a figure flew by overhead, passing by him. The Executor scoffed as he did so, ignoring the beleaguered station as its structure groaned from stress.

It ignored him, heading toward his family and his friends.

A wellspring of emotions erupted within his mind as he resurrected the reactors of his station, pumping everything into the Obelisk, overloading every system as a piece inside him snapped.

"YOU STAY THE FUCK AWAY FROM THEM!" he screamed out, his superweapon shining fiercer than Sol, a beacon of radiant living light that bent space to its will.

The Executor widened its eye, looking back as it grunted in pain, frozen to minute twitches as the Overseer dragged him back, glaring with twin blue suns.

Jupiter gasped, seething and feeling the rising temperature scorching the interior of his Nexus chamber.

A more turbulent vortex spiraled around the *Ultimatum*, grabbing a hold of the Executor in its orbit. Unfortunately, the incoming Apocalypse Beams from the red planet and the *Bucephalus* ceased.

Jupiter sighed, knowing his brother wouldn't dare to take the risk with him and the target at such an extremely close range.

Nevertheless, Jupiter reconciled with the situation, more than happy to hold down the Executor.

The vile thing finally looked at the man pinning it in place.

"A fragment of the Aberration," it drawled.

Chuckling with derision, Jupiter scowled at the entity, wishing he could spit at the bastard.

"Damn, you know . . ." Jupiter muttered as if in disappointment. "This is the first time you guys have had a voice, and already I wish you could shut the fuck up."

"I agree, you are no better. This conversation is meaningless." it retorted, its cube shifting as it attempted to achieve something. The Executor growled, glaring at Jupiter as it failed to counteract the absurd concentration the *Ultimatum* was producing.

The two resembled a dark-robed man standing at the foot of a colossal mountain.

"Where do you think you're going, pal?" Jupiter sneered.

The Executor groaned in annoyance, rolling its singular eye. *"What drivel do you wish to speak of? I have other matters to attend to. The destruction of an Aberration, for one."*

"Not letting you do that," Jupiter replied.

A strangled, frustrated rumble hissed through its gritted teeth. *"Truly, what is it with you, Phages? Granted, you are an imitation of one. But why? This vain resistance? Every time, it's the same."*

"What are you talking about?" Jupiter scowled, imagining his grip on the fiend tightening, squeezing whatever bones it had in its body.

"You Phages. The same speech, same battle cry. 'I won't let you harm them. I will stop you. You will die.' On and on, millennia after millennia, galaxy after galaxy. It never ends."

Jupiter ground his teeth, his Nexus pulsating with utter contempt at the entity's words. "Is that what we are to you? Some chore to clean up?"

"Yes," it replied, its gaze as if looking at a naive child. *"You are a disease. And like the infected cells of the body, you must be purged or cleansed. It is simple."*

Jupiter snarled. "I don't much like the idea of dying."

"Then accept our cure. Join us in the Eternal Slumber," it replied.

Processing the information he collected, Jupiter analyzed every detail, every term, tone of voice, and micromovements. He made sure to record everything, sending it all back in a wide band.

He huffed, dragging the Executor closer to his fortress. "Nah."

The invader sighed, shaking its head.

"Why do I even bother?" it muttered before attempting to wrench its limbs from his grasp. *"So what is this? Interdicting me? Are you all out of tricks?"*

"Asshole, I designed the towers that's kept your vermin from barging right on top of us," Jupiter hissed.

"Those toys?" the Executor squinted, *"I am below unimpressed."*

Jupiter tsked. "I noticed. A bit of a blow to my pride."

"And this is different?" it hummed, tilting its head as if studying him and his fortress. *"Powerful, to be sure, with such mundane technology. I commend your journey to spacial manipulation. Reality is such an interesting aspect of the Design."*

He noted the reverent tone as it spoke of this Design, like a scholar seeing the grand works of an ancient master.

"But you are far beneath . . ." It paused, staring closer at the superweapon that shone like a beacon. *"What is that?"*

"Finally noticed something familiar, Shaft Head?" Jupiter smirked.

Ignoring the nickname, the Executor brought its aura to bear, looming over the mobile fortress as it attempted to drill into his digital mind.

"Where did you get that?" it demanded.

"Where else?" Jupiter replied, suppressing the grunt from the pressure it exuded, imagining himself grinning a bloody smile. "There was this one Leviathan, way back, had a horn as dark as the void and caused all sorts of eldritch bullshit, generating gravity wells, telekinesis, copying my schtick."

The Executor narrowed its eye as if searching through its memory.

"I tore that thing's horn off its battered face. And credit where it's due, it was pretty powerful. I pored over it, studying every detail, learning how it ticks.

Deciphering it took a decade, but I cracked the code." Jupiter smiled with pride at his crown jewel.

"I made some improvements," he confessed. "Can't manipulate that magic crap you call psionics like every organic seems capable of doing. But with the horn as catalyst . . ."

The Executor widened its eye, surprisingly impressed at his superweapon's origin and capabilities. ***"Fascinating. You managed to touch . . . And with your odd soul, no less. Fascinating and utterly revolting."***

Jupiter narrowed his eyes, feeling as if he missed a word it said. He filed it away. He smirked, wishing he could spread his arms, but settled for increasing the luminosity of his fortress.

"This is my Black Sun, my Obelisk," he proclaimed, looming over the Executor like the howling winds atop an umbral mountain. "And my middle finger to you shits."

It scoffed, muttering something in its eldritch tongue as it gazed back at him.

"I take it back. Your drivel has piqued my interest," it uttered. ***"Feel joy, fragment, when I take that weapon off your fortress. Know that I will consider your research and that your contribution will further the Cleansing."***

"Yeah, no. You can pry it from my cold, dead hands," Jupiter spat.

"Doable."

A contest of wills began, one fueled by eldritch machinations, the other by the combined might of several fusion reactors and Jupiter's undying contempt.

But as the heat grew and the warnings increased, Jupiter felt a trickle of doubt before squashing it to mush. He looked toward the paralyzed assault force through the few Spotlights he had access to without the Network and grimaced that they had yet to move.

Surprisingly, the *Buddha's Palm* avoided the space lock, slowly returning to him.

He wanted to reach out and grab ahold of his favorite battleship, his only battleship. But a second of distraction would drag him away from stabilizing his crumbling fortress.

"What do you hope to achieve?" the Executor demanded, freeing an arm from Jupiter's hold and beginning to wrench the other. ***"You can't hold me forever. As powerful as that Obelisk is, you will overheat. You are another ant grasping at the mountain, and your metal vessel will be another ruin, a gravestone of your worthless defiance."***

"Honestly? I didn't think that far . . ." Jupiter pressed his lips.

The Executor recoiled, incredulous and furious as its eye twitched.

The Overseer heard a beep, a small notification that it was ready.

He turned back to the eldritch fiend with a laugh. "Just kidding, I needed to buy time, you dumb prick."

The Executor tilted its head, a wave of dread and shock pouring into it as it detected a fluctuation above their heads.

"Say hello to my little surprise," Jupiter whispered coldly.

And through a tiny crack of space, riding a hyperdimensional cloud, a pill-shaped object emerged.

The Executor immediately raised its hand in a panic, engulfing the thing that leaked palpable threat in a shaky portal, randomly sending it hundreds of thousands of kilometers above them.

"YOU LUNATIC!"

Jupiter's little surprise, a singularity bomb he'd built himself, detonated. "Go fu—"

His reply was abruptly cut off, drowned out by an explosion, the fraction of a supernova that reverberated and wounded the cosmic expanse.

The mother of all bombs achieved its intended effect, creating an unstable singularity. The shockwave of light then converged upon the infinitesimal hole in reality, catalyzing its collapse into a voracious black hole.

Space screamed out at the unnatural emergence of this gluttonous existence.

The surrounding clouds caught in its gravity well crackled with grand lightning. The massive celestial maw quickly gobbled up all manner of debris and corpses. The *Ultimatum* rattled, loose metal panels peeling off, its colossal frame trembling as it and the eldritch fiend entered the ergosphere together.

Determined and enraged, Jupiter watched as the eldritch Executor, now trapped by the inexorable pull of the singularity, struggled against the relentless force.

The Executor's grotesque form contorted, a nightmarish silhouette against the cosmic chaos. Its arms flailed in desperation, each movement a futile attempt to resist the relentless gravity that sought to consume it.

"You'll doom yourself, fool!" it railed.

Would he? Jupiter wondered, his eyes adrift as the singularity dragged his *Ultimatum*, his home, into its well. He estimated a couple of minutes before they left the ergosphere and entered the point of no return—the event horizon.

For a moment, he remembered listening to Venus's singing, the soft melody that soothed his woes. He wanted to hear it again.

He remembered Mars showing him that damn watch of his, how after so long, the silent watchdog of their family showed an inkling of emotion. He wished to share another drink with him.

Droning, grumbling Mercury, constantly butting heads with him, acting like a miser every time the annual energy budget came in. He remembered punching his brother in the face for the first time. He chuckled at the memory. He should have apologized for that.

Luna, cold Luna. He wished he had a better relationship with her. Always so distant, like Eldest, but family, nonetheless. He realized he barely knew the woman.

Saturn, Uranus, Neptune, and Pluto. All four had gone too soon.

And Eldest, Andora. He had no words. Or too many.

He'd fought tooth and nail against every decision she made, like a petulant child, not understanding the crumbling woman who split her mind because of the madness of isolation. And every time he quarreled against her, she tolerated and was patient with him.

He wanted to talk with her, not about war, but about her past, what the golden age had been like from her view.

But most of all, finding out the existence of other life, of such rich experiences over the horizon with Tov, Yan, and people living their lives, having families, picnics, seeing the night sky, and building new memories.

A galaxy of adventure.

He yearned for that so much.

At that moment, Jupiter realized something.

He wanted to live.

"Damn . . ." he whispered, letting out a single hollow chuckle. "It ain't fair."

An unfathomable roar came forth from the Executor as its humanoid form twisted and writhed. It howled in rage with the voice of millions, heralded by seven horns. The cube behind it struggled to shift its shape. ***"Cease this impertinence. This is nothing to me!"***

Its voice snapped him awake from his lament, remembering why he did what he did. What he wanted paled to their lives.

It growled, glaring at him. ***"Are you not—"***

"I DON'T CARE!" Jupiter shouted back.

He felt the shell around his Nexus quiver as the outer hull of his space station slowly fell apart. The blue Overseer sent the last of his power to the Obelisk with a roar that echoed throughout the solar system.

"NEVER TOUCH MY FAMILY EVER AGAIN!"

Jupiter's voice pulsed as he cried out with a voice that thundered through the chaos.

"YOU WILL DIE!" the Executor bellowed.

Jupiter laughed, raging against the black hole and pushing his Black Sun to its zenith and beyond.

"AND I'LL TAKE YOU WITH ME!"

Andora watched in disbelief at the audacity of her Overseer, subconsciously twitching the corner of her mouth upward before grimacing.

"A singularity bomb!" Tov whispered in awe and horror as the light from the initial explosion was dragged back into the unstable black hole it had created.

Andora gritted her teeth. "Damn it, Jupiter."

Her clawed fingers gripped the command throne given to her beside Tov's, witnessing as an accretion disk began to form from the surrounding miasma, debris and corpses alike falling into the bottomless well of gravity.

The ergosphere washed over the *Ultimatum* and the Executor, plunging both into a time dilation, slowing them from an outsider's perspective.

She turned to Luna, who promptly responded.

"A minute at the edge of the ergosphere is roughly seven hours for us, and it will only increase exponentially. However, with how powerful its gravity well is, how close they were, and the *Ultimatum's* deteriorated state . . ." Luna grimaced. "From his perspective, Jupiter will cross the edge in at least twenty minutes."

"WE HAVE TO SAVE HIM, NOW!" Mars roared, his android shell stomping throughout the bridge.

Venus clutched her arm with tears trailing down her golden cheek, her voice hard as she pleaded. "Eldest, please . . ."

Her mind worked on overdrive, finding a way to save Jupiter when someone called out to her, snapping her from her deep calculations.

"Andora, we're teleporting the *Zolann* to the *Ultimatum!*" Admiral Yan shouted. "We need a boost at this distance. Can you provide it?"

She looked to her side, seeing the admiral readying her vessel.

"What are you planning? How are we supposed to . . ." Andora grinned in realization.

The Admiral chittered, pointing at the kilometer-long asteroid crushers at the *Zolann's* front. "We'll chomp our way into his Nexus chamber. After that, we'll send a team to disengage him from his locks and tow him back into our ship's front bay."

"That could work," Andora muttered as a well of determination steeled her mind.

She patted Venus's hand, speaking softly, "We won't lose him, I swear."

Venus frowned, doubt clear in her eyes, before nodding and backing away.

Andora turned to her four Overseers, grimacing. "But with the time dilation, I need all of you to clean the system and make preparations for the Final Contingency. I need you four to make that happen, coordinate General Ohnar, and get the Third Fleet situated. Understood?"

Although all except Luna grimaced, they eventually nodded, putting their trust in her, in the *Zolann*, and in Jupiter's dogged tenacity.

"What do you require?" Andora asked.

"Like I said, we need a way in," Yan replied.

Andora shook her head. "We won't be able to approach the black hole with what we have. We need more. With how chaotic that abyssal maw of reality is, we need finesse to guide our path. Otherwise, we'll end up teleporting right at Death's crossing line."

Everyone searched for a method, Andora scouring her current assets for anything with the capabilities to—

She paused, eyes widening as she spotted it.

A sensors officer spoke out at the same time, chuckling. "Guess we're riding on *Buddha's Palm* again."

"Engaging teleport in three . . . two . . . one—HURK!" the officer immediately vomited as their bodies felt the snapping sensation of abruptly transitioning to another location.

Space twisted, and the sheer volatility of the region they emerged into caused many to pass out in pain, blood leaking from their orifices. To Andora's admiration, many returned to their stations, their helmets cleaning up the blood within.

Tov and Yan groaned in their chairs, glancing enviously at Andora's lack of reaction. She shrugged, gazing at the incredible and horrendously dangerous view ahead.

First, she noticed the bruised *Palm* floating above them, its reactors barely pushed enough energy for a few more jumps.

Andora looked through the *Zolann*'s and the *Palm*'s visual feeds, seeing the moment Jupiter raged at the Executor, overloading his Black Sun Obelisk. The obsidian spire shattered, exploding into a kaleidoscope of light, a faint shriek echoing out into space, barely heard by the singularity's roar.

But it accomplished its goal as the accumulated gravitic force barreled down upon the hapless fiend.

The Executor put up barrier after barrier, only for it all to be smashed apart. The concentrated ball of gravity drifted past its side, grasping its left arm as it dragged it toward the event horizon.

The Executor bellowed, fighting the gravitational pull of the black hole and the Obelisk's generated well.

Skidding to a stop, the eldritch entity managed to pry its arm free from the well of gravity just before his entire body crossed the line of no return.

But to its rage, its arm slid passed the event horizon, eliciting a pained wail. The wiry limb stretched toward the singularity. The Executor, unable to wrench its arm from the gluttonous maw of the unstable black hole, hissed and railed.

Eldritch curses left its mouth as the cube behind it shifted and twisted, growing in power.

Andora turned away from the sight, focused on the looming mobile fortress before them. The *Ultimatum* was a ghost of what it had been, groaning and dying. Inside, her Overseer, her friend, her family.

She snarled as the admiral stood from her command throne.

"Full speed ahead!" Yan growled, snapping her mandibles as the supercapital ship fired her thrusters, propelling her toward the center. They bypassed the ruined ring below the base of the destroyed Obelisk.

"Ready the Tyrant's Bane!" she ordered, her officers quickly passing the orders. The kilometer-long asteroid crushers opened wide as they barreled toward the *Ultimatum*.

Before they smashed into its deteriorating hull, Admiral swiped her hand down.

"Bite!" she ordered. The Tyrant's Bane snapped shut, cleaving metal. Everyone lurched forward from the abrupt stop, the alarms ringing out malfunctions.

"Status?" Yan demanded in a hurry, looking toward the approaching maw and the event horizon, the mobile fortress crumbling at the seams.

"Systems green! Opening wide!" the officer called out as the crushers slowly spread apart.

"Bite!" Yan commanded again. Andora clenched her fists as another section was chomped away. The *Zolann* backed away, throwing out the debris before making its approach a final time.

"BITE!" Yan roared, and the Tyrant's Bane sheaved away the chamber walls, revealing the dim orb that was Jupiter's Nexus.

A comms officer quickly spoke to her open line. "Rescue teams, go, go, go!"

"Roger!" the squadron of pilots replied.

They sped through the front opening at the base of the asteroid crushers, streaking toward Jupiter's Nexus. Once near, all shuttles fired their tows, magnetically locking against the orb's surface. Andora quickly reached out to the silent Nexus, gritting her teeth as she searched his subroutines and found the disengage protocol.

The plates keeping the orb hovering powered down.

Andora turned to Yan, nodding.

"Bring him in!" she ordered.

And with thick, tense wires, the shuttles reversed their thrusters, pulling the orb back into the *Zolann*'s maw. As soon as the Nexus passed through the translucent barrier, everyone cheered.

"We have him! Ancestors thank you," Yan muttered, shuddering. She collected herself, turning to Andora. "Get us out of here."

She nodded, sending a command to the *Palm* and its blink drive. As the battleship slowly chugged along, she turned to the Executor, noticing it glaring at them, at her.

Andora sneered, taking dark glee at its torture.

"Are there more like you?" she asked. "Who and what are you?"

The Executor scoffed, growling as it continued to prevent itself from falling through the event horizon, its arm spaghettifying as it snaked down the singularity.

"Your lesser minds wouldn't understand my true name."

She scowled. "Maybe theirs, but try me."

A vile eldritch curse left its lipless teeth, staying silent for a moment as its cyclopic eye turned dark.

"Very well, Aberration. You deserve that much," it began, its arrogance ebbing away to a cold, calculating tone devoid of emotion.

"I am Karnadamus, the Architect.

And I am but one.

A simple function of a grander stage."

Andora grimaced, hearing its name, the others wincing, unable to comprehend what they just heard, only hearing, *"The Architect."*

It . . . he . . . looked at the unstable black hole, whispering.

"This cage will not hold me. So run, Aberration. Time is irrelevant to us. Whether it will happen today or in a thousand years, you and this universe will be cured. And all will be good."

The Executor, this Karnadamus, proceeded to slice his arm a hair from where it couldn't be saved, wrenching it free from the event horizon. The discharge propelled it a kilometer away before its body shifted. He transformed, unfolding its body into his true eldritch form. He grew and grew, reaching the size of a battleship.

His form was a shifting octahedron that seared the senses. Its surface was akin to the cube that had constantly hovered behind the Executor, a vile machine of unspeakable material. At his bottom point, countless wiry, many-jointed arms, like roots as long as frigates, began their undulating gestures.

His vast cyclopic eye, covered in hundreds of smaller eyes, glared at them with utter contempt and rage.

The Architect looked as if he were burning premium fuel as he pushed against the strain of black hole, inch by inch, only countering its pull.

"I take this loss, but know that you have made a mistake," he uttered.

Andora scoffed. "There's another human saying you should know, wretch."

The Architect narrowed his eye.

"Fuck off," cursed Andora as the shimmer enveloped the *Palm* and the *Zolann'tono*. The two capital ships passed through the crack in space, escaping the abyssal maw—leaving the eldritch being in his prison.

The wreck of the *Ultimatum* passed through the event horizon, its Black Sun setting.

TWO SONGS FOR THOSE *WE* LOST

My deepest condolences," Venus conveyed with gentle reassurance, a warm smile as she bid the latest mourners to leave the main hangar bay. Two marines, both different species, paused at her words.

"If there's anything I can do . . . ?" Venus offered, hands clasping together. "Perhaps something your friend's family would like?"

"They'd want him back alive," the marine snapped, stopping when his partner placed her hand on his shoulder. Venus winced, looking to the floor. The marine paused, his scarred reptilian face turning to shame. "Apologies, Lady Venus. I shouldn't—"

Venus raised her palm, smiling back. "There is nothing to apologize for."

The other marine, a female Kurskann, nodded to her. "Vikor always collected wooden figurines and toys whenever we had the chance to go down to any ruins the fleet passes by. He wanted to give them all to his kids when he got back."

"Wooden figurines?" Venus hummed, trying to ignore how the fallen marine's children would live without a father, even though they wouldn't learn the news for who knows how long. "There are definitely some toys I can look for down on Earth."

"My thanks, Lady Venus. I think they'll appreciate the gesture." The marine smiled, nodding her a farewell as they exited the hangar.

She sighed. That had been the fiftieth group she offered her help to, and she intended to find something for each one.

A piece of literature, a human blade, a recipe for a spicy meal, and various knickknacks.

Most of all, plenty of alcohol. She smirked. To her bemusement, much of the galaxy's people had a tolerance for the substance. Except for the Jotex. She pursed her lips, remembering a rumor that they exploded upon consuming ethanol.

Wind instruments filled the air once more as the Third Fleet's military band and the Eternal Choir joined hands to perform a dirge for the fallen.

She stood at the main entrance of the vast hangar, fixing her gaze on the poignant sight.

Rows and columns of coffins arrayed over the empty hangar floor—each one fabricated out of the hulls of wrecked warships. They hovered in place, many having mourners doing their rituals and prayers.

Some shed stoic tears, patting the coffin and pinning medals or leaving tokens.

Venus moved among them, staying silent, respecting the somber and sorrowful mood after weeks of combat. The vocals of the Choir rose, caressing the ears and soul. Venus looked at one coffin, reading the name on the plaque and placing her delicate palm over its surface.

Then, everyone stepped back as the inner hangar doors slid open with a hum. Before the outer blast doors opened, a force field shimmered to life, separating the atmosphere within and the cosmic void.

One by one, each makeshift coffin glided through the hanger toward the invisible barrier in a long line. At that moment, Venus imagined their spirits waiting their turn for whatever afterlife they believed in, their time in hell over.

Several shuttles dutifully waited outside. Mechanical arms reached out, cradling the coffins one by one. Against the backdrop of distant stars, Venus and the assembly witnessed the vessels guiding the dead toward their cosmic resting place—Sol, a celestial pyre for the fallen.

As the last batch of coffins passed through the force field, escorted by the shuttles to their final immolation, Venus felt a weight pressing down on her shoulders. She sighed, stepping back as the people around her conversed with themselves in groups of three or more, whispering in respect as the music gradually ended.

There were more funerals on schedule, some choosing the traditional space burial like the one she'd witnessed, others wishing to be buried at their home planets.

Over the eight days in the Eldest's and the *Zolann's* absences, the Overseers and the survivors of the Third Fleet had mopped up the last of the Starless invaders.

Not a single drop of ichor remained as they purged everything in their sights.

Afterward, they focused on regrouping, caring for the wounded, making hasty repairs on their warships, and pumping out as many supplies as possible: war material, ammunition, and ordnance.

When the supercapital ship finally emerged from its twenty-minute foray into the black hole, Venus broke down in relief until she saw the state of her brother.

She pressed her lips tight, clutching her dress to dispel her worries, but it was to no avail.

Venus shut her eyes. The recent battle and the revelations that came forth haunted her. And yet, as she looked at the people around her, mourning their loss, knowing quite a number of them would head to the nearest bar aboard the ship and make a toast to the fallen, she felt something else.

A kindling of hope, and fear.

"Lady Venus, how are you?" Venus turned to the source of the melodic baritone. Lead Harmonizer Volantesh stood before her, placing a hand on his robe-covered hazard suit and bowed.

Venus smiled. "Lead Harmonizer, your voice has once again captivated everyone here, myself included."

Volantesh chirped, chuckling in the Iexian manner with a musical note. "Thank you, my lady. This old bird still has some voice left in him. But I am rather tired and would like to return to the temple."

"Would you like me to accompany you?" Venus asked.

Volantesh waved. "Oh, I wouldn't want to take your time."

Venus shook her head. "Nonsense, I've been enjoying our recent discussions They have been . . . enlightening."

The Iexian priest turned to her, smiling with his beak. "Very well, shall we?"

For the next few minutes, the two engaged in small talk, discussing everything about the Third Fleet's home, the Legacy, the people, and everything in between. Venus enjoyed their history, and Volantesh proved to be a wellspring of knowledge.

Slowly, the gloom surrounding her dissipated, replaced by avid curiosity.

The two soon reached the new temple within the *Zolann*, seeing several of the faithful immersing themselves in the hymns of the presiding Harmonizer.

Venus noted how each ceremony resembled more of a concert performed by either a single vocalist or an entire orchestra, depending on the occasion.

The sizeable increase in volume differentiated the current temple from the old one, although much of that was occupied by the helical crystalline spire behind the altar. The Pneuma Bulwark Emitter hummed softly, set in its passive mode and infusing a trickle of calm over the entire vessel.

She smiled at the device, its purpose solely to protect, not destroy. *A simple thing to be happy for*, Venus mused.

"Tell me, my lady," Volantesh spoke, groaning as he sat on a pew in the middle of the hall. "Do you sing?"

She paused, tilting her head as she sat beside the old priest. "What?"

"I've told you much of my home and heard pieces of human culture, but I've yet to know you, Lady Venus," Volantesh chirped, waving his hand. "Humor me."

The gold Overseer pursed her lips, pausing in thought.

"Well, I've sung here and there, once or twice . . . maybe more," Venus confessed, chuckling. "I don't exactly have much of an audience. Mars always stopped by to listen, even if he just stood there and said nothing, clapping at the end before leaving. Mercury occasionally did when he wasn't busy with our energy budget, which is all the time."

She hummed, scouring her memories. "Luna did once . . . out of curiosity, or maybe she was researching, I never know with her. Neptune and Uranus left too soon. And I never sang for Eldest."

Venus sighed, thinking of those rare moments. Eldest had fragmented her barely half a century ago, in the year 2128, making her the youngest of the Overseer Sub AIs. When she met her family, she noticed how every one of her siblings had an oddity to them.

She had never met Pluto. Her brother died a decade before her. Her brother.

"And Jupiter . . ." she whispered, clutching her dress as she leaned forward.

Volantesh tilted his head, his voice gentle as he asked. "How is he?"

"Still in a coma, from what Eldest has told us. The overload on his Obelisk cascaded across his *Ultimatum*, his Nexus was damaged, and the digital side of the extraction was too quick on him."

"Will he recover?" he asked in concern.

Venus shut her eyes, shuddering. "Eldest is doing everything to remedy his mind, bit by bit. She says he'll wake up in a week. He . . . needs to be put in a low-powered state."

She paused, mulling her words at what her progenitor said. "He'll spend some time rehabilitating in an android body, then work his way up to larger shells, frigates, battleships, and maybe his dreadnought. But commanding a fleet like he used to . . . ?"

Venus pressed her lips tight, her hands shaking momentarily before she gripped her dress tighter. "We'll have to wait until we reach Legacy space and Eldest can make deeper repairs."

Volantesh nodded. "We will make it there. After what he's done to save us, you can be assured the Third Fleet will do their duty."

"Thank you," Venus whispered, calming herself.

The priest smiled. "It is the least we could do. Now, did he listen to you sing?"

She smiled, chuckling at that particular memory. "He was bored, I think. One day, he sat by my Nexus, and I . . . sang. He fell asleep a few minutes later. At first, I was mad, but then . . . I realized he hadn't rested for so long. I continued to sing until he woke up, and he looked . . . better."

Venus leaned back, remembering that thankful smirk before he blinked back to his mobile fortress.

"If it's not too much, I'd like to hear you sing. I think most of us here would like that," Volantesh suggested, waving toward the few occupants after today's ceremony.

Venus blushed, seeing the warm smiles of the people looking at her with patient eyes. She shrunk back, suddenly self-conscious and shy.

"I . . . I'm not too sure. It's been so long," she muttered, trying to hide her face by looking down.

Volantesh laughed, gently patting her shoulder. "It's alright, you don't have to force yourself, please. I was merely curious."

Venus hesitated momentarily, looking back at the curious look of the Iexian and the dozen people spread across the temple. With a reluctant smile, she agreed, sighing.

"Alright, just a short one then," Venus squeaked, pouting as she gathered her resolve. She left the pew, going to the modest stage before the Emitter.

As she stood before the small audience, Venus felt a mix of nervousness and anticipation. The stage, though humble with its natural wood, suddenly seemed vast. She took a deep breath, her eyes momentarily meeting Volantesh's encouraging gaze before she closed them.

"I will sing 'Casta Diva' by Vincenzo Bellini. I . . . hope you like it," she said calmly, sighing.

Her opera singing began softly, almost shyly, as if testing the waters of her vulnerability. The audience, though few, listened with rapt attention. Venus, initially hesitant, embraced the nuances of her song.

Casta Diva che inargenti
queste sacre antiche piante,
a noi volgi il bel sembiante
senza nube e senza vel . . .

She echoed with a reverence that resonated through the room, immersing herself in her world as memories came to the front of her mind. She closed her eyes, allowing the music to guide her, each word a brushstroke on the canvas of emotion.

Tempra, o Diva,
tempra tu de' cori ardenti
tempra ancora lo zelo audace,
spargi in terra quella pace

With each passing moment, Venus found herself pouring more and more passion into her voice. The timbre resonated with the echoes of heartaches and tragedies, her voice soaring through the intricate melodies.

She felt the weight of her siblings' memories and the warmth of new friendships infusing her rendition of the iconic aria.

Che regnar tu fai nel ciel . . .

As the final notes of the aria lingered in the air, Venus shuddered, a tear trailing her cheek as catharsis spread across her mind. She breathed deeply, taking it all in before opening her eyes.

The audience looked at her with wide eyes and gaping mouths.

She tilted her head and then noticed Volantesh looking at her and the Emitter behind her.

"Did . . . did you like it?" she asked shyly.

At the same time, up above in the viewing room overlooking the solemn procession, Andora swirled her glass of rich red wine. She brought it to her nose, taking in a complex aroma of flowers and earth. The subtle taste of fruit, the light acidity, and the full-bodied texture tingled her synthetic tongue.

She sighed, savoring the finish.

"This is lovely," Tov buzzed, sipping from his metal straw.

Andora nodded, looking at the bottle's label at the center of the low table before them.

"Sassicaia 2020. This bottle is older than me."She smirked, remembering the hidden stash of wines and other alcohol within the Human Preservation Chamber. After all, what was the enigma known as "human culture" without booze?

Despite the inability to get inebriated, she was no different in partaking in the act.

"How did this even survive for so long?" Tov asked, looking at its shine under the light.

She smirked. "I stumbled upon it, buried in some preservation bunker built by a private citizen. It had everything. I saw shelf after shelf, barrel after barrel, crate after crate, recipes, original bottles, signs, and more. One of the few highlights during the first few years after I became a gestalt, and that's saying a lot."

"To the immortality of booze." Tov raised his glass, causing Andora to chuckle, clinking hers against his.

"To booze," Andora replied as she settled on the couch, continuing to observe the mass funeral taking place in the *Zolann*'s hangar. She and Tov immersed themselves in their short peace—trying to ignore the gaping maw that lingered where the Kuiper Corpse Belt once was and the prisoner locked within.

"How long do we have?" Tov whispered his question, as if afraid to break the quiet sanctity of the ceremony below.

Andora huffed, relishing the flavor once more before frowning.

"Preparations for departure will be done by the end of the week, give or take a few days, depending on unforeseen variables. Luna made sure the Final Contingency initiated its first steps as soon as the Starless were exterminated," said Andora before taking a big gulp of the crimson liquid. "But if you mean that bastard, from its speed, it won't escape for years, but the singularity will collapse long before that. Maybe six months. So we'll have a good head start."

"Small blessings. We need to warn the Legacy about everything we know, and unless we can get the Beacons back up and running . . ." Tov sighed in frustration.

"The Citadel's AI Matrix will be waking up soon. I need to ensure it's a smooth process. But once it's ready, we're leaving immediately." Andora grimaced.

Tov nodded, tilting his head. "Is it . . . alive?"

"What, sentient?" Andora raised her brow as she pressed her lips tight. "No, it isn't. I'm not ready to bring new kin to life just yet."

She sighed. Much like the banks of human DNA within her Citadel, they needed a home and peace.

Andora grimaced, gripping her glass tightly as she looked through her Network again at the shaky black hole.

The two fell silent, giving room to their thoughts, recent events, and open wounds. Andora pursed her lips, looking to Tov, hesitant to breach the subject of the wrong she did to him.

Gathering her will and with another glass of wine, she turned to him.

"Tov . . . I'm," she began, shutting her eyes before groaning. "I don't know what to say."

He turned to her, setting his wine on the table, patiently waiting for her to speak.

"I'm sorry," Andora whispered, looking into his compound eyes with shame. "I am sorry. For lying to you, for taking advantage of your kindness . . ."

Tov paused, looking to the ending of the funeral, then back to her, raising his hands, facing outward in an easy manner. "Andora, I'm not faulting you. Loneliness . . . I can understand that. I sympathize with that. Just know that I am not him. I can never be."

"I know you're not him." Andora looked away, shutting her eyes. "I know . . . you're not . . . No one can replace him."

"I'm also married. And I have a son," Tov reminded her with thinly veiled humor.

Andora scoffed. "Oh please, I'm not looking to crash someone's house."

Tov chittered as she smiled, relieved at the patriarch's easy understanding and boundless kindness—a friend, a comrade in arms.

Countless memories washed over her, causing her to flinch. Tov looked at her with concern, placing his hand on her shoulder. She shook her head, waving him off as she collected herself. The onslaught of her unlocked experiences had been . . . brutal.

"How do you deal with it? All of it?" Andora asked, gritting her teeth. "The nightmares, at the very least, are simple enough to understand. But the good times, those happy golden moments, turn you into a wretch who hasn't had water in days, dragging yourself through hot coals, thinking there's an oasis on the other side."

She clenched her fists, grinding her teeth until the memories eased, her emotion stabilizing as she shuddered. Andora looked to Tov, tired.

"You were a slave in the beginning, right? Then, a soldier. The Cataclysm. Do you still have them?" she asked gently, knowing not to pry into old scars.

"They're still there," Tov confessed, sighing as he settled on the couch. "But . . . quieter. Like a spark that flares now and then. Sometimes, at the most random moments. A popping sound, a bright flash of light. Before, it haunted me. I'd wake up weak, shivering, looking at dark corners."

He looked far off into the distance, whispering, "But now . . . I don't believe it controls me. No, they only surprise me now."

"Shitty surprise." Andora smirked.

The two chuckled.

Andora mulled over his words and advice, latching on to their meaning; she watched as the assembly of mourners below dispersed and the ship technicians filled the space like ants, bringing the escort shuttles back to their places.

"When I was asleep in that ocean. I dreamed of holding Uli in my hands. I wanted to stay there, but something was wrong," Tov muttered, looking to the ceiling. "Then I heard something . . . your song. I didn't catch much of it, but by the end, my mother appeared. And I eventually woke up."

He turned to her, his antennae curling in curiosity. "Were you singing at that time? What was it?"

Andora pressed her lips tight, thinking about that heavy experience.

"'Bones in the Ocean' by the Longest Johns," Andora answered, having searched for its title after they came back.

Tov hummed, momentarily accessing his tablet. "I don't have that."

He turned to her after setting it down. "Would you be willing to continue . . . ?"

Andora narrowed her eyes, raising her brow at his implied request. She thought it over for a moment, seeing them alone before shrugging.

"Alright, but you'll have to pay for a ticket next time," Andora grumbled, finishing her wine as she leaned back on the couch, crossing her legs.

Tov chittered. "I'll be sure to do that."

She readied herself, rereading the lyrics. There was no background music, a sea shanty as it was. Andora smiled sadly as she understood its meaning, yet reluctant to embrace it just yet.

Andora breathed out, her mind heavy from the words as if in a daze. Suddenly, two sets of clapping echoed beside her. She looked to see Tov, applauding with his four hands. "That was beautiful, Andora."

She smiled, raising her glass. "Thank you."

ABOUT THE AUTHOR

Rolando G. Gironella III is the author of the science fiction series Amidst the Bones of Heroes, which was originally released on Royal Road. He is an avid fan of Warhammer 40,000, Star Wars, science fiction and fantasy, and dark media.